KU-022-649

Tara's Destiny

Also by Geraldine O'Neill

Tara Flynn
Tara's Fortune
The Grace Girls
The Flowers of Ballygrace

Tara's Destiny

Geraldine O'Neill

First published in Great Britain in 2007 by Orion Books,
an imprint of The Orion Publishing Group Ltd
Orion House, 5 Upper Saint Martin's Lane
London WC2H 9EA

An Hachette Livre UK Company

1 3 5 7 9 10 8 6 4 2

Copyright © Geraldine O'Neill 2007

The moral right of Geraldine O'Neill to be identified as the author
of this work has been asserted in accordance with
the Copyright, Designs and Patents Act of 1988.

All rights reserved. No part of this publication may be
reproduced, stored in a retrieval system, or transmitted
in any form or by any means, electronic, mechanical,
photocopying, recording, or otherwise, without the
prior permission of both the copyright owner and the
above publisher of this book.

All the characters in this book are fictitious, and any resemblance to
actual persons living or dead is purely coincidental.

A CIP catalogue record for this book is
available from the British Library.

ISBN (Hardback) 978 0 7528 7256 8
ISBN (Trade Paperback) 978 0 7528 7257 5

Typeset by Deltatype Ltd, Birkenhead, Merseyside

Printed in Great Britain by Clays Ltd, St Ives plc

The Orion Publishing Group's policy is to use papers that are natural,
renewable and recyclable products and made from wood grown in sustainable
forests. The logging and manufacturing processes are expected to
conform to the environmental regulations of the country of origin.

www.orionbooks.co.uk

Tara's Destiny is dedicated with
love to my mother-in-law, Mary Hynes

Acknowledgements

Thanks to Kate Mills, who has been with me since my very first book, and also to Genevieve Pegg who is always so supportive and helpful. I am very grateful to all the Orion staff who work behind the scenes selling and promoting the various editions of my books.

A very warm thanks to my agent Mandy Little for her advice and dedication to my writing career, and to James, Isabel and all the staff at Watson, Little Ltd.

Thanks also to Sugra Zaman for the early years we spent working closely together and for believing in me from the start.

Thanks to Mark Tavini of the Alma Lodge in Stockport – and staff member Zoe Fairclough – for being so helpful with the research about the hotel business back in the 1950s.

Thanks to Ber Owens from Tullamore for information about the court systems in Ireland in Tara Flynn's time.

Thanks to my own family and Mike's family, and all our dear friends who have given me constant support and encouragement in both Ireland and the UK.

Thanks to all my readers from all over the world who give me the reason to keep on writing the books!

And, as always, thanks to Mike for his enduring love and patience.

PART ONE

*It is not in the stars
to hold our destiny
but in ourselves.*

WILLIAM SHAKESPEARE

Chapter 1

Tara opened the bedroom curtains of the big bay window. After looking at the grey October sky for a few moments, she let her gaze wander down into the garden of Ballygrace House. Everything was still and calm this morning, but the evidence of the previous weekend's storm was obvious.

She had spoken to her father on the phone several times before she and William, her young brother-in-law, had set off from Stockport for the boat journey to Ireland yesterday morning. William was on half-term from school in London, and Tara was taking a long over-due week off from running her small hotel.

'The worst of the weather is over now,' her father had informed her in the last call, 'so ye should have a reasonable journey across. Now, don't be drivin' too fast through Wales, and take it easy on those oul' winding roads down from Dublin. They're not like the English roads; they can be greasy and treacherous at this time of the year. And make sure you have your spare tyre well pumped up.'

Tara had raised her eyes to the heavens and listened patiently to her father's advice about cars and driving and roads – which Shay Flynn actually knew nothing about. But she listened because she knew he meant well, that he was trying to advise her in the way that Gabriel, her husband, would have done. But Gabriel had been dead for over three years now, and although she still missed him every single day, Tara had learned to look out for herself when it came to practical matters.

'Don't worry, I'll be careful,' she had said.

She looked down now at the bigger fallen branches that Shay had dragged into a damp pile, where they were waiting until they had dried sufficiently to be sawed into manageable logs. Then, they would be carried in a wheelbarrow into one of the outbuildings to dry out completely, and used later for fuel on the house fires.

Her gaze moved further back to the fence which bordered the garden, and the field behind where two lively children's ponies had once run. One for Gabriel and one for his sister, Madeleine.

But that was a long time ago. The field was now let to a neighbouring farmer for grazing sheep. As far as Tara could see, the once-sturdy fence had been damaged by the high winds in at least two places. The elderly farmer had obviously done a patch-up job on the fence with branches and bits of wood, but it would have to be done properly.

Tara would have to organise somebody to do the work, and she would have to do it *today*, otherwise her father would be doing it himself. If it hadn't been for the constant rain over the last few days, he would have been out to start on the job already.

No matter how many times Tara told him to get a local handyman in to do any extra work – or to give him a hand – Shay always ended up doing the job by himself or with Mick, his brother. But the fact was, they were getting too old for heavy work. Both men were now in their sixties, and while Tara's uncle Mick was prepared to listen to his wife, Kitty, about what he was still capable of doing – or not – her father certainly wasn't. Tara's stepmother, Tessie, could warn him until she was blue in the face, but it made no difference.

Tara stared out of the window for a few minutes, a thoughtful look on her face, then she walked back across the bedroom to put her warm velvet dressing-gown over her pyjamas, and went downstairs.

As she laid the kitchen table for breakfast, Tara heard a noise from upstairs. She smiled. It was a sure sign that William Fitzgerald was growing up, when she was awake and moving before him in the mornings.

When he was younger – on their trips over to Ireland or when William came to Stockport – he would have been waiting for her and Gabriel in the kitchen or dining-room. But he was now exhibiting all the traits of a normal, growing teenager – eating more and sleeping longer.

The first thing Tara had done when she came downstairs was switch on the radio, then rake out the range and get it fired up again. Ella Keating, the local woman who helped out in Ballygrace House, had set the fires in the other rooms, ready to be lit, and she had left bacon, sausages and black-and-white pudding in the fridge. Ella had also offered to come and cook the breakfast, but Tara had told her not to rush up early every morning. It was good for her and William to do things for themselves. She heated up a griddle pan and started cooking.

In truth, although she was grateful for help around the big, old rambling house, Tara was happy to have some time there on her own. She often sat in the cosy kitchen, remembering the days and nights she and Gabriel had spent in the house during their short marriage, and her mind would wander further back, to when she came to Ballygrace House as a young girl and Madeleine Fitzgerald's best friend.

The sausages, bacon and pudding were soon cooked, and she put them in a dish to keep warm in the oven.

'Something smells good,' William said, coming into the warm kitchen. He ran his hand over a clump of dark hair that was sticking up at the back of his head.

As Tara turned to look at him, she was suddenly startled to noticed he was wearing Gabriel's old blue tartan dressing-gown. Why she should have been surprised she didn't really know, because she had loaned it to William the last time he was here and it must have remained hanging in the spare room wardrobe.

Flustered, she went back to the slices of soda bread that were now frying in the pan alongside two eggs. 'There's tea in the pot,' she told him, 'or orange juice in the white jug.'

'Great,' William said, reaching first for a small glass and then to the centre of the round table for the jug of juice. After pouring his drink, he lifted the white paper napkin that was at his place and spread it over his lap. 'These are useful things, Tara,' he said, running his hands across the square of stiff tissue. 'I suppose you can just throw them away after using them. My mother still has the old-fashioned kind that have to go to the laundry every week to be washed and starched.'

Tara turned the eggs in the pan, then glanced over her shoulder at him. 'We have lots of linen napkins, too,' she told him, 'but it's easier to use the disposable ones when there's only the two of us here.' She gave a little shrug. 'It's the same as us eating in the kitchen; it's easier than waiting for the fire in the dining-room to warm the place up and then having to carry all the food through.'

'I think it's nicer eating in here,' William told her. 'It's more cosy and relaxed. We always eat in the dining-room at home – breakfast, lunch and dinner.' He looked around the kitchen now. 'Being here feels like being on holiday.'

'I'm glad you enjoy it,' Tara said, smiling warmly at him. 'I love coming back to Ballygrace House, too, and it's lovely having company.' She stopped. 'But you're lucky that you have such a nice stepfather. Harry is very good at going to rugby and cricket matches with you, and taking you and your mother out for drives or up to the West End for the theatre and that kind of thing.' She checked that the eggs and bread were fully cooked, then moved the frying pan to the edge of the range, away from the strongest heat.

'Oh, Harry is very good to me,' William quickly agreed. He took a drink of his orange juice. 'It's just that everything is more relaxing here in Ireland ... I don't have to think about schoolwork or anything like that.'

Tara was glad now that she had offered to bring the boy with her. It killed two birds with one stone, giving her the chance to check on Ballygrace House and see William at the same time. The only drawback was the time of year, with the late October mornings and evenings becoming darker and longer. It was not the best time to have a holiday. But, Tara wryly told herself, beggars can't be choosers. She had to take the time off from the hotel when it was convenient for the business and not for her own personal life. She knew when she bought the Cale Green Hotel in Stockport that she would have to commit all her time to it for the first few years.

'I can't promise anything very exciting this week,' Tara said now, as she lifted the dish from the oven, and began dividing the sausages, bacon and black-and-white pudding between two plates. 'I've got to do a few jobs around the house, and have to organize work to be done outside before the winter sets in.'

'I was looking out of the upstairs hall window earlier, and I noticed that the fence at the back of the garden is broken.' William started to laugh. 'Could you imagine what would happen if all the sheep escaped from the field?'

Tara felt a sudden stab of annoyance. It was the sort of thing she dreaded might actually happen.

'They would demolish the whole garden!' William went on, with a childish gleefulness. He shook his head. 'I can just picture Shay running about and swearing his head off as he tried to herd them back into the field.'

'I'm afraid I don't find that very funny, William,' Tara said, a touch snappily. 'It just adds to the list of things I need to have done around the house.' Then, seeing the chastened look on the boy's face, she softened her tone. 'With the hotel and everything, I feel as if I'm neglecting Ballygrace House. I'll have to try to get as much done as I can this week. Next year I'll try to spend a bit more time here.'

'Maybe I could help you with some jobs?' William ventured. 'Last time I helped Shay mend the door of the turf-shed.'

Tara slid the eggs and fried bread on to the plates. 'That's kind of you, William, but there's been quite a bit of storm damage around the house. I'm going to have get proper workmen in.'

William raised his eyebrows and smiled. 'Shay won't like that.'

'I don't think it's fair to leave all the work to him,' she said, trying not to sound irritated again, 'and I'm going to have a chat with him about it later today.'

Jim Reeves was singing 'I Love You Because' on the radio, and Tara hummed along to it as she brought the hot plates to the table. 'Do you like this song?' she said, trying to move to a more light-hearted subject.

'Not really, but my mother does,' William said. 'Harry bought the record for her last birthday. Do you like it?'

Tara put a plate down in front of William and one at her own place. 'I suppose I do,' she said, 'I've never really thought about it.'

William lifted his knife and fork and started to cut up a sausage. 'What's your favourite group?' he chattered. 'I think I like Herman's Hermits and the Beatles the best.' He suddenly laughed. 'I suppose you like the Bachelors because they're Irish?'

Tara's shook her head and laughed, too. 'To be honest,' she told him, 'I haven't got a clue about music at the moment. I'm a bit out of date compared to a teenager like you. Sometimes I hear a song and I like it, but I don't know who sings it, and then I get the groups all mixed up.' She reached for the teapot and poured herself a cup, then poured William one, too.

'Don't you listen to the radio?' he asked incredulously. 'Or watch *Top of the Pops* on television?' He popped a piece of sausage into his mouth, then pierced the yolk of his egg with his fork.

'I'm so busy at work that I never have the radio on, and when I'm at home I'm usually in the dining-room catching up on the hotel accounts, or occasionally reading or playing the piano.' She gave a little sigh. 'I never really get the chance to watch television, either. I don't think I've ever seen *Top of the Pops*, although I have heard about it.'

'You are very out of date, Tara,' William told her with a grin. 'You'll have to get more with it or you're going to be left behind with all the oldies like my mother and Harry – or even Shay!' He was giggling now, so much so that he almost choked on his mouthful of food, and tears started streaming down his cheeks.

'I didn't think I was *that* funny,' Tara said, rolling her eyes and laughing with him in spite of herself. 'I suppose I'm going to have to get *you* to bring me up to date. The next time you're in Stockport or I'm down in London, we'll sit down together and watch this *Top of the Pops*.'

William nodded, wiping his damp eyes with his napkin. 'Have you ever thought of getting a television here, Tara?' he asked now.

She shook her head. 'There would be no point,' she said. 'I wouldn't have the time to watch it. Sure, I hardly have the time to read the newspaper when I'm here.'

'Shay was delighted when he got it in last year, wasn't he?' William said. 'He said it was about time everyone in Ireland came out of the Dark Ages and got the telly.' He took a bite of soda bread and chewed it thoughtfully. 'I remember him saying that Ballygrace was in a better spot for the BBC than Tullamore, and that you should get a television here as you'd get a great reception.'

Tara shook her head. 'If I paid heed to every suggestion that my father made,' she told him now, 'I'd be running around like a headless chicken.'

Another song came on the radio and William said, 'Now, Tara, that group is called the Kinks and the song is called "You Really Got Me"'.

'OK,' Tara said. 'Let's stop chattering now and get on with eating our breakfast while we're listening to it.' She lifted her teacup and took a sip from it, glad of the excuse to have a few minutes' peace from her young brother-in-law's entertaining – but constant – chatter.

Later, as they were clearing the table, William suddenly stopped in his tracks, pointed at the huge kitchen dresser and yelled, 'A mouse! A mouse has just run under the cupboard!'

Tara closed her eyes and took a deep breath. She'd have to go out today and buy new mousetraps and poison, otherwise Ballygrace House would soon be completely over-run. She wasn't one of those women who screamed and ran at the sight of a mouse – it was part and parcel of living in the country.

But it was another thing to feel guilty about. She knew she was neglecting the beautiful old house that she loved. And it was one more thing to add to her ever-growing list.

Chapter 2

❧

STOCKPORT, LATE NOVEMBER

Tara looked in her wardrobe, trying to decide what was appropriate to wear to the opening of a new boutique. She had already had Bridget on the phone that morning asking the same thing. They, along with Tara's half-sister, Angela, had received invitations to the launch of Mersey Style in Princess Street in Stockport. The owner, Liz, was a business aquaintance of Tara's friend, Kate Thornley.

'It's all right for Kate and Angela,' Bridget had said, sounding harassed. 'They're both up to date with all the latest fads and fashions. They'll be all dressed up to the nines in their short skirts, bell-bottoms and dangly earrings. What on earth are *we* going to wear?'

Tara had burst out laughing. 'Well, whatever they wear, they can't wear the skirts and trousers at the same time! And you make us sound like a pair of ancient lost causes, Bridget Roberts. Surely we're not that bad?'

If it had been anyone else, she might have taken offence, but Bridget was Tara's oldest and most trusted friend. Together they had fled from Ballygrace in Ireland when they were only eighteen. They had both overcome personal difficulties and worked hard for their now successful lives, and a strong bond remained between them.

Bridget seemed to realise that she'd put her foot in it, as usual. 'I'm not saying *you* don't dress up to date, Tara,' she rushed on. 'It's just that you dress very professionally for work most of the time, and the majority of my clothes are for cooking and cleaning or going to school concerts.' She was sounding breathless now. 'This is going to be a really trendy do – it has to be with George Best opening it – and all the top fashion people in Stockport will be there. I can't believe we're going to see *George Best*. Even though he has that untidy long hair, he's absolutely gorgeous!' She gave a little dreamy sigh. 'Don't you think he's lovely, Tara?'

Tara laughed. 'Of course I do. He's one of those types that all the women like, whatever age we are. We needn't expect him to notice *us*, though; he'll probably be there with one of his gorgeous model girlfriends.'

'I was lying in bed last night thinking about it,' Bridget went on. 'I'm really delighted that Kate asked me but I'm a bit nervous at the same time ... I don't know if I'll fit in with all those fashionable types.'

'You'll be grand,' Tara said, her voice light and encouraging. 'What about that nice black tunic with the red chiffon blouse you wore to the Grosvenor a few weeks ago? It looked lovely with those long black beads and earrings, and your black boots.'

'D'you think so?' Bridget's voice sounded hopeful.

'Definitely,' Tara told her. She knew that Bridget's confidence fluctuated. 'I've seen a few younger girls wearing that sort of thing at the minute, but it's flattering for our age group as well.'

'I'll go and check if I need to iron the blouse now,' Bridget said, 'because it'll be a bit of a rush for me after I get the lodgers fed and the kids ready for bed. Did Angela tell you that she's coming down to give me a hand tonight before we go out?'

'She did,' Tara replied. 'And she said she was bringing her outfit with her to change into at your house. Kate is calling for me at around half past seven, and then we'll be down to pick up you and Angela.'

'I'd better get my skates on, so,' Bridget said, 'or I'll be running late as usual.'

Tara didn't feel quite so hopeful herself now as she searched through her neatly arranged wardrobe. Fashions had changed a lot recently, and the women's magazines that she occasionally flicked through told her that she hadn't been keeping up.

Angela, who worked in the Cale Green Hotel and also lived in Tara's house, had called in for a few minutes before going down to help Bridget with the evening meal in the lodging house.

They had chatted about the boutique opening and then Angela had shown Tara the outfit she had planned to wear: a short, white, belted skirt with a multi-coloured, Bri-nylon stretch top, and patterned stockings with white boots.

'My goodness!' Tara said. 'You've certainly gone for the new styles.'

Angela had tilted her blonde head to the side in a thoughtful manner. 'Wouldn't you think of buying something like that, Tara?' she said. 'You have the figure for it.'

'It's gorgeous on *you*, Angela,' Tara told her honestly, 'but too young for me.'

Angela raised her eyebrows. 'You can wear anything. You don't look much older than me, and your hair and figure are fantastic.'

Tara laughed and turned away. 'Oh, I think I'd be better with something tried and tested, although you never know – I might go mad and buy a few things at the opening tonight.'

Tara lifted out a brown trouser suit now, held it up for a few moments with a cream blouse then put it back on the rack. It was too stiff and official-looking – as Bridget had said. Then, she lifted out a long green evening dress with bishop-style sleeves that she'd bought for a dinner-dance the previous Christmas. She quickly dismissed it as too fussy and formal for the occasion. She picked out a few more outfits before eventually settling on a gold, unfitted shift dress with cutaway armholes and a bronze sequin decoration on the high neck. It would be warm enough on its own as it was made in a fine woollen material. The hem stopped a couple of inches above her knee, and although it wasn't as short as some of the newer outfits, it was as short as Tara was prepared to go. She held it up to herself in front of the mirror and was reminded that she had bought it because the colours complemented her Titian hair. It will do, she told herself. People would be wearing all sorts of outfits and it would be silly to waste more time agonizing over it. Besides, the idea of the boutique launch was to show off all the latest styles and encourage people to buy them. She would enjoy looking at everything and everyone, and discussing it all with her friends.

Tara looked at her watch now and gave a little gasp. She had three-quarters of an hour to bath, dress and put her make-up on before Kate Thornley was due to pick her up.

Tara came hurrying down the stairs, her black bag with the long gold chain handle in one hand and her warm black coat over her arm. She came out of the front door, then stopped in her tracks when she saw that it wasn't Kate's familiar Beetle that was waiting for her. Instead, a sleek, maroon Jaguar was idling outside the gate.

It was Frank Kennedy, the only serious boyfriend that Tara had had before marrying Gabriel. The boyfriend who had deceived her into thinking he was a single man when he was in fact married with a family back in Ireland. He had explained he had been long separated at the time and waiting on a divorce – and had done everything he could to make it up to Tara – but she had been unable to forgive him. The wound he had inflicted had cut deep.

But that was all water under the bridge now, and the successful businessman had been courting Kate Thornley for the last couple of years. Tara wasn't entirely comfortable with the situation, but she had grown used to it. She would have preferred to have no contact with him, but inevitably their paths occasionally crossed.

Tara stopped for a few moments to put on her coat, then took a deep breath and walked out to the car.

Frank's dark head bent forward as he stretched across to open the front passenger door for her. 'Kate had to rush down to give them a hand doing the window in the shop,' he explained, 'so she rang me and asked me to pick up you, Bridget and Angela.'

Tara sank into the car's soft leather upholstery, immediately aware of the subtly expensive smell of Frank's cologne. And without looking at him, she knew he would be dressed exactly right for the smart-casual occasion. 'If I'd known,' she said a touch sharply, 'I could have driven the girls down in my own car.'

'Not at all,' Frank said in his rich, Irish accent. He turned to look at Tara, his manner easy and unruffled; he was well used to her cool manner. 'There's no point in us taking two cars, and, sure, it's a pleasure to give you ladies a lift into town.' He put the car into gear again, and they set off on the short distance down to Maple Terrace.

'I thought the boutique opening was women-only,' Tara said, unable to stop herself from sounding short and snappy.

'Sorry to disappoint you,' he said lightly, 'but there will be a few men there tonight, including Mr Best.' He chuckled. 'I'd say they're guaranteed a good crowd with him opening it.'

'I suppose it will be something different,' Tara said, looking out of the car window, 'and it was nice of Kate to put us on the guest list.' She knew she should have been more friendly and enthusiastic, but, no matter how hard she tried, she could never be completely relaxed in his company.

Bitter experience had taught her to be wary where Frank Kennedy was concerned. In fairness, he had never been anything other than a gentleman and a business colleague to her in the last number of years, and she knew that his serious relationship with Kate should have removed her reservations about him. But her feelings were too deeply ingrained, and created a brick wall between them.

They pulled up outside the large, well-kept house in Maple Terrace, and, a few moments later, Bridget and Angela came down the steps of the boarding house.

'I thought the fashion show was in the boutique?' Frank joked as they climbed into the car. 'I hardly recognised you, Bridget. You look more like a teenager in your fancy outfit.'

'Oh, there's still life in the old dog yet,' Bridget retorted, delighted by the compliment and digging Angela playfully in the ribs. 'And I scrub up well – especially when there's a chance of meeting someone as famous and good-looking as George Best!'

'I think we'll have to join the queue,' Tara said, feeling free to sound more light-hearted now she had company. 'Most of the women will be there to see him.'

'June said she saw him walking down the street in Bramhall a few weeks ago, and he was mobbed by a load of fans all looking for his autograph.'

June was Bridget's rough-and-ready helper in the boarding house and her main babysitter. Whenever anyone had a story to tell, June could always go one better. If she didn't know anything about the subject herself, she would speak on behalf of someone else who did.

'And do you know what?' Bridget went on. 'He had a load of signed photographs in his pocket and gave them out to anyone who wanted them, and then he stood and posed with his fans for anyone who had a camera.' She raised her eyebrows. 'According to June, he's right down-to-earth and ordinary.'

Frank glanced over his shoulder and smiled. 'Well, I hope you're not in a hurry to get home tonight, because if he stands to have his photograph taken with everybody there, it could be a very long queue.'

'Oh, some of the women might be more interested in the fashion than in a footballer,' Tara said.

'Will we be able to buy things tonight?' Bridget asked. 'Fred was feeling generous and gave me some money to treat myself.'

'Lucky you,' Tara said. 'And yes, I think Kate said that there was a special opening sale tonight.'

Angela sat quietly in the back seat. While she felt totally at ease with Bridget, she always felt she had to be on her best behaviour when she was with her older sister on a night out. And while she had come across Frank over the years at the boarding house, or at meetings in Tara's hotel, she didn't know him that well.

They drove through Shaw Heath, then down King Street and into the centre of Stockport town. When they came to the beginning of Princess Street, Frank slowed down to look for a parking place.

'There's going to be a good turn-out for the launch if the cars are anything to go by,' he said. He crawled along until they reached the only shop-front on the street that was lit up. They could hear music and see figures moving around behind the window display.

'If I'm not mistaken, this is Mersey Style,' Frank said.

'Look at all the fancy cars!' Bridget gasped. 'There's two sports cars and another Jag like yours, Frank ...' She paused, not quite sure of the makes of the other vehicles. If her Fred had been with them, he would have named each one without any trouble.

'Tell you what,' Frank said, coming to a stop in the middle of the road outside the new boutique, 'why don't I drop you off here and go and park the car? There's a few drops of rain coming down and I don't want you getting wet in all your finery.'

Tara lifted her handbag, felt for the door handle and opened it carefully, making sure she didn't hit the car parked next to them. 'Thanks for the lift,' she said, swinging her long legs out as elegantly as she could manage.

'It looks fairly full already,' Angela said as they walked towards the boutique to the loud strains of the Rolling Stones' 'I Can't Get No Satisfaction', 'and it's more like a discotheque with the music and the flashing lights.'

'My God!' Bridget exclaimed as they slowed up outside the double-fronted shop. 'Look at that ...'

They all stopped now to gaze at the bedroom scenes in both windows. In one an antique wardrobe, tables, chests of drawers mingled with Art Nouveau lamps and mirrors, and a collection of peasant-style floaty dresses jostled with short skirts and colourful stripy tops on the dark-green patterned backdrop. In the other window, a variety of colourful bags and hats were draped across the end of a small wrought-iron bed, while necklaces, pendants, earrings and bangles hung from a navy-blue coat stand.

'That window display is absolutely amazing,' Tara gasped. 'It feels more like London than Stockport.'

'The inside of the shop looks as if it's done up in the same way,' Angela said, standing on tip-toe to see as much as she could.

'You go first,' Bridget said, moving behind Tara. 'You'll know more people than me and Angela.'

When they stepped inside the large boutique, it did indeed have the air of a night-club or a discotheque with low lighting, throbbing music and a twirling ceiling spotlight that threw out different colours as it moved around. There were antique chairs and sofas in mulberry velvet, tall, fringed lamps, and Eastern vases filled with gold-painted twigs and peacock feathers.

There was a good crowd in already – mainly young, fashionably dressed women, as Bridget had predicted, and a number of equally fashionable young men with longish hair and Beatles-style round-neck suits, or suede jackets and casual trousers. There was still room to move around and look at the rails of clothes that lined the walls, however, and through the groups of people they could see a disc jockey in the corner, gyrating behind a turntable and large speakers.

A trestle table stood to the side, a girl and a young man serving glasses of red and white wine from it, and there were trays of crackers with cream cheese, cocktail sticks of cubes of cheese and pineapple, tiny pickled onions, and bowls of crisps and nuts.

'Imagine them having food and drink in the shop,' Bridget commented in a low but impressed voice. 'I don't suppose a small glass of wine would do us any great harm ...'

Tara smiled. 'No, I don't suppose it would.' She knew her friend was making a point by checking with her, because they had crossed swords over Bridget's heavy drinking in the past. But it hadn't been an issue in the last year or two, and there were times when Tara felt slightly irked at the way Bridget sought her permission to have a drink when they were out. There would be no problem with alcohol if Bridget kept it to a reasonable level and didn't drink when she felt worried or depressed.

As they walked to the table, Tara caught sight of Frank at the door. She hesitated, knowing that out of courtesy she should wave him over to join them, but before she had time to think, two girls went rushing towards him with exclamations of delight. Tara turned back to her friends, grateful that the situation was taken out of her hands.

After picking at a few of the nibbles, the three women wandered towards the back of the shop, glasses of white wine in hand.

'Tara!' Kate Thornley came rushing across to greet them, dressed in a purple sweater dress, which finished several inches above her slim knees, black fishnet stockings and long black boots. She wore several rows of long onyx beads with matching earrings, which complemented her heavy-fringed, strawberry-blonde bob. 'Well, what do you all think?' she asked, her hand sweeping the room.

'Fabulous!' Angela said her, long blonde hair swinging as she nodded. 'The clothes look absolutely brilliant.'

'The changing rooms are open at the back if you want to try anything on,' Kate informed her. 'And there's a fifteen per cent discount off everything bought tonight.' She leaned forward in a conspiratorial manner. 'If anything catches your eye, I'd go for it now, because it might not be there by the end of the night.' She nodded towards the door, and they all turned to see another group of people coming in to join the crowd.

The disc jockey's muffled tones came over the crackly speakers, followed by Sandie Shaw singing 'Long Live Love'.

Angela turned to Bridget. 'Will you come with me while I try on those checked trousers?'

'Go on,' Bridget said. 'And you can help me to pick out something with the money Fred gave me.'

As they crossed the shop floor, Tara said to Kate, 'The whole place is absolutely amazing. I hear that you were helping out with the window-dressing earlier on. You certainly made a good job of it.'

'Oh, I only helped with the finishing touches,' Kate told her. 'They were rushing at the last minute and needed an extra pair of hands. Sorry about not being able to pick you up, but I knew I could rely on Frank to do it.'

Tara looked at her friend for a moment, wondering how she could put the words 'Frank' and 'rely' together. But she said nothing. Presumably he had changed, otherwise his romance with Kate could not have lasted for so long.

They stood chatting for a while and admiring the clothes displays, as more and more people arrived. Then gradually, the two friends moved into a quieter corner to the side of the drinks table. They were engrossed in a discussion about the people who had designed the shop when a tall, dark-haired figure appeared behind them.

'I suppose this place must be every woman's shopping fantasy,' Frank Kennedy said, his voice confident and easy. 'And I've just heard that George Best has arrived, so that should make them even happier.'

'Oh, I'd better go and let Liz know he's here!' Kate exclaimed. 'She was terrified he was going to let her down.' She gave Frank a quick peck on the cheek. 'Sorry for leaving you stranded, but we'll have time for a drink later.' She disappeared into the crowd.

Frank turned to Tara. 'Can I get you another glass of wine while I'm getting my own?'

'Yes, thanks,' Tara said, her manner deliberately distracted as she scanned the crowds to see if there was any sign of Bridget and Angela coming back from the changing rooms. She hoped they would catch up with her again before the official launch started.

A few minutes later Tara glanced up to see Frank making his way back to her, and for a fleeting moment their eyes met. She quickly averted her gaze, but in that short space of time she noted his well-cut hair – fashionably longer than he usually wore it – the expensive, round-necked, tan leather jacket, and toning shirt and trousers. The latest style but discreet enough for his age.

Tara was still making reluctant small talk with him when the popular Manchester United football star was brought through the packed shop. Tara took a sip of her wine and stifled a sigh of resignation at being stranded without her friends. She wouldn't have minded if she had been stuck with anyone else, but there was nothing she could do.

'How is business going at the hotel?' Frank asked her during the small lull in the proceedings as they hooked up the extra microphones. 'It always looks busy enough any time I've called in.'

'Grand,' Tara told him, distracted by a kerfuffle at the door, as a group of four young girls made their noisy, giggling way into the boutique and barged through the crowd to get near to the football idol. Everyone moved – tutting and sighing – to let them past, but as a woman stepped backwards, she knocked Tara off balance and into the drinks table.

Tara attempted to steady herself by grabbing onto the edge of the table, and was suddenly aware of the wine splashing out of her almost-full glass, while the glasses on the table started shaking and clinking into each other. She watched in horror as two empty glasses actually tumbled over and fell onto the carpeted floor.

Then, Tara felt a strong pair of hands take hold of her shoulders and put her gently but firmly back on her feet. Without turning to look, she knew instinctively that it was Frank. Her face burned with embarrassment as she stepped back into the corner while he quietly took control of the situation, steadying the flimsy table and picking up the unbroken glasses, murmuring, 'It's all right, no harm done,' to anyone who had seen the small incident.

Thankfully, the few people who had noticed went back to their own conversations while Tara closed her eyes and took several deep breaths to restore herself.

'Are you all right, Tara?' Frank asked, his face and voice concerned. He touched her shoulder lightly. 'Those silly girls could have caused a nasty accident.'

Tara looked up at him. 'I'm fine, thanks.'

'You're sure?'

'Honestly,' she said, feeling her face start to flush, 'I'm absolutely fine.'

Mercifully, she saw Angela and Bridget making their way through the crowds towards her.

'We got stuck in the queue for the changing rooms,' Angela told her in a heated whisper, 'but thank God we made it out in time for the speeches.'

'It was mad through there,' Bridget said, her face glowing with excitement. An assistant came up to them with more glasses of wine for the launch toast, and Tara took one to replace the wine she had spilled. Then, out of the corner of her eye, Tara saw Bridget lift two glasses. She put one on the corner of the table and took a long drink on the one she was holding, almost emptying the glass.

'I got a lovely pair of trousers,' Angela told Tara, 'and Bridget bought a gorgeous black skirt with a low belt.'

The disc jockey came to the microphone then, and called for order. An official from the local council gave the opening speech, then introduced the owner of Mersey Style, Liz, a small, exotic-looking girl with a halo of dark curls and wide, slanting eyes outlined with black kohl. Liz thanked everyone who had been involved in the establishing of the new business, including her friend Kate Thornley, and Frank Kennedy, who had overseen the renovation of the building.

Bridget immediately turned round to beam at Frank, but Tara gazed straight ahead, thinking how typical it was that he should be involved in anything new in the town, and not even feel the need to mention it as they were driving down. Then she felt a stab of guilt and grudgingly had to admit that he never boasted or bragged about any of his business deals. He never had.

The thought suddenly struck Tara that, for all his success and money, Frank Kennedy was still a modest man. But favourable thoughts about him always made her feel uncomfortable, so she banished them and instead joined in with the frenzied clapping and cheering, as a smiling but slightly embarrassed George Best was ushered towards the microphone.

When the speeches were over, everyone was asked to raise their glasses and join in a toast to the success of Liz and Mersey Style. And it was then that Tara glanced to smile at Bridget and saw her lift a full glass of wine to her lips. She had obviously downed the first one and was now starting on the second.

'That was a great night,' Bridget said, as Frank Kennedy's car pulled up outside the boarding house, 'and Michael will be delighted that I got George Best's autograph for him.' She paused. 'And will you please thank Kate, Frank, for asking us all.'

'You've already thanked her,' Frank reminded her, 'but I'll tell her again when I catch up with her later. We're going back to Liz's house for a nightcap.'

Bridget got out of the back seat of the car and went around to the driver's side, her handbag on one arm and the Mersey Style carrier bag on the other.

Frank rolled down his window. 'Are you all right, Bridget?'

'I'm the finest,' Bridget said, leaning on the edge of his window. 'And I just want to thank you, too, Frank – for the lift. She smiled and shook her head. You're a gentleman – a thorough gentleman.'

She paused. 'And I'll tell you something, Frank – and I'm not meaning anything bad by it, for my Fred would agree – you could give that George Best a run for his money. You were as well-dressed and every bit as good-looking as he was, and you and Kate make a lovely couple.'

'Well, thank you for that nice compliment,' he said, smiling.

Tara felt herself cringe with embarrassment as she listened to Bridget's tipsy rambling.

'And thanks again for the lift,' Bridget repeated.

Frank patted her hand. 'It's my pleasure,' he told her. 'Goodnight now, and tell Fred I'll be in touch about that wrestling match in Bolton next weekend.'

Tara and Angela got out at the house in Cale Green and thanked him for the lift.

'It was nothing at all,' he said, 'and, as I said to Bridget, it was a pleasure to take you all.'

'He's a lovely man, isn't he?' Angela said, as they walked up the short path to the house.

'Yes,' Tara said non-committally as she put the key in the lock, 'he certainly can be.'

Later, as she sat in front of her mirror, taking off her make-up with tissues and Ann French cleansing milk, Tara thought back to the incident in the boutique where Frank had calmly saved her from falling over and making an embarrassment of herself. Then she thought how diplomatic he had been with the obviously merry Bridget. Whether it was the glass or so of wine she had drunk herself, Tara found herself in a very rare, retrospective mood about her old lover.

She had to admit that he hadn't put a foot wrong tonight. As Bridget had said, he had been a thorough gentleman. And even though he was a good few years older than George Best, there wasn't a man in his own age group who came near Frank Kennedy for looks, dress and impeccable manners. In addition, he was one of the wealthiest building contractors around. And yet, he retained a quality that allowed him to mix easily with people of every background, from business colleagues to labourers on his building sites. He had remained a good friend to the down-to-earth Fred and Bridget, yet had no difficulty mixing with all the top business people in Stockport and Manchester, and had been accepted by Kate Thornley's family, who were from old money.

And there was a time when he could have been the mainstay of Tara's life – until he had ruined it all.

Tara finished her nightly ritual by applying her hand cream, then she got into bed and switched off her bedside lamp. As she lay in the dark she told herself that things between herself and Frank Kennedy had turned out the way they had for a reason. A very special reason.

If she had continued her romance with Frank, she would never have married Gabriel. And that was unthinkable. Her few short years of marriage to her teenage sweetheart had been the most fulfilling of her life. It was the relationship that had given her security and confidence, and had made her feel more content than she had felt at any period in her life. Gabriel had filled a gap that no one else could have filled.

Her passionate romance with Frank Kennedy was never meant to last.

He was far more suited to Kate – and that was how things were meant to be.

Chapter 3

❧❧

STOCKPORT MARCH, 1966

Tara took a deep breath, trying hard to keep her patience. Her father was on the other end of the office line.

'Look, Daddy,' she told him, 'just tell the man to put the new boiler in and I'll send him a cheque for whatever it costs to fit it.'

'Sure, they're daylight robbers, Tara,' Shay argued. 'That fella took one look at the size of Ballygrace House and doubled the price. I know he's takin' liberties. Me and Tessie had a new boiler put in the oul' cooker two years ago, and it wasn't anywhere near that expensive.'

'But the range at Ballygrace House is far bigger that the one you have,' Tara argued.

Shay made a clucking sound. 'That fella's nothing but a cowboy,' he said, 'a feckin' robber. He's well known for it. I'm sure you could get it done for half the price somewhere else.'

'Look, Daddy,' Tara said, a real edge to her voice now. 'You've said he's the only one in the Tullamore area that can do the job this week, so I don't think we've much choice. The house will get damp at this time of the year if we don't have some heating in it.' She closed her eyes and slowly counted to three. 'Please give him a ring back and ask him to come out first thing in the morning.'

'Ah well,' Shay said, his voice suddenly sounding very cool, 'if that's your decision, then it's not up to me to be interferin' in yer business. It's your house and you have to decide where the money goes.' There had been a silence for a few moments. 'But if you want my opinion ...'

Five full minutes later Tara put the phone back down in its cradle, then slumped back in her office chair. She gave a weary sigh, her forefinger pressing into her temple. Ballygrace House seemed to be haunting her at the moment. Shay had filled her in on every tiny detail about the plumbing job that needed to be done at the old house.

She hadn't dared ask Shay to book a skilled workman to do the fences, because she knew it would lead to the same rigmarole.

Tara knew in her heart of hearts that she would soon have to take time off from the hotel to organise a proper system for the maintenance of the old Georgian house back in Ireland. She couldn't leave it all to her father. He had neither the capability to do it himself nor the ability to organise someone else. And she knew perfectly well that it wasn't his fault. The caretaker job had just fallen to him by dint of Tara's prolonged absences from Ireland.

A short while later Tara came out of her office with a sheaf of papers in her hand and headed towards the reception of the Cale Green Hotel.

'Could you check the number of the company that we buy the bed linen from, please, Angela?'

Angela reached under the desk for the hotel phone directory, and flicked through the pages until she came to the correct one. 'Oh, by the way, Tara' she said, 'Frank Kennedy came on the other line when you were taking the last call. He said could you ring him back as soon as possible.'

Tara raised her eyebrows but said nothing. What on earth could he want? He very rarely phoned her, had no reason to be in touch. If there was any kind of social thing where their paths might cross, it would always be Kate who made the arrangements.

'Tara.' Frank's voice was warm. 'Thanks for calling me back. I suppose you're wondering what I'm after.'

'Well, yes,' Tara said candidly. There was a small pause as she waited for him to explain.

'It's about the Grosvenor,' he said. 'I wondered, have you heard anything in that direction?'

'The *Grosvenor*?' Tara repeated. She leaned back in her chair. 'No ... I haven't heard anything about it.'

'Well,' he told her, 'I have it on good authority that it's going on the market very soon.'

'You're joking,' Tara said, suddenly sitting to attention.

The Grosvenor Hotel in Stockport was where Tara had learned all the tools of the hotel trade. She had worked there evenings and weekends as a receptionist, to earn extra money to help pay her mortgage. It was also the hotel that had trained Angela so well, as well as one of the oldest and grandest hotels in the area, with a solid reputation among business people in the north-west of England.

'No joke,' Frank went on. 'It's fairly definite.'

'How did you hear?'

'I happened to be in there last night when the company group came out of a meeting,' he told her, 'and I got chatting in the bar to a few of them later.'

'Is there any particular reason that they're selling it?'

'Seemingly, they're investing in two brand-new, bigger places in Manchester.'

'That is news indeed ...' Tara said.

There was a pause at the other end of the line. 'Would you be interested in it?'

Tara's brow creased. 'In what way?'

'Buying it,' he said, laughing.

'Now, you *are* joking,' she snapped. 'Where would I have the money even to think of buying a huge hotel like the Grosvenor?'

'Tara, Tara,' he said now, his tone placatory. 'You always have that same reaction when something new is put to you.' His voice became soft. 'You were the very same when I suggested you buying your first house.'

Tara's hackles started to rise now. She hated it when he alluded to their past relationship. 'That was a long time ago, and I don't think there's any comparison between that and buying a huge hotel now.'

'You've never put a foot wrong so far in all your property investments, especially since you bought the Cale Green Hotel. You have a fantastic business head on you – better than most of the men I know.' Tara was sure she could hear a note of humour in his voice.

Tara gave a long, low sigh, which indicated that she wasn't going to get involved in any light banter with him over the differences between men and women in business. 'Frank,' she started again, 'not in my wildest dreams could I even *think* of affording a place like the Grosvenor. You must know that. Where could I get that kind of money?'

'The big house back in Ireland,' he said simply. 'You could sell it. You don't use it very often.'

Tara felt a sudden, physical jolt. *Sell Ballygrace House?* How could he even dare suggest selling the house where she and Gabriel had lived? It held so many memories.

When he got no reaction, Frank moved swiftly on, clearly presuming that Tara was thinking about it. 'Now you have the Cale Green running well, you could re-mortgage on that as well.'

He suddenly became aware of the icy silence.

'Tara?' he said. 'Are you still there?'

'Yes,' she finally answered. 'I am.'

'What do you think?' he asked.

'I think you're totally mad for even thinking I would be interested in buying another bigger hotel, and, for your information, I have no intention of ever selling Ballygrace House.'

He paused. 'OK,' he said, 'it was only a suggestion. No harm done.'

'Since you're so interested,' she told him sharply, 'maybe *you* should think of buying it. A wheeler-dealer businessman like you would have no trouble coming up with the money. I'm surprised you haven't already put an offer in.'

'They're looking for big money, Tara,' he said, his voice sounding more serious now. 'They've put a lot of money into it in the last few years and they'll want to recoup that.' Then he took a deep breath. 'You wouldn't consider going into a partnership to buy it?'

'What do you mean?'

'You and me, and possibly a few others,' he said. 'Between us all we could come up with the money, and you and I both have the same approach to business. I'd be happy to be the main investor. You just come up with whatever you can afford.'

Tara was almost speechless. 'No, Frank,' she said stiffly, 'I wouldn't consider going into any kind of partnership with you. After all that happened between us, I can't believe you'd even think of asking me.'

'This is *business*, Tara,' he told her.

'Does Kate know about it?' Tara suddenly asked.

'No,' he said. 'Why should she? As I've just said, it's business, my work. She has no interest in that side of things.'

A knock came on Tara's office door. She could see the shape of the hotel chef through the glass, obviously waiting to discuss the following week's menu with her. 'I have to go,' she told him briskly. 'I have someone waiting for me ...'

Later, when Tara thought about the conversation, she realised the significance of the fact that he hadn't discussed his business proposition with Kate. How high-handed of him, she thought.

Tara knew that Kate had hopes of eventually marrying Frank, and, if that happened, his work projects would certainly affect her. Surely he should have talked things over with her before sounding Tara out on such a venture? And although she and Kate had got over the initial awkwardness regarding Kate's romance with Frank, if the truth be told, neither of them was truly comfortable with it.

Even if Tara could put things completely behind her, she was always aware that Kate felt insecure, and even a touch jealous, that Tara had repeatedly turned Frank Kennedy down, both before and after her marriage to Gabriel.

Tara shrugged and gave a little sigh. She was sure that Kate wouldn't be happy if she knew that Frank had contacted her about the Grosvenor, but it wasn't her fault. She certainly had never encouraged him, and had no interest in going into any kind of business with him.

Chapter 4

❧❧❧

The following day, when she finished work, Tara drove down to Maple Terrace to Bridget and Fred's boarding house. As she pulled up outside, she knew that she had instinctively headed here because it was the one place she could safely talk about Frank Kennedy.

Tara had only reached the second step leading up to the house when Bridget's son, Michael, opened the door, calling back to his mother.

'Come in, Tara. I'm delighted to see you,' Bridget said, coming along the hallway to greet her friend, and drying her hands on the bottom of her flowery apron.

'I've probably come at a bad time,' Tara said, realising that the children would only just have come in from school and Bridget would be busy getting the evening meal ready for the boarders.

'Not a bit of it,' her friend said, taking both of Tara's hands in hers. 'I'm glad you came. I wanted a chat with you, and I was going to call down to the hotel later on this evening to see you. I had Angela in helping me for a few hours earlier on, so I'm ahead of myself for a change. I suppose I should feel a bit guilty – the poor girl has a day off from working in your hotel, and spends half of it slaving down here. June had a hospital appointment so she couldn't come in this afternoon.'

'I don't think Angela sees helping you as work,' Tara told her. 'She's very fond of you and the children, and she loves coming to Maple Terrace. She sees it as a second home.'

'Well, we're very fond of her, too,' Bridget said. 'Although I think it's better for her that she comes as a visitor now, rather than living here.'

'Oh, definitely,' Tara said. 'It's all worked out well, and she can still come up and down to you easily.'

Tara's house was only a few minutes' walk from the hotel, and having Angela living with her meant that Tara could keep a close eye on her younger sister. Both Bridget and Tara felt it was best to keep her away from the lads in the boarding house, given the mistakes

26

she had made with her first, very unsuitable boyfriend. In fairness to Angela, she hadn't put a foot wrong since in that department, but it was better to be safe than sorry.

'The kettle's boiled, so I'll make us both a cup of tea or coffee, whichever you prefer. Or I have a nice big pot of home-made soup if you'd prefer a bowl of that?' Bridget suggested. 'I'm just going to pour some out for Michael and Helen to have while they're watching television in the sitting-room.' She pointed towards the ceiling. 'Lucy's having a little sleep in the cot upstairs, so we should have a few minutes' peace and quiet before she reappears.'

'Just a cup of coffee would be lovely, Bridget,' Tara said, giving her a warm smile.

As they walked into the kitchen, Tara took off her coat and scarf, then pulled out a chair at the table. 'I had my lunch only a short while ago, so I'm not that hungry.' She could always be sure of a warm reception from her friend, and the older Tara became, the more she valued that.

They chatted generally, as Bridget ladled the soup into bowls for the children and cut several thick slices from a large bloomer loaf. She placed everything on a tray and took it into the sitting-room.

When she came back she put a pan of milk on to boil, then she took the coffee jar down and put a spoonful of Maxwell House into two mugs, with a spoonful of sugar in Tara's and two in her own.

As the milk boiled, she lifted down the chocolate-biscuit tin from one of the cupboards and put it on the table in front of her friend. Then she poured the hot milk into the mugs, stirring well as she did so.

'So,' Bridget said, handing Tara her mug of milky coffee, 'anything new or exciting?'

Tara knew their conversation could be interrupted by the children or the phone at any point, so she decided not to waste any time. 'I got a call from Frank Kennedy yesterday. He rang to tell me that the Grosvenor is up for sale.'

Bridget nodded. 'So I believe. Fred mentioned it the other night.' Fred was the head barman at the Cale Green Hotel, but he still kept tabs on what was happening in the Grosvenor, where he and Bridget first met. 'Seemingly, the staff knew nothing about it, so they were all shocked when they heard.' She looked at Tara. 'I suppose Frank Kennedy heard before anyone else?'

Tara rolled her eyes heavenwards. 'Doesn't he always? But you'll laugh at this. He phoned because he thought I might be interested in buying it. With *him* – and possibly some others. Can you believe that?'

Bridget stared at Tara for a few moments. Then she said, 'And *are* you interested?'

'*Me*?' Tara said incredulously. 'Now, don't tell me you're as bad as Frank Kennedy! Where would I get the money to buy a big hotel like that? Things have just started to pay for themselves in the Cale Green in the last year, and that's only a small place compared to the Grosvenor. How on earth could I even consider it?'

'If anyone could make a go of it,' Bridget said quietly, 'it would be you. Every single thing you try always succeeds.'

'You really are codding me now,' Tara said, taking a mouthful of her coffee. 'But you won't believe what he had the cheek to suggest I do to raise the money.'

'What?'

'*Sell* Ballygrace House.' Tara's voice was high with indignation. 'Can you believe it? The bloody cheek of him!'

A smile broke over Bridget's face. 'Did you actually swear at him?' Tara never swore or used any kind of bad language, but Frank Kennedy was the one person who could push her towards it.

'I say as little as I can to that fellow,' Tara said, looking all bristly now.

'Maybe it's not such a bad idea,' Bridget ventured. 'You're not there very often these days, and it's just sitting empty.'

'That's only because I've been busy with the hotel,' Tara said defensively.

'True ... but, be honest, Tara: do you think you'll ever go back to live there full-time? And would you even want to? Ballygrace House is a big oul' barn of a place for a single woman. I mean, it's not as if it is your own home-place or anything like that. You only married into it.'

'Well, thank you very much,' Tara snapped, the hurt evident in her eyes. 'I didn't expect *you* to agree with Mr Big-Shot Kennedy. I thought my oldest friend might have had a bit more loyalty to me than that.' Her voice dropped. 'I'm really surprised at you, Bridget. How can you even think of suggesting that I sell Ballygrace House? You know that's the only thing I have left of Gabriel.'

'Now, you know I didn't mean anything against poor Gabriel,' Bridget said quickly. 'I only meant that it would give you the chance to move into a much bigger business league with the Grosvenor.'

She paused, wondering if she dared remind Tara about the awful things that had happened to her in that rambling old house in the village where they grew up. Whether she should mention the housekeeper who had treated Tara disgracefully, and Gabriel's father, whose terrible actions had been the cause of Tara leaving Ireland in the first place. But a glance at Tara's face told Bridget not to go there.

'Gabriel would want you to do whatever makes you happy,' Bridget said, trying to placate her friend. 'And if that meant getting a *really* fresh start, then I'm sure he would be all for it.'

'Well, I think I've made enough fresh starts already,' Tara said quietly, 'and I'm not ready, or willing, to make any more for the time being.'

'Fair enough,' Bridget said, smiling. 'But you should be looking on it as a compliment, that people think you are up to buying and running a place like the Grosvenor.'

'Subject closed,' Tara said in a brusque manner, but she was smiling now, which meant they weren't going to fall out over it. She stood up, reaching over the table to collect her coat, handbag and car keys. 'You've hardly touched your coffee,' she said, noticing Bridget's half-full mug.

'Actually, that's what I was going to come down to tell you tonight ...'

Tara's brow creased in confusion. 'Tell me what?'

'I'm pregnant again. I found out for definite yesterday.' Bridget pointed to her mug. 'I went off coffee with Lucy for the first couple of months.'

'Oh, my God!' Tara said, going over to hug her friend. 'I'm delighted for you – and for Fred.'

Bridget flushed. 'It'll be the last one now – four's enough for anyone these days.'

Tara held her at arm's length, looking directly into her eyes. 'You're a very lucky woman, Bridget Roberts. A very lucky woman indeed.'

'I know, Tara, I know,' Bridget said in a hushed voice. She knew a baby was the one thing that Tara had wanted but had been denied. Suddenly, her eyes started to fill with tears.

'What's wrong, Biddy?' Tara asked, inadvertently calling her friend by her childish nickname. 'Are you not happy about the baby?'

Bridget searched in her apron pocket for her hanky and dabbed at her eyes. 'No, no … it's not that. I'm pleased about it, and so is Fred. It's just that …'

'What, then?' Tara asked, sinking down into the chair next to her, an arm around her shoulder. 'It's not that silly difference we've just had over the Grosvenor, is it?'

Bridget shook her head. 'No, no,' she said, tears streaming down her face now.

'What's the matter? What else could be upsetting you like this?' Surely, she asked herself, there couldn't be anything wrong between Bridget and Fred? Three-year-old Lucy – still asleep upstairs – had caused a few ripples of concern when she was born. Her lovely, coffee-coloured skin had placed serious doubts over her paternity, and Tara sincerely hoped that there weren't any doubts with this next child.

'I've been having a lot of bad dreams recently …' Bridget's voice trailed off miserably.

'What about?' Tara asked, trying not to show her relief that Bridget's worries were of such an ordinary nature.

She snuffled into the hanky. 'The baby.'

Tara looked at her baffled. 'Do you feel all right? You don't think there's anything wrong, do you?'

'Not *this* baby,' Bridget whispered in a shaky voice. 'The little one back in Ireland. The one I left to be adopted.'

Tara's hand flew to her mouth. This was something she didn't need to hear. And something that Bridget definitely didn't need to think about.

The baby in Ireland was from the past. Their shared past. It was something they'd left behind a long, long time ago.

Another lifetime ago.

'I can't stop thinking about it these past few days,' Bridget sobbed. 'And you're the only one I can tell, the only one who really knows all about it. I couldn't bring it up with Fred. We never spoke about it after all the carry-on before the wedding when I had to tell him.'

'It'll pass,' Tara said firmly. 'It's only because you're in the early stages with the new baby. It's bringing it all back.' She rubbed a comforting hand over Bridget's shoulder. 'I promise you it will pass.'

Then, her voice a little softer, she added, 'It will *have* to pass, Bridget. No good can come out of you raking all that up again now. No good at all.'

The sound of footsteps could be heard out in the hall, and, a few seconds later, Helen came into the kitchen, carefully carrying the tray with the soup bowls on it.

Bridget made a great show of pretending to blow her nose so that her daughter wouldn't notice her red eyes and her blotchy face.

'Good girl, Helen,' Tara said, getting up to take the tray from her. She put the bowls and spoons in the sink and the tray down at the side of the cupboards with all the others. 'You're nearly as handy as your mother already.' She playfully tousled the little girl's hair. 'I could do with you helping down in the kitchen at the hotel. Do you think your mum would let you come down and work for me?'

Helen giggled, enjoying Tara's teasing.

'Now, come here, I have something for you.' Tara reached into her handbag, and came out with two half-crowns. She walked the child back towards the door. 'One for you,' she told her, 'and one for Michael.' She glanced anxiously over her shoulder at Bridget, who was now up at the sink, turning taps on, squeezing washing-up liquid and generally making herself look busy.

Helen, gleefully clutching the two half-crowns, went running down the hallway towards the sitting-room. Tara closed the kitchen door behind her then turned back to her friend.

'You'll just have to put it out of your mind,' she said quietly, 'and concentrate on the lovely children you have with Fred.'

Bridget put the washed bowls onto the dish-rack, then dried her hands on the towel hanging by the sink. 'I know, I know.' She met Tara's eyes now. 'I have no idea where this has all come from; normally I can just put it out of my mind.' She folded her arms tightly over her chest, almost hugging herself.

Tara felt her throat tighten. 'I'm sure you had these same feelings when you were expecting Lucy. It must be a little phase of depression, brought on by your pregnancy.'

'It's not just havin' a new baby ...'

'Do you think about it often?' Tara asked quietly.

Bridget nodded. 'It's always there. I've never really forgotten, no matter how hard I've tried.' She halted. 'Do you ever think back to the way things were at that time?'

31

Tara's face darkened. 'I try not to,' she said. 'What's the point in going over old hurts and wounds? Isn't it better to look at the good things we have in our lives now, rather than harking back to the bad times?'

Tara was beginning to feel a little alarmed at Bridget's train of thought. She hadn't brought this subject up, or even alluded to it, for a long time. Gabriel's tragic death a few years ago had overshadowed everything that had happened to her and Bridget in their early life. And that was how Tara had looked at it. The loss of her kind, gentle childhood sweetheart had broken her heart, and, since it had happened, Tara had not been able to see beyond it, or feel that any other hurt in her life had ever compared to it.

'The thing you told me about Gabriel's father,' Bridget said, 'do you ever think about that?'

'No,' Tara said, her voice suddenly brittle. A horrible darkness was starting to descend on her now, transferring itself from Bridget's troubled mind to her own. 'And I'd prefer you not to remind me about it. It's a part of my life that I made a big effort to forget.' She paused, trying to pick her words carefully. 'You must know that, Bridget. Sure, I only told you about it in the last few years. It was something I kept a total secret for years.'

Bridget's eyes were downcast now, and she was unconsciously rubbing her arm, as though desperately seeking some kind of comfort. 'I'm sorry to be bringing all this up again,' she whispered. 'But I haven't anybody else who would understand.'

Tara took a deep breath. 'Oh, Bridget, believe me, I *do* understand,' she said, her voice full of sympathy. 'I know some terrible things have happened to you, but you can't let the past spoil the wonderful life you have now, with a, decent man and lovely, lovely children …' She stopped. 'Have you any idea just how lucky you are? You know I'd give anything to have a husband and children to come home to.'

Bridget looked up at her now, her eyes brimming with tears. 'I'm so sorry, Tara … I'm making you miserable now.' She gave a small, shuddering sob. 'And you're right – I'm being totally selfish going on like this.'

'There are dark bits in all our lives that we have to try to forget,' Tara told her, feeling rather overwhelmed by the conversation.

'I shouldn't have said anything about it,' Bridget said, wiping the back of her hand over her damp face. 'I promise ... I promise I won't mention it again.'

Tara felt a little wave of relief, which was quickly followed by a wave of guilt. Deep down she knew that the right thing would be to allow Bridget to pour it all out and get to the bottom of her misery about the baby. But it was all too uncomfortably close to Tara's own past.

She went over to her friend now and put her arms around her. Then they just stood silently, each wrapped their own thoughts, as the ghosts of Ballygrace reached out once again.

Chapter 5

The following Friday afternoon, Tara was in the kitchen going over the weekend menus with the chef, when Angela came through to say she had finished her early shift and was heading home.

Angela was now the main receptionist in the small, busy hotel. She took great pride in her job and in wearing the nice navy suit and white blouses, which she washed, starched and ironed every evening.

'Can you hang on another few minutes?' Tara asked her. 'I wanted to check something with you before you go.'

'I can, of course,' Angela said, slightly startled. It was rare that Tara asked her to stay late at work. She went back to the reception area, her mind quickly running over any possible areas that her conscientious half-sister might raise. Something always made her jump to attention the minute Tara summoned her into the office or asked her to do anything, as though she were still a naive, impetuous girl, although her older sister had never had cause to reprimand her about her work.

Tara quickly finished her discussion with the chef, then checked the meat, fruit and vegetable orders for the following week. Satisfied all was in order, she hurried back to the main desk where Angela was busily going over the booking lists for the weekend with Carol, the receptionist who had taken over the evening shift.

'Oh, I'm sure she's left it well in order for you, Carol,' Tara said, smiling at them both, then she said to her sister, 'Shall we step into the office for a few minutes?'

'Is there anything wrong?' Angela said anxiously, closing the door behind them.

'No, not at all,' Tara said, giving the younger girl a quizzical smile. 'Why on earth should you think there's anything wrong?'

Angela's shoulders slumped in relief. 'I just wondered.'

Tara went to sit at her desk, then lifted her large diary and started to flick through the pages. She indicated the comfortable leather chair on the opposite side of her desk. 'Sit yourself down for a few minutes. I only want to ask you about the dates of your trip at Easter.' She paused at a page in the diary. 'I see Easter Sunday is in the middle of April this year.'

'I was going to book off a full week,' Angela volunteered. 'Going over to Ireland on the Wednesday or Thursday and coming back the following week ... if that's OK?'

'Grand, grand,' Tara said, a studied frown on her face. She glanced up from the diary. 'You haven't booked the boat yet, have you?'

'I was going to do it tomorrow,' Angela said, wondering now where all this was leading.

Tara smiled. 'How do you fancy a travelling companion?'

'Who?' Angela asked, her voice high with surprise.

'Me, and maybe William.' She closed the diary and sat back in her chair. 'It's only an idea, but I was just thinking that it was time I took a trip back home. I want to catch up with all the family and check on the state of Ballygrace House. I thought that maybe William could get the train up to Stockport and I could bring him over with us. It would kill two birds with one stone. If I'm going to Ireland at Easter, I wouldn't have time to go to down to London as well, so bringing him along would mean I could spend time with him and visit Ballygrace, too.'

Tara didn't give her two other reasons for going over to Ireland. She didn't say that it would fill a gap in her empty social life, or that she had recently felt a need to visit Gabriel's grave in Ballygrace Cemetery. She hadn't even said those things to Bridget. She had hardly said them to herself.

Over the last couple of years, Tara had been so busy with her hotel that she'd had no time for socialising, and now that the place was up and running, she discovered she had no place to go and, worse still, no one to go with.

She met Kate Thornley every few weeks for Sunday lunch or the theatre, and Bridget often came down to the hotel on a Friday or Saturday night to have a meal with her, but apart from that, Tara's life was all work.

Realising that she needed to get out more often, Tara had recently started accompanying some of her lodgers to the cinema or, occasionally, to one of the local restaurants. But the women in the house weren't really the most suitable company. They were either too old and dowdy, like Vera Marshall, or too young and giddy, like Angela. When she was out with the younger girls, she felt that they were always on their best behaviour, and she had a horrible, sneaking feeling that they thought she was more like the spinsterish Vera than themselves.

All very different from the life she had led before as a single woman and then as a wife. Now, as a young widow, life was the quietest it had ever been, and it didn't look likely to change.

Even if she had more female company, Tara certainly had no interest in going dancing or into pubs or anything like that, where she might have to deal with the attentions of men. She found that a problem even now if she was in a restaurant or around the bar in her own hotel; she never imagined that men would approach her with obvious intentions in such places. But they did. And Tara knew she wasn't ready to get involved with another man. In fact, as time went on, she wondered if she ever would be.

Work would have to fill any gaps in her life. That, and regular trips back to her family in Ireland.

William had already been on the phone over the last few weeks, checking whether Tara was coming down to London for Easter, or whether he could come up to Stockport to help around the hotel. He had told Tara that his mother and her husband were staying at home for the holidays, as Harry had strained his back and had been told by the hospital that he shouldn't travel anywhere for the next few months.

Tara had felt sorry for Gabriel's younger brother, knowing he would be bored stiff at home if Harry wasn't able to take him anywhere.

Tara's mother-in-law, Elisha Fitzgerald, still suffered with her nerves, and Harry, who was a marvellous stepfather to William, was the one who organised any family activities. Besides, Tara knew the boy loved going over to Ireland with her, and enjoyed helping her father around the grounds of Ballygrace House.

'I've been thinking,' Tara said to Angela now, 'that we could head over on the Tuesday night and come back a week or so later, perhaps the following Friday or Saturday.' She paused. 'Probably travel overnight on the Friday to give us the rest of the weekend to get over the journey.'

'Are you sure it's OK for me to have that long off work?' Angela asked, sounding surprised.

'Yes,' Tara said, smiling at her. 'You've a week owed to you since last year, so it would give us a decent length of time. By the time we travel over and back, it only leaves us just over a week in Ireland.'

Angela looked delighted. 'Oh, that would be grand, Tara,' she said, her eyes shining. 'I'd love the company, because it can be a fierce long journey on your own, and I think William's a lovely young fellow.'

'I'll take the car,' Tara said, having now made up her mind. 'So that'll save you a few pounds on your fare.' She knew her sister had been saving for her trip, so she could now use her travel expenses for something else.

'Oh, no,' Angela said, 'I'd have to give you something towards the boat fare or the petrol. I couldn't expect you to pay for everything.'

'You'll pay nothing towards the travelling,' Tara said in a definite tone, 'because I would be paying to bring the car over for myself.' Then, thinking that she might be making the girl feel childish, or as though she had no say in things, she added, 'Maybe you could pay for a meal on the boat, or if we stop off somewhere in Wales on the way to Holyhead?'

'Grand,' Angela said.

'You head off to Bridget's now,' Tara said, looking at her watch, 'and I'll give William's mother a ring.'

William was predictably delighted by Tara's suggestion. He was at home when she called his mother about the arrangements, and, within minutes, he was on the phone chatting to Tara himself.

'Can I come up to Stockport as soon as the school holidays start next weekend?' he said. 'I could help you out at the hotel until it's time for us to go to Ireland.'

Tara was momentarily taken aback. She had been going to suggest that he travel up from London the day before they left, so that he could catch his breath overnight before setting off again. 'I'm not too sure about space at the moment,' she hedged.

'Oh, don't worry if you haven't room for me in *your* house,' he said quickly. 'Bridget and Fred have told me tons of times that I can stay with them. She says they usually have one spare room, and if they haven't, I can always share a room with Michael.' There was a little pause. 'Don't you remember?'

Tara smiled to herself. William was always a step ahead. Always planning, always working things out to get what he wanted. He was so very different from the easy-going Gabriel. Different in looks – dark whereas his older brother had been blond – and different in nature. 'I don't mind when you come,' she told him. 'Just check things with your mother and Harry first. They might prefer to have you at home for some of the holiday.'

'Oh, I'd already asked them if I could come up at Easter,' he replied, 'so there won't be any problem there.' He paused. 'D'you think we might go down to that house in County Clare again?'

'No,' Tara said, 'the people will be using it, and anyway, I've only got ten days off work, so we can't fit it in.'

'What about going to see Joe in Cork?' he suggested. On a previous trip, Tara had taken William down to visit her brother Joe, who was a curate in a parish just outside the city. 'Or maybe Dublin for a day out?'

Tara took a deep breath, feeling slightly overwhelmed by the young boy's enthusiasm. 'We'll see,' she said. 'We might just take things as they come, see what the weather's like.'

'Brilliant!' he said. 'It'll be like a surprise holiday, then.'

'I've got to go,' Tara told him. 'Give me a ring when you've organised your train times.'

After she had put the phone back in its cradle, Tara sat in her office chair staring thoughtfully at nothing in particular. Then she made herself tidy her desk and put things away in the filing cabinet.

Afterwards, she looked at her watch and decided that she might as well stay on in the hotel for the evening meal. She had nothing else planned, and it was better than going back to the house. She reached for the phone again.

'Bridget,' she said, when she heard her friend's voice. 'Do you fancy joining me for dinner down in the hotel tonight? My treat.'

'Oh, Tara, I wish I could,' Bridget said, 'but we've to be out the door at half past six tonight. There's a thing for Cubs that me and Fred need to attend. Michael's going on a weekend camp at Easter.'

'Oh, don't worry about it,' Tara said casually. 'It was just a spur-of-the-moment thought.'

'I've never had a day like it,' Bridget told her, sounding more than a touch harassed. 'Poor Helen has been off school with a bad cold, and all she's wanted is to be nursed all day, so I've hardly been able to get a thing done in the house. June was in for most of the day because we had planned to change all the beds, but by the time we got the breakfast things cleared up and the beds all stripped and the fresh bed linen back on, it was time for her to go and collect Michael. And when she got back she only had a few minutes to tidy the bathrooms for me, so I'm runnin' about like a headless chicken now, trying to finish the upstairs rooms and get the dinner ready for the lads comin' in from work.'

'Angela is on her way to help you,' Tara said, hoping that would ease things for her friend.

'Thanks be to God,' Bridget sighed. 'And she's going to stay on and mind Helen and Lucy while we're out at the Cubs meeting.' She paused for a moment. 'How would tomorrow night suit you for the meal? Fred is going to a wrestling match and June said she's available to babysit for a few hours.'

'Yes,' Tara said, 'that would be grand. I'm free tomorrow night as well.'

Then, as she hung up, Tara thought, I'm free tonight, tomorrow night – and every other night.

Chapter 6

'Here comes the cavalry!' Bridget said delightedly, when Angela walked into the kitchen of the boarding house. She gestured to the piles of carrots and potatoes that needed peeling, and the slices of fish that had to be coated in bread-crumbs then fried. She shook her head. 'It's been one of those days. I've never been so behind in me life.'

'Oh, we'll soon catch up,' Angela reassured her. 'If we get the lads' dinner going first, then we can do all the other bits and pieces while it's cooking.'

She still loved coming to Maple Terrace, enjoying the hustle and bustle of the daily routine. There was always someone to chat to, whether it was the young-at-heart Bridget, who loved a good gossip and a laugh, the brassy June, the lodgers, or even the children. Angela felt it was a real home-from-home place, and while she quite enjoyed living in Tara's elegant house in Cale Green and found it handy for work, she loved the lighter, more homely atmosphere in the boarding house.

Angela hung her black suit jacket on the back of one of the kitchen chairs, then took her blue nylon overall from the hook on the door and put it on. She absolutely hated wearing the overall, thinking it made her look dowdy and as old-looking as Bridget and June, but it was a necessary evil to keep her receptionist's white blouse and suit skirt clean. She would get all the dirty jobs over and done with early, so that she could have the overall off and in the washing by the time the younger lads came back from work. It wasn't really that she fancied any of them enough to care how she looked, but in the last year or so – since meeting all different kinds of men through her receptionist job in the hotel – Angela Flynn had become very conscious of her appearance.

'It's all hands on deck this evening, as me and Fred need to get off early,' Bridget said, filling the basin with water for the potatoes.

'I'll do those for you,' Angela said, taking the basin and the potato-peeler from her. She carried them over to the table. 'Did you say it's a Cubs meeting you're going to?'

Bridget nodded. 'It's about their weekend away at Easter. They want to talk to us about the clothes the boys have to bring and that kind of thing.' She ran a carrot under the tap to make sure it was clean, then started to peel it with a small sharp knife. 'Michael's delighted, so he is. It's only the second time he's been away from home on his own. He's in the sitting-room, writing out a list of all the things he has to take with him.' She shook her head and laughed. 'He keeps reading it out to Helen, and she keeps telling him to be quiet and to let her read her comic. I looked in a few minutes ago and he was even reading it out to Lucy, who doesn't understand a word of what he's saying.'

39

'Oh, God love him,' Angela said. She picked up a potato now and started to peel it, letting the long, curly skins fall back into the warm water. 'Talking about kids being away from home, William Fitzgerald is coming up to Stockport next week, and guess what?'

Bridget stopped peeling the carrot. 'What?' she asked, full of curiosity.

'He's coming to Ireland with me and Tara for a week.'

'*Tara's* going to Ireland?' Bridget said in surprise. 'Since when?'

'She called me into the office just before I left the hotel,' Angela explained, 'and told me that she had decided to come over to Ireland with me.'

'She never mentioned it when we were on the phone,' Bridget said, feeling slightly hurt that Angela knew something about Tara that she didn't. 'She called to see if I fancied meeting her tonight, so she was probably going to tell me when we met up.'

'Did you fancy coming as well?' Angela said. 'Tara's taking the car, so there would be plenty of room.'

'No, no ... not at all,' Bridget said, taken aback at the suggestion. She started scraping away at the carrot again. 'Sure, how could I, with the children and everything?' The very thought of returning to Ballygrace was enough to make her feel sicker than she already felt this evening.

'Could you not get June or somebody in to help you?' Angela suggested, thinking that it would be a real laugh to have Bridget with them in the car and on the boat journey. 'What about Fred's sister or his parents? Didn't the children stay a weekend over the Christmas holidays with them?'

'They did,' Bridget confirmed, 'and they would be good enough to have them anytime we need them, but I really have no interest in going back to Ballygrace.' She paused from scraping carrots again, a distant look in her eyes. 'You see, I don't have the same happy memories of County Offaly as you do, Angela. I don't have any family or a home-place to go back to.' Her voice faltered a little. 'It would be no holiday for me. It would only depress me to go back to Ballygrace again, to have to remember all the terrible times I had there when I was growing up.'

'Oh, that's a shame,' Angela said, feeling very awkward now and wishing she'd never made the suggestion.

Sensing the younger girl's discomfort, Bridget said, 'Even if I did want to go, I don't think it would be too sensible going on a boat when I'm already feelin' squeamish every morning and at various times during the day. If the sea was rough it would finish me off entirely.'

'Is the sickness that bad?' Angela asked, always intrigued about babies and pregnancies. Her mother and the other women back in Ireland were very secretive about it, but Bridget was always very open about things like that. As she was getting that little bit older herself, Angela reckoned that she needed to become more acquainted with that part of life.

'I suppose I'm no worse than I was with the others,' Bridget said, 'but a boat is the last thing you need in the early weeks.' She paused, a thoughtful look in her eye. 'But you're right about havin' a break away. I might suggest to Fred that me and him should have a few days in Blackpool on our own when the weather improves.'

Even as she said it, Bridget knew that it was highly unlikely she and Fred would get around to doing that. Even if Fred's parents had the kids, she would have a lot of organising to do so that the boarding house ran properly in her absence. There was so much to be done, and each day seemed to offer less time in which to do it.

The two of them chatted as they peeled the potatoes and carrots and put them on to boil, then Angela dressed the fish in breadcrumbs while Bridget opened a catering-sized tin of processed peas. She put them into a large pan ready for heating when the rest of the meal was near completion. Then, leaving Angela to set the table and keep an eye on the proceedings, she went to sort out Michael's Cubs uniform for the meeting.

As she mounted the stairs, Bridget felt a sudden heavy weight in her chest and stomach. Any talk about Ireland always left her feeling low. And lately it seemed almost to envelop her. She had felt slightly better talking to Tara about it the other night, but as soon as she got into bed – into the darkness of the room – the ghosts and the memories of Ballygrace came flooding back.

How could she really explain to Angela and Tara why she felt this way? Sure, she could hardly explain it to herself. All she knew was that when she went back to Ireland for Gabriel's funeral, she felt she had had a narrow escape, that she had been lucky no skeletons had leapt out of cupboards at her. That no one had said there was no point in pretending she was a well-to-do landlady from Stockport, when everyone knew she was one of Lizzie Lawless's poor orphans from Ballygrace. One of the girls who had been half-starved and neglected, who went with any man to give her a good look or a kind word.

And Bridget Hart was the one who, rumour had it, had had an illegitimate child and dumped it in an orphanage run by the nuns, then disappeared over to England.

How could she walk back into that lion's den again? Was it any wonder that she wanted to keep as far away from Ireland as she possibly could?

Chapter 7

I t was the night before William was due to arrive in Stockport when Frank Kennedy walked into the Cale Green Hotel. He was immaculately dressed as usual, in a grey herring-bone coat over a dark pin-stripe suit and a sky-blue shirt. If he had been any other man, the well-chosen outfit would have caught Tara's appreciative eye. But he wasn't any other man. And there was not one single thing about him that she could find to appreciate. Apart from, perhaps, his unfaltering business sense.

She was standing at the bar, chatting to Fred, when she saw the four smartly dressed businessmen walk in, heading in the direction of the restaurant. And although she hadn't had more than a sidelong glimpse of the group, she knew that Frank Kennedy was one of them.

Even in a crowd Tara could pick him out, could always tell when he was in a room. And each time, her hackles rose.

Fred waved cheerily. 'And how's Mr Kennedy?' he called

After a few words with his companions, and gesturing towards a free table, he came across to them.

'Fred,' he said, smiling warmly at the barman, 'I'll have a large Jameson's.' Then he turned to Tara, 'And whatever Mrs Fitzgerald will have.'

'Nothing, thanks,' she said, lifting the file she had placed on the bar. 'I've still some things to sort out in the office.'

Fred turned towards the drinks gantry to select the Irish whiskey.

'That's a pity. Well, maybe I could catch you for a drink after our meal?' Frank ventured. 'I wouldn't mind having a few words with you.'

Tara frowned. 'What about?'

'This and that,' he said lightly. 'Just some developments that have cropped up regarding the Grosvenor.'

She shrugged, holding herself back from being obviously rude to him in front of her barman, although she knew Fred was well aware of her feelings for Frank Kennedy. 'I already told you I had no interest in it.'

Frank raised his eyebrows. 'When you hear what's in the air, you might just change your mind.'

'I seriously doubt it,' Tara said dismissively.

The stocky barman placed the glass of whiskey on the bar now, along with a small jug of water bearing the Jameson's emblem and name, and took the pound note proffered by Frank. 'Sorry for interrupting you,' he said, 'but what time did you book your meal for tonight, Tara?'

Tara's eyes flitted towards the clock above the bar which said it was just a few minutes past seven. 'Eight or even half past will be grand,' she said casually. She looked down at the file she was holding and flicked through the top few sheets, to emphasise just how busy she was.

'Look, Tara,' Frank said, when the barman had gone to the till for his change, 'why don't you join the group of us in the restaurant now?' He looked her straight in the eye. 'They're all very influential men in Cheshire, and it wouldn't do you any harm to get acquainted with them. You never know where it might lead with regard to business.' He gave a little shrug. 'It would also do no harm for them to hear how you can cater for business lunches and meetings, or provide accommodation for business clients who prefer the smaller type of hotel.'

Tara glanced up at him. 'I don't think it would look too good me having dinner with you. People – Kate – might get the wrong impression.'

'Fine,' he said. 'If that's how you feel then I'm not going to argue with you.' He began to walk away then suddenly stopped. 'However you feel about me, Tara, I can assure you that I would only ever have your best interests at heart. And I have to tell you, there's not a man in town who would talk to me the way that you do. And there's no businessman or woman that I know of who lets all this personal stuff stand in their way.' He shook his head. 'Our differences happened a long time ago, and I think you should do yourself a big favour and let it all go.'

And then, before Tara had a chance to voice a sharp retort, he turned on his heel and walked away.

Tara stood for a few minutes absolutely fuming, then she composed herself and went back to her office. How dare he? She thought. How bloody well dare he? And yet, when she had simmered down and thought the conversation over, in her heart of hearts she knew he was right. If one of her good customers, or even someone using the hotel for the first time, had overheard the way she had spoken to him they wouldn't have been at all impressed. And she would only have herself to blame.

She would have to try to find a better way of handling things.

A better way of handling Frank Kennedy.

A short time later there was a knock at Tara's office door.

'The group has now left the restaurant, Mrs Fitzgerald,' the young waitress told her, 'and your own table is ready.'

'Thank you, Marie,' Tara replied, lifting her handbag from her desk. She was absolutely famished, having not eaten since lunchtime, but would rather have missed a meal entirely than have to share a table with Frank Kennedy and his business cronies.

She went quickly past the busy, Friday-night bar and on into the three-quarters-full restaurant, pleased that there was still a good crowd in at this time of the evening. She sat down at her usual table for two by the window and picked up the menu. In deference to her Irish Catholic upbringing, and through sheer habit, she always went for fish on a Friday. There were two dishes on offer – cod in batter with a parsley sauce, and salmon steak with hollandaise sauce.

'I'll have the salmon with sauté potatoes and the vegetable selection,' Tara told Marie, 'and a glass of the house white wine, please.'

While she waited for her meal, Tara sat looking around the restaurant, weighing up the type of customers they were attracting. Tonight it was mainly residents, with a number of local people who lived within walking distance. Mid-week it was usually just the residents, plus any corporate clients holding meetings or seminars in one of the two function rooms.

Things would start to get much busier in the next week or two with the Easter break approaching, and then it would pick up until the summer season started. All in all, the Cale Green Hotel had done better than Tara could ever have hoped, but she knew there was still room for improvement.

When Tara had finished her meal she headed back to her office to collect her coat. As she passed through the bar, she caught sight of the group of businessmen sitting at a corner table, so she turned her head and carried on walking. She had a quick word with Carol on reception, checking all was well for the night, then she went into her office.

She had locked her office door and was just pulling on her coat when she saw one of the men from Frank's group coming towards her. He looked mid-to-late thirties – at least a few years older than Tara – with sandy-coloured hair starting to fleck a little with grey at the temples. The way that Gabriel's blond hair would probably have gone if he had grown older.

'Mrs Fitzgerald?' he said, holding out his hand. 'Gerry McShane.'

Although she immediately thought that this was yet another ploy of Frank Kennedy's to involve her in the Grosvenor project, Tara smiled and returned his firm handshake. Business was business, and she couldn't afford to dismiss someone just because they might know a common party. She would have to hear him out.

'I want to compliment you on the lovely job you've done with the hotel,' he told her. His voice was warm and his hazel eyes were bright and friendly. 'I haven't been here since you took it over, and I must say that I'm extremely impressed.'

'Thank you,' Tara replied, in an even but cautious tone. 'I'm delighted you think so.'

'You've improved it in every way,' he continued. 'The work you've carried out is evident throughout, from the stonework outside to the very tasteful furnishings.'

Tara kept smiling, politely waiting to see if there was a point to the conversation.

'I wondered,' he said, looking directly at her now, 'if you'd be interested in joining a little business discussion that we're having in the bar? You've heard about the Grosvenor going up for sale?'

Tara deliberately glanced at her watch. 'I know about the sale, Frank Kennedy put me in the picture, but I don't really think I could add anything to your discussion.'

'Please?' he said, raising his eyebrows. 'It wouldn't take very long.'

She took a deep breath, intent on refusing. Then, she saw something in Gerry McShane's eyes. Something that reminded her of Gabriel, something that told her he was innately decent and honest. She softened. 'I don't have much time,' she told him. 'I have a visitor arriving from London in the morning, and I've things to prepare.'

They walked back into the bar, and Tara felt her face tighten when she saw Frank Kennedy's eyes light up as he saw her. But she was grateful that he sat quietly as Gerry McShane introduced her to the two other men, a balding architect called Eric Simmons and an older man called John Burns.

He left Frank until last. 'I believe you and Frank are already acquainted,' he said, and Tara gave a brief nod. The barmaid appeared at the table to see if they were ready for another round of drinks. Instead of stepping in to check what refreshment Tara wanted, Frank ordered his own drink and left Gerry McShane to sort her out with a small glass of sherry.

Then, when the barmaid had bustled back to the bar, the oldest man in the group, John Burns, looked over at Tara. Gerry McShane had introduced him as the owner of the biggest local newspaper. 'You're here by popular demand, Mrs Fitzgerald,' he said, smiling warmly at her. 'We feel we could do with a bit of feminine input, so to speak, and there's a scarcity of women running hotels in the area.'

'I'm not at all sure I could be of any help to you,' she said, with a slightly bemused smile. 'I've relatively little experience in the business.'

Frank sat up in his chair. 'But you've single-handedly turned this place around, Tara,' he said. 'You've restored every little detail.' He ran his hand over the carved wood of his armchair. 'You spent a lot of time checking out the exact style you wanted, then sourcing people who could restore and renovate the things you wanted to keep.'

Tara looked back at him. 'Yes, I did do all that,' she said quietly, 'but it was a very small project in comparison to a town or city centre hotel. And even though this place is small, it took a lot of effort.'

Gerry McShane turned to her now. 'You know that there is a business group putting a bid in for the Grosvenor Hotel?'

Tara nodded. 'I've heard various rumours,' she told him, 'but I wouldn't be that up on the business goings-on around the town.'

'Well,' John Burns said, looking directly at her again, 'we are the four people involved in the takeover.' He studied her for a moment. 'We think your expertise on refurbishment and style is just what we need – and we wondered if you would consider being a fifth member of the group?'

Tara felt a red heat rising to her face. 'I'm afraid I wouldn't be in the financial position to join any kind of a business group.' She was more than a little annoyed with Frank Kennedy for putting her in this embarrassing situation, where she had to explain her finances to a group of strangers. 'The money I have is already tied up in the hotel and in other properties.' She paused, a picture of the newly landscaped hotel gardens suddenly coming into her mind. The bill would be arriving the following week and would be waiting for her when she came back from Ireland. 'If you need a fifth person, I think it would be advisable to look elsewhere.'

'We've done a very good deal – and I'm sure it's not as expensive as you think when there are so many people involved,' the older man said. 'And there are always ways to release or raise money.'

'If we gave you some figures,' Gerry McShane suggested, 'would you take the time to have a look at them?' He lifted his briefcase from the floor and started sorting through various papers.

Tara pursed her lips. What harm could looking at the figures do? And even though this certainly wasn't the time for getting involved in a high-flown business venture, it was impossible to know what might happen in the future. 'I'll look,' she told him, 'but I'm not promising anything more.'

Chapter 8

William had grown since Tara had last seen him. She was momentarily surprised, then realised that she shouldn't have been. He was at that in-between stage, still a child but not for much longer. She hoped his childish enthusiasm wouldn't disappear. He had come running along the platform at Stockport station, calling, 'Tara,' one hand securing his hold-all on his shoulder and the other hand waving excitedly. Then he came to a standstill in front of her and put the bag down on the ground. There was a moment's hesitation, where he wasn't quite sure whether he should hug her or shake her hand. Excitement took over and he flung his arms around her neck, landing an awkward kiss somewhere between her ear and her cheek.

'It's lovely to see you, William,' Tara said, hugging him back. The close physical contact suddenly brought a lump to her throat, and it crossed Tara's mind that she hadn't been this close to another human being in a happy way since Gabriel had died. On odd occasions she had put her arms around Bridget to comfort her, and on other occasions she had kissed or hugged people in greeting, but that had been the extent of it.

'Thanks for letting me come up to Stockport,' he said, 'and for inviting me to Ireland.'

Immediately Tara felt a wave of guilt that the boy should be so grateful to her. He was, after all, Gabriel's younger brother, and it shouldn't be that big an effort to include him in her life. 'I'm delighted that I could get the time off work to spend with you, William,' she told him as they walked along the platform together. 'And it will be lovely having you in Ireland with me again.'

'Who will we see when we go to Ballygrace?' William asked eagerly.

'I should think we'll see my father, Tessie and all the family, and of course Angela will be there with us.'

'What about Father Joe?' William asked. 'Do you think we might see him again?'

Last summer, Tara's brother Joe had taken a few days off from his parish work to come up to Ballygrace, and he had taken William to a couple of football matches and swimming in the outdoor pool in Tullamore. These were all things the boy enjoyed, and Joe knew that most of his time was spent with elderly adults in London.

Tara took a deep breath. With all the rushing around, organising things in the hotel before she left, she hadn't really given a thought to Joe or anyone else she might see when she was in Ireland. She supposed she was just going to take things as they came, do things the way they did back home, casually and without any prior organisation. But Joe would need a bit more warning. He couldn't just up and leave his parish commitments at the drop of a hat. 'I'm actually going to ring Joe this evening,' she told William, 'so we'll know then whether he can come up for a few days.'

'Brilliant!' William said, his eyes shining. 'I've brought a sports jacket and trousers, and training shoes for playing football with Joe, or for going to the park with Michael.'

'Very sensible,' Tara said, smiling warmly at him. 'We don't go to Ireland until next Tuesday night, so you'll have plenty of opportunities to play out and enjoy yourself.'

'I want to help you in the hotel, too,' he said, his face serious now. 'I'll help Fred around the bar again, picking up the glasses and that kind of thing.'

'You'll be sorry you said that,' Tara joked. 'We'll have you run off your feet with work.'

They drove up the hill from the station and straight to Bridget's boarding house, where Tara knew there would be the kind of welcome that William would love.

'My God!' Bridget exclaimed when she opened the door. 'Would you look at the size of you?' Then she swept him in, calling for Michael, Helen, Fred and June to come and see him.

As always, the two younger children were slightly shy and awkward for the first ten minutes, and it was left to the adults to do the chatting and ask William all the right questions about what he'd been up to since they'd last seen him. Then Bridget turned towards a cupboard. 'I've made your favourite fruit cake,' she told the boy, 'and since it's Lent and our two aren't allowed chocolate or biscuits, I went mad and iced it all for you.'

'Oh, thanks!' William said when the rich cake was produced. 'Can I have a piece now?'

By the time the cake had been sliced and glasses of lemonade poured, all three children were laughing and chatting together. Michael was puffed up with importance as he told William all about his Cubs trip over the Easter weekend.

'It's amazing how William just fits in again every time he comes back, isn't it?' Bridget said quietly.

Tara nodded and gave a little wry smile. 'I suppose he's a little bit like myself,' she said. 'He likes to feel that he's a part of a lively, happy family every now and again.'

Chapter 9

BALLYGRACE

They were only ten minutes into their journey from Dublin docks to County Offaly when Angela was asleep again in the back of the car. William, refreshed from his few hours' sleep on the boat overnight, was bright-eyed and chatty all the way down to Ballygrace.

As soon as the car pulled up outside the familiar white-washed cottage, Tara's Uncle Mick – a stocky man with a ruddy face – and his neat, bright-eyed wife, Kitty, came rushing out to greet them. Tara always felt a strong sense of nostalgia at the old cottage, because it was where she spent her childhood years with her granda, widowed father, and Uncle Mick. In spite of the little pangs of sadness she suffered when remembering her grandfather, it was a happy house to visit, and Mick and Kitty, who had married late in life, were one of the most contented couples she knew.

A short while later they were all sitting in the warm kitchen, drinking tea from Kitty's shamrock-sprigged cups and eating slices of freshly baked soda bread, while waiting for the bacon, sausages and black-and-white pudding to finish frying in the pan. Angela had gradually woken up and was just coming round properly.

'Any exciting news around Ballygrace since I last saw you?' Tara asked, as she reached across for the jar of marmalade.

There was a small, awkward silence, then Mick put his cap on and patted William on the head. 'How would you like to have a look outside at the babby chickens?'

Immediately, Tara knew that there was indeed news and it wasn't good.

After the door closed behind them, Tara looked at her aunt. 'What's wrong?'

'I didn't want to say anything in front of William,' Kitty said, her gaze flickering from Tara to the sleepy-eyed Angela, 'but we heard some bad news yesterday. The body of a young girl has been found up in the bog.'

Angela's eyes opened wide. 'A dead body! Imagine something like that happening in Ballygrace.'

Kitty looked at Tara. 'I could have rung you, but you were due to leave, so we decided to wait and tell you when you got here. We thought we might have more news by then.'

'Oh, dear God,' Tara said in a low voice. 'Have they any idea who it is?'

'Not so far,' Kitty explained. 'It would seem that it's been there for a good number of years.' She shrugged. 'It was some men from Bord na Mona who found her, up near the bog railway tracks.'

Angela sat forward, her elbows resting on the pine kitchen table, her chin cupped in her hands. 'Can they tell what's happened to her? Does it look like she's been murdered or something like that?'

Kitty pulled a face. 'It would be very hard to know at this stage,' she said, 'and we didn't get to hear what kind of condition the body was in. The Guards had the whole area sectioned off. The people who examine the body are due to arrive from Dublin today. I think they were waiting until it was daylight to check the area before they moved her.' She shrugged. 'They'll probably have to do all sorts of tests on the body to find out what age she is and how long she's been there.'

'The poor soul,' Tara said, shaking her head. 'I wonder if she's a local girl.'

Kitty got up from the table to check the pan, then called Mick and William to come back in as the breakfast was now ready.

William came through the door very carefully, carrying four new-laid eggs in the rolled-up rib at the bottom of his jumper. 'Two duck and two hen eggs,' he informed them, as though he had been collecting eggs all his life.

'Pick the one you want and we'll put it straight into the pan,' Kitty told him.

Whether it was because she was tired from her long journey or because of the startling news, Tara felt herself beginning to wilt by the time they had finished their meal. 'I hope you don't mind us heading off so quickly,' she told Kitty and Mick, 'but we've got to drive into Tullamore now and drop Angela off at my father and Tessie's house.'

Kitty looked in surprise at Angela. 'I thought you would be staying at Ballygrace House?'

Angela immediately coloured up, because she knew that Tara would probably have liked her company in the big empty place. 'I might come back over later in the week,' she said. There was an awkward pause. 'It's just that I'd written to Mammy and Daddy ages before Tara said she was coming, and I told them I'd be staying with them in Tullamore.'

'Ah, well, I suppose it's understandable that they would want to see you,' Kitty said, smiling warmly at her young niece. 'I know they still miss having you around.'

Angela nodded. 'I'll be back and forth to Ballygrace anyway,' she emphasised.

One of the main reasons Angela had decided to go home was to catch up with her friends and have a few nights out dancing or at the pictures. In all honesty, after the town life she had become used to over in England, she now found Ballygrace House a bit remote and quiet. And it wasn't as if she knew any young ones in Ballygrace or Daingean who she could go out with, even for a bit of a walk in the nice evenings.

And although it wasn't the size of Stockport, Tullamore had plenty going on, and she knew every second person in the place. Going to Mass and the other Easter church services was as good as any social event, with people stopping to ask her how she was getting on over in England and if she had any plans to come back to Ireland in the future.

Angela was also looking forward to having a break from her more formal lifestyle. And although she enjoyed her job and was happy enough with her small room in Tara's house, she felt stifled at times and liked to escape back home where she could let her hair down with her old friends, and allow her mother and father to mollycoddle her at home.

If she were to spend the whole week in Ballygrace House she would inevitably feel that she had to revert to her housekeeper role for Tara, the job she had done for a while before moving away. Not that Tara would expect it, but Angela knew Ella Keating wasn't available to spend every single day at the house, and she would feel guilty just sitting around while Tara looked after her and William.

Angela would, on the other hand, have no qualms about having her mother wait on her hand and foot, cooking her a nice fried breakfast with her favourite black-and-white pudding every morning, and all the familiar meals she enjoyed in the evening.

Now that the others had all left home, Tessie enjoyed doing things for her, and Angela didn't feel the slightest bit guilty about being spoiled.

Tara, however, was a different kettle of fish altogether, and, if Angela were honest, there were times when it was a bit draining having Tara as both her boss in the hotel *and* her landlady. At times she felt she had to be on her best behaviour night and day. Besides, she really felt she'd worked very hard in the Cale Green Hotel these last few months and she just needed a few days away to think only of herself. To *be* herself.

As William and Angela were settling back into the car for the drive to Tullamore, Tara lingered at the cottage door for a few moments with Kitty and Mick.

'You always have everything so perfect and orderly around here,' Tara said, indicating the rows of late daffodils and the purple and yellow crocuses.

'Sure, what's there to keep tidy?' Mick said, rolling his shirt-sleeves up to the elbow. 'You'd fit this whole place into a corner of Ballygrace House. You'd certainly know you were working if you were looking after a place that size.'

Tara felt a pang of guilt at the mention of the workload out at her house. 'I hope my father has agreed to get some of the local lads to help him out this year, with jobs like cutting the grass and the hedges,' she said now. 'I told him last year that it was getting a bit much for one man to do on his own.'

'Now, you know how bull-headed Shay Flynn is,' Mick said, shaking his head. 'We've all told him recently that he needs to slow down, but he's the kind of a lad that won't take a warning.' Then he glanced over in his wife's direction, and the look on Kitty's face brought him to a sudden halt.

Immediately, Tara sensed something. 'What's wrong?' she asked, her gaze moving from one to the other.

'It's nothing really,' Kitty said, her face flushing. 'It's just that your father ...'

'What about him?' Tara urged.

'He's not been the best recently,' Mick said in a low voice, regretful now that he'd put his foot in it, and knowing that Kitty would take him to task when the visitors were gone. 'A few oul' funny turns, that kind of thing.'

Tara's face suddenly darkened.

'It's not our place to be telling you,' Kitty said, looking anxiously towards the car to check that Angela couldn't hear them. 'I don't think they wanted to worry you. You know what your father's like about being sick – he makes little of anything along those lines. But I do know that Tessie was going to let you know if it happened again.'

'What sort of funny turns are you talking about?' Tara asked, her frown deepening.

Mick's face reddened now as it was wont to do when he felt any kind of spotlight was on him. 'Ah, he took kind of weak a few times, dizzy spells, and said he couldn't see too well. He was a bit mixed-up as well … but sure, it passed after a while and he was grand.' He shrugged. 'Oul' blood pressure or something like that, the doctor said. They've given him some tablets, and if it happens again they're sending him up to the hospital for some kind of tests.'

'Now, don't be worrying yourself,' Kitty told her, putting a comforting hand on her shoulder, 'because he was out here the other day and he was as right as rain.'

Tara felt a chill run through her. 'How is it, Kitty,' she said in a low voice, 'that just when you think things are getting onto an even keel, something always seems to happen?'

Chapter 10

As soon as the car pulled up outside the house, Shay appeared at the door to help lift any luggage out. 'Well, girls,' he said, grinning delightedly as the car doors opened, 'how was the trip over? Did youse have decent weather for the boat?'

'Grand,' Angela told him, as she got out of the car. 'Not a bother at all.' She gave her father the gesture of a hug, for they were not a family given to open demonstrations of affection, then she moved to the car boot to locate her various bags.

Tara went towards her father, trying not to look as though she were checking him. She made the same gesture as her half-sister, then gave him a peck on the cheek. 'You're looking well,' she told him, because, in all honesty, she could see no great difference in him from the previous October. Smaller than his tall, elegant daughter, Shay still had a reasonable head of curly dark, greying hair, and he moved more quickly than a lot of men half his age.

'Ah, sure, I'm holding up well,' he told her, giving her a sidelong smile. 'Me and Tessie are the finest.' He looked back towards the house now to see if there was any sign of his wife. 'She was busy taking a bit of baking out of the oven when you pulled up. You know what she's like with those kind of things.' He caught sight of William in the back seat of the car. 'Young Mr Fitzgerald, how the hell are you!' he exclaimed with the over-dramatic welcome he knew the boy would like.

William opened the back door now and got out, his face beaming. 'I'm very well thank you, Mr Flynn,' he said, going over to shake Shay's hand.

Shay grabbed his hand and gave it a hefty shake. 'I only hope you're fit enough to eat all these cakes that Tessie's been baking all morning,' he said, winking.

William made a funny face. 'I'm afraid there's only one problem,' he said. 'We've just eaten a gi-*normous* breakfast out at Kitty and Mick's.'

Shay pretended to look very serious now. 'Well,' he said, putting his hands on his hips, 'if you're half the man I think you are, you'll manage at least a half a dozen of them, no trouble.'

William looked over at Tara and rolled his eyes dramatically. 'I don't think you would want your passenger to be sick all over the car, would you, Tara?' he said.

'Welcome! Welcome!' Tessie said, rushing down the path towards them. Apart from the obvious lines and wrinkles that would be expected at her age, Tessie looked very well. Her thick, slightly greying hair had obviously been washed and set for their arrival, and her still buxom figure was warmly dressed in a hand-knitted pink sweater, which went well with her wine-coloured slacks.

'We thought we'd call in for a few minutes before heading over to Ballygrace House,' Tara told her, giving Tessie a hug. She hoped she'd be able to grab a few minutes with her stepmother later to talk about her father's health.

'Thought you'd drop in on the oul' ones, and see if they're still the same as you left them last?' Shay joked.

'Don't mind that fella,' Tessie told her, tutting and pulling a face at her husband. 'Sure, we're grand, Tara,' she said, in almost the same tone that Shay had used earlier, 'and grander still for seeing you all.' She ushered them all towards the house now. 'Come in, come in. I have the kettle boiled and some nice fresh scones and buns.'

The visitors and Shay all sat down at the kitchen table now as Tessie continued to bustle around, putting a plate of hot scones in the middle of the table, along with butter and a jar of home-made strawberry jam, then passing around plates for them all.

'You're both looking very well,' Tara said.

'She's rushin' about too much, as usual,' Shay said, prodding a finger in his wife's direction. 'She walks around the town two or three times a day, getting shopping and doing errands for some oul' couple that she hardly knows.'

'Don't listen to him!' Tessie cut in, her voice exasperated. 'He's only saying that because we've all been getting on to *him*. It's a case of attack being the best form of defence.'

'You *are* running about helping this one and that one,' Shay persisted.

'The couple I've been helping aren't people I hardly know,' Tessie corrected. 'Yourself and meself have seen them at church for God knows how many years, and now the poor craturs are housebound and have no family near them.'

'She never sits down for more than five minutes,' Shay said, sailing on blithely. 'And if she's not runnin' after them pair, she's back and forth on the bus to Mullingar to visit Molly twice a week.' Molly was Shay's aunt who had helped to bring up Joe.

'Oh, shush,' Tessie said, rolling her eyes at her husband. 'You'd be giving out to me if I wasn't busy. And you'd be thinkin' there was something wrong if I didn't give a damn about dear old Molly or any other poor cratur that needs a bit of help.'

'How is Molly?' Tara asked.

'Just the same,' Tessie replied. 'She knows you one day and doesn't the next. But she's happy enough with the nuns in the nursing home and her old friend, Peggy Coulter.'

'So, what's the news in the town?' Angela asked. The last thing she wanted to hear about was boring old people that Tessie knew from church and her father's old auntie. 'Have any of the girls called round asking about me?'

'Indeed they have,' Tessie said, smiling now. 'We had Rose Fox here during her lunch break from the shop wondering when you were due home, and Carmel Malone called the other night to tell you that there was a crowd cycling over to a dance in the Roseland in Moate on Easter Monday night if you fancy going.'

Angela's eyes lit up. 'I'll call round to Carmel's house later,' she said, her mind flitting to all the nice outfits she'd brought home with her from England, which she would wear around the town over the next week. She was also delighted that her blonde hair had grown since her last visit, and she knew she would attract a lot of attention from the lads. 'The dances in Moate are always great,' she said, unconsciously running her fingers through her hair. 'We'll have to go early, though, as there's usually a good crowd at them.'

'Did you know that Rose is doing a line with a fellow from Durrow?' Tessie said.

Angela rolled her eyes to the ceiling. 'She writes about nothing else in her letters,' she said. 'According to Carmel Malone, he's a farmer, a very old-fashioned type of a farmer, and he's got two left feet on the dance floor.'

Tara suddenly laughed. 'Now, Angela,' she said, 'there's plenty to be said for old-fashioned farmers. They're solid and dependable. Many a girl would be delighted to settle down with one.'

Angela started to laugh now. 'You didn't exactly settle with a farmer yourself, and neither did Bridget.'

Tessie shot her younger daughter a warning glance. Tara could be very touchy when it came to personal matters and even now, several years later, everyone still felt very awkward alluding to Gabriel in her presence.

A faraway look came into Tara's eyes. 'True,' she said, nodding. 'But that's not to say it doesn't suit other girls.'

Tessie turned to Tara now, relieved she hadn't been offended by Angela's tactlessness. Maybe she was starting to move on, getting her life back to normal. 'We could look after William if you fancy going to the dance as well, Tara,' she said now. 'Girls of all ages go to Moate, don't they, Angela?'

Angela's face dropped, but before she could say anything, William suddenly cut in, 'Could we go for a walk out to Charleville Castle again?' he asked Shay. 'I really enjoyed hearing all the ghost stories the last time you took me there.'

'Of course we can,' Shay told him, his face lighting up. 'Sure, I've a hundred more stories about that place, an' every one of them true.'

Angela's heart sank as she listened to them making plans so that Tara could go to the dance. Surely she wasn't going to have to spend a night out with Tara? She had planned this holiday to have some time away from the confines and constraints of work and the house she shared with her kind but uppity half-sister. Surely to God she wasn't going to be saddled with her over these few precious days back home? She shot a warning glance at her mother, who looked back at her vacantly, oblivious to her thoughts.

'Wouldn't she be welcome to go along with you and the girls, Angela?' Tessie prompted, smiling from her daughter to her step-daughter.

Angela frowned. 'I'm not too sure if it would be Tara's cup of tea … You often get young lads in there who've had a bit too much to drink and they start messing around.'

Tara immediately got the message. 'I'm sure it's only for the younger ones,' she said lightly. 'And anyway, I wouldn't really have the time for that kind of thing. I have Joe coming up over the weekend and we'll have to go out to visit Auntie Molly and maybe take William for a run up to Dublin.'

'But it would do you the world of good, Tara, an' William would be grand out here with us for the evening,' Shay joined in now, much to Angela's consternation. 'A bit of an' oul' dance to let your hair down would be like a tonic for you. Sure, you and Biddy Hart used to have a great time going around the dance halls when you were young.' He pointed his finger in Angela's direction. 'If you were asked up for half the dances them pair were asked up for in their early days, you'd be in heaven. The lads were only mad for them.'

Angela gave a tight little smile. 'I think Tara might find it's changed a bit these days,' she said vaguely.

'I'm sure it has,' Tara said, nodding. 'It was a long time ago.'

'Ah, Tara, you can't go burying yourself in that big oul' house every time you come home,' Shay stated. 'Sure, it's not natural for a young woman like yerself. A bit of an oul' dance would do you the world of good.'

'I'm perfectly happy to spend a few days in Ballygrace House. That's the reason I came home,' Tara told him, but there was an edge to her voice, revealing that Shay's words had hit a raw nerve. 'I have plenty to keep me busy back in Stockport, so it's nice to have a bit of peace and quiet when I come back.'

'There's times when Ballygrace House is more like a mausoleum than a house,' Shay announced. 'It's grand enough, but it's the kind of place that needs a half a dozen childer running around in it to give it a bit of life.'

An awkward silence suddenly descended at Shay's tactless words, which Tara eventually broke. 'Well, it's my home and I happen to like it exactly as it is.'

Tessie looked across at Angela now, wishing she would speak up and encourage Tara to have a night out. She couldn't fathom why her daughter hadn't welcomed the idea of Tara going out with her and her friends, especially after all the good turns Tara had done her. 'Well, I think Tara should go to the dance hall with you,' she said to Angela. 'From what I've heard down in the hairdresser's, there's plenty of people Tara's age going to Roseland.'

'Mammy,' Angela said in a high, clearly irritated voice, 'Tara's more than welcome to come to the dance if that's what she wants, but she just said she's quite happy to stay at home.'

Tara reached for her handbag. 'I think it might be a good idea for William and me to head back to Ballygrace House now.' She stood up, smiling encouragingly at her young brother-in-law. 'Ella said she would have the fires all ready for us, and by the time we unpack and have a bit of a rest, the day will be nearly gone.'

'Sure, we'll see you shortly,' Shay told her, standing up, too. 'I've a few little jobs I want to do out at the house. We need to cut that feckin' oul flowering creeper that's startin' to grow into the walls and the window frames.'

'Shay ...' Tessie shot her husband a withering glance.

'Excuse the language,' he mumbled in Tara's direction, 'but I don't want it causin' any damage to the roof slates or the window sashes.' He sucked in his breath, conscious of having to measure his words more carefully. 'An' I want to have a word with you about a couple of oul' trees at the back that might need taking down.' He shook his head. 'Sure, if the weather got up very blowy again, they could easily cause someone a fierce bad injury.'

Tara's face darkened as she immediately remembered the falling tree that had killed Gabriel's sister and father some years back, but she said nothing, as it was obvious that neither her father nor stepmother had made the connection.

'You'll have to get someone that knows something about trees to take a look at them first,' Tessie told Shay. 'If it's a big enough tree it might even take two or three men to do it.'

Shay's eyes widened in indignation. 'Since when did you become an expert on taking trees down?' he demanded. 'Haven't I been looking after the trees at Ballygrace for the last number of years without any help or advice from you?'

'Please yourself,' Tessie told him, 'but if a tree falls down on top of you, or you have a heart attack trying to saw it all on your own, don't say that nobody warned you.'

'A heart attack, me arse!' Shay said, laughing now. He looked over at Tara. 'Have you ever heard the likes of that for exaggeration?'

Angela gave a great sigh. 'Would you listen to yourselves arguing, and I'm hardly in the door a half an hour,' she complained. 'I came home for a bit of peace and quiet, not to listen to the pair of you going at it hammer and tongs.' Just as she said it, she caught a frown of disapproval on Tara's face at her childish manner and Angela felt herself blush. God, she thought, I can't even let my guard down at home in front of my own family without Tara judging me.

'Sure, we're only chatting,' Tessie said in, a hurt tone. 'Me and your father get on just grand, don't we, Shay?'

'Begod, we do! Left to ourselves, we get on the finest,' Shay agreed, all smiles.

Tessie been looking forward to Angela and Tara coming home; and had been imagining all the little get-togethers the three women would have at their own place in Tullamore and at Ballygrace House. In the last year, Tessie had begun to picture Angela as a professional, grown-up woman who would meet a nice, well-to-do Englishman over in Stockport, get married and buy a nice house.

Angela – being her own daughter and more easy-going than Tara – would naturally have a more relaxed and down-to-earth house than Tara's, which they would be inclined to visit more often. Tessie could imagine herself and Shay paying regular trips over the water to visit Angela and her husband in their lovely house, with probably two or three little grandchildren running around.

But now, as she looked at the petulant pout on Angela's face, she realised that her daydreams were not grounded in reality. The time that Angela had been away from home had dimmed her memories about her daughter's prickly nature and the clashes that often occurred between them.

'Why don't you all come out to Ballygrace House on Good Friday?' Tara suggested, moving towards the front door, 'If you come to the church in Ballygrace for the Kissing of the Cross at three o'clock, then I'll do a meal for us all afterwards. Kitty and Mick will probably come, too.'

It would give her a chance to talk to Tessie on her own while her father and Mick did their usual tour around the gardens. Then she would find out if Shay Flynn really was as well as he looked.

Chapter 11

꧁

As soon as Tara's car pulled away, Angela felt as though a big weight had lifted from her. She walked back into the house, her arm tucked companionably through her mother's, all previous friction with her parents now forgotten. 'So,' she said, 'did you say that Rose and Carmel were calling around here or that I should call to see them?'

'Rose won't be finished working in the shop until after five,' Tessie reminded her, 'and Carmel has to be at home all day to give Mrs Malone a hand with things around the farmhouse.' As they walked into the kitchen she glanced at the clock. 'They'll probably just be dishing up lunch for the lads.'

Angela suddenly thought of Carmel's two older brothers. She usually had a bit of oul' craic with them. Joe and Pascal weren't the type of lads she would fancy – being plain-speaking and plain-looking farmer types – although she was well aware they definitely had an eye for her, which she used to her advantage. Being good dancers themselves, they were happy enough driving her and Carmel in the old family car to halls in the further flung areas, and the girls could always rely on them if they were stuck for dancing partners.

Angela wondered now if either of them had got themselves a girlfriend yet. While they weren't exactly to her liking, she knew that both boys were well regarded by a lot of girls in the area. If she hurried now, she might catch them at the end of the lunch break and have a cup of tea and a chat with them all.

'I think I might just take a walk up and see Carmel now,' she said.

'Would you not be better having a few hours in bed first?' Tessie said, throwing an eye to Shay to see what he thought of Angela disappearing as quickly as she had arrived. 'You can't have had much sleep on the boat.'

'I'm grand,' Angela said distractedly, going over to the sideboard to get her handbag.

Shay shrugged, signalling that it was nothing to do with him, and picked up the newspaper he had been reading before both his prickly daughters had arrived. How was it that he always managed to forget how difficult life could be when the house was swamped with women? A few years of being on their own had made all the arguments fade away. He and Tessie got on just grand – for most of the time.

Years ago he would never have imagined being so content with just the two of them in the house. When Shay was younger he had always been on the lookout for something exciting to happen. Something to lift him out of the mundane family life that most working men silently endured. But unlike the other men, he had done just that. He'd had a colourful life, and had been quite a ladies' man during his few years in England. But that was all in the past, and Shay Flynn was more than happy with the hand that life had dealt him as he headed into his twilight years.

'Mammy, would you plug the iron in for me?' Angela asked, turning towards her bedroom to get ready. 'I want to press a dress for going up to Carmel's.'

'Sure, you look fine as you are,' Tessie told her.

Angela gave her mother a withering look. 'I've been travelling all night in these things. I'm not going up to the Malones' looking like a tinker.'

'Get the dress and I'll iron it for you,' her mother said, rolling her eyes to the heavens.

A short while later, Angela emerged from her bedroom. After a thorough stand-up wash, she had changed into a blue flowery dress with a matching short jacket and cream, high-heeled, sling-back shoes.

Shay glanced at his daughter from behind his newspaper. 'Whose wedding are you going to all dressed up to the knockers like that?'

'Very funny,' Angela said, making a face at him. She turned to her mother. 'I'm looking forward to hearing all the girls' news,' she said, sounding bright and breezy now. She took her compact, a pale-blue eye-shadow and her lipstick, then moved a few sidesteps to look at herself in the oval mirror above the fireplace. It was an old, slightly mottled mirror, the border decorated with etched ribbons and bows, and had once hung in Shay's father's cottage in Ballygrace. With one eye opened wide and the other half-closed, Angela proceeded to brush the blue powder on her eyelids and, when that was finished, she applied a thick coat of pink lipstick.

Tessie glanced over at her daughter. 'Don't you think you're a bit made up for a visit out to the farm?'

Angela whirled round, her brows knitted in a frown. 'What d'you mean, *made up*?'

Tessie hesitated for a moment, trying to pick the right words. 'I just meant that they don't usually wear lipstick and the like during an ordinary day.'

'You had lipstick on when we arrived,' Angela challenged.

'Well,' Tessie said her face reddening, 'that was because Tara was coming to the house and she always looks well. You always feel you have to make a bit of an effort for her.'

'So, what's wrong with *me* wearing it?' Angela's voice was high with indignation now. 'Are you saying that it's fine for Tara to wear it but not me?'

'Indeed and I'm not saying that,' Tessie said, sighing loudly. She felt cornered now. 'It's just that Carmel might feel a bit awkward if she's in her oul' farming clothes.' She indicated her daughter's fancy outfit. 'She's used to seeing you dressed plainer and without any make-up during the day.'

Angela gave a shrug. 'It's hardly my fault that she's doing heavy, dirty work,' she said. 'And surely that doesn't mean I've to dress and look the same to make her feel better?' She started to comb her blonde hair.

'I'm not saying that,' Tessie said, moving to clear the table. She started to gather up the knives, forks and teaspoons.

'Carmel and the others know I've been living and working in England these past few years,' Angela went on, 'and they know I have to dress smartly for work. It's different to the work I did back here, and the girls I work with all dress nicely, too, so I'm used to making a bit of an effort.' She looked over at her mother now, a petulant look on her face. 'I'm not going to suddenly change into an oul' country yokel just because I've come home for a few days. And there's no point in having saved up for decent clothes not to wear them.'

'Please yourself,' Tessie said in a weary voice. 'Wear what you like.'

'That's exactly what I intend to do,' Angela replied curtly.

Shay sat up straight in his chair, suddenly aware of the tension in the room. 'There's no need to take that tone of voice with your mother,' he said sharply. 'Sure, you're hardly in the place five minutes and you're already giving out to everybody and causing trouble. We thought you'd left that kind of nonsense behind when you went across the water.' His brows came down now into a deep, disapproving V. 'You're not a twelve-year-old schoolgirl now, you know, and if you're fit to act the lady over in Stockport then you should be acting it towards your mother and showin' her a bit of respect.'

'Well, I feel as if I'm not five minutes in the house and the pair of ye are both onto me,' Angela retorted. 'As far as you're concerned, I can't do right for doing wrong. One minute I'm being told off for acting like a child and the next minute I'm being told that I'm too made up to be seen around the town.' She shrugged, looking on the verge of tears. 'What harm am I doing by going up to see Carmel in my decent clothes and with a bit of make-up?'

'Do what you like,' Shay told her. 'That's what you've always done.'

Chapter 12

As she walked along the main road and over the Kilbeggan Bridge towards Carmel's farm, Angela felt a pang of guilt at the way she had spoken to her mother. She had been childish and rude, and had spoiled the start of her first day back home for her parents. Even as she had been arguing with them, making petty points, she knew she should have been kinder and warmer. And she also knew that her mother had meant well when she reminded her that most of the girls here at home wouldn't dream of wearing lipstick or mascara during the day.

As she stepped along the Daingean Road, Angela became conscious of the stares she drew from other girls and the over-enthusiastic greetings from boys around her own age, as well as older men. She had lived too long in Tullamore not to know what was drawing the attention. And while she might have got away with her fancy outfit and her high heels for a walk in the town on a Sunday afternoon, it was definitely out of place for this time of the day. Angela found her confident stride slowing a little as she drew nearer to her friend's house, her mother's advice about her clothes and make-up ringing in her ears. And if she was truthful, she was regretting having worn the cream slingbacks, which were not suitable footwear for the bumpy, tractor-rutted farm lane she was now treading.

Just as she turned into the driveway to the Malones' farmhouse, she ducked behind a big bush. Quickly she opened her handbag and took out her powder compact and one of her initialled hankies. Very gingerly, she ran a corner of the hanky around both her eyes to remove most of the blue eye-shadow, then pressed a fresh part of the hanky to her lips to blot her lipstick to just a light cover. She held the little mirror at arm's length to check and immediately felt better at her toned-down face. But there was not a thing she could do about her outfit, so she took a deep breath and picked her way up the uneven path towards the front door, determined not to feel apologetic or awkward about how she looked.

Mrs Malone opened the door to her, wiping her wet hands on a tea towel. 'Angela Flynn!' she exclaimed, her eyes lighting up with delight. 'You're heartily welcome.' She ushered her into the kitchen. 'Come in, come in. Believe it or not, but you're the *second* unexpected visitor we've had today.'

'Hello, Mrs Malone. I thought I'd drop in and see how you're all doing,' Angela said, smiling warmly at the older woman. Mary Malone was always the same friendly way, whatever the circumstances.

Angela stepped into the kitchen to be met by a chorus of welcomes from the short-haired, bespectacled Carmel, her father Jimmy, her brothers and a farm worker, who were all sitting drinking tea and eating slices of soda bread with home-made jam to finish their main meal.

'Oh, the life in England's obviously suiting you,' Pascal Malone said, winking at her. 'You've always dressed well, but you're surely looking like a *real* lady now.'

'You're looking great, Angela,' Carmel told her, lifting a dish of discarded potato peelings off the table. 'How long are you home for?' Carmel was a short, elfin-faced girl with slightly prominent teeth, steady and old-fashioned in her ways, but she and Angela had always got on well, and the Malones' farmhouse was always one of the first places that Angela made for on her visits back home.

Although Carmel never had any exciting news about herself – boys always saw her as a friend and confidant rather than a girlfriend – she usually kept well up to date on the news in the town. And Carmel was always happy to fill Angela in on everything when she came home, or to pass it on in the long, descriptive letters she sent to her friend in Stockport.

'Exactly a week,' Angela replied, then she caught sight of a dark-haired young man sitting at the end of the table, dressed in a smart business suit and a dark tie. As she heaved a discreet little sigh of relief that she wasn't the only one in the room not attired for farm work, his deep brown eyes locked with hers. Angela suddenly caught her breath.

'Angela,' Jimmy Malone said, indicating the stranger, 'this is a young cousin of Mary's from Birr, Aiden Byrne. He was out at a funeral in the town and thought he'd call in on us.'

That, Angela realised, was obviously the reason for his formal attire.

Immediately, Aiden Byrne rose out of his chair and came around the table to take her hand in a warm, firm handshake. 'It's a pleasure to meet you, Angela,' he said, smiling and not taking his gaze off her.

As soon as he touched her, Angela felt something like a small electric jolt run through her. 'Nice to meet you, too,' she said, her face starting to burn up. Then, she became aware that their hands were still joined and she quickly withdrew hers. She felt so clumsy and awkward, and was sure all the Malones were wondering what on earth was wrong with her.

'Here,' Carmel said, pulling a chair out at the opposite end of the table from her mother's cousin. 'Sit yourself down and tell us all your news.'

Angela broke into an embarrassed but relieved little laugh. Obviously nobody had noticed her awkwardness. 'I don't know where to start ... I think the walk out in the fresh air has done something to my brain,' she said. 'Either that, or the fact I've not slept since leaving England yesterday afternoon.'

'Pour the cratur a cup of tea,' Mary Malone instructed her daughter. She patted a comforting hand on Angela's shoulder. 'Sure, you must be worn out with all the travelling.'

'Oh, I'm grand,' Angela said, giving a weak smile. 'A cup of tea will buck me up.'

'Which part of England were you in?' Aiden Byrne asked, his handsome face full of curiosity. His voice was deep with a lovely richness to it.

'Stockport,' Angela replied, conscious that her own voice sounded a little tight.

'Whereabouts?' he continued, all ears. 'I was over there a few years ago myself.' His eyes narrowed, calculating. 'I suppose it was ten or twelve years ago, when I think about it. Time goes by so quickly.'

'I'm living just a few minutes' walk from the town centre,' she told him. 'Cale Green. It's around the Shaw Heath, Davenport area.'

He nodded his head, smiling. 'I know it well. I was working in Levenshulme one summer, making deliveries out to builders' yards all over Stockport.' His brow deepened. 'What are you doing over there yourself?'

'I'm a receptionist in a small hotel.' Angela suddenly became conscious that their conversation was excluding everyone else. She turned now to look around the table and smile at the others.

Carmel came around the table and placed a mug of tea in front of her friend. 'Angela's being very modest now,' she said in a slightly teasing tone. 'What's she's not telling you is that her sister actually *owns* the hotel in Stockport, and she also helps out a friend who has a boarding house.'

'Couldn't you tell she's off big-moneyed people the way she's got up in her finery?' Pascal said, winking across at Angela.

'I could certainly tell she was no ordinary woman when she walked in the door,' Aiden Byrne said, his eyes lighting up with humour.

'I only work in the hotel and boarding house,' Angela told them.

'I don't own them.' She lifted her mug in both hands, feeling that the ice had now been broken with the Malones' visitor. 'And I'm going to be walking back *out* the door if I hear any more jeering out of any of ye.'

'Pay no heed to them,' Carmel said, putting her arms around her friend. 'And you can stay as long as you like, because Mammy has a list of jobs the length of your arm that have to be done around the house for Easter – and the longer you're here, the less work I have to do.'

'Oh, no,' Angela said, waving a finger at her friend. 'I only came up for a quick chat while ye were all having your lunch, and I won't be staying long enough to be blamed for keeping you back.'

'You may go back to England, so!' Carmel told her. 'I was hoping for the afternoon off at least.'

'Tell that to all the beds that need clean sheets putting on them,' Mary said, raising her eyebrows.

'Many hands make light work,' Carmel said, glancing over at Angela and grinning.

'You needn't look at me,' Angela laughed. 'I came over here to get a break from work and have a good time. I need a bit of pampering myself and I'm looking forward to my mother running after me for the week.' She checked her watch. 'You have a half an hour left and then I'm heading home, so you'd better talk quick.'

There was a ripple of good-humoured laughter now and the conversation took a more general direction with everybody joining in. Carmel emptied the lukewarm tea leaves from the large teapot, then made a fresh pot. She pulled a chair up beside Angela, and within a few minutes they had caught up on each other's news, although Angela was still acutely conscious of the newcomer at the end of the table. Her curiosity about him was surprising. But then, she'd never come across anyone like him at home before.

In fact, she'd never come across anyone so attractive and confident back in Stockport – although there were similar business-looking types who came in and out of the hotel regularly, but none of them had ever caught her eye. Back home she'd always gone for working lads – farmers or factory workers. But then, those were the types of lads she had grown up with.

But whatever it was about this Aiden Byrne, Angela had enough experience of lads to know that he was more than interested in her.

68

The Malone boys chatted away to him, and, from the snippets of conversation she overheard – while Carmel was describing a tedious-sounding church concert she'd been to recently – they were discussing some land that was due up for auction in the area.

The buying and selling of land was always a lively topic of conversation, especially amongst farmers, but it wasn't a subject that Angela knew too much about. Shay had never owned any land in his life apart from the few yards surrounding his small house in the town.

Jimmy Malone looked at the kitchen clock and suddenly stood up. 'Now, lads,' he said, 'talk won't get the work done.' He looked over at Aiden Byrne. 'We've a field out there that's going to take us a good week to turn over, so you'll have to excuse us. They're giving rain for the next few days, so we need to make a start before we're washed out of it.' He gestured towards his wife. 'We'll have to leave you in the capable hands of the women.'

'Ah sure, I'm grand,' Aiden Byrne replied. 'I'll have to be getting back to the office shortly myself.'

Angela's ears suddenly pricked up at the word 'office'. He couldn't be a farmer after all.

'Oh, we'll look after him all right,' Mary Malone said, smiling at her cousin. 'I can't let him go until I've heard all the news from Birr.'

He smiled back at her. 'Sure, there's very little that happens in that neck of the woods – it's the same old thing all the time.'

'Oh, I wouldn't say that at all,' Mary laughed. 'It's often the smallest places that have the biggest scandals. You'll have another cup of tea and a slice of fruitcake?'

He checked his watch. 'Go on,' he said, 'you've twisted my arm. Anyway, I'm sure the women in the office will be delighted to have me gone for half the afternoon. One of them is getting married shortly, and she's in and out with pictures of wedding dresses and cakes and God knows what.'

'Ah, most women love all the fuss around a wedding,' Mary said. She placed two mugs on the table. 'Are you very busy out there in the office in Birr?' she asked, lifting the heavy teapot and pouring them both fresh mugs of tea.

'We're kept going,' he said, nodding. 'There's a big farm out towards Terryglass that came up for sale, and we've been handling the accounts for them.'

An accountant, Angela immediately deduced. He couldn't be anything else. Smart, good-looking, good sense of humour – and a good job. She reckoned he must be around thirty, or maybe late twenties, from what he'd said about working over in England. At his age, and with all those fine attributes, surely he would be well married, she thought. And to someone from the same class as himself – probably a big farmer's daughter, or a teacher, or someone professional like that.

The conversation carried on between Mary Malone and her cousin, and although she kept her ears pinned back for any incidental information, Angela heard nothing to confirm his marital status. Then the phone rang out in the hall and Carmel went to get it, leaving Angela with her mother and her cousin.

Once again, Angela became aware of Aiden Byrne's eyes lingering on her as all three made light conversation about the weather and the difference between living in the town in England and the country in Ireland. Every so often she had to pull herself up short because she was enjoying the unspoken attraction between them, and she had to remind herself that she could be flirting with a man that was already spoken for.

Then Mary started clearing the dishes from the table. 'Is your mother still helping to mind the little one?' she asked her cousin.

'Oh, she is,' Aiden said, his voice faltering slightly. 'I don't know where we'd be without my mother's help. I drop her out to the farm in the morning and pick her up in the evenings on my way home.' His eyes flickered over to Angela again, but there was a serious look in them now.

Angela suddenly realised that Aiden Byrne and Mary were talking about a child – *his* child. There could be no doubt about it. He was not only married but a *father* as well. And yet he had sat there, eyeing her up as though he were a single man – and she had been silly enough to feel flattered by it.

Well, she decided, she certainly wouldn't be giving him any further encouragement. She moved from her chair now and started to pick up cups and cutlery, depositing them in a pile on the pine worktop beside the enamel sink.

'Clare has plenty of company out at your mother's place,' Mary went on, lifting a large dish, which contained the greasy remnants of a joint of ham, from the table across to the sink. 'It's a bit like our own house with people coming and going.'

Aiden nodded his head. 'That's exactly what she needs to keep her occupied. And my mother is very good; she often brings Clare into the office when she's shopping in the town.'

'Angela!' Carmel called along the hallway. 'Rose Fox is on the phone from work and wants to have a quick word with you about the weekend.'

Without a backward glance, Angela put the bundle of knives and forks on the draining board and went out to the hall.

By the time that Angela had finished her phone call and come back into the kitchen, Aiden Byrne was out in the yard with Carmel and Mrs Malone, preparing to set off. Angela walked across the kitchen and stood casually leaning against the doorjamb with her arms folded, making sure that she didn't look in any way interested as they said their goodbyes.

'Make sure you tell your mother I was asking for her,' Mary Malone said. 'One of these fine Sunday evenings, myself and Jimmy will take a run out to see her.'

'Do,' he said, taking her hand and patting it. 'And call up to us while you're there. I don't think you saw the house since we did the bit of renovating last year.' He gave a small sigh. 'I did a good bit of it myself; it helped to pass the long winter nights.'

'I'd love to see it,' Mary said.

He checked in his jacket pocket for his car keys, and when he located them he turned towards the doorway. 'Nice to meet you, Angela,' he said, looking directly at her.

Angela averted her gaze this time, her eyes fixed on the field in the distance behind him. She wasn't going to give any encouragement to a ladies' man. 'Nice to meet you, too,' she said in a polite but cool manner.

Half an hour later Angela gave her second yawn in five minutes. 'I think I'd better make a move and head back home. I could do with a couple of hours' sleep before Rose calls to the house after work.' She stood up now and lifted her handbag from the farmhouse kitchen table.

'So we're all set for the dance on Sunday night?' Carmel said, getting to her feet to see her friend out.

'I'm really looking forward to it.' Angela said goodbye to Mrs Malone and the two girls walked out to the door together. 'I'd better get a move on,' she said, glancing at the darkening sky. 'If it starts raining now, I'll be like a drowned rat by the time I get home.'

'You'll be grand,' Carmel told her. 'They didn't say anything on the radio this morning about rain. All the lads were listening to it to check on their work for the day. It's a pity that we have to wait until Sunday for a dance,' she added in a low voice and out of earshot of her mother. 'Holy Week is the worst week of the year. All prayers and no craic – and the shops shut for most of the weekend.'

'We'll make up for it at the dances on Sunday and Monday,' Angela said. 'And anyway, you always get to catch up with people at Confession and Kissing of the Cross on Good Friday.'

'True,' Carmel agreed. 'And I suppose we can always go for a bit of a walk around the town or down by the canal. There's nothing much else to do.'

'Why don't you call on me this evening? We can go to Stations of the Cross first then we could go for a walk if it's fine?' Angela suggested. 'Rose is coming down at around half past seven.'

'Grand,' Carmel agreed. 'See you then.'

Chapter 13

Halfway home, Angela was again regretting wearing her high-heeled shoes. While they were suitable for the short walk from Tara's house in Stockport to the Cale Green Hotel, they were decidedly unsuitable for walks like this. When there was no one around she took it slowly and carefully to ease the burning feeling in the balls of her feet, taking up her more usual confident stride when she saw a car or someone coming towards her on a bike or walking.

As she neared the end of the Daingean Road, the dark clouds suddenly opened and heavy drops of rain came down. Angela had to speed up. She turned towards the canal bridge, cursing the fact that she hadn't brought an umbrella with her, when a car came to a halt beside her. Some kind soul was stopping to give her a lift! A little wave of gratitude washed over her.

She halted, trying to see who the driver was, as the rain was running down the car windows. Then the driver's window slowly wound down and Angela found herself looking straight into the eyes of Aiden Byrne.

'Jump in,' he told her, 'and I'll run you home.' He paused, waiting, then, when he saw her hesitation, he said, 'I'm not going to take a bite out of you – and you're going to be soaked through by the time you get into town.'

For a few seconds Angela just stared back at him, then she found herself stepping around the other side of the car and sliding into the passenger seat. Again, this close to him, she felt the same electrical jolt, but now she knew it was a feeling she would have to bury.

'I'm sorry I didn't catch you earlier,' he said, turning towards her. 'I've driven up and down several times but I didn't see you.'

'Why', she asked, incredulously, 'have you done that?'

'Because I wanted to see you,' he said. 'I wanted to speak to you.'

He looked in the car mirror and saw another car coming up over the bridge behind them. He moved into gear and quickly accelerated. 'Where do you live?' he asked, as they drove along. 'Unless you fancy going for a little drive somewhere? We can have a bit of a chat.'

Angela sat up straight in the passenger seat, hot anger rushing over her. 'What about?' she demanded. 'What on earth d'you want to chat about?'

'You,' he said.

'I'm sure there's nothing very interesting about me,' she snapped. She took a deep breath, trying to calm down without making a total fool of herself. 'I live behind the Guards barracks, and I'd be very grateful if you'd just drop me off there.'

He moved the car up to the Kilbeggan Bridge and turned left towards the centre of the town. 'Have I said or done something wrong?' he asked in a puzzled tone. 'You seem very different from how you were earlier on.'

Angela flushed, embarrassed. He had obviously noticed her awkward, flustered reactions when she first met him. What on earth could she say to him now? If she brought up the fact she knew he was married, it would look as though she were accusing him of leading her on when they'd hardly even spoken. And it wasn't as if he had actually said anything to suggest he had some kind of notion about her.

And yet, every instinct in her told her that there had been a real spark between them.

'Look,' he said, driving very slowly down the Main Street, 'I think you're a lovely girl, and I'd really like to get to know you better.'

Angela sat silently in the seat beside him. One half of her knew that she should speak up and give him directions straight to her parents' house, but the other half wanted the journey in his car to go on for a little bit longer. Even though she knew it couldn't possibly lead anywhere. Common sense took over. 'Look,' she said, 'I don't think you should be saying things like that to me.'

He steered the car in towards the kerb now and pulled up. Then he turned towards her, smiling. 'Don't tell me that you're not used to men saying nice things to you?'

Angela swallowed hard. 'I'm just not used to *married* men saying them,' she told him pointedly.

'Ah ...' he said. 'I didn't realise—'

Angela cut him off. 'And don't bother denying it,' she told him, 'I heard you talking to Mrs Malone about your little girl. You should be ashamed of yourself. You're both a husband *and* a father.'

He was silent for a few moments, then he sat up very straight in the car seat. 'I feel very embarrassed now ... I thought Carmel or her mother had told you,' he said in a low voice.

'Told me what?' Angela said, feeling more confused than ever.

'I do have a little daughter,' he said, 'but I'm actually a widower.'

Angela's shoulders slumped, the wind completely taken out of her sails. Her hand flew to her mouth. 'Oh, no,' she said. 'I'd no idea ... I'm so sorry.'

'It's OK,' he told her. 'It's an easy mistake. How could you know if nobody had told you?'

She shook her head. 'Trust me to put my big foot in it. I can't believe I said all that to you.'

'Forget it,' he said, shrugging. 'You're bound to have felt annoyed at me showing you attention, when you thought I had a wife and a child waiting back at home.'

Angela bit her lip now. There were questions she wanted to ask him, but she was afraid of saying the wrong thing. But she had to say *something* to try to make amends for misjudging him so badly. 'I'm very sorry about your wife ... That must have been terrible for you, especially when you have a little girl.'

He nodded slowly. 'There's no point in saying anything else. It was terrible all right.'

'Do you mind me asking what happened?'

'She died having Clare,' he told her in a low, monotone, a voice weary from explaining the same story time after time. 'She'd had a weak heart when she was a child, but they didn't realise it had worsened over the years. She had trouble with the birth and, by the time they got her into theatre for a Caesarean section, her heart wasn't up to the anaesthetic.'

Angela felt tears springing into her eyes. 'Oh, my God,' she whispered. 'I'm so, so sorry ...'

'It was just over four years ago,' he told her quietly. 'And just so as you know – you're the first girl I've looked at since.' He reached over and lightly touched her hand. It was just for a moment, just enough to show her he was sincere. 'I wouldn't want you to think that I got over it easily, or that I don't think about Elizabeth, because I do. Of course I do ...' His voice trailed off.

Even in the midst of her sadness at the tragic story, Angela felt her heart miss a beat when his hand touched hers. And she was truly relieved that he wasn't the womanising cheat she had imagined him to be. 'I understand,' she said. 'You only have to listen to you to know how sincere you are ... and I'm sorry for thinking otherwise about you.'

He nodded. 'No need for that,' he said. 'It was an obvious and genuine mistake.' He took a deep breath, then exhaled very slowly. 'Now,' he said, 'where does this leave you and me? Since we've cleared the decks about me, and I've found the courage to tell you that I'd like to meet up with you again, what do you say?'

Angela looked at him, all sorts of thoughts running through her mind. The fact that he was older than her for one, and the fact he had a daughter another. She pushed another niggling thought to the back of her mind. The one that told her she wasn't good enough or interesting enough to be going out with somebody like an accountant. Her previous boyfriends hadn't exactly been professional types.

She paused for a moment, then she suddenly smiled. 'Yes,' she said, pushing all those reservations to the back of her mind. 'I'd like to meet up with you again, too.'

'What about tonight?'

Angela shook her head. 'I've already arranged to meet my friends tonight,' she told him.

He looked thoughtful for a few moments. 'If I took the day off work tomorrow,' he suggested, 'we could take a trip in the car to Dublin ... or Galway, or anywhere you like. My mother has Clare for the day, so it won't need any more organising than usual.'

Angela stared back at him. Could this actually be happening? she thought. Nothing as exciting and unexpected as this had ever happened to her before. Her mind whirled. What should she do? What would her mother and father say when she told them she was going out for the day with a stranger she'd only just met? An older stranger who was a widower with a child. 'I'd love to go to Dublin,' she said, trying not to smile too excitedly.

'Excellent,' he said, grinning back at her. 'We'll make a day of it. I'll have a look at the paper tonight and see if there's anything on in the cinema or theatre – and we'll go somewhere nice for lunch.' He started up the car up again and drove towards the centre of the town. 'I know it's a bit quick suggesting tomorrow, but given that it's the Easter weekend, there will be nothing open Friday, and I might not find it as easy to get away on Saturday or Sunday.'

'I've already arranged to go out dancing with Carmel and the girls on Sunday and Monday,' she told him.

'I did overhear some of your arrangements,' he said, smiling, 'so I thought I'd better get my stake in for a few hours of your time before you had it all planned.'

'I'm glad you did,' she said, smiling back at him.

As he turned the corner towards their house, Angela suddenly said, 'If you drop me at the Guard station, that'll do just grand.'

'Are you sure?' he checked. 'It's still raining. I can take you to the door.' He slowed the car as they came towards the station.

'No,' she said in a decisive tone. 'It's only a couple of minutes' walk and it would be best if I get out here.'

The car came to a halt. 'Would ten o'clock be OK to pick you up?' he asked.

'Yes,' she said, 'ten will be fine.' She turned to open the car door.

'Angela?' Aiden Byrne said, a huskiness in his voice now. When she turned back towards him, he leaned across and kissed her lightly on the cheek. 'I'm really looking forward to us spending the day together.'

Once again she felt a shivery shock run through her whole body. 'So am I,' she said. Then she opened the door, swung her legs out of the car, and hurried home without looking back.

Chapter 14

❧❦❧

Tara walked up the steps to Ballygrace House with a strange sense of trepidation.

Her young brother-in-law stood on the top step waiting for her, grinning from ear to ear. 'I can't wait to be back inside,' he told her. 'I want to help you with things around the house, like bringing in the wood and the turf for the fires. And I've told Shay that I'll help him fix the old outhouses.'

'Oh, you'll find plenty to keep you busy,' Tara said, feeling inside her handbag for the keys.

The older he became, the more interested William was in returning to the house where his elder brother and sister had grown up. And he was constantly asking Tara what Gabriel had been like as a teenager, wanting to know the sorts of things he had been interested in. And Tara had discovered that she was happy enough to reminisce with William about their schooldays and recount little stories about seeing Gabriel and his sister, Madeleine, at church on Sundays, or to talk about the ponies they had as children.

But since the conversation with Bridget last week, Tara found her memories of the house were slightly tainted. In spite of the happy years of marriage that she'd spent in the old Georgian building, she now felt that the darker memories she'd successfully pushed away were threatening to return.

But she wouldn't allow it. Tara Flynn, now Fitzgerald, had endured too many difficult things in her life to give into self-pitying behaviour. It's only a house, she told herself as she located the keys in a small pocket inside her handbag.

Just as she went to put the key in the lock, the door suddenly opened.

'I thought I heard voices,' Ella Keating said, her face lighting up at the sight of them. 'Welcome home, Tara,' she said, sweeping the door wide open. 'And a warm welcome to you, too, William.'

'Hello, Ella, it's nice to see you,' William said, stepping back to let Tara in first.

'This is a surprise,' Tara said, smiling at the housekeeper who had once been an old schoolfriend. 'I didn't expect you here. I thought you would have just done your bits and pieces and gone home.'

Last year Ella had married a farmer from just outside Daingean, and was happy to have the time in her own home when Tara was away. She was kept busy enough cooking dinners every day for all the farmhands, tending to the chickens and ducks, and cycling in and out to Ballygrace to see her elderly parents. But she said she would always be glad of the few weeks' work any time that Tara was back in Ballygrace House, and that the extra money would give her a little bit of independence.

'My mother-in-law came to give me a hand at the farm this morning, and we got everything done that bit earlier, which meant I had time to myself this afternoon. So I thought I'd do a few extra little jobs that needed doing.'

'The house feels nice and warm,' Tara remarked as they walked down towards the kitchen. 'You must have got the fires going early this morning.'

'I did the range when I arrived around ten o'clock,' Ella said, 'and I lit the fires a couple of hours ago.'

Tara walked into the kitchen now, and when she smelled the warm, freshly baked bread and the cinnamon buns mixed with the familiar turf scent, she felt herself beginning to relax. 'Everything looks lovely,' she said, looking around the large, airy kitchen.

Very little had changed over the years, apart from a new coat of paint every so often and several thorough cleanings every year. There had been very little done to the kitchen since it was originally built. But it was the type of kitchen – the type of house, in fact – that didn't need improving. As long as it was given the bare maintenance it required – and Shay Flynn did his best to make sure it was – the house just seemed to look the way it always had.

'I have the kettle boiled,' Ella said going over to the range. 'Do you want tea or coffee?'

'Oh, a cup of coffee would be lovely,' Tara said, taking off her coat.

She went to the cupboard to get the cups and saucers. 'What will you have, William?'

'Coffee, please,' he said.

'I have a bottle of your favourite red lemonade in the pantry for you,' Ella told him, 'if you'd prefer that.'

He hesitated for a moment. 'Actually, I'll just have the coffee now, and I'll probably have a glass of it later … Thank you for going to the trouble of getting it for me, Ella.'

In that moment, Tara realised William was growing up. Before, he would have gone for the sugary drink, the sort of thing he would never have been allowed back in London.

'I know you told me in your letter that you'd be having a bit of lunch out at your relatives,' Ella said, 'but I baked some bread, and a few cakes and buns, which I thought would keep you going for a couple of days.'

'That's very good of you,' Tara said, glad that she'd left the bags of bread and cakes in the car; both Kitty and Tessie had pressed them upon her.

'Should I take my bag upstairs now, Tara?' William asked. 'Or can I wait until we've had our coffee?'

'Oh, you can leave it,' Tara said. 'There's no big rush about any-thing. We have all evening to get ourselves settled in.'

'I wasn't sure who would be staying,' Ella said, pouring boiling water into the big coffee pot, 'so I aired all the bedrooms just in case, and lit all the fires.'

'Oh, that was a lot of extra work for you, Ella,' Tara said, looking concerned. 'There's only ourselves and Father Joe, who'll be coming for a few days at the beginning of next week.'

'I thought Angela might be staying the odd night, like last time,' Ella said, 'so I made the bed up in the back room for her just in case.'

'You're so good,' Tara said, smiling warmly. She didn't like to say that there was little chance of Angela staying out at Ballygrace House on this occasion. Tara had got the message, loud and clear, that Angela wanted to have time to herself, to mix with her younger, more exciting friends.

'I try to get out once or twice a week to light the fires during the colder months,' Ella told her, 'just to stop things from getting too damp.' She waved her hand around the kitchen. 'This part of the house is always grand and dry, but you feel the upstairs and the drawing-room need warming up. You know, I think it could do with a family in it again, to give it that lived-in feeling.'

Tara caught her breath, wondering if Ella realised what she'd said. Then, just as she had earlier that day with her father, she dismissed it as an insensitive but unintentional comment. It was amazing how people could say things without thinking them through. How could there possibly be a family living in Ballygrace House? There was only herself now that Gabriel had gone, and that wasn't likely to change in the future.

Ella brought the coffee-pot over to the table. 'I don't suppose you've any plans to come back home yet?' she asked, oblivious to the fact that she was driving a very sharp point through Tara's sensitive skin.

'Not at the moment,' Tara said quietly. Then, seeing Ella's brow crease, she perked up, not wishing her old schoolfriend, or William, to think she had taken offence, because she knew quite plainly that Ella would never dream of offending her. 'It's still early days with the hotel and I can't really expect anyone else to run it for me just yet.'

'True,' Ella said. 'I was forgetting you have so much to do over in England. Still, you never know what the future holds.' She gave Tara a beaming smile. 'Ballygrace House will always be here waiting for you, whatever happens.'

Chapter 15

Tessie Flynn paused in the middle of rolling out pastry for an apple tart. 'You're going *where* for the day tomorrow?' she asked in a high, surprised voice.

'Dublin,' Angela repeated in a heated whisper. Her eyes darted towards the back door in case Shay walked in on their conversation. She had waited until he was safely out of the house – mending a hole in the roof of the turf-shed – to tell her mother. 'And I don't want you to go telling Daddy all the details, because he'll only start giving out to me and I'm not in the mood for another big row.'

'And who did you say this lad was?' Tessie asked, dusting the flour from her hands. 'Is he from Tullamore?'

'He's not a lad,' Angela corrected. 'He's a grown man and he's actually from Birr.' She got up from the armchair and went over to the mirror to check her newly-washed hair was sitting correctly.

'And how long have you known him?'

Angela shrugged, preening herself in the mirror. 'He's a cousin of Carmel's mother,' she said evasively. She ran a finger along each eyebrow to check there wasn't a stray hair out of place, then she turned sideways to check there were no hairs clinging to her blue cardigan.

'Sure, Carmel's mother is in her fifties,' Tessie calculated. 'So how old is he, if he's her cousin?'

Angela picked up a magazine from the top of the polished sideboard. 'He's not that much older than me,' she said, starting to thumb through it. He was definitely older than any other fellow she'd ever been involved with, but in truth she didn't know his exact age. She had already decided that she wasn't going to give any more details than she needed to, because she had discovered long ago that the more her parents knew, the more they found to complain about. And whatever it was that she already felt about Aiden Byrne, Angela wasn't prepared to jeopardise it just yet.

There was definitely something different about him, because, since she'd clapped eyes on him this afternoon, she'd been unable to stop thinking about him. Even talking about him to her mother had made her feel excited and somehow more alive and energetic than she'd ever felt before. Even before they spoke a word, his dark-brown eyes had somehow drawn her towards him.

'He must be doing well if he has a car,' Tessie said, starting to cut the pared apples into thin slices for the tart. 'What does he work at?'

'He's an *accountant*,' Angela said casually. She walked back to the armchair and sat down with the magazine, flicking idly through it.

'An accountant?' Tessie repeated, sounding both surprised and impressed at the same time. 'He's an accountant in Tullamore?'

'No,' Angela replied. Her mind worked quickly, because she knew her mother would have Aiden Byrne's seed and breed tracked down in a matter of days, and she didn't want that to happen. 'I think it's somewhere out towards Portumna or Birr.' She gave a shrug. 'Sure,

I'm not bothered where it is, I'm only having a day out in Dublin with him.' She paused at a fashion page in the magazine.

'Well, he must like you to have asked you to go out for the whole day,' Tessie said. 'Especially since you've only just met him.'

Angela felt a warm glow run through her at the comment, but she felt she had to throw a little cold water on it to keep her mother in the dark. 'Well, I could have met him before at Carmel's house. There's always people coming and going at the farm.'

'They're a very decent family, the Malones,' Tessie mused. 'So if he's related to them I suppose he must be decent enough, too.'

'Well, I wouldn't be going out with him if he wasn't decent,' Angela said, raising her eyebrows. 'What type of girl do you take me for?'

'Don't get too cocky,' her mother warned. 'Anybody can make a mistake when it comes to men.'

'I know that. It even happened to Tara, didn't it?' Angela said. 'She made a mistake with that Frank Kennedy fella back in Stockport, didn't she? Bridget Hart told me all about it.' She shook her head. 'It's hard to believe that Tara could be such a fool not to know he was already married. When she's in the hotel she gives the impression of knowing everything, as though she'd never made a mistake in her life.'

Tessie glanced at the back door now, then she put her knife and the apple she was paring down on the table. 'You shouldn't be saying things like that about Tara,' she said in a low voice. 'That was a long, long time ago, before she married Gabriel Fitzgerald.'

'I'm only telling the truth,' Angela pointed out. 'And it was you who brought the subject up, saying that anybody can make a mistake.'

Tessie looked silently at her daughter for a few moments. 'Just be sure *you* don't go making any mistakes, m'lady,' she finally said.

'I won't,' Angela promised, 'but don't go saying too much to Daddy. We'll just tell him that I'm going out in the morning and he'll think that it's with the girls. If we tell him where I'm going and who with, he'll only start giving out about it and wanting to know everything.'

'Don't look at me,' Tessie told her. 'I'm not going to be making up lies for you.' She gave a little sigh. 'He's got a few bits and pieces to do around the town tomorrow, and, if I know him, he'll likely take a cycle out to Ballygrace House in the afternoon to see how Tara found the place. He'll probably be too busy to notice what you're up to anyway.'

The gate gave its familiar creak when pushed open, and Angela threw her magazine to the side of her chair. 'That'll be Rose or Carmel,' she said excitedly. She got up and was halfway across the floor when she suddenly halted in her tracks. 'Don't say anything to Carmel about me going to Dublin tomorrow with Aiden Byrne,' she whispered urgently to her mother. 'I don't want to say anything just yet until I see how we get on.'

Tessie gave another sigh and shook her head. 'I don't like all this secrecy,' she said. 'First I've not to mention a word to your father, and now we've got to keep it quiet from Carmel Malone.'

Angela looked beseechingly at her mother. 'Oh, don't say anything to her, Mammy. I don't want to tell anyone just yet ... He's different from the other lads I've known, and I'm only home for the week ...'

Tessie's face softened. She should be flattered that Angela confided in her. She had trusted her mother more than her friends, and that had to be a good thing.

Angela sat between Rose and Carmel in the church pew, her hands joined in her lap as she stared straight up at the priest and the altar, not hearing a single word about the atrocities that Christ suffered during the week leading up to the Crucifixion. Her mind was full of Aiden Byrne, and every time she replayed the scene when he leant over in the car to kiss her cheek, she felt the same stab of excitement that she'd felt at the time.

She found herself running miles ahead in the relationship, imagining him begging her not to go back to Stockport and even offering her a job in his accountant's office in Birr. Of course, she wouldn't be in a position to accept anything straight away, and since she didn't have a car she couldn't travel that distance from her parents' house in Tullamore every day. It was too far away to cycle, and there wasn't a bus that would take her there and bring her back in the evenings.

But there were ways around it. She could always find a room in Birr until they got married ... She brought herself up abruptly when she got to that particular stage – she was getting totally carried away. On several occasions that evening her daydreams about Aiden Byrne had been abruptly disturbed, as Carmel or Rose dug her in the ribs when they saw lads from school or the local dances. But it was strange how, in the space of a few hours, the younger lads had suddenly lost their attraction.

The priest came down from the altar now and, followed by a group of sombre altar boys, started on his journey through the church, halting at each Station of the Cross to recite the relevant prayer.

As he neared their pew, Angela lifted her prayer book and joined the rest of the congregation in the recitations, but minutes after the priest passed them, she was lost once again in a romantic scenario.

'Shall we go for a bit of a walk around the town?' Rose Fox suggested, as they filed out of the church. 'It's turned into a nice enough evening and you never know who we might see.'

'I hope you're not thinking of looking at other lads, Rosie,' Carmel said, 'when you're as good as engaged to Tommy Kelly.'

'Go away,' Rose said, rolling her eyes in horror, but looking delighted at the suggestion. 'Sure, that fellow's so slow and careful I'll be well over thirty by the time he gets around to proposin'.' She gave a little laugh. 'I wasn't talking about getting up to anything we shouldn't ... but there's no harm in having a bit of craic now and again.' Rose also knew that both she and the plain-looking Carmel would get more attention than usual from the local lads if they had the lovely Angela Flynn with them.

'Grand,' Angela said, giving the girls a beaming smile. 'A walk out would be lovely.'

During the church service she had debated whether she would go out with the girls, or go home and have a nice hot bath and an early night, so she could lie in the darkness and the quietness of her bedroom for a while just thinking. Thinking about Aiden Byrne.

In the end she decided that she would do both. It would make the night pass more quickly to have a walk, then go home and have her bath and an early bed.

It would make both the morning and Aiden Byrne appear more quickly.

'Angela, I meant to ask you, what did you think of our visitor yesterday?' Carmel asked, as all three girls strolled along William Street.

Angela looked at her friend, frowning as though trying to remember. 'The fellow in the suit?' she said, as if there had been half a dozen fellows out at the Malones' farmhouse.

'Isn't he very good-looking and nice to talk to?' Carmel continued. 'You wouldn't think he's Mammy's cousin when he's so young-looking.'

Angela felt herself starting to blush now at her little deception, but she just couldn't tell Carmel that she had met him later and had a date planned with him for tomorrow. 'You get that in families,' she said vaguely. 'Mammy has cousins that are years older than her, and Tara has her young brother-in-law over from England; he's only a young teenager and Gabriel was in his thirties.'

'How is Tara?' Rose Fox put in. 'Is she still as glamorous and posh as ever?'

'She always looks very nice,' Angela confirmed, feeling uncomfortable at her friend's derogatory description of Tara, but she knew it was all her own fault. Angela had complained to her friends many times that Tara was uppity, and had often imitated Tara's formal way of talking, so it was no wonder that Rose felt within her rights to say anything she liked about her. And while, years ago, Angela had enjoyed the bit of jeering at her serious half-sister, she suddenly realised that she had grown out of that type of talk. In any case, Tara had been very good to her over the last few years. 'Tara's changed a lot these days,' she added. 'She's far more easy to talk to and down to earth than she used to be.'

'Indeed?' Rose pulled a face as though not quite convinced, but she said no more.

'D'you know something?' Carmel said, her eyes narrowed in thought. 'I think Aiden Byrne and Tara would make a grand couple. They're both widowed and, from the sound of how Tara gets on with that young Fitzgerald lad, I bet she'd make a great stepmother to little Clare.'

Angela felt as though she'd been punched in the stomach. Tara was in her *thirties*, a good decade older than herself. Had Aiden Byrne really looked Tara's age? Was he that much older than her?

'Sure, Tara's not in the least interested in any other man,' she said sharply. 'I think it will be years before she looks at anyone else – if she ever does.'

'It's a pity,' Carmel mused, 'but then Aiden's never looked at anyone else, as far as we know, since Elizabeth died.' She pushed her glasses up on her nose. 'Isn't it sad to see two nice people on their own? Especially when there's a poor child with no mother.'

Angela looked around now, anxious for a diversion. 'Isn't that Sarah Gilligan across the road?' she said, spotting a girl she knew from school who was walking along arm in arm with a young man.

'Shhhh.' Carmel looked around to check there was no one close enough to hear. 'Didn't I tell you in one of my letters that she'd got married in February?'

'No,' Angela said. 'I'm sure I would have remembered. Who did she marry?'

'A fella from Durrow,' Carmel whispered.

'She's in the family way,' Rose Fox said, rolling her eyes meaningfully. 'And it's a disgrace because she was only going out with that lad for less than six months when it happened.'

Angela shrugged. 'We shouldn't be so quick to judge. She was always a nice girl ... and I suppose it could happen to anyone.'

'Yes,' Rose said, 'if you're stupid enough to let a lad tamper with you before you get married.' She shook her head, and her eyes grew big and very serious-looking. 'If that Tommy Kelly dared put a hand on me he wouldn't live to tell the tale.'

'You needn't worry,' Carmel told her. 'He's a decent lad. He's not the type that would try anything on with you. You'll be safely married before he goes anywhere near you.'

'The very thought of it terrifies me anyway,' Rose said, huddling close to her friends. 'If it's anything like I've heard, I think I'm happy to wait for a few years.' She pulled a face. 'What d'you think, girls? Can you imagine letting a lad paw all over you?' Her voice dropped lower. 'Imagine letting anyone touch you *down below*!' She gave a shudder, then went into peals of laughter. 'Tommy Kelly needn't be gettin' any ideas in his head about *that*, I can tell you.'

'Oh, Rose!' Carmel squealed. 'You're the limit, talking like that. Sure, we're all terrified of what it's like, aren't we, Angela? But if you get married, it has to be done.'

Angela looked back at her two friends now, amazed at their childish attitude to boys and sex. By the sounds of it, they hadn't moved on an inch since they were at school.

Surely they didn't think she had the same old-fashioned views that she had as a teenager? Would they still feel like that if they were with the right man, someone they found really, really attractive?

Angela knew she should keep quiet and just agree with the girls, but she felt a total hypocrite and couldn't stop herself. 'It can't be all that bad,' she said, 'or else there would be no one in the world. The whole human race would die out. And when you come to think of it, every child that's born means that the mother and father must have done it.'

'It's the men,' Rose said, speaking with all the confidence of an older, wiser woman. 'It's because *they* enjoy it so much. It's different for women; we're not made the same way. It's us who have to do our Catholic duty and put up with it to have the children.'

Angela couldn't let it go. 'But what about all the great romances we've read about in books like *Jane Eyre* and *Wuthering Heights*? What about the romantic films like *Gone With the Wind* or *Casablanca*?' she said, trying not to sound too serious or to make it too personal. 'You don't get the impression that those women were just gritting their teeth and putting up with it, do you?'

'Sure, they're only oul' films, not real life,' Rose said, laughing. 'If you take all that stuff seriously and expect your own life to turn out like that, you'll be sadly disappointed. Who do you know that acts like that in real life?'

'Well, I think Tara and Gabriel were quite romantic,' Angela said, 'and she was heartbroken when he died. And I think that Bridget and Fred back in Stockport get on very well, too.' She shook her head. 'I don't think they'd put up with *anything*.'

'But you don't know,' Carmel told her, as if she were explaining something to a child. 'They're not going to start talking about things like that in front of anyone, are they?'

A picture of Aiden Byrne's handsome face flashed into Angela's mind and she felt a warm glow move through her. 'Well, I hope I can enjoy it,' she suddenly said. 'I really don't think it can be *that* awful if you meet the right person.'

'Would you just listen to Miss Angela Flynn,' Rose said, her voice still light-hearted, but with a derisory note. 'You can tell that living in England has certainly turned your head about men.'

'Not a bit,' Angela said, determined not to be talked down. 'Long before I left home I thought that the physical side of life was bound to become natural as you got older. Surely we're expected to get a bit of pleasure out of it at some point? You couldn't live your whole life either hating it or avoiding it.'

'Don't tell us you've met somebody over there that looks like a film star?' Carmel said.

'*No*,' Angela said in a high voice, still laughing at their silliness, 'and will the pair of ye stop going on? I'm only saying that things *can't* be as bad as you're saying, or else there's no hope for us all.'

Although she made a valiant effort to be cheerful and chatty, Angela was glad to escape back home to prepare for her day out in Dublin with Aiden Byrne. She was also relieved to have got away with not mentioning what she was doing tomorrow, because they had been keen to make plans for meeting up any time she was free. She had made vague references to going out to Ballygrace House over the next few days, so the girls had obviously been satisfied that she was tied up with family business or was helping Tara out at the house.

Tessie was sitting with her knitting in front of the television, having cleared up the dinner things and prepared a large round loaf of soda bread and a fruit loaf to go in the oven first thing in the morning.

Angela put a blanket on the end of the table and plugged in the iron, then she went into her bedroom and took her cream Capri pants and a tan, boat-necked sweater from her case, bringing them back into the kitchen to press.

Tessie lifted her head from the yellow and white matinée jacket she was knitting for another forthcoming grandchild. 'Are you wearing trousers to go out for the day?' she asked in a surprised voice.

'Why? What's wrong with them? They're my brand-new Capri pants; they're the height of the fashion,' Angela told her, licking her finger to test the temperature of the base of the iron. 'Why, do you not like them?'

'I just thought that since he's an accountant, you might want to dress up a bit. Wear a nice frock or a suit. He's probably used to going out with girls who can afford the best.'

'I was wearing a dress when he saw me earlier on, and anyway, Tara often wears trousers when she's going out, and you always say she's one of the best-dressed women in Tullamore,' Angela said, feeling irritated with her mother. What on earth did *she* know about fashion? Most of her clothes came from the same shop in the town. 'And I bought these trousers in Manchester in a posh shop called Kendal's when I went shopping with Tara. As a matter of fact, she has the very same pair in green.'

'OK,' Tessie said, holding up her hands, 'I get the point. The trousers are grand for Dublin.' She looked at the clock. 'You'd better get a move on if you want your hair to be dry before you go to bed.'

'Did you get the hairdryer fixed?' Angela asked. It had blown up on her the last time she was at home.

'Your father had a look inside it,' Tessie explained, knowing that it would be another thing for her daughter to complain about, 'but he said the workings had all melted together and there was nothing could be done.'

Angela gave a loud sigh. 'You might have bought a new one to replace it.'

'They're not cheap, Angela,' Tessie said, sounding wounded. 'And it's only used when you come home.' Tessie had her hair washed and set once a week in her local hairdresser's, and only combed it out in between or, if it was really bad, dampened it and shoved in a few rollers.

'That means I'll either have to sit brushing it out in front of the range,' she moaned, 'or go to bed with it damp.' She shook her head. 'You'd think we were still in the Dark Ages over here.'

Tessie bit her lip and kept her gaze focused on her knitting.

Angela carefully pressed her Capri pants, putting a damp tea towel on top to save marking them, then she did the same with her sweater, all the while wondering if her mother was right and she should have chosen a dress, or a skirt and blouse. 'Do you think the water is hot enough for a bath now?' she asked, wishing that she could ask Tara's opinion, as her old sister always knew the right thing to wear for any occasion.

'It should be. The range has been roaring for the last couple of hours, and it's still very hot,' Tessie said.

'Have you any of that nice bubble bath left that I got you for Christmas?' Angela asked, her voice lighter and easier now she was asking for a favour.

'Yes, there's a good bit of it still left. It's on the window ledge in the bathroom, behind the curtain,' Tessie said, relieved she could give an answer that would please her daughter.

Half an hour later Angela appeared back in the kitchen dressed in a lilac quilted dressing gown with a towel wrapped around her wet hair. She pulled one of the kitchen chairs across to the range and opened the small door at the front to allow the heat to flow out.

Then she unwrapped the towel and proceeded to rub it briskly over her long blonde hair. Satisfied that she had blotted the worst of the dampness, she started carefully to brush her hair out, holding her head close to the range to help it to dry more quickly.

'Would you like a cup of tea or maybe some cocoa?' Tessie said, putting her knitting down. She had enjoyed the half an hour of peace and quiet with both her daughter and husband occupied.

'Oh, cocoa would be lovely,' Angela said, smiling gratefully. Lying back in the scented bubbles, thinking of the handsome Aiden Byrne, had restored her good humour. Remembering when he had leaned over in the car and kissed her cheek was like running a lovely romantic film over and over in her mind.

Tessie went over to the cupboard and got out a small pan. She half-filled it with milk then put it on the range to warm. 'While we're on our own,' she said in a quiet voice, her eyes flickering towards the back door, 'I just wanted to let you know that your father's not been too well recently.'

Angela felt a little pang of alarm. For all her father drove her mad at times, he had a good heart, and underneath all their verbal sparring she loved him clearly. 'What's wrong with him?' she said, halting her brushing.

'Well,' Tessie said, trying to pick her words carefully, 'he's had a few little blackouts when he doesn't remember what's happened to him. The last time, he fell outside and bruised his face and shoulder.'

'Do you think it's serious?' Angela asked, her voice low and anxious now. She started brushing her hair again, very vigorously.

'I don't honestly know,' her mother replied. 'We'll just have to wait and see. The doctor has put him on tablets and they seem to be helping him all right. But they've told him he's to take it easy and not be lifting heavy things.'

'Have you told Tara yet?' Angela said, putting her brush down and running her fingers through her hair to separate the drying strands.

'I didn't really get a chance,' Tessie said. 'Your father was hovering about the whole time she was in, but I got the feeling that Kitty or Mick might have said something, because I noticed her watching him.'

'What about you?' Angela asked, looking at her mother closely. 'Are you feeling OK? You seem quieter than usual.'

'Oh, sure, I'm grand,' Tessie said, sitting down at the table with her hands joined under her chin. 'I'm just not as able for things as I used to be. I suppose we're all getting that bit older.'

Angela stared at her mother, not quite sure what to say. Tessie rarely complained about anything. 'I think Daddy looks the same,' she said, 'He doesn't seem sick or anything.'

'There are times when he drives me mad, but I wouldn't be without him,' Tessie said. Tears suddenly welled up in her eyes. 'I'm probably worrying about nothing ...'

Angela felt a wave of guilt. She knew her mother would have been looking forward to her coming home, and all she'd done was complain about everything. She swallowed hard now, trying to decide whether she should acknowledge that she'd been awkward, or whether to say nothing and just make more of an effort to be cheery and nicer to her parents.

She knew she didn't mean half of the things she said to them. She was just reverting back to her familiar, grumbling, teenage ways, because she wanted her parents to react the way they had always done, which was to try to placate and please her. The way that made her feel loved.

The thought of anything actually happening to either of them suddenly cut to the core of her, and she found herself instinctively going over to her mother and putting her arms around her. 'I'm sure it'll be all right,' she said, kissing her lightly on the top of the head. 'And I'll try to help you more about the house while I'm here.'

Tessie reached up to pat Angela's arm. 'You're a good girl,' she whispered, 'and we're delighted to have you back home.'

The back door opened and Shay came in. He stood, leaning on the doorjamb watching his wife and daughter in an unusually affectionate pose. 'Oh-ho,' he said, taking his cap off. 'What's all the kissing and making up about now?'

Chapter 16

❦

Tara was lying, wide awake, at quarter to four on Thursday morning. She had woken up from a dream about the Grosvenor Hotel, and was now ruminating over the business proposition that had been put to her before she left for Ireland.

The whole idea of getting in over her head financially terrified her. Plus there was the thought of becoming involved with such high-flying businessmen. She wasn't at all sure if she would be able to hold her own. They were all very wealthy – and, apart from Frank Kennedy, who, in the early days, had worked physically hard for the money he had earned – professional men who had been used to handling large amounts of money for most of their lives.

There was no comparison between her own little hotel and the Grosvenor. The Cale Green Hotel could fit into a corner of it. And the rebuilding and refurbishment of it had not been much bigger than the work some people did on their houses. In addition, there was a possibility that she had just been plain lucky with the timing, the fact the hotel had been on the market for a while, the people who had been involved in re-designing the hotel, and her business contacts in town, whom she had met through working as a receptionist in the Grosvenor.

And then, of course, she'd had Mr Pickford's guidance. Her old boss in the estate agency had pointed out that the small hotel had filled a gap in the market for smaller functions and business meetings in a quiet part of the town. And his advice had been spot on. But the whole venture could just as easily have turned out to be a big mistake. So far it had been every bit as successful as she had hoped, but that wasn't to say it would continue.

She couldn't even conceive of buying into another hotel, a big hotel, now or in the foreseeable future. She had more than enough on her plate running the Cale Green, and she really couldn't afford the time or the huge amount of money that it would take.

Tara felt awkward about the fact that she had been officially approached by the whole group. When it had just been Frank Kennedy she felt she could brush him off without a thought, but it was a very different matter when he was with several well-respected businessmen. Brushing *them* off could harm her reputation and maybe even her business. She would have to handle the refusal with tact and good grace.

And then Frank Kennedy floated into Tara's mind.

How was it that she could never feel totally free of him, no matter how hard she tried? It was bad enough that he was courting Kate, because it meant that there was always the link of her friendship to tie them all together. And, although Tara tried to avoid him, there were often occasions that she was obliged to attend, like the boutique openings or the fashion shows that Kate asked her to. If the occasion were suitable for a man to attend, Frank was guaranteed to be there.

When she got back to Stockport, Tara decided she would look at the business proposal for the Grosvenor very carefully, then come up with a cast-iron reason for not being involved. She would ring Gerry McShane and explain it to him, and then the matter would be closed.

She forced herself to think of more pressing concerns, such as what she would do with William that day. Good Friday would take care of itself, with the church service and then the family coming out for dinner. It would be well into the evening by the time they left, and Tara knew that until then, her father and Mick would keep William occupied checking the grounds outside and playing dominoes or cards with him.

On Saturday they would go into Tullamore for bits and pieces of shopping, and to buy a few chocolate eggs for Tessie's grandchildren and a box of chocolates to take out to Kitty's, as they were having Easter Sunday dinner there. On Monday, Joe was travelling up from Cork to spend a few days at Ballygrace House, and they would take a trip out to visit Auntie Molly in the nursing home in Mullingar.

But that still left today, Thursday, to fill, and Tara knew that the first day of the holidays would set the tone for the rest of the week. If it was a flat, boring day, it would be hard to pick things up from then on. She considered a few possibilities – the Wicklow mountains perhaps, or maybe Kilkenny – but dismissed them, as they would be dependent on the weather, and it was unlikely to be warm and sunny.

She came back to the first place she'd thought of – Dublin. It had plenty of indoor things, apart from shops, to keep William amused if the weather let them down. Tara had a list in her desk drawer downstairs from previous visits to the city. Off the top of her head – without checking what matinées were on in the theatre or the cinema – she knew that she could easily fill the day with visits to the National Art Gallery and the Museum. They would have lunch in one of the nice city centre hotels, and, if it were dry, a walk around St Stephen's Green.

Although she felt easier that she had now decided how they would spend the day, Tara gave a weary sigh, wishing that she could have just spent the day pottering around the house and visiting Ballygrace Cemetery.

She would take William out to Gabriel's grave at some point over the weekend, but would make sure she got a visit on her own. She wouldn't feel she had visited him properly if she went with other people. As long as she did that, she didn't mind whatever else she did with William or the rest of her family.

As she lay back on her white embroidered pillows, she wondered if her life would always be like this – planning to fill the endless hours when she wasn't working.

When she looked back on it, Tara realised that, even when she was married, she had always found time hanging heavy on her hands when she wasn't with Gabriel. In the quiet darkness now she recalled the period they went through when she was desperate to have a child. Part of it was to fill the hours during the day when Gabriel was working, but the overwhelming reason had been the natural urge to have a child with the husband she loved. And Tara Fitzgerald had felt that urge very strongly, right up until Gabriel's death.

She had so longed to hold their child in her arms, and it still broke her heart to know that it would never happen. And yet, having lost her beloved Gabriel, she knew it was for the best. Having never known her own mother, she would not have wanted a child of hers to bear the loss of a parent.

She had been lucky to have had most of the void in her life filled by a loving grandfather, and quiet but steady relatives like her Uncle Mick and his wife, Kitty. Shay, in his early days, hadn't been a good father, but, as the years had gone on, he had redeemed himself, and Tessie had been a good friend to her. And although Joe had spent his early years away from her in the seminary, they were now as close as many brothers and sisters who had been brought up together.

Finding something to pass the time had never been an issue when she was younger. Things had always taken care of themselves. Growing up in Ballygrace, she had had a busy life keeping house for her granda and Mick. She had always had her friends, and interests such as her music and tending to her little poultry farm. Life had been simple but full.

When she first moved to Stockport, her work in the estate agency had filled her days, while her evenings and weekends were occupied teaching music or working in the reception at the Grosvenor Hotel. And even now, Tara knew it was easier to fill her time in Stockport with work. The Cale Green Hotel took up as many hours up as she cared to spend there, and there was always something she could find to do, whether it was in the office, the kitchen or even in the hotel gardens.

But here, back in Ballygrace House, there was no place to hide from her loneliness. It was fine when other people were around and she was organising things for them. But when she was on her own, the loneliness was constantly there, waiting for her around every corner.

Having planned the day, Tara turned over again, trying to sleep, but there was a restlessness within with her that wouldn't go away. Her mind moved to the situation with Bridget, then flitted back to the Grosvenor. She came to no conclusions about either, apart from deciding that she would spend more time going to her friend's, and offering to help in any way she could.

She gave another loud sigh, then buried her face in the white pillow, suddenly feeling exhausted.

When William came down for breakfast he was delighted to hear Tara's plans. 'I'd love to go to the Museum again to see all the stuffed animals,' he told her. 'We went there a few years ago, but it was near closing time and we only had a very short while to look around.' He lifted the box of Kellogg's Cornflakes and poured himself a big bowlful, then liberally sprinkled a spoonful of sugar on top before adding the milk. Even now that he was a teenager, his mother would still tell him off for having so much sugar, and he was always gratified when Tara always said it didn't matter what he had, as he was on holiday.

'Grand,' Tara told him. 'We'll start off at the Natural History section and see where the rest of the day takes us.' She turned back to the grill where she was cooking four slices of bacon and some black-and-white pudding.

A knock came on the back door and William jumped up to get it. It was Shay, cap in hand as usual.

'You're surely on the go early,' Tara said. She picked up the now empty kettle and moved to the sink to refill it and make her father a cup of tea. 'It's only nine o'clock.'

'Sure, I've been up since seven,' Shay said, as though he had been a regular early riser all his life. 'Since it was dry this morning, I decided I'd cycle over to see how you two were gettin' on out here.' He made a pretence of swiping at William's head, which always made the boy duck and laugh. 'They're giving out showers on the radio for later on, so I thought I'd make a move and not get caught in it.'

'Will you have a bit of bacon or some bread or cinnamon buns?' Tara asked him. 'Ella baked them for us.'

'I wouldn't thank you for any more fried stuff,' Shay said, sitting down at the big wooden table. He'd obviously been well fed by Tessie already this morning. 'But I'll try one of Ella's buns.' Tara went off to the small pantry where Ella kept the buns in a deep, sealed biscuit tin.

It crossed Shay's mind, as he watched his elder daughter, how well she had adapted to running Ballygrace House entirely on her own. When she and Gabriel were living in it, they had Ella most days and Angela Flynn as well. Things had been far more formal then. Of course, he reasoned, that was the way Gabriel had been brought up, and that was what he had been used to. And, in the early days, Tara herself had taken to the grander things in life like a duck takes to water. But, he supposed, the novelty had worn off, and since she was a hard worker by nature, it would be no problem to Tara to do the odd bit of cooking and cleaning.

Shay had never held with all the old formality that was the order of the day in places like Ballygrace House. When he had first visited the place he immediately felt like a fish out of water, and preferred coming in through the back servants' entrance than up the front stairs with the family. And if he hadn't initially felt it, the gimlet eye of the old housekeeper had certainly left him in no doubt as to his station in life. Ballygrace House had not been built for the likes of Shay Flynn.

And then Tara had married Gabriel Fitzgerald, and, within a short time, the pair of them were the owners of the old Georgian house. Imagine, Shay Flynn's daughter the mistress of Ballygrace House!

Never, in a million years, could he have imagined such as thing happening. Just as he would never have imagined himself sitting here now, quite comfortable and content, drinking tea and eating buns in the big old kitchen, without fear of a housekeeper or an owner running him for his life.

But time had changed a lot of things recently, Shay reckoned, and the world was no longer as cut and dried as it had been. Sure, you only had to pick up the newspaper to read all that was happening.

The 1960s were seeing big changes in Ireland, with showbands taking over from the traditional music, and more and more people getting the television channels in. Shay had been entranced by television when he had lived over in Stockport, but he had never dreamed of affording one himself. But there he was now, with his own little black and white television back in the kitchen at home. Who would ever have believed it?

Shay winked at William. 'And how are they all back in London and Stockport?' William politely swallowed the mouthful of cornflakes he was eating, then put his spoon down. 'Very well, thank you,' he replied. 'My mother and Harry have gone to Stratford-upon-Avon with some friends for the Easter weekend.'

'Begod,' Shay said, 'isn't that where that Shakespeare fella came from?' He turned to take a bun from the biscuit tin that Tara was now offering him. 'Thanks,' he murmured, dipping his hand into the tin. As she went to take it away, he suddenly dipped into it again. 'I'll chance two since they look so nice.'

William nodded. 'I think they're going to see one of Shakespeare's plays while they're there.'

'Well, wouldn't they be fools to miss it when they're in the very place itself,' Shay commented, as though he were very well acquainted with the English playwright's work. 'And how are poor Fred and Bridget and all the little ones?' he asked, taking a good bite from one of the cinnamon buns. Shay always referred to Fred as 'poor Fred' since his brain injury in the wrestling ring, even though Bridget's husband had, more or less, made a full recovery. Shay had always been fond of Fred, and often recounted stories of their outings to wrestling matches at Bellvue Hall in Manchester.

'I was up at their house a few times this week,' William said, 'and they were all fine. Michael was getting ready to go away for the weekend with the Cubs.'

'Was he now, begod?' Shay said, taking another bite of his bun.

'Do you still have two sugars in your tea?' Tara asked as she poured a cup for him.

'The very same,' he confirmed. 'And a good splash of milk.'

'William and I are going up to Dublin today,' Tara said, turning back to the grill to lift the bacon and slices of savoury pudding onto two plates.

'*Today*?' Shay exclaimed. 'Sure, you must be mad driving all the way up there after only driving down from the boat yesterday.' He shook his head. 'And I believe Angela has similar plans to yerself.' He shrugged. 'Not that she said anything to me about it, but I heard it from Tessie.'

'Angela's going to Dublin as well?' Tara's voice was high with surprise. 'Who is she going with and how is she travelling?' She put a plate in front of William and one at her own set place.

Shay rolled his eyes to the ceiling. 'Now, you might as well be askin' the wall as askin' that lady anything.' He took a sip of his tea. 'Seemingly she met up with an old friend yesterday who has a car, and the pair of them are heading up there for the day. What the attraction is about Dublin, I do not know. It's one place you wouldn't catch me in if I could help it.' He shrugged. 'Dublin, how are ye?'

'So there's no point in asking you to join us?' William asked, with an impish grin on his face. He loved the way that Shay went on and the odd, funny sayings that he had.

'Not if you paid me a million pounds!' Shay stated. 'Not if you sat it down on that table this very minute would I go up to that hell-hole.'

'Oh, well,' Tara said, lifting her knife and fork, 'we wouldn't dream of putting you through that misery, so we must make sure we never ask you.'

'And what, might I ask,' Shay demanded, 'is taking ye back up there again?'

'We're going to the Museum,' William told him, 'to look at the stuffed animals.'

'What, in the name of God, would you be going to look at things like that for?' Shay said. 'Oul' dead, stuffed animals – nothin' but dirt, the lot of it!' Smiling, he started on his second bun, enjoying the banter now.

'It's actually very interesting, Shay,' the young boy said. 'Honestly, if you came with us you'd really love it. You see wild animals there that you'd never see in real life.'

Tara shot her young brother-in-law a warning glance. She certainly didn't want her father coming up to Dublin with them.

Shay shook his head, silent for a few moments while he finished off his bun. 'Not for a million pounds,' he repeated. 'Sure, I can walk up the bog and see all the wild animals I need to see without ever stirring outside of Tullamore.'

Due to Shay's unannounced visit they set off for Dublin later than intended, but Tara felt it was better that the time went more quickly rather than finding it drag. Having seen Shay up and about early, and in such good humour, had eased her mind.

William chatted all the way to Dublin, telling Tara about school and all the other things he was involved in.

'Have you any idea what you want to do when you leave school, William?' Tara asked him as they drove along the country roads. 'Have you any plans for college or university?'

'My first plan is to get away from school as early as I can,' he replied. 'I really hate it.'

Tara looked at him quickly. 'Are you serious?' she asked.

'Yes,' he said, his gaze moving firmly in front of him to look out of the car window.

'What's wrong?' Tara asked. 'Has something happened?' She kept glancing at him while trying to keep one eye on the winding roads.

'Sometimes the other boys tease me for being Irish.' Then he laughed. 'Actually, it's not that serious … I'm only half-joking. They tease everyone, and that's the only thing they can find that's funny about me.'

'William,' Tara said, 'you sounded serious to me. Is there some kind of a problem at school you're not telling me?'

'No, honestly,' he said. 'It's just that at times I find it very boring and I wish I was old enough to get out in the world and do whatever I want.'

'And what would you like to do?'

He frowned. 'I haven't made up my mind yet . . . I'm not at all sure what direction I should go in.'

'What subjects do you particularly like?'

'Well,' he said, 'I used to think I'd like to do law or accountancy, or the sort of estate agency work Gabriel and my father did, but recently I've been thinking that I might like to do something a bit more exciting, like hotel management, with a view to running my own hotel some day.'

'*Hotel management*?' Tara said, completely astonished. 'I've never heard you say anything about that before. Have you mentioned it to your mother or Harry?'

'No, you're actually the first person I've told.' He glanced up at her now, and she detected a look of anxiety in his eyes.

An ominous feeling crept over Tara. A feeling which told her that she might well find herself on the wrong side of Elisha Fitzgerald, and being blamed for encouraging William to follow her own example.

'I've still a few years to go at school,' William went on, 'so it's only an idea at the moment, but I really would prefer to do something with a bit of variety, and I think a hotel would be brighter and livelier than working in a dull old office.'

'Is this because of all the time you've spent in the Cale Green Hotel?' Tara said quietly. 'Because if it is, I have to warn you that it's not all fun. I know you enjoy helping Fred and helping out in the kitchen during your holiday, but it's very, very different when you're doing it for a living, and it's harder again when you know that you are responsible for all the people working for you. When you actually *own* the business, you have to find the money if anything goes wrong. You have to maintain everything inside the building, like furniture and bedding, as well as the gardens and the exterior of the building, too.'

William smiled and nodded. 'I've been reading up on it,' he said. 'We had a careers day for the older boys in school and I got a brochure with details about courses and that kind of thing. That was actually what gave me the idea. I didn't realise you could train for that kind of work.'

'I'm not sure if it's the sort of work that your mother would approve of you doing,' Tara ventured. 'I'm sure she's hoping that you'll go into something more professional.'

'I was actually hoping that you might have a word with her about it sometime,' he told her. 'I'm sure she would listen to anything you have to say. I know she admires you enormously for what you did with the Cale Green Hotel. I've heard her say it to Harry loads of times.'

Tara took a deep breath. 'Well, as you say, it's a long time off. You don't have to decide for a few years.' She wasn't at all sure how Elisha would react to the news that William wanted to go into the hotel business. And while she might well admire Tara, she was well aware of Tara's humble beginnings and would probably feel that it was an appropriate business for her. But Tara had the feeling that it might be an entirely different ball game when it came to her own son.

Chapter 17

Angela could see Aiden Byrne's car waiting opposite the Guard station as she turned the corner, and she deliberately slowed her step to a stroll so that she wouldn't appear too keen.

Tessie had walked to the gate, still chiding her for not eating her breakfast. 'Two cups of tea and half a slice of bread isn't a way to start the day,' she said, her arms folded high over her chest.

'I'm grand,' Angela had said distractedly, wishing that her mother had stayed in bed, or had gone out to Mass or the shops, to let her get ready in peace. She had forced down a few bites of the buttered soda bread her mother had placed in front of her, just to keep her happy. But eating was the last thing on her mind. Since meeting Mrs Malone's cousin yesterday her appetite had completely and in-explicably vanished.

Thankfully, her hair had turned out well and was sitting beauti-fully, with the help of a few rollers earlier this morning and a light spray of lacquer. She had carefully made up her face and then applied a small touch of Shalimar perfume between her breasts and on her wrists. It was her favourite perfume – a bottle that Tara had bought for her last birthday – but she had learned to be very sparing with the spicy fragrance, as too much was overpowering.

Before she left the house, she had listened carefully for the weather forecast. It was exactly as she had reckoned – mild with light showers. She decided to wear her smart beige raincoat, which would match her cream and brown outfit very nicely.

As soon as he spotted her, Aiden Byrne leaned across the passenger seat to open the car door. 'Good morning, Miss Flynn,' he said as she slid inside, his dark-brown eyes appraising her. And from the appreciative smile that followed, she knew that he was very satisfied. 'You look and smell lovely. I'm delighted that you've come. I was afraid you might have changed your mind.'

'You needn't have worried. I'm not the type to do something like that,' she told him.

His face suddenly became serious. 'To tell you the truth,' he admitted, 'I was worried that you might have had second thoughts … or that you might have been persuaded not to go out with me.'

'By whom?' Angela asked. Then she turned to look at him and, when their eyes locked, she had a strange feeling of familiarity, as though she had known him for a long, long time.

He gave a little shrug. 'Your family or your friends.'

She raised her eyebrows, then shook her head. 'No, I wouldn't let anyone talk me out of something, if that's what I wanted to do. Anyway, I'm old enough now to make up my own mind about things.'

It wasn't worth going into the discussion she'd had with her mother. It would only make her look young and incapable of making her own decisions. And anyway, Aiden Byrne had seemed impressed yesterday by the fact that she was an independent young woman living over in England, so it wouldn't do to have him think she still had to answer to her mother and father when she came back home.

'You didn't have any trouble getting away yourself?' she asked lightly.

'No,' he said, 'I'm often up in Dublin for meetings, so nobody thought any more about it.'

'Well, that's grand, isn't it?' She unbuttoned her coat now and slipped it off. The car was already warm and comfortable, the nice smell of leather upholstery mingling with the very subtle cologne that Aiden was wearing. 'Do you mind if I throw this in the back seat?' she asked.

'How would I?' he said, laughing. Then, impulsively, he leaned across and kissed her lightly on the lips. He moved back a few inches and waited for her reaction. When she looked up at him and smiled, he bent forward again and gave her a much longer, lingering kiss, and was delighted when her arms came up to twine around his neck.

'That was lovely,' he breathed when he eventually pulled away.

'It was,' she agreed, 'but I think we'd better get moving or we'll have some of my nosy neighbours calling the Guards to come and remove us for making a spectacle of ourselves at this ungodly hour of the morning.'

'I think I might be willing to take a chance on that,' he grinned. 'But then, nobody really knows me around here, so it wouldn't do *me* a great deal of harm.' He touched her lightly under the chin. 'But you, on the other hand, Miss Flynn, might well lose your carefully guarded reputation, and we couldn't possibly allow that to happen.'

Reluctantly, he started up the car engine and they set off.

'Have you any thoughts on where you'd like to go in Dublin?' he asked as they drove out of Tullamore and up towards Kilbeggan.

'I don't mind,' Angela said. 'Why don't you surprise me?'

Aiden Byrne started to laugh. 'I think it's you who are doing all the surprising, Angela,' he said. 'You've surprised me since the very first moment we met.'

'How?' she asked, turning round in her seat to look at him properly.

He took his eyes off the quiet road to look at her. 'You're not like any other girl I've ever known.'

'How?' she repeated, curious now. Of course she knew he was bound to say something nice and flattering – most lads did say things like that to girls, even if they didn't mean it – but she felt that Aiden Byrne might say something she'd never heard before.

'Well, to start with,' he said, 'you're brighter and more sophisticated than most of the girls your age.' He paused. 'But that's not all. You've definitely got *something* that sets you apart. Something very different that I can't quite put my finger on.'

Dublin was bright and busy and noisy, and, as they drove along The Quays, Angela felt a surge of excitement. She'd only been to Dublin half a dozen times in her life, and she didn't know it all that well. Aiden Byrne, on the other hand, was well acquainted with the city, and she was looking forward to seeing it with someone who knew their way around.

Angela had to admit to herself that she would have been excited going anywhere with Aiden Byrne, whether it was a city, the country or even the seaside. She wondered, as they drove along, whether he felt the same, whether men thought the same things as women in these circumstances, but came to no conclusions.

Aiden drove over one of the smaller bridges before the bridge at O'Connell Street. 'There's a quiet spot just off Grafton Street,' he told her. 'That will suit us fine for parking and for the main area. Is that OK with you?'

Angela smiled and nodded. Anything he suggested was OK with her. 'That'll be absolutely grand.' She'd only ever come up to Dublin on the train with her friends or in the car with Tara, and she'd just followed everyone else.

They parked the car in a small cobbled street, then strolled back towards the main shopping area. 'Would you like to stop for tea or coffee now at the Westbury Hotel?' Aiden asked. 'It's just off Grafton Street.'

'Grand,' Angela said again. She hadn't been in that particular hotel before, but Tara had taken her into places like the Gresham Hotel in O'Connell Street and the Midland Hotel in Manchester when they were out shopping, so she wasn't as over-awed by them as other girls of her own age and background might be. To be honest, she never really understood why people like Tara were so impressed by the bigger, expensive hotels. She was happy enough in the smaller, more homely places.

When they came to the entrance of the hotel and Angela saw the doorman dressed in his fancy blue and red outfit, she suddenly wondered if she would look terribly out of place in her Capri pants and sweater. Then, as they walked up the grand, winding stairs to the big airy lounge, Angela felt Aiden Byrne's arm slip casually around her waist. 'You look and smell really lovely,' he told her once again, giving her a small, appreciative squeeze, and all her fears about being dressed appropriately disappeared.

A waitress met them at the top of the stairs and guided them to two comfortable armchairs on either side of a small elegant table, by one of the tall windows. As they looked at the morning menu, Angela glanced around the lounge, and was delighted to see two sophisticated-looking, dark-haired women about Tara's age coming up the stairs laden with shopping bags and both dressed in a similar style to herself.

The waitress brought them to a table close to Angela and Aiden, and, after they had disrobed themselves of jackets and bags, they sat back in their chairs. One of the women caught Angela's eye and gave her a warm, friendly smile. Angela smiled in return, then moved her gaze back to the menu, but out of the corner of her eye she glimpsed the woman motioning to her friend to look across at her and Aiden. The other woman lifted her head and stared, her eyes cool and appraising. Instinctively, Angela knew that the focus of their attention was Aiden and not her.

She suddenly felt Aiden's hand stroke the back of hers. 'Have you decided yet?' he asked.

Angela looked up at him blankly, then realised he was asking what she'd like to order. 'Coffee, please,' she said, blushing.

He indicated the menu 'Would you like anything to eat? It's a bit early for lunch, but they do nice pastries and scones.'

She hesitated. She really wasn't at all hungry, the little knot of excitement in her stomach was still there, damping her normally healthy appetite. 'I think I'll wait until later,' she said. 'A coffee on its own would be lovely.'

'You're not one of these girls who watch what they're eating in case they get fat, are you?' he joked.

'Definitely not,' Angela said. 'I love eating, and my weight has hardly changed since I left school.'

He closed the menu and put it back down on the table. 'And can I be so bold as to ask exactly when that was?' he said, raising his eyebrows and smiling.

'You mean you're asking how old I am?' she said, her voice slightly teasing.

He nodded his head. 'I've a good idea, since you're Carmel's friend, but I think it's a little thing we might just want to get out of the way, rather than get any surprises later.'

'I'm twenty-three,' she said. 'I'll be twenty-four in July.'

Aiden Byrne pressed a thoughtful finger to his lips. 'Nine years' difference,' he said, 'I'm going on for thirty-three.' He looked directly at her. 'Does it seem a big age gap to you?'

Angela stared back at him, not quite sure how to answer. Too big an age gap for what? she wondered. To be sitting here with him in a fancy hotel in Dublin? To be seen out together in public for a one-off date? He couldn't be meaning anything more serious, could he?

Even if she'd had her own silly fantasies since yesterday, it was much too early to think of things like that. She gave a little shrug, but the question was written on her face.

Aiden leaned forward in his chair. 'I just wondered if you thought the age gap was too big for us to be friends,' he told her. 'And especially with me having been married, and being the father of a child.'

Angela suddenly became conscious of the two elegant women looking over at them again and knew that they would both love to be in her shoes. Any woman would. He was a handsome and successful man, had been honest with her about his situation, and was now being upfront about his age.'

Angela wondered how Tara would react in the same position, and, in a flash, the answer came to her. Tara had not let anything stand in her way when it came to men. There had been a much bigger social divide between her and Gabriel than there was between Aiden Byrne and herself. The fact that her half-sister owned Ballygrace House and the land that went with it, plus a hotel and boarding houses in Stockport, meant that she was much better connected than Tara had been at that age. It hadn't held Tara back, had it? She'd still married Gabriel Fitzgerald, and it had worked out fine.

And then there was Frank Kennedy. Proof that Tara had done it twice. She had found another successful man, and not only did he have plenty of money, he was also older than Tara. Angela didn't know by how much, but even though he was a good-looking man, she thought he must be somewhere around forty. The age difference between herself and Aiden Byrne was probably not a great deal more.

Angela looked back at him now and smiled. 'The age difference doesn't bother me in the slightest,' she said.

'You're an amazing-looking girl,' he told her, gazing deep into her eyes, 'and you're amazing in every other way as well.'

Chapter 18

❧❧❧

Tara found a parking space up by the side of Trinity College, then she and William walked along to the Museum. Since they had both had a fairly hefty breakfast, they decided to go straight there, then walk around the corner and have lunch in the Shelbourne Hotel afterwards.

As they walked around the exhibits that had excited William so much a few years ago, Tara noticed a marked difference in the boy's attitude. He still enjoyed looking at the items on display, but was more subdued in his appreciation of it. Instead of the gasps of amazement, he used the dry sense of humour that he was cultivating.

They came to stand in front of a large stuffed giraffe. 'I wonder if Shay's ever seen anything like this around Tullamore? I must remember to ask him when I see him tomorrow.'

Tara stifled her laughter in the quiet, austere room. 'Oh, don't,' she whispered to William. 'There are times when I could kill him. He says the most ridiculous things.'

'I find him funny,' William said, 'and entertaining. In fact, I like Shay very much.'

Tara looked at him. 'Do you really?' she asked, suddenly curious.

'Yes, he's a lovely man. He always takes the time to talk to me and explain things to me, and I enjoy playing cards and dominos with him and Mick. They've both got a good sense of humour as well.'

Tara realised that she had never seriously asked William's opinion before. She had always presumed to know how he would feel about things, how a child would view them. But the fact was, William Fitzgerald was no longer a child. He was a boy certainly, but one swiftly heading towards manhood.

The Shelbourne Hotel was busy, so they had to wait in the bar until a table for two was available. Tara ordered a glass of white wine for herself and a lemonade shandy for William.

'Harry lets me have a glass of wine with my meals now,' he told Tara, sipping at his drink, which he had used to gulp. Then he grinned. 'But my mother tells him off and says it'll be his fault if I get a taste for it.'

'How is your mother these days, William?' Tara asked. 'I must visit her in London soon.'

He looked thoughtful for a few moments. 'Better in some ways,' he said, 'and worse in others. She worries far too much – especially about me.' He paused. 'But then she lost two of her children very young, so I suppose it's only natural that she would worry about the only one she has left.'

Tara lifted her glass to her lips, quite taken aback by William's matter-of-fact statement. She swallowed a mouthful of the wine, trying to push the picture of the young, blond Gabriel and his tragic sister, Madeleine, that had just flown into her mind. Not that it was unusual for her to think of Gabriel – there were days when everything reminded her of him – but she had learned to avoid thinking of him at times like this.

A waiter came into the bar to inform Tara and William that their table was ready. As Tara moved to lift her bag and handbag, she gave a deep, silent sigh, and realised she had been holding her breath.

By the time they came out of the Shelbourne Hotel, the afternoon had brightened considerably. 'Shall we have a bit of a stroll around St Stephen's Green?' Tara suggested, indicating the park across the road. 'It's lovely now, so it might be best to take our chance rather than wait until later in case it rains.'

'D'you mean a constitutional?' William said, laughing. 'That's what Harry always calls it. He says it helps old fogies digest their food better.'

'What a thing to say!' Tara exclaimed. 'And I hope you're not suggesting that I'm an old fogey?'

William's face immediately turned serious. 'No, no,' he said. 'I was just repeating Harry's silly joke.' He touched Tara's arm now. 'I would never say or even think such a thing about *you*, Tara. You could never be an old fogey, not in a million years. I couldn't imagine you ever getting old.'

'That's very nice of you,' Tara said, guiding him across the road now towards St Stephen's Green, 'but we will all get old some day. It's the natural order of things.' But again, she fleetingly thought of her poor Gabriel, and his sister who hadn't been given the chance to grow old. 'We'll all get older if we're lucky,' she added.

William made no further comment, and they both walked into

the beautiful city centre park in silence.

'I should have stopped and bought some bread for the ducks,' Tara said.

'It doesn't matter,' William said, his voice unusually flat. 'We can enjoy just looking at them.'

Tara glanced at her young brother-in-law. 'Are you all right William?' she said, coming to a sudden halt. 'Is something the matter?'

The boy's face flushed, and Tara was alarmed to notice his eyes were welling up with tears. She took him gently by the arm and guided him to an empty bench situated in a more secluded area of the park.

'I feel *really* stupid now,' William said, reaching into his jacket pocket for a hanky.

'What on earth is the matter?' Tara said in a soft, concerned voice.

William rubbed his eyes dry with the folded square of cotton. 'I shouldn't have said that thing about old fogeys,' he mumbled, his shoulders hunched and his gaze glued firmly to the ground. 'I'm so, so stupid. What a ridiculous thing to say to someone like you. Why do I always get things wrong?'

'William,' Tara said, putting her hand under his chin to make him look at her, 'you said nothing wrong. Sure, I was only codding you that I was offended. It was a joke.'

His eyes met hers now. 'I'd never, *never* say or do anything to hurt you, Tara.' His eyes filled up again. 'You're the best person in the whole world. I don't know what I'd do without you.' He shook his head. 'I love you very, very much.'

Tara reached out to him now and pulled her close to him, her arms wrapped tightly around him. 'And you know I love you, too, William.'

'I wish I were older,' William said now, his voice choked and hoarse. 'If I were twenty-one, I could ask you to marry me.'

Tara's heart almost stopped. Had she heard him correctly? She sat there on the bench, completely frozen with shock, with William Fitzgerald's damp face pressed against her shoulder. She had never imagined in her wildest dreams that any young boy – William especially – could feel like that about her. It was wholly and completely inappropriate. Apart from his age, he was her husband's brother.

And then a horrible realisation dawned on her that her husband's father had said and felt the exact same thing. Is it me? Tara wondered, carefully easing away from the boy. What unknown encouragement did I ever give them? But she could not answer her own questions. As far as she knew, she had only been herself. She had neither preened nor flirted, neither said nor done anything to warrant that type of attention. And, frighteningly, she had not been the slightest bit aware that William Fitzgerald senior *and* junior could possibly have romantic notions about her until it was too late to do anything about it.

Tara moved now until she was sitting a decent distance away from the boy. And although all her instincts made her want to walk away from the situation, she knew she could not. She looked at William now, as he dabbed at his eyes, and she realised that she, as the adult, was going to have to take control. She was going to have to say something to him to defuse this awful, uncomfortable situation.

'William,' she said, lightly touching his arm, 'you know that was a very silly thing you just said? You know, even if we were the same age, that I couldn't possibly dream of marrying you? You are Gabriel's brother, and I could never, *ever* think of you like that – even if we were the same age.'

He sat up, rubbing the hanky over his eyes again and nodding. 'I'm so sorry, Tara,' he said again. 'I didn't really mean it the way it sounded. I just mean I'd like to live with you and see you every day. You make me feel safe. Being with you, whether it's here in Ireland or in Stockport, makes my life more predictable. I feel I know where I'm up to.' He took a deep, shuddering breath. 'Back in London with my mother ... I never know how she's going to be from one day to the next. I never know what to expect.' He shrugged. 'I know she can't help it. It's her nerves; it's just the way she is. And there are times when I'm not all that happy at school ... Since Gabriel died, you and the hotel and Ballygrace House are the only truly happy things in my life. You are the one person I can always depend on.'

A wave of pity washed over Tara. Compared to other boys – compared to her own upbringing – he had everything that money could buy, but he lacked his mother's interest and devotion.

'And I will continue to be dependable, William,' Tara reassured him. 'As long as you put those silly thoughts about me completely out of your head.'

He nodded miscrably. 'I really didn't mean it,' he repeated. 'It was just the way it came out.'

'That's grand, then,' Tara said, smiling at him. 'We can put it to the side and forget all about it.'

They continued on their walk around the park, stopping to look at the ducks and commenting on the various features.

'Shay told me that this park was actually built in the late eighteen hundreds', William said, sounding more like his old self. 'It's amazing to think that it's almost the same now as it was back then, isn't it?'

'It is amazing,' Tara agreed, wondering where her father had got that little nugget of information, considering he had probably never been to St Stephen's Green in his life. She smiled at the boy, feeling herself start to relax again. She loved walking around the park, taking in the beautiful flowerbeds, the fountain and the lake with all the ducks and swans.

At one point they stopped to lean on a bridge and just people-watch. Then William's brow creased in confusion and he pointed to a distant grassy area where children were playing with a ball and several groups of people were sitting on benches. 'Tara,' he said, in a low voice, 'am I imagining it, or is that Angela sitting on that bench?'

'Actually, it may well be her,' she said, 'because my father mentioned that she was coming up to Dublin with a friend today.' Tara scanned the benches, searching for two women, but she couldn't pick her out. 'I don't see her,' she said, moving up the bridge to get a better view. 'Whereabouts is she?'

'On the bench under the big tree,' William said. 'I'm certain it's her.'

Tara's eyes narrowed in concentration. Then she spotted the familiar blonde hair. It was indeed Angela. No doubt about it. She moved to look at her half-sister's companion now, and was taken aback to see it was a man. A very smart, well-dressed, *older* man. Not an old schoolfriend.

'Should we go across and say hello?' William asked.

Tara hesitated, watching now as the dark-haired man slipped his arm around the back of the bench and pulled Angela closer to him, then bent his head and kissed her on the lips. 'No,' she said, 'I don't think we should. Angela has obviously travelled up to Dublin today to get some privacy. She wouldn't be expecting to see us or anyone else she knows around here.'

William looked surprised but said nothing. He'd made one mistake today already, and he didn't want to make another.

Tara checked her watch now. 'I think we should head back to Grafton Street to get a newspaper and find out what's on in the theatre or the cinema this afternoon.'

'Great!' William readily agreed.

As they turned and walked out of the park in the direction of the shops, Tara hoped that Angela had not seen them. Angela kissing a total stranger in broad daylight? At least, Tara *presumed* he was a stranger. He certainly wasn't anybody she knew from Tullamore or from any of the outlying villages. And yet, Angela had only come home yesterday and wouldn't have had time to meet anyone new, so she must have known him from before. Whatever the circumstances, Angela and the man certainly looked as if they knew each other, the way they were carrying on.

Tara sucked in her breath, not knowing what to think. Hopefully, Angela wasn't up to anything stupid or wrong, but why had she told her parents that she was going to Dublin with an old friend? It sounded suspicious, as though she were trying to hide something. Hopefully, Tara thought, Angela wasn't slipping back into her old ways.

Chapter 19

On Thursday afternoon, Frank Kennedy stood by the bar in the Grosvenor Hotel, chatting to the barman. Every so often he looked at his expensive watch, then cast a glance at the door. A short time later Gerry McShane appeared in the bar and, after ordering a drink, both men went to sit at a quiet corner table, away from the lunchtime hubbub.

'Are you home or away for the Easter weekend?' Frank asked, his manner easy and casual.

'I'm spending the weekend with my family in York,' Gerry replied. 'They're all very sensitive about the bachelor son and brother spending Christmas or Easter on his own.'

'That's nice of them,' Frank said, nodding. 'And York's a lovely city.' There was a pause as both men sipped at their pints of beer. 'You wanted a word with me?' he finally said.

Gerry looked him square in the face. 'It's about Tara Fitzgerald.'

Frank sat up straight in his chair. 'What about her?'

'I wondered if you knew anything about her financial situation, how she was fixed with regard to joining our group.' He cleared his throat. 'She's a hard woman to get through to, but I hear you know her better than most people.'

Frank hesitated. 'We used to be close,' he said in a low voice. 'But that was some time ago, before she got married.'

Things didn't work out for you and her?'

'Unfortunately, no ...' He debated whether to say any more, but decided to leave it at that. From what he knew of Gerry McShane, he was a decent fellow, straight and honest in business dealings, but Frank didn't know him that well. And even if he had known him better, he probably wouldn't have said much more. Tara was not a subject he'd discussed with anyone apart from Bridget Roberts.

'Did you know her husband well?' Gerry asked, his voice full of curiosity.

'I met him on a number of occasions,' Frank said, 'but I wouldn't say I really knew him. He was a quiet, reserved sort of bloke. Public schoolboy type, from old Irish stock.' He was tempted to add that Tara and Gabriel were not a suitable match, that Tara had worked for everything she had in her life, while Gabriel Fitzgerald had been born with a silver spoon in his mouth. That Tara and himself were much more alike; both had come from nothing and had climbed their way up the slippery pole of business success.

Gerry nodded, getting the picture. 'No harm in public school – I went to one myself. I find a lot of the best people do.'

Frank raised his eyebrows but said nothing.

'So, how long ago is it since he ... since she lost him?'

Frank tilted his head to the side, calculating. 'It must be three years.'

'And is she involved with anyone else at the moment?'

'Why do you ask?' Frank said, frowning. He looked at his business acquaintance now, not at all sure if he felt comfortable with the direction of the conversation.

'No particular reason,' Gerry said, lifting his glass. 'It's just that I might ask her out to dinner to see how the land lies with regard to the offer we've made her.'

'And is that the only reason you're asking her?' Frank said, trying to keep his voice light. Even as he said it, he knew the answer.

Gerry shrugged. 'I think any man would enjoy sitting across a table from Tara Fitzgerald. She's a very striking, beautiful woman, and highly intelligent as well. There aren't too many of her type around. And she's known throughout Stockport as an excellent businesswoman. She must be to have turned the Cale Green Hotel around.'

Frank felt the blood rushing to his face. 'I wouldn't go getting any ideas about her,' he warned, his manner blustery and awkward. 'She's a hard person to get to know, and she doesn't let her guard down easily.' He pursed his lips together. 'Losing her husband has changed her. She's never been the same since it happened.'

'So what's changed?' Gerry quizzed, all interested. 'What was she like before she was married?' He paused. 'What was she like when you knew her?'

Frank looked at Gerry McShane, and wondered how on earth he could answer that question without completely breaking down and making an utter fool of himself. How could he begin to explain how Tara Flynn had been, how he knew she still was, under that layer of cold steeliness that she wore like a suit of armour? Where would he start?

Should he tell him that he never knew the meaning of the word 'love' until he set eyes on Tara Flynn, and that his feelings for her had never changed through all the years. And if they had changed, they had only deepened until they consumed his whole life. She was with him night and day, and no matter how hard he tried, he could never escape from her.

How could he tell Gerry McShane that he carried Tara Flynn around inside him every single day, like a bleeding wound in his heart?

Eventually, he lifted his glass and took a deep drink from it. 'Tara's not like any other woman I've ever met in my life,' he said now. 'And I wouldn't know how to begin describing her.'

Gerry McShane stared back at him, then his face broke out into a big smile. 'That's a good enough recommendation for me,' he laughed. 'Most of the women I meet seem interesting, but underneath they're predictable. Tara Fitzgerald has real class, which is a very important quality, and rare enough these days.' He raised his eyebrows. 'I like a bit of a challenge and I'm looking forward to our little get-together.'

'She's not open to people,' Frank told him. 'Especially men. Since Gabriel Fitzgerald died it's as if she's built walls around herself to keep everybody out. You won't find her easy to spend an evening with.'

'I'll take a chance on it,' Gerry said. 'I've nothing to lose and I just might be able to persuade her to join the group.' He paused, as though studying his business associate. 'Sometimes when there's a history between people it makes things tougher. She might be more open when it's somebody new.'

Frank downed the rest of his drink in one gulp and stood up. 'I must go,' he said abruptly. 'I have another meeting that I can't be late for.'

Chapter 20

'Well?' Tessie said, when Angela came through the door just after six o'clock. 'How did it go?'

'Grand,' was Angela's fairly muted response, but the glow in her cheeks and the sparkle in her eye said it all. She dropped a large brown carrier bag on the floor and took her raincoat off, hanging it on the hook on the back of the kitchen door.

'Where did you go?' Tessie asked, full of curiosity. 'Did he take you somewhere nice?'

Angela threw herself down in the armchair at the side of the fire. 'We parked the car behind Switzers, then we went to various places around the centre of Dublin.' She ran a hand through her blonde hair. 'We started off in the Westbury Hotel off Grafton Street.' Her eyes crinkled up at the memory. 'It was absolutely gorgeous ... We had coffee and Danish pastries there, then we went for a walk down to Trinity College and along O'Connell Street.'

'Very nice,' Tessie said. 'Then what did you do?'

'We had a look around the shops, went to a nice restaurant near the theatre for lunch, then walked around St Stephen's Green.' She shrugged. 'We went to a little pub after that, then drove back home.'

There was a little silence. 'So what's the story now?' Tessie eventually asked. 'You're not going to see him again, are you?'

'I am,' Angela declared, looking defensive now. 'Why would I not be seeing him?'

'It's the Easter weekend and we're out at Tara's all tomorrow afternoon,' Tessie reminded her, 'and you've already said you'll be out with the girls at the dancing and that kind of thing.'

'He's calling for me on Saturday morning,' Angela said. 'He said he wants to see me as much as possible while I'm at home.'

Tessie looked at her incredulously. 'I don't want to tell you your business, Angela, but it sounds as though you're wastin' this fella's time when you'll be back in England the weekend after this.' She shook her friends. 'And if you let the girls down after them runnin' backwards and forwards to see you, they're not going to be too pleased, either. If you do that too often, you'll end up with nobody to go out with when you're back home.'

Angela's face suddenly crumpled. 'But I really like him, Mammy. He's the nicest fella I've ever met.'

'But what do you know about him, Angela?' Tessie said, coming to sit in the chair opposite with her hands clasped in her lap. 'You must have found out a bit more about him by now, after spending the whole day with him.'

There was an air of tension in the kitchen now, as Angela debated whether to trust her mother completely or not. She couldn't bear it if it led to a massive row, with her father involved as well. 'Now, Mammy,' Angela began, 'before I start to tell you anything, will you remember that I'm a grown woman, that I'm nearly twenty-four years old?'

Tessie sat silently and listened, as Angela told her all about Aiden Byrne being a widower with a child and that he was a good bit older than her. 'I don't know what to say,' she said when she'd heard it all. 'It's a difficult situation to give any opinion on when you're going to be going back to England next week.'

'What if I wasn't?' Angela cut in. 'Just supposing I was to stay on here and to continue going out with him, what do you think Daddy and Tara and everybody would say?'

'But you've only just met him,' her mother said, shaking her head. 'Surely you wouldn't give up your good job, and you'd be letting Tara down as well ...' Her voice trailed off now.

'I didn't actually say I was going to give up my job for him,' Angela stressed. 'I was just asking what Daddy and everybody else might say, just supposing I did.'

'Has he said that he wished you would stay on?'

'No,' Angela said. 'Sure, we've only just met, I wouldn't expect him to say anything like that.'

'Well, what's there to say if nothing is happening?' Tessie sighed.

'I just wondered ...' Angela said weakly, suddenly realising how silly the conversation now sounded. 'With him being older and having a child ...'

'It would all depend,' her mother hedged, not knowing the right thing to say, 'on his situation and how things went.' Her brow creased. 'Would it do any good if *I* mentioned it to your father?'

'Don't say anything yet,' Angela decided. 'There's no point in making a big issue when it might all come to nothing.'

'Angela,' Tessie said, her daughter's name coming out as a long, exasperated sigh, 'there's no *might* about it. If you want my opinion – for what it's worth – it's only a holiday romance. I don't mean to slight you or anything, but you need to watch out for older men. Often they only have the one thing on their minds.'

Chapter 21

Given that it was Good Friday, the breakfast in Ballygrace House was scant: a boiled egg and bread and butter for Tara, and a bowl of cereal for William. At around eleven o'clock Ella Keating came in, and she and Tara worked together getting the plain, traditional dinner of fish, potatoes and vegetables ready to have straight after Mass. There would be no dessert today. Bread and butter with tea would be the only thing allowed.

While Ella went around the rest of the house lighting fires, cleaning and polishing, William tinkered about at the piano and Tara sat at the dark wood dining-table, checking her Irish bank account and any bills or documents that needed attending to. Things usually ran very smoothly, as her local bank in Tullamore handled most of the business for her, and would contact her in England if there was anything she needed to sort out.

Every so often, she paused and stared out of the window to the gardens that Shay tended. The flowerbeds were now showing their shy spring colours, and the leaves on the trees were coming into full bloom. Tara was conscious of the piano in the background and, as she listened to William's fairly accomplished playing, she hoped and prayed that the awkwardness of the day before in Dublin was well and truly behind them.

Thinking of the day out in the city, her mind flitted back to Angela and the man she had been with in St Stephen's Green. She was still amazed when she thought about it. Tara shook her head. How naive she had been to imagine that Angela had matured in the last few years. She had certainly given that impression, both in the house in Cale Green and at work in the hotel. She was a good, dependable worker and had given them nothing to complain about. Her private life was very obviously a different matter. It had to be. How else could it be explained that she had arranged to meet up with a man – whom she had never mentioned to anyone – and keep it a total secret?

Tara sighed, suddenly realising that she was acting as though she were responsible for her half-sister and her young brother-in-law. As if she were their keeper, constantly checking they were on the right path and ready to pick up the pieces if it all went wrong.

Why should she? she thought then, a tiny seed of resentment creeping in. William had a mother and a stepfather who should be meeting his needs, and Angela – a grown woman now – still had her parents. Why did Tara feel the role of keeper had fallen to her?

Who had been *her* keeper when she was Angela's age? If she were honest, there had been no one she could turn to, apart from poor Bridget, who had been struggling against far greater odds than Tara had even known.

As Tara followed that particular train of thought, she found herself going back over the mistakes she had made with Frank Kennedy. There had been no one she could turn to for advice when it all went wrong. A hot, burning feeling washed over Tara just thinking about it. How could she have been so trusting? To have been involved with a married man who had a family? She would never have believed such a thing could happen to her. She had always been careful in her choice of men, had veered on the side of caution about most things in life. But even so, she had been fooled – and fooled big-time – so it would stand to reason that it could just as easily happen to Angela, if she were conducting clandestine affairs with men she hardly knew.

Tara shrugged now. If Angela wanted her help then she could ask for it. If she didn't, then grand. She could take the consequences of her adult decisions.

Tara wasn't at all surprised when the afternoon at church, and then back at Ballygrace House, came and went without Angela mentioning her day in Dublin.

Shay had referred to it, saying that he'd hardly seen his younger daughter since she'd come home as she'd been so busy gallivanting here, there and everywhere.

Angela had merely rolled her eyes and said, 'Daddy, sure you'd only be complaining if I was in all the time, saying I was only under your feet.'

Everyone had laughed, but Tara had felt a sense of disappointment in Angela. She'd thought that, after everything she and Bridget had done for her, the girl would have felt she could trust her and confide in her.

Chapter 22

STOCKPORT

On the Saturday morning, Fred and Bridget's household was a hive of activity as Michael prepared for his trip away with the Cubs.

'Have you got everything on your list?' Fred asked, lifting the stone-coloured rucksack from the kitchen table, as well as the small carrier bag containing sandwiches, a packet of crisps, a chocolate biscuit and a drink for lunch. The Cubs would eat on arrival at Pott Shrigley, where they would set up camp.

'I'll check again just in case.' Michael dug deep into the pocket of his navy Burberry school coat and fished out a small square of folded paper, now grimy with several weeks' use and starting to fray at the corners. He carefully unfolded it and spread it out on the kitchen table, a serious frown on his face as he studied it.

Fred walked out into the hall. 'Are you ready, Bridget?' he called upstairs. 'We need to get going or we'll be late for the coach. Akela said they won't wait for any latecomers – you know how strict she is with time.'

Michael pushed up the sleeve of his green Cubs jumper to glance anxiously at his leather-strapped Timex watch. 'It's only half-past nine, Dad,' he said, as Fred came back into the kitchen. For all he was on the lazy side at home – Bridget was constantly on at him to do things – Michael hated getting into any kind of trouble outside of the house, particularly if it was to do with school or the Cubs. 'The coach doesn't leave until quarter past ten, so we've still got plenty of time. It'll only take us five minutes to drive up to the hall.'

Fred gave his son a conspiratorial wink. '*I* know that, son,' he said, 'and *you* know that, but your mother is always running at the last minute and we've got to get you checked in at the hall and put your rucksack into the boot of the coach, and all of that.'

Michael nodded and went back to scrutinising his list. 'I ticked everything off last night when me and Mum were packing: sleeping-bag, plate and mug, cutlery, jeans, spare trousers and shorts, under-wear—'

'Give it here,' Fred said, 'and I'll check it again for you.'

It was only Michael's second trip away with the Cubs, and he had learned about packing the hard way on his previous outing, when his rucksack had been left in a puddle in the corner of the tent on the first night, and he had to wear damp spare clothes. He had com-plained for weeks afterwards to his mother, so this time everything was packed and double-packed in waterproof bags, and Bridget had warned him several times to check for puddles before putting his rucksack down.

Fred scanned the list, looking at the ticks beside each item, then he handed it back to his son. 'Good lad,' he said. 'You seem to be all organised.'

Fred's car pulled up outside the Scout Hut on the Stockport Road at quarter to ten, Bridget and the two girls in the back seat, and Michael and his father in the front. There were several other cars parked in the grounds beside the small coach, plus various families that had come on the bus or walked to the meeting place.

'You go into the hall and sign in,' Fred instructed his son as they all got out, 'and we'll bring your rucksack over to the coach.'

Michael lifted his precious lunch bag, then looked at the coach and back towards the hall, trying to see what the other Cubs were doing. 'Akela and Baloo are over at the coach, Dad,' he said, starting to hop from one foot to another. 'I'd better just go over to them and check what I'm supposed to do.'

Bridget lifted little Lucy up in her arms. 'We're supposed to introduce ourselves to the new second-in-command, Baloo – it said it in the last note Michael brought home. You hang on there with Helen and the bags, and I'll go across with Michael and have a word with them.'

Fred gently grabbed Helen around the neck in a mock-wrestling hold, which he knew would make her giggle. 'See if they have a space in the boot for a little one while you're at it,' he joked to his wife. 'We could have total peace at home for the weekend without the pair of them.'

Helen squealed now, trying to struggle out of Fred's grasp.

'Don't, Dad!' Michael hissed, swinging his lunch bag in Fred's direction. 'If Akela sees you messin' around like that we'll get in trouble.'

Fred immediately released Helen and put his arm casually around her shoulder. 'Sorry, sir,' he said, saluting with two fingers. 'Dib, dib, dib, an' all that.'

'Da-ad!' Michael's eyes opened wide to show he wasn't joking. 'You're showing me up.'

'Don't pay any heed,' Bridget said, ruffling her son's dark hair. 'He's only kidding you.' She shot Fred a warning glance. 'You and Helen stay here by the car until we get back, and try to behave yourselves.' She guided Michael across the grass verge to where the two leaders stood, fully decked out in their Cub Leader outfits and busily checking lists and forms on their clipboards.

Akela was a small, heavy woman with curly red hair and glasses, and Baloo was a tall, gangly young man in his twenties with Brylcreemed black hair and a rather prominent nose.

'Good morning, Mrs Roberts,' Akela said, giving them both a welcoming, approving smile. 'All present and correct with Michael, and thankfully in plenty of time.'

'Good morning,' Bridget said, smiling back. Although the Cub Leaders were, in her opinion, officious and petty over small issues, she had a grudging admiration for the great work they did with the young boys. 'Where do you want him?'

Akela looked at her list. 'I think Michael should actually be in the hall now, finding which group he's assigned to and collecting his name badge.'

Bridget just stopped herself from tutting aloud at the inference that they were running late, when they still had a full half an hour before the bus was due to leave. She told herself not to take it personally, that it was the way the woman dealt with everyone.

Akela looked over her spectacles at her assistant. 'Would you accompany Mrs Roberts and Michael, Baloo, and check how things are going generally?' Her brows came down. 'The first group that went in seem to be taking an awful long time to come back out and get on the coach. At this rate, we'll be leaving half of them behind at quarter past ten.'

Michael looked alarmed. 'Quick, Mum,' he whispered, tugging at his mother's sleeve and pointing towards the hall. 'We'd better hurry or they won't let us on the coach.'

'We're grand,' Bridget reassured him as they walked back across the grass. 'Sure, we've plenty of time. You run on ahead if you want to, and I'll tell your dad.'

Michael went off at a quick trot in the direction of the hall, the lunch bag swinging against his legs.

'So you're Michael's mum?' Baloo said as they walked along. He seemed to bounce on the balls of his feet, which added another inch or two to his already tall height.

'I am,' Bridget said distractedly, stopping to put Lucy down on the ground to walk; then, as the little girl made to run away, she gripped her tightly by the hand.

'I'm Richard Freeman,' he said, grinning broadly. 'I can say my real name now that there are no Cubs around.' He was much more relaxed now he was out of earshot of Akela. 'I think we're going to have a great weekend with the boys. They're a good bunch of kids.'

'I don't think Michael got too much sleep last night he was so excited,' Bridget told him, thinking that Richard Freeman was one of these strange kinds of lads who would probably talk and act just the same when he was twenty years older. The type who would be a Cub or a Scout Leader into old age.

'They're all like that,' he laughed. 'I was the same myself when I was a Cub and a Scout. You always have that feeling the night before you go away from home.' He looked at Bridget. 'To tell the absolute truth, I could hardly sleep myself last night. It's my first time to go away as a group leader.'

'Is it?' Bridget said, surprised. He suddenly sounded very young and inexperienced, almost like one of the Cubs himself. She looked him up and down, then turned her gaze back to Lucy, checking she didn't trip up, as some of the paving stones were uneven around the hall. 'You have to do some kind of training to be a leader, don't you?' she asked, hoping that he was mature enough to be responsible for such a big group of boys.

Baloo's face was suddenly serious. 'Oh, yes, we have to do lots of training. Open-fire cooking, tent-erecting, First Aid – the lot.'

Bridget looked visibly relieved. She called over to Fred, 'I'm just going into the hall to make sure Michael gets his name badge. I'll be back in a minute.'

'Is that your husband?' the young man asked, nodding to Fred.

'Yes,' Bridget confirmed, 'and that's Michael's sister, Helen, with him.'

'And who's this little one?' he said, indicating Lucy.

'This is Lucy,' Bridget replied, 'our youngest one.' She nearly added *for the time being*, but stopped herself just in time. It wasn't the sort of thing she should be saying to such a young, gawky lad.

Baloo's brow creased in confusion. 'Is she a neighbour's child?'

'No,' Bridget said. She suddenly felt a tight knot forming in her stomach. 'Didn't you hear me just say that she's our youngest child?'

He looked at Bridget and back at Fred. Then, suddenly, he smiled and nodded, as though having worked something out. 'Is she *adopted*?' he said, mouthing the words quietly.

'*Adopted?*' Bridget gasped, an incredulous look on her face. She stared down at Lucy. 'Indeed and she's not *adopted!* She's the same as the other two – the same mother and the very same father.' She pointed her finger over to where Fred stood patiently by the car, holding Helen's hand, the rucksack dangling from his other hand. 'That's Lucy's father back there with the same black hair as herself. *Adopted?* she repeated. 'What on earth made you think such a thing?'

'I'm sorry,' he mumbled. 'I just presumed—'

'Presumed *what?*'

He shrugged. 'I don't know ... it's just that she looks so different.' He looked down at Lucy, who was now staring back at him curiously. 'She's got a different colour skin from the other two, and her hair's like a West Indian fellow I knew at college.' He shrugged again. 'I suppose that's why I just guessed she might be adopted.'

Fred, seeing a heated discussion was taking place, came towards them now.

'Well, you're wrong!' Bridget said, shaking her head furiously. 'And you're the first person ever to pass a remark like that. Nobody's ever said such a terrible thing to me before.'

The Cub Leader stood looking at her now, lost for words.

Bridget opened her mouth to continue then suddenly halted in her tracks as she became aware of her husband and daughter just a few feet away.

'What's up?' Fred said, his face dark with concern. He eyed Richard Freeman up and down. 'Is there some kind of a problem? You look worried or annoyed – or something'

'We're grand,' Bridget said, her heart starting to thump furiously. What if Fred had overheard what the stupid young Cub Leader had been saying? 'I was just asking him about the arrangements for the weekend,' she said, hearing her own voice sound lame and weak. Hearing her own voice lying.

'Sorry about that mix-up,' the Cub Leader said now. 'But I suppose you must get people saying things like that all the time. I didn't mean to cause offence or anything.'

He turned to Fred, and Bridget could immediately see that that this naive, overgrown schoolboy was ready to launch into a blow-by-blow account of their conversation.

She suddenly felt as though she couldn't catch her breath, and her legs began to feel weak. Then, mercifully, she heard Akela calling, 'Baloo!' and the exchange between them was halted in its tracks. She turned towards the coach and saw Akela signalling furiously to her understudy. 'Check the hall, please!' she called. 'Time's marching on and so should you be.'

A look of alarm crossed Baloo's face. 'Have to go,' he said, and went off, bouncing on the balls of his feet, towards the Scout Hut.

'I'm not sure that fella's the full shilling,' Bridget announced as she watched him disappear into the hall. 'He was talking the biggest load of rubbish just before you came.'

'What do you mean?' Fred said. 'What's he been saying?'

Bridget scanned her husband's face to see if he had heard any part of the conversation. There was no evidence of the kind of upset she would have expected to see if he had. She finally managed to take a deep breath. 'Oh, nothing worth repeating,' she said, adding an exaggerated sigh to emphasise the fact she couldn't be bothered with the subject.

'D'you want me to go and sort him out?' Fred asked.

'Indeed and I don't,' she said, forcing a bright smile. 'Sure, he's only a young lad ... Right,' she continued, handing Lucy over to Fred, 'you wait here. Me and Helen will go to the hall now and see if that lanky eejit has managed to sort Michael out yet.'

At quarter past ten exactly the coach of Cubs pulled out of the Scout Hut car park.

'I hope he'll be all right,' Bridget said, as she joined all the other families in enthusiastically waving the boys off, 'and that he looks after his things better than he did on the last trip.'

Helen took little Lucy by the hand now and led her in the direction of the car. 'He'll be as right as rain,' Fred said reassuringly, putting an arm around his wife's shoulders. 'He's a good lad and he'll do whatever he's told.' They walked back to the car. 'If you don't mind me sayin,' you're lookin' a bit peaky, love. Maybe a bit of a rest might do you good.'

'I'll be grand when I get home and have a cup of tea,' Bridget said, smiling gratefully at him. 'I didn't sleep too well last night. I suppose I was worrying about him going.'

Fred gently squeezed her shoulder with his big hand. 'You're always worrying about the kids, you are. If it's not one of them it's another.' He lowered his voice. 'You're a beltin' mother. You know that, don't you?'

A wave of raw guilt washed over Bridget. Poor Fred ... poor, decent, good Fred. Her eyes filled up with scalding tears.

'Why don't we call in at the Grosvenor and have a cup of tea there?' Fred suggested.

Bridget indicated the two children. 'We can't take them in there,' she said in a choked voice. She wiped a tear away with the back of her hand, wishing she'd put a hanky in her coat pocket.

'We can get them a glass of lemonade and a packet of crisps,' he said. 'There's often kids around in the morning with the guests, and the staff all know us, so there won't be any problem.'

'If you don't mind,' Bridget said in a strained voice, 'I'd rather go straight home.'

He looked at her now and saw the silent tears streaming down her face. He brought her to a halt. 'What's wrong, Bridget?' he asked. 'What's upsetting you so much? This isn't just about Michael going, is it, love?'

Bridget rubbed her eyes with her fingers now. 'It's nothing,' she said. 'It's just that I had a bad night … Oh, ignore me. Some women get very weepy when they're having babies.'

'But you were so bright and cheery with the others,' Fred told her, looking seriously worried. 'You were as right as rain when you were carryin' Lucy.'

Bridget gave a loud, shuddering sniff, which made Fred dig into his trouser pocket for the initialled white hanky he always carried. 'Well,' she said, 'I don't know why I feel like this and I can't help it, but I'm sure it'll pass. When I get home and busy myself with the cooking and cleaning, it'll take my mind off it.'

'Maybe that's the trouble,' Fred said, handing her his handkerchief. 'Maybe it's all gettin' a bit too much for you.' He paused. 'You're not getting any younger, you know … and it's your fourth one. You're running around after three kids all day and running a business at the same time.'

Bridget buried her damp face in the big hanky. It's not my fourth baby, she thought. It's my fifth.

Chapter 23

A s soon as they got back home, Fred rang June's neighbour and
asked if he could have a quick word with June. She couldn't
afford a phone herself, but she often babysat for the family;
in return, they let her use the phone and took messages for her.

Fred waited for a few minutes until the neighbour's child ran to
June's house and brought her back to speak on the phone. 'I know
it's your day off,' he said apologetically, 'but I'd be very grateful if you
could come in for the rest of the day. I'll pay you over and above the
usual. I don't feel that Bridget's up to doing too much today.'

'I'll come in, no problem,' June said. 'I hadn't much on today in
any case. But I don't want owt extra for it. Bridget's always good to
me, so I'm more than happy to help out.' She'd paused. 'D'you mind
me askin' what exactly is the matter with her? I hope there's nothing
wrong about the baby, like.'

'No, no. It's nothing like that. She's not been herself recently,' Fred
explained in a low voice, so as not to be heard. 'She's been a bit down
these last few weeks and isn't sleeping too well. I think she might
need a bit of a break.'

'Well, you know I'll help out any way I can.'

June could always be relied upon. When she had first started helping out at the boarding-house a few years ago, Bridget had her doubts
about her tall, thin, peroxide-blonde appearance. But underneath
her cheap-looking exterior, June was a warm-hearted, hard-working
woman, who had brought up four children on her own. After two
disastrous marriages and plenty of experience of men, June now gave
the opposite sex a wide berth, preferring to look after herself. But she
often entertained Bridget with outrageous stories of her past.

'Thanks, June,' Fred said. 'I'll see what I can work out.'

Then he went into the kitchen and told Bridget what he'd done.
'June will be here in the next half an hour,' he said, 'to sort the
dinner and clear up afterwards. I'm here with the kids, so you can
take yourself upstairs to bed for the afternoon and get a good rest.'

Bridget's brow creased in annoyance. 'But I'm grand now,' she
protested. 'You shouldn't have bothered June. I can manage just fine

on my own. It's not as if we have a houseful in at the minute. There's only a couple of men, and Michael's gone, too ...' Her face suddenly paled as the awful memory of Baloo and what he'd said about Lucy came flooding back.

Fred pointed towards the ceiling. 'Upstairs,' he repeated, in an unusually firm tone. 'You need a good rest. And it's not just yourself you should be thinking of. There are two of you now.'

Half an hour later Fred and June were sitting in the kitchen, heads bent over a large calendar that usually hung on the back of the door. Fred's brow was furrowed as he studied the dates that were already marked, while June puffed away on her cigarette and nibbled at the edge of a ragged thumbnail.

Bridget was meticulous in writing things on the calendar: the children's school holidays and dentist appointments; her own ante-natal appointments; the days that Angela was on a late shift and free to help out in the boarding-house; the dates that Tara and Angela were away.

'I'm trying to find a good weekend to take Bridget away for a few days,' Fred said, a look of deep concentration on his face. 'But it looks as though it's going to have to be the end of the month, or early *next* month before it can happen.' He gave a sigh. 'That's the thing with working in hotels; weekends are always the busiest time. And then we have to take this place into account. There's got to be somebody here at least for breakfast and the evening meal, even if there's only a couple of the lads in.'

'Between me and Angela,' June told him, running her finger over the calendar, 'we'll sort everything out here.' She took a deep drag on her Benson & Hedges cigarette. 'You've got absolutely nowt to worry about here.'

Fred nodded. 'It would be beltin' if we could get away for a break. Me mam will have the kids for the weekend, so you won't have to worry about them.'

June's brow creased in thought. 'Then we only need to be in for breakfast, leave sandwiches for lunch and then be back in again around five o'clock to get the dinner ready.' Her face relaxed. 'It'll be a bleedin' dawdle – in fact, I can manage it easily on my own. As you say, there's usually only a couple of the lads around at the weekend.'

'I'll have a word with Tara about the best time to take off,' Fred said, 'and then I'll make enquiries about a bed and breakfast.'

June's face suddenly brightened up. 'I've got a mate who was goin' on about a place she stayed at in Blackpool last summer,' she remembered. 'Well, not exactly a mate as such, a nice woman I did a bit of ironin' for. A little bit uppity but nice in her own way. It sounds like the type of place you and Bridget would like.' She bit at the annoying nail again. 'I'm sure she said it was right opposite the pier and just up from the Pleasure Beach. I'll find out about it for you.'

'That would be great, love,' Fred said. 'It would save me the trouble of having to go into town.' Fred hated having to go into busy travel agencies or look things up in the paper, as people always tried to rush these things, and he found it hard to take in too much new information in a short time since his accident. He winked at June now. 'I've a feeling a little break away will do Bridget a power of good. She'll come back a new woman.'

Chapter 24

TULLAMORE

On Saturday afternoon Aiden Byrne picked up Angela at the top of the town. This time they stayed within County Offaly, travelling out to the old monastic site at Clonmacnoise. Given that it was the Easter weekend and a reasonably fine day, it was busy with visitors ambling around the old stone crosses and ruined churches, and having picnics amongst the numerous small hills.

They spent a while walking around in the weak sunshine, ostensibly looking at the ancient ruins, then came to stand by an old stone wall, looking out over the Shannon river.

'When do you go back to Stockport, Angela?' Aiden asked quietly.

'At the end of next week,' she replied, keeping her gaze firmly fixed on the shimmering water in front of her.

'I'm going to miss you very much,' he told her. 'I feel everything has suddenly changed since we've met.'

'How?' she asked, trying to sound casual.

'I keep thinking about you all the time,' he said. 'I can't concentrate on the smallest of things … I feel I'm just living from hour to hour, waiting to see you.' He put his arm around her shoulders and drew her towards him. 'Maybe I shouldn't be saying this to you so soon, but I'm anxious to know how you feel.'

'I feel exactly the same as you,' she confessed. 'And I really wish I didn't have to go away so soon.'

There was a silence as they stood, still leaning on the ancient wall, heads bent together.

'I know there's no point in asking you to stay longer, because you already have your plans made,' he told her. 'So I suppose I can only ask when do you think you'll be home again?'

'Summer,' she replied, her voice flat and resigned. 'I usually have a few weeks at home then.'

'How would you feel if I came over to see you in England for a few days in May?' he suggested, touching the side of her face gently. 'Do you think that might be a good idea? Give us a chance to spend a bit more time together?'

'That would be lovely,' she told him, turning her head to look at him, and when their eyes met he pulled her even closer to him and kissed her on the lips.

A ripple of delight ran through Angela, and she could feel from the way he was holding her, and from the hard intensity of his kiss, that Aiden Byrne felt exactly the same.

Droplets of rain started to fall and people began to scatter in search of shelter, or to head back to cars and coaches.

'Shall we go back to the car?' Aiden suggested, looking up at the grey clouds sweeping the sky. He pointed to one of the ruined buildings that stood on a small hill, with an arched doorway that was several feet thick. 'Or we could try one of the old churches over there that has a roof. It would shelter us until the rain stops.'

Angela took his hand and they started to run towards the building, laughing as they slipped up the incline towards it. When they reached the shelter of the doorway, they came to a halt, brushing the raindrops off their coats. Aiden then took a few steps inside to check the interior of the old ruin, much of which was open to the sky. When he saw that it was completely empty, he reached forward and grasped Angela's hand, then quickly drew her into the small building and into his arms.

130

'You are so, so beautiful,' he said, crushing his mouth down on hers. Then he carefully guided her backwards so that she was resting against the church wall. Cupping her face in his two hands, he kissed her. His hands moved to reach behind her neck and down over her shoulders, then he leaned towards her again, his hard body moulded tightly against hers, and kissed her for what seemed to be an eternity.

As she clung to him, Angela felt herself almost overcome with the sensations that were racing through her, making her body move in time with his. Then he adjusted his stance slightly and pressed his very obvious male hardness against her. Angela suddenly froze. Her mind was suddenly full of the conversation she'd had with Carmel Malone and Rose Fox the other night. The conversation about the girl from school who had had to get married very quickly. She could almost hear Rose's scathing words in her ears about girls who were easy, who were a disgrace to their families because they'd let fellas have their way with them before they were married.

'Are you OK?' Aiden checked, moving back a little.

'I'm grand,' Angela lied. 'I just thought I heard someone ...'

He pulled away now, looking to check they were still alone. 'There's nobody around,' he told her, his voice husky from wanting her.

Angela straightened up now, checking her hair and smoothing down her coat. 'Maybe we should go back to the car,' she said in a low voice. Then, before he could say anything, voices echoed outside the old church and several sets of footsteps could be heard coming towards the entrance.

Aiden took Angela's hand and they headed out in the opposite direction through a gap in the wall. When they got outside into the open air they could see the rain had eased.

'That was lovely back there,' he told her, a slightly embarrassed grin on his face. 'Although I felt a bit like a teenager, as though we were getting up to something we shouldn't have.'

Angela looked at him, then she started to giggle. 'I'm glad you felt that,' she said, 'because I did, too. I thought somebody was going to come in and tell us off for our terrible behaviour in such a holy place.'

He shook his head and made a funny little noise that was neither a laugh nor a sigh, but somewhere in between. 'I never imagined that if I started courting again it would be like this. It almost feels as if we're doing something wrong.' He shrugged. 'How can that be? I'm sure I shouldn't feel this at my age – or yours, for that matter.'

'Perhaps it's because we're in a public place,' Angela said as they came down a little hill towards the parking area. 'I suppose anybody would feel like that.'

'Of course,' he said. 'We should really have some privacy, but that's not an easy one, either.'

Again Angela felt a pang of alarm. Did Aiden Byrne really think that she was the type of girl who only needed somewhere private to let him do anything he wanted? Surely he didn't think she was that easy?

Even though she felt Aiden was very different from any other boyfriend she'd had, she had survived until now with her virginity still intact – and she intended to keep it that way. Angela had decided that she'd save it until she got married.

They reached the car and Aiden opened the passenger door for her, then he went around to his own side. He took off his damp coat, folded it and threw it in the back seat, waiting while Angela took hers off then did the same for her.

'Angela,' he said, turning towards her now, 'how would you feel about coming back to my house with me?'

'Now?' she asked, her voice high with surprise. 'Do you mean we should drive there now?'

'Why not?' He leaned across and took her hand in his, gently stroking it. 'There's nobody there. Clare is at my mother's for the day. In fact, she's actually staying the night there. She often stays on Saturday nights and I said I'd be up there in the morning to go to Mass with them. No one will disturb us.'

Angela bit her lip. 'I don't think so,' she said quietly.

'But why?' he asked, lifting her hand to his lips. 'It would be lovely to have a bit of time on our own, especially when we know how little time we have left together.'

Angela looked straight at him. 'I don't think it would look right,' she said, a tightness evident in her voice. 'We hardly know each other ... and I wouldn't want you to go getting the wrong idea about me.'

'My God,' he said, letting out a low, embarrassed sort of moan. 'You didn't think I expected you to ...' He put his hands over his face. 'If I've given you the impression that I expected us to jump into bed straight away, or anything like that, I'm really sorry, Angela. I wouldn't expect that of any girl, let alone someone like you.'

It was Angela's turn to be embarrassed now. 'And I didn't mean that to sound the way you've taken it,' she said quickly. 'It was just in case I gave you the wrong impression.' She joined her hands chastely in her lap. 'I had a bad experience with a lad a few years ago ...' Her eyes darted to meet his for a few moments, then she stared straight ahead again. 'Nothing very serious, thank God, but enough to give me a bit of a fright ... and I'm afraid of anything like that happening again.'

'Angela,' Aiden said now, stroking her long blonde hair, 'I've always behaved like a gentleman where women are concerned, and I promise you that I'll never, ever harm you.' He paused, his eyes dark with concern. 'You do believe that, don't you?'

Chapter 25

The ringing of the phone shattered the early-morning silence in Ballygrace House on Easter Monday.

Tara woke with a start, then, realising what the sound was, she quickly got out of bed, grabbed her dressing-gown and ran downstairs barefoot. She glanced at her watch as she quickly padded along the hallway. It was only eight o'clock. Was it Joe? she wondered. When she spoke to her brother last night, he'd said that he would be up early and setting off from Cork after breakfast.

'Hello, Tara,' her Aunt Kitty said. 'I know it's very early, but I thought you would want to know the news that Mick heard down the town last night.'

Tara's heart started to beat quickly. She had no idea what Kitty could have to tell her at this time of the morning. Her mind started to race. 'Go on,' she said.

'The young girl who was found up the bog,' Kitty said, 'is the other little orphan who lived with Bridget Hart. Mick said her name was Nora. I didn't know the girl myself, or the woman who looked after them, Lizzie Lawless, wasn't it?'

Tara felt the hairs prickling up on the back of her neck. 'Oh, dear God ...' How would Bridget react to her dark past suddenly rushing into her life again?

'Now, it's only hearsay at the minute,' Kitty went on. 'But I'd say there's more than a grain of truth in it, for the news came from the Ballygrace Guards, and if anybody is going to know anything about it, it will be them.'

'What makes them think that it's Nora?' Tara asked in a hushed tone. 'Was there anything to identify her?'

'I don't know any more details,' Kitty said. 'But no doubt they'll come out in the fullness of time.' There was a moment's pause. 'Mick was anxious I let you know what's happened. He said you'd probably remember the girl from when she was young.'

Tara nodded. 'I knew her all right, but not that well,' she said. 'She was a couple of years older than Bridget, but I used to see her at Mass and at school. I only spoke to her a few times.' She searched her memory. 'I think she used to help the priest's housekeeper after she left school.' Tara suddenly shivered and drew the collar of her dressing-gown tighter around her neck. The hall was always the coldest spot in the house at this time of the morning.

'Do you have any idea what happened to her after she left Lizzie Lawless's house?' Kitty asked. 'Mick can't remember much about her.'

'I really don't know.' Tara said. She frowned, remembering 'I have an awful feeling she ran away, just disappeared ...'

There was a silence on the line now.

'Do you think Bridget will know anything about what happened to her?' Kitty asked eventually.

'I honestly couldn't tell you,' Tara said. 'It seems so long ago. Bridget never says much about those days. Both girls had a very hard life with Lizzie Lawless, and I think she hates to be reminded about it all.'

'How do you think she'll take the news?' Kitty asked.

'Not too well at all,' Tara said. Her friend was often fragile, but this pregnancy seemed to be making her worse. 'The whole thing is very strange.'

'Oh, dear God,' Kitty whispered. 'You have to ask how a young girl could end up buried in the middle of a bog unless something terrible had happened to her.'

When she'd finished on the phone, Tara went quickly down the hallway and into the comforting warmth of the kitchen to put the electric kettle on. She needed a cup of hot tea or coffee, as she couldn't seem to stop shivering, and while she knew that the cold morning was enough reason, receiving such shocking news had contributed to it as well.

The kettle filled and switched on, Tara went over to the range and opened the top of it, giving the mound of orange and grey cinders a good rake to bring it back to life. Then she threw in some small sods of dry, brittle turf to start it off for the day. As she heard the electric kettle rumbling into life, Tara was grateful that they no longer had to wait for the range to liven up sufficiently to boil and cook things on. When she looked at all the modern conveniences that she now had in Ballygrace House and in Stockport, Tara often thought back to the early days in her grandfather's cottage, when they didn't even have the range and had to cook and bake things on an open fire. When she thought of all the things like fridges and televisions which William, and Bridget's children, took for granted, she wondered how on earth she had managed in the small, basic cottage where everyday living was such hard work.

Ella Keating would be due shortly to get breakfast for her and William, set the fires in the front rooms, and generally tidy up. Joe would arrive early afternoon, and Ella would leave a lunch of sliced cold meat and salad ready for them. For the evening, Tara had booked a table in a restaurant in Tullamore for herself, William and Joe. She hadn't asked her father and Tessie to join them at the restaurant, because they had told her time and time again they didn't like eating their main meal in the evenings, and thought restaurants were nothing but a pure waste of money. On the occasions that Tara had insisted they come out, she had ended up not enjoying the meal herself as they were so uncomfortable about the whole thing.

Tessie had asked the rest of the family to come out for a cup of tea and a light supper later on, saying it would give Joe a chance to catch up with Angela and some of the others, and William something different to look forward to.

Tara made a full pot of tea and left it on top of the warming range to brew while she went to get the jug of milk from the fridge. She was debating with herself whether she would take the tea back up to bed or stay downstairs in the kitchen. Even though she had been wakened out of a deep sleep, she knew she wouldn't be able to sleep again now. Her mind was too full of the disturbing news that Kitty had just told her, news that would bring turmoil and upset to her dear friend.

Chapter 26

As soon as he heard the car tyres on the gravel path, William came rushing out of the sitting-room. 'Tara!' he called in his strange, half-adult voice as he headed towards the front door. 'It's Joe – he's here!'

'Good God!' Joe said, when he saw Tara's brother-in-law coming down the steps. 'Where did you shoot up from? Look at the height of you – you're as tall as myself now! Where did the little fella go?'

William laughed, blushing. He came towards the young priest with his hand outstretched. 'Good to see you again.'

Joe shook his hand. 'And you, young Mr Fitzgerald.' The priest went to the back of the car now and lifted his small weekend case out of the boot. He set it down on the ground, then turned back to the car and lifted out a large brown parcel, which he handed to William. 'An Easter present for you,' he said, smiling.

'Oh, that's very kind of you.' William said, his eyes lighting up with delight.

'My pleasure,' Joe said. He winked at the boy. 'We'll find somewhere to set it up later.'

Tara came forward now and put her arms around her brother. 'I've missed you very much,' she told him, 'and I'm so delighted that you could make it up while we're here.'

'Not half as delighted as I am,' the young priest grinned. He went back into the boot and came out with a colourful bouquet of flowers. 'To the main woman in my life,' he said, handing them to her.

'Oh, Joe,' Tara said, her voice full of emotion, 'they are absolutely beautiful.' And as she inhaled the scent of the flowers, it suddenly dawned on her that her brother was the main man in her life since Gabriel had gone. He was the only man she could talk to as an equal about anything, without having to monitor each word. Father Joe

Flynn was a patient, kind and intelligent man. She was immensely proud to have him as a brother.

William stood politely, waiting until Joe had finished lifting things out of the car, then all three walked up the stairs and into the house, William trying not to look as though he was desperate to open the parcel he was clutching to his chest.

Joe went straight upstairs and put his stuff in one of the spare bedrooms, while William helped Tara to bring the lunch dishes through from the kitchen and into the dining-room.

'You needn't have gone to all this trouble,' Joe said, when he came in to join them. 'The kitchen table would have been just grand.'

'Indeed it would not,' Tara said light-heartedly. 'It's a bad day when your sister can't make an effort to entertain you properly.' She glanced up at him, a little glint in her eye. 'Especially when you have all the women in the parish inviting you into their dining-rooms on a regular basis.'

'Now, Tara,' Joe said, shaking his dark curly head and laughing, 'I've come up to Offaly to get a bit of a break from those kind of women. Don't be reminding me about it.'

'I'm only codding you,' Tara said. She gestured towards the sliced ham and beef, the potato salad, and the dish of tomatoes, lettuce and hard-boiled eggs. 'Help yourself now. You must be starving after that long drive.'

Joe glanced over at William. The parcel was on the table, still unopened. 'Go on,' he said, indicating it. 'You must be dying to see what's inside.'

William's eyes lit up. 'Great,' he said, immediately starting to untie the brown string around the package.

Tara handed her brother a bottle of chilled white wine and a corkscrew. Then, almost without thinking, she said, 'This was one of Gabriel's little jobs ... it's nice to have another man here to do it for a change.' She looked across the table at William. 'I still miss him every single day for even the little things.'

William kept on working away at the string. 'Maybe you might meet another nice man some day soon, Tara,' he said in a low voice. 'I'm sure there are lots of men who would like you for their wife.'

Tara felt her throat suddenly tighten. Say nothing, she told herself. William was, in lots of ways, young for his age, and youngsters were apt to blurt out the odd tactless remark. She didn't want to over-react after the incident in St Stephen's Green. 'Do you think so?' she said, trying to sound as though his comment hadn't struck a vulnerable chord.

Joe shot a concerned glance at his sister. He deftly removed the cork from the bottle and put it down on the table, then he reached across to give Tara's hand a reassuring squeeze.

'A dartboard!' William exclaimed. 'Absolutely brilliant. I've always wanted to learn how to play darts.'

'I'll teach you,' Joe said. 'I've become quite an accomplished player since we set up the boys' guild in the parish.' He rolled his eyes to the ceiling. 'Darts, as well as card games and pool, for my sins.'

'Where can we set it up, Tara?' William asked eagerly. He was delighted that Joe had arrived as it would liven things up in Ballygrace House, although even if Joe hadn't come, he still liked to be in the quiet big house in Ireland where at least things were predictable. But with Joe here – who knew exactly the sort of things that boys of his age enjoyed – it just made things much, much better.

Tara looked at him with bemusement. 'I wouldn't have a clue,' she said, holding up her hands. 'I think we'll have to leave that to the expert. All I would ask is that I'm out of the line of fire.'

'You're OK, Tara,' Joe laughed. 'I'd already thought it all out. We'll put it up in the old stable. My father and Mick cleared it out last summer, so it would be ideal to hang the board up there, where it wouldn't be in anybody's way.'

'Fine by me,' Tara said. 'We never use the stables.'

'That's a brilliant idea, Joe,' William said, clearly thrilled with the gift and the whole idea. 'I'll be able to practise out there without disturbing anybody or stabbing them to death with a dart!'

Tara looked at her young brother-in-law. 'If you want, you can leave it here, then you'll always have it any time you're over.'

William's face fell a fraction. 'I might . . .' he said, hesitating. 'But I might just bring it back to Stockport to show Fred and Michael.'

Tara had to put her hand up to her mouth to hide her amusement. 'Well, that's grand, too,' she said. 'It's your dartboard and you can decide what you want to do with it.'

Later that afternoon, when William was out in the stable practising darts, Tara and her brother sat chatting over a glass of wine in the drawing-room in front of the fire.

'William has fairly stretched,' Joe commented, taking a mouthful of the chilled wine. 'He's really grown up since the last time I saw him.'

Tara's face darkened. 'Joe,' she said, getting up to close the drawing-room door properly. She came back to sit in the armchair opposite him. 'I need to talk to you about William ... I feel you're the only person I can really tell. You have an understanding about people – especially younger ones – being a priest.'

'What's wrong?' he said, leaning forward, the wine glass held between his cupped hands. 'Has something happened?'

'Nothing major,' she told him. 'But we had a conversation, which I found rather uncomfortable ... and even a little worrying.'

'Go on,' Joe said quietly. 'I'm listening.'

And then Tara told him about William's declaration of love for her and his wish that had he been older he would have asked her to marry him.

'Oh, dear,' Joe said, raising his eyebrows and giving a wry little smile. 'Sounds like typical teenage angst to me.'

'Do you think so?' Tara frowned. 'You don't think it's anything to worry about?'

'Not really,' Joe said, his voice reassuring. 'I hear worse when I'm asked to come in and help with families.' A little sigh escaped from his lips. 'An awful lot worse.'

For a fleeting moment Tara felt an urge to pour out all the terrible stuff about Gabriel and William's father. About the fact that he'd raped her when she was only eighteen years old, when she was drunk and incapable of refusing him.

She'd told no one about that apart from Bridget.

But, she wondered, what good would it do pouring all that out to Joe now? William Fitzgerald senior was dead and gone, and digging up all those dark memories now would do no one any good. In her own way, Tara had come to terms with it soon after it was over, feeling that he'd punished himself afterwards for reading a situation so wrongly. In any case, there was nothing that could be done about it now.

Even as a young girl, Tara knew that she could either hang on to the dreadful episode and allow it to ruin her life, or let it go. And while she'd never forgotten it, by putting it to the side, she'd been able to move on with her life and do all the things she'd planned. She had made a fresh start for herself in Stockport, become successful in her property deals and in her career. And when she had established herself, she had been reunited with and eventually married to her teenage sweetheart Gabriel, without his ever knowing how obsessed his father had been with Tara.

'To be honest,' Tara said now, 'I think he only sees me as an older sister, or even a mother figure. I don't think he's worldly-wise enough to realise exactly what he was saying.'

'I think you're right,' Joe agreed. 'He absolutely worships you, Tara, and you heard what he said earlier about you meeting a new man and maybe getting married again in the future.' He took another sip from his glass. 'How do you feel about that?' he asked.

'How do you think I feel?' Tara said, her voice a low whisper. 'As if I'd even consider such a thing … How could I even *think* of replacing Gabriel? I know he's still only a young boy, but you would think he'd be a bit more sensitive. It's his own brother we're talking about …'

There was a silence.

Joe reached for Tara's hand. 'It's not a question of replacing him, Tara. No one thinks you should do that. But I do think William is right, and sometimes it takes the young and insensitive to say what everyone else is thinking. Surely you don't intend to live on your own for ever?'

'What do you mean?' Tara said, her brow wrinkling. 'Lots of people live on their own for different reasons.' She pointed her glass in her brother's direction. '*You* live on your own.'

'Ah, Tara,' Joe said, shaking his dark, curly head and smiling, 'c'mon now. We're talking very different situations here.'

'No, really,' Tara said. 'I have my work to fill the gap in my life that Gabriel left, and you fill your life with the Church.'

Joe took a drink from his glass and shrugged. 'I have to admit that, as time has gone on, I'm more and more satisfied with the life I've chosen. I've grown into it and I feel very fulfilled.' He raised his eyebrows. 'I have a different life from most people, but God fills any little gaps within me.'

'That's a wonderful thing to be able to say,' Tara told him, feeling glad for her brother; she had often worried about the loneliness of his life. 'A lot of married people don't feel that.'

'I'm not saying it's for everyone,' Joe went on, 'and occasionally, there are times when I wish I was married and had a family around me, but I've come to realise that the parishioners are my family in a way. It's lucky I feel like that, because, really, I don't have much option.' He smiled. 'You, on the other hand, have plenty of options.'

'Well, maybe I don't want options,' Tara said, a touch petulantly.

'I think it's what Gabriel would have wanted,' Joe told her, quite bluntly. 'And I think you've spent long enough on your own.'

To change the subject, Tara asked her brother's advice about William's planned career in hotel management.

Joe shrugged again. 'It's as good as a job as any, better than most, and William is a very gregarious boy who loves mixing with others. He would be very suited to that type of work. He enjoys being amongst people from different backgrounds, and he treats them all with the same respect.'

Tara had smiled. 'You make it sound a bit like your own vocation.'

'Well, the best advice you can give anyone about work is simply to do the job you love. It means you get paid for something you would do for free.' He raised his eyebrows. 'Like the way William comes up to Stockport to help you in the hotel. I saw him when I was over last year, helping Fred pick up the glasses and stock up behind the bar. He was positively animated. What more can you ask for?'

Tara pulled a face. 'I'm afraid Elisha and Harry are going to feel that the money they spent on an exclusive education will have been wasted. Hotel management is not exactly the sort of top-drawer career they will have expected William to go into.'

'He may change his mind by the time he finishes school,' Joe mused. 'But if he doesn't, then I'm sure they'll come around to it. Don't you think Mrs Fitzgerald would be delighted for Gabriel and his sister to be working in a hotel if she could have them back?'

Tara bit her lip and nodded.

Joe was so very wise in many ways.

Over the next few days Tara and Joe visited all their relatives, including Auntie Molly. They had gone to the nursing home in Mullingar laden with flowers, fruit and chocolates. Molly had been asleep when they went in, her small, shrivelled body looking like more like a young child under the blankets than an adult.

One of the nurses came and gently woke her, but she was

disorientated and only interested in asking where her breakfast was, even thought it was three o'clock in the afternoon.

'She doesn't know me at all this time,' Joe had whispered, his face solemn and resigned.

As a child, Tara had lived with her grandfather, but Molly and her sister, Maggie, had raised Joe, after their mother died. The two old spinsters had taken great joy in his years at the seminary, and their cup had been full and running over when he was ordained.

'It's very hard when they don't know you,' Joe sighed. 'I suppose I should have been prepared for it; I have it every other day when I visit the elderly parishioners at home or in hospital. But it's very different when it's your own relatives.'

'She's very well looked after,' Tara said, patting his arm. 'And you've always done your best for her.'

Joe just nodded, but the sadness was evident in his eyes.

When Joe went back to Cork, Tara missed his solid, reassuring company very much. While she got on well with Kitty and Mick, and her father's family, she found her brother's presence more invigorating and challenging. She felt they were both on the same level, while everyone else, including William, looked to Tara to take the lead.

She and William filled the remainder of their holiday around the house, going to Tullamore, and once to a classical music concert in Athlone. Then, suddenly, it was time to go back to Stockport, and Tara found herself reluctant to leave Ballygrace House.

She had a silly feeling about it that she'd never had before, a sensation of loneliness. Even though she knew it was ridiculous, she felt as though the house knew it was about to be left empty yet again. It made Tara feel guilty.

Any time that William was outside in the stables practising his darts, or when he had gone out for a cycle or was helping Shay, Tara had found herself wandering around the house, standing at the thresholds of rooms or staring out of the windows.

She had become very conscious of the fact that the house had only been used for a few short visits every year since Gabriel's death. She was also aware that she was relying on other people, like her father and Ella Keating, to maintain both the interior and exterior of the building. And for what exactly? she found herself wondering.

Was she planning to return there at some point? And if she did, what sort of life was she going to have? Would she be returning to the lonely life she had when she was newly widowed a few years ago? She had no answers to any of the questions, but she knew it was something she would have to address in the not-too-distant future.

Chapter 27

Angela's week at home slipped by very quickly, seeing her friends and family one day and Aiden Byrne the next. Soon, there were precious few days left before she, Tara and William took the overnight boat back to England on the Friday.

'How about a trip to Galway on Thursday?' Aiden had suggested. 'Since it's your last full day, I'm taking the day off so that we can spend it together.'

'Won't it take an awful long time to drive there?' Angela had asked. 'We usually go on the train.'

'We'll set off early,' he told her. 'I've already said that I've got a business meeting down that end of the country and I won't be back until late.' He stopped. 'It's not a problem for you, is it?'

Angela shrugged. 'No, not really. I've already said to my mother that I would probably be seeing you.'

His eyes suddenly narrowed. 'Have you told people about us?'

'Just my mother,' she replied. 'But I haven't gone into any real detail.'

He nodded. 'Have you said anything to Carmel or any of your other friends?'

She shook her head. 'I didn't think there was any point in making a big issue of it, when we only had the week together.'

'Is that how you see it?' he said quietly. 'Just the week?'

'It's how things are,' she replied. 'I've got to go back to England.'

'Don't you think we'll be able to keep in touch by writing and phoning every few days, until we see each other again?'

Angela's face lit up. He had obviously given their romance some thought, which meant that he was taking it seriously. As seriously as Angela hoped and prayed he would, although she had been very careful not to let him know that. She didn't want to appear too desperate or enthusiastic. 'When you put it like that,' she said, 'I suppose the distance between us doesn't sound quite so bad.'

They continued their discussion about keeping in touch on their way to Galway on Thursday.

'Do you think it would be OK to phone you at work?' Aiden checked. 'Are you allowed private phone calls?'

She thought for a moment. She would have to tell Tara who was phoning her from Ireland, whether it was at the hotel or at the house, but eventually she would have to tell Tara all about Aiden anyway. 'I'm sure it would be fine,' she said.

'I can make the calls to you from my office, so it wouldn't cost you or the hotel anything.' He looked at her and grinned. 'I know only too well what it's like running a business and having staff making sly calls, so I don't want to get you into any trouble.'

'I get into enough trouble as it is,' Angela said.

'Do you?' he said, sounding most surprised. 'I can't imagine it. Since I've met you you've been nothing but the perfect young lady.'

Angela looked at him and saw a little glint in his eye. 'I do try,' she said, laughing. 'Although I don't always get it right.'

They parked in Eyre Square in the centre of Galway, and then, since it was mild, they took a stroll around the city, Angela's arm tucked through Aiden's. And as they walked along, she occasionally caught sight of their reflection in the big shop windows and was surprised to see how well-suited they looked as a couple. She wondered then how she had ever been attracted to boys her own age. Aiden Byrne was ten times more interesting than anyone she'd ever gone out with, and she didn't feel any difference whatsoever in their ages.

When they stopped for lunch in the Great Southern Hotel in the centre of the city, Aiden ordered a special bottle of Italian red wine to mark their last day together and, as they clinked their glasses together, he looked deep into her eyes. 'I'm going to miss our days out,' he told her, his face serious and his voice slightly choked. 'I feel I've rediscovered a part of me that I thought had gone for ever ... I feel like a real person again.'

Angela took a mouthful of the wine, which she found quite different from the white wine she'd had, before. 'Has it been very hard bringing up Clare on your own?'

He nodded. 'It's unbelievable. It's something you can't conceive of happening. You can't prepare for it,' he said, his gaze shifting to the window behind her. 'I don't mean to cut you off, Angela, but I find discussing the past a very depressing subject. It's natural you should be curious, but it's something we can talk about next time we meet up, if you don't mind.' He looked back at her now. 'I'd much rather we had this last day together without anything spoiling it.'

'Of course,' Angela said quickly, suddenly feeling that she had ventured somewhere forbidden. She took another gulp of her wine, then felt a huge wave of relief when she saw the waiter coming with their steaks and dishes of sautéed potatoes and vegetables.

Over lunch the conversation quickly returned to normal and afterwards they walked down to the cathedral on the outskirts of the city. Angela felt much more relaxed after two glasses of the warming red wine. They went into the dark, cool building and sat in one of the empty pews at the back, looking around at the statues, organ and stained-glass windows, and whispering to each other.

'I'd like to light a few candles before we go,' Angela said in a low voice, lifting her handbag.

Aiden stood up. 'I'll come with you,' he said, checking in his pockets for change to put in the box beside the candle-stand.

They walked to the front of the cathedral together and then over to a small alcove on the right, where a large, lifelike crucifix hung over the wrought-iron candle-holders. Angela put her coins in the box at the side and picked up three small white candles. She placed them in empty holders and then, picking up one of the candles that was already lit, she touched the flame from it to each one in turn to light all three.

Then, while Aiden lit his candles, Angela went over to a nearby pew and knelt down. She blessed herself, then closed her eyes and wondered what three things she should pray for. She started by asking that her father would be returned to the whole of his health again, then moved swiftly on to pray that everything worked out for her and Aiden. Her third candle was reserved for Tara – that she wouldn't be too cross if and when she found out that Angela was seeing an older man with a child.

They walked out of the cathedral into the watery afternoon sunshine.

'Angela,' Aiden said, putting his arm around her shoulders, 'if you have no objections, I'd really like to buy you a little gift to take back to England with you. Something to remember me by until we meet again.'

Angela's heart leapt at his suggestion. If she'd had any lingering doubts about his feelings, they were now dispelled. 'Sure, there's no need to do anything like that,' she said, making a token effort to dissuade him.

He pulled her gently to a halt, then cupped her face in his hands. 'I really, *really* want to buy you something. It would make me happy to know you'd gone back with something to remind you of the lovely days we've spent together, so please don't argue with me.'

Angela felt a surge of emotion so strong that tears rushed into her eyes. 'You're so nice, Aiden,' she said, in a stumbling fashion. 'I still can't believe you'd be interested in somebody ordinary like me.'

He swung his arm around her again, hugging her close to him. 'Angela, darling, the last thing you are is *ordinary*.' He gave a little laugh. 'You are stunningly beautiful and very, very good company. You make me feel as though I've known you for years.'

'Well, that's lovely to hear,' she said, warmed by the generous compliment, but still needing more reassurance. 'You don't think I'm too young or immature for you?'

'Do *you* think you are?' he said, amusement dancing in his eyes.

Angela shook her head, sending her long blonde hair tumbling over her shoulders.

As they neared the more crowded shopping area, Aiden stopped to give her a light kiss on the lips, then he moved his arm from her shoulder, slid Angela's arm through his, and they walked on in a more dignified fashion.

After a while they came to a stop outside a jeweller's shop. 'Would you like a necklace or maybe a locket?' Aiden suggested.

Angela's eyes scanned the window display. She was initially drawn to the pads full of glittering rings – engagement rings – but she quickly chided herself and made herself look at the other things on display.

'What do you think of that?' Aiden asked, pointing to a single display card which held a rectangular-shaped locket, with a small garnet set in each corner and a bigger one in the middle.

Angela's eyes widened. 'It's beautiful,' she whispered, 'but it'll probably cost an absolute fortune.'

'Let's go in and see what it looks like on,' he said, taking her hand and gently guiding her into the shop.

A few minutes later Angela was looking at herself in the shop mirror, the gold locket nestled comfortably just below the hollow of her neck. 'It is really lovely,' she said.

'We'll have it,' Aiden told the shop assistant.

'But you haven't even asked the price,' Angela protested as the woman went to get a box.

'That's not a problem,' he told her, giving her a beaming smile, 'and not your concern.' He touched his fingers along the side of her cheek. 'It looks even nicer on you than I imagined.' Then, as he saw her making to take it off, he reached around the back of her neck and lifted her hair up to open the catch for her. He paused for a few seconds and then he bent down and planted a tender kiss on the nape of her neck, which made Angela close her eyes with delight.

The shop door opened, making the bell ring, and Aiden and Angela both turned towards it as a middle-aged couple came in, the door swinging closed behind them.

'Aiden ...' The woman stopped in her tracks, her eyes wide with shock. 'It *is* you ...' Her gaze moved to Angela now and her whole body stiffened.

Aiden put the locket down on the glass counter, his face dark and serious.

'Josephine,' he said, nodding at her, 'and Patrick. I'm surprised to see you down this part of the country. How are you both?'

The man put his hand on his wife's shoulder now, looked very awkward and embarrassed. 'We were looking in the shop window and Josephine thought she saw you. We didn't realize ... We're down visiting Margaret for a few days ... with her having the new baby.'

The woman's face was now tight and pale. 'You're the last person we expected to run into down here.' She looked directly at Angela, a cold, studying stare. 'And we certainly didn't know that you had a new lady friend.'

Chapter 28

Aiden turned to Angela. 'I'd like to introduce you to Angela Flynn,' he said in a tone that was fairly steady, considering the situation was so obviously awkward. 'Angela, this is Patrick and Josephine O'Shea, my father- and mother-in-law.'

'I'm pleased to meet you,' Angela said, her voice just above a whisper. She automatically put her hand out but when neither of the couple took it, she had to withdraw it.

'Well, Aiden,' Josephine O'Shea said, her eyes narrowed, 'you might have had the decency to tell us, and not let us find out like this.' She shook her head. 'Kissing and canoodling in broad daylight in a public place ...' Her voice dropped to a low hiss. 'It's nothing but a disgrace to Elizabeth's memory.'

The shop assistant came from the small backroom into the shop, and then, sensing a personal conversation, she discreetly disappeared again.

A hot wave of guilt and acute embarrassment rushed over Angela, making her legs feel weak and her stomach a tight knot.

'We weren't doing any harm, Josephine,' Aiden said, glancing at Angela. 'I know you're upset, but there's no need to take it like this.'

'There's every need,' the woman said, 'especially when you're the father of my granddaughter.'

'I've hardly left the house for the last few years,' he told her. 'Surely you don't expect me to become a total recluse?'

She gave a sardonic little laugh. 'Oh, I hardly think there's any likelihood of that happening. You're conveniently forgetting the little episode last month in the County Arms Hotel when you made a complete show of yourself.'

Aiden raised his eyes to the ceiling, his whole body tense now. 'This is neither the time nor the place—'

'Leave it, Josephine,' Patrick O'Shea said, taking her arm to move her back towards the door. 'This is not our business.'

'Oh, yes, indeed it is,' she said, and looked at Aiden as though he were something that had just crawled from under a stone.

Aiden took a deep breath. 'Look, I am not prepared to stand here defending myself to you or anyone else. I know that I've done nothing wrong, and if I want to have a day out with a friend, it's no business of yours.' He turned now and, seeing the stricken look on Angela's face, placed a comforting hand on her back. 'If the time comes when you need to know anything about our relationship, then I'll make sure you and the family know it. Angela and I have been friends for a very short time, and I didn't feel it was right to say anything to even my own family just yet.'

'So your own mother doesn't know what you're up to?' she said, shaking her head in despair. 'But then you were always like that, Aiden. You've always played your cards very close to your chest, even when Elizabeth was alive.'

Patrick O'Shea took a firm grip on his wife's elbow and propelled her towards the door of the shop. 'You've said your piece,' he said in a manner that brooked no argument. 'We need to go now.'

When the door closed behind them, Aiden turned to the white-faced, trembling Angela. 'I am so, so sorry that happened. Are you all right?'

'I'm fine,' she said, clearly not fine at all. She looked down at the locket. 'Maybe it's best if we leave it.'

'No,' he said. 'Certainly not. We came in to buy you a present, and that's precisely what we're going to do.'

The lady came through now from the backshop, looking busy and efficient, as though she hadn't heard a single word of the heated conversation.

'Would you like the locket gift-wrapped?' she asked, looking from one to the other.

'Yes, please,' Aiden said decisively.

When they came out of the shop they walked back to the car with an awkward silence and space between them. Eventually, as they came towards Eyre Square, Aiden reached for her hand. 'Please, Angela,' he said. 'I beg you not to let this come between us.'

Angela opened her mouth to say something, but the words wouldn't come. Big tears formed at the corner of her eyes and she pulled her hand away from his grasp to scrabble in her handbag for a hanky.

'Josephine O'Shea has always been a difficult woman,' he said. 'She was like that even before Elizabeth and I got married. Elizabeth found her hard to get on with and even left home to live in Dublin.'

'You don't have to explain all this to me,' Angela croaked.

'But I want you to know and to understand.' They arrived at the car. Aiden let Angela in first, then came around the other side to slide in beside her.

'If there's anything you want to ask me,' he continued quietly. 'I'll gladly answer it.'

Angela shook her head. 'It's none of my business, Aiden,' she told him. 'And I think you have enough people interfering in your life without me adding to it.'

Later on that evening, as Aiden stopped to drop Angela off at the usual place, he turned towards her. 'Please don't let today spoil things for us, Angela.'

'It wasn't spoiled,' she said. 'It was another lovely day – just like all the others we've spent together – apart from the last bit.'

'And can we forget that?' He looked at her now, almost holding his breath.

Angela nodded and smiled. 'Yes. I think that would be the best thing to do.'

He reached in his pocket and brought out the small parcel. 'I want you to think of us and all the good times we've had,' he told her, handing it to her, 'every time you wear it.'

Angela's eyes filled up with tears again as she held on tightly to the beautifully packaged gift. 'I'm going to miss you very much,' she whispered.

'But we will keep in touch,' he told her. 'I'll be on the phone to you on Sunday to make sure you got back home safely, and I'll be in the travel agents on Monday to check out flights to Manchester for next month.'

'And I'll be counting the days until I see you,' she replied.

Chapter 29

On the drive up to Dublin on Friday evening, Angela thought of approaching the subject of Aiden Byrne with Tara, but it never seemed to be the right time. Cautious of approaching her at the best of times, she'd noticed that Tara seemed quiet and distant, and Angela was wary of getting on the wrong side of her.

As they drove along the quays towards the ferry, William leaned forward from his back seat. 'I really enjoyed that day we had at the Museum, Tara,'

'When was that?' Angela said, her mind only half on the conversation as the other half was back in Birr with Aiden. 'I didn't know you were in Dublin.'

'It was the day we saw you in St Stephen's Green ...' William suddenly stopped, realising he'd put his foot in it.

'Me?' Angela said, her face creased in confusion. 'When did you see me?'

There was an ominous silence as the car slowed down, then Tara pulled up at the traffic lights. She turned towards the passenger seat. 'We were in Dublin the Thursday after we arrived,' she said in a low voice, 'and we were actually in St Stephen's Green the same afternoon that you were there with your ... friend.'

Angela's face drained of colour. 'I didn't see you.'

'No,' Tara said, 'you didn't.'

Angela swallowed hard, her throat suddenly dry. 'I was going to tell you about Aiden ... when we were on our own. I was waiting until the time was right.'

The lights changed. Tara put the car into gear again and moved off without saying a word. She knew she had put Angela in a most uncomfortable position but she was so hurt that her half-sister had not told her about her new romance that she didn't really care. If Angela was old enough to make decisions to cut people out like that, then she was old enough to take the consequences.

'It's a difficult situation ...' Angela attempted to explain, feeling acutely conscious that William was in the back seat and probably listening to every word, 'and it happened so quickly I haven't had

151

a chance to tell anyone apart from my mother ...' She stopped. 'Honestly, Tara, I had every intention of telling you. I was just waiting for the right time.'

The silence returned, then Tara, also conscious of her young brother-in-law's presence, said, 'There are occasions when we have to make the right time. And if we don't, then we run the risk of people finding out for themselves.'

Angela's mind flew back to yesterday and the scene in the jeweller's shop in Galway. That had happened because Aiden hadn't told anyone that he was seeing her, and now she had gone and upset Tara by doing the very same thing herself.

'You're right,' she said, giving a little, shuddering sigh. 'I should have asked to speak to you on our own and not left it until you found out the way you did. I'm really sorry.'

'Forget about it,' Tara said, but there was still a distinct edge to her voice.

'Wow, it's getting really windy!' William said when they pulled up at the docks in Dublin. 'Look at the flags going mad up on the boat. We'll have an exciting trip if it keeps up.'

'Don't say that,' Tara told him, rolling her eyes. 'The last thing we need is a rough crossing.'

An hour later, as they drove onto the boat, the wind had increased, and by the time they were out into the Irish Sea it was obvious they were indeed in for a rough crossing.

'I feel a bit sick,' Angela said, her face wan.

'Maybe a cup of tea will help,' Tara suggested. 'I was just thinking that a sandwich or something might steady our stomachs.'

'I'll go,' William offered. 'It might be safer. I've just seen an elderly woman stagger and spill a drink all down herself.' He bit his lip. 'I know I shouldn't laugh, but she swore out loud and I couldn't help it. She reminded me of Shay and the way he goes on.'

'And are you suggesting that Angela and I are elderly women incapable of carrying a drink?' Tara said, pretending to be insulted.

William grinned. 'Of course I'm not,' he said. 'You certainly aren't elderly, but unfortunately you are women and therefore incapable.'

'I'd give you a good kick up the backside if I didn't feel so sick,' Angela moaned, putting a hand to her stomach, 'so give us some peace and go and get the tea.'

Tara went to give William some money, telling him to pick plain ham sandwiches that wouldn't be too hard on their stomachs.

Angela reached for her bag. 'No, Tara,' she said in an unusually decisive voice. 'We agreed that I would pay for any food on the journey.' She caught Tara's eye. 'Please. It's the least I can do after all you do for me.'

When William went off in search of the food, Angela turned to Tara. 'I'm really, really sorry for not telling you about Aiden sooner.'

'You're a grown woman, Angela, and you are entitled to your own privacy.' She gave a little shrug. 'You must live your life the way you want.'

The boat gave a lurch now and both women gripped the edge of the table to steady themselves in their chairs.

'Tara, please,' Angela said, leaning forward with her elbows on the table. 'I want to tell you, and I would really value your advice.'

'Angela,' Tara said, reaching for the table again as the boat gave another dip, 'you don't have to confide in me just because we're sisters, and anyway, I know you feel much more comfortable talking to Bridget or June or the younger girls at work.'

Angela felt her cheeks start to burn. She hadn't realised that Tara knew she confided in other people, and it made her feel terrible that it had been so obvious. She began to deny it, then realised that she might as well tell the truth, since Tara was being so straight with her. 'I think I feel a bit awkward talking to you about personal things like boyfriends, because you're my boss and also,' she felt embarrassed now, but made herself continue, 'because if you're not happy about it, you might feel you have to tell my parents.'

Tara looked down at the Formica-topped table, considering Angela's words for a few moments. 'Fair enough,' she said. 'I think I can understand that.' She then smiled at Angela. 'And I appreciate your honesty.' She just stopped herself from adding, *albeit belated*. There was no point in prolonging the awkwardness between them.

Angela looked back at her now, half-surprised by how easy it had been to get Tara to understand. 'If it's not too boring for you to listen,' she ventured now, 'I would really appreciate your opinion about my . . . my friendship with Aiden.'

Tara reached out and touched Angela's hand. 'Go on,' she said. 'I'm all ears.'

Angela had just got to the part in the story when Aiden Byrne's in-laws had walked into the jeweller's shop when William came back carrying a tray full of sandwiches and drinks.

'I've just got to go back for the milk and sugar,' he said, putting the tray down on the empty table next to them. 'And while I'm gone again,' he said, looking from one to the other, 'I'd like you to note that there hasn't been a single drop of tea spilled, even though the boat was heaving while I was carrying the tray.'

Tara and Angela gave great exaggerated sighs and then started laughing.

When he disappeared again, Tara turned to Angela. 'Thank God for that,' she said, 'I can't wait to hear what happened next.'

Delighted by Tara's genuine interest in her romance, and even more delighted by her new-found closeness with her older half-sister, Angela happily picked up the saga of Aiden Byrne where she'd left off.

Halfway across the Irish sea, the storm got into full swing, and Tara and Angela found themselves treading a rocky path to the ladies' toilets on several occasions, during which the sandwiches and tea unfortunately made an unwarranted and unwelcome reappearance.

William spent most of the time kneeling up on a bench, watching the crashing waves, as the boat rocked its way towards the Welsh coast.

'Never again,' the ashen-faced Angela said, as the car drove through the port in Holyhead. It was Saturday morning and dawn was breaking. 'I'll never go on a boat again as long as I live.'

'Surely you don't mean that?' Tara said, her lips curving into an amused little smile. 'I was sure you'd be checking the holiday rota in the hotel when you got back, to book your next trip home to see Aiden.'

Angela glanced at her sister, and smiled shakily. 'Well,' she said, 'I suppose you should never say never ...'

Chapter 30

❦

Bridget gave a little sigh of satisfaction as she looked around the bathroom. The white enamel sink and toilet bowl were shining, and so was the bath. The brass taps and window-lifters were newly polished, and the soap dishes washed and dried. There were clean towels on the ends of the newly changed beds, and every carpet in the house was hoovered. When the boarders who went home for the weekend came back on Sunday night, everything would be spotless and fresh for them.

For once, Bridget felt ahead of herself. She and June had done a very good day's work and it showed.

June had gone off to the shops to pick up the leg of pork for the Sunday dinner, as well as a few other bits and pieces, taking all three children along with her since it was a nice sunny afternoon. It was rare that Bridget had the house to herself these days, so she decided to give herself a little break and read her new magazine in front of the sitting-room fire.

She put her glass of lemonade down on the coffee table and sat flicking through her *Woman's Weekly*. She was totally engrossed in a short story about a woman whose son had disappeared, when the doorbell rang. She sighed as she realised that, since she was the only one in, she would have to answer it.

'Tara!' Bridget said, her voice high with surprise, as she opened the door. 'When did you get back?' She hadn't expected to see Tara until tomorrow or the day after.

'A couple of hours ago.' Tara followed her friend along the hallway and into the sitting-room. 'I took William down to the hotel to get some lunch and I've left him helping Fred out in the bar, stacking bottles of beer.' She unbuttoned her coat. 'Since it was nice and sunny out, I thought I'd give my legs a bit of a stretch and walk down to see you. You get all cramped up sitting in the car for hour after hour.'

'You're great to do it,' Bridget told her. 'There's not many women who would drive a big car all the way over to Ireland and back.' She noticed the dark circles around Tara's green eyes. 'Did you get any sleep on the boat at all?' she asked in a concerned voice. 'You look fierce tired.'

'I had a couple of hours on the boat,' Tara told her. 'And I had a lie-down when we arrived back at the house.' She took off her coat and sank down into the corner of the sofa.

'Was it an easy crossing?' Bridget asked, remembering the weather from the night before. 'I was up with Lucy around one o'clock and it was fairly windy.'

Tara sighed. 'To be honest, it was a bit rough … very rough at one point. Angela and I were both really sick. Poor Angela was worse than me.'

'How is she now?'

'When we got back to the house, she went straight to bed,' Tara told her. 'She's totally washed out.'

'Oh, that's terrible,' Bridget said, pulling a sympathetic face. 'The poor cratur. There's nothing worse than being seasick – it's like morning sickness only worse.'

'It gradually eased off,' Tara told her, 'but we were glad to arrive in Holyhead and get off the boat.'

'Well,' Bridget said, joining her hands together in her lap, 'how did it all go?'

Tara raised her eyebrows. 'Angela met a new boyfriend.'

'Did she?' Bridget looked fascinated. 'A young lad she knew before?'

'No, no,' Tara said. 'He's not a young lad – he's an older man. More our age than Angela's, and he's a widower with a child.'

'I don't believe it,' Bridget said, shaking her head. 'I can't imagine Angela with an older fella. She's always gone for young pipsqueaks.'

'Well, this one is no pipsqueak,' Tara told her. 'Far from it. He's an accountant with an office in Birr.' She smiled now. 'I actually saw him when we were on a day out in Dublin, and although it was from a distance, he seemed very smart and good-looking.'

'I don't believe it,' Bridget said again. 'How did this all come about?'

Tara smiled now, although there was a weariness in her eyes from the journey, and she was dreading having to tell Bridget about Nora. Although she knew it had to be done, she put it to the back of her mind for now. 'Look, I won't spoil it. I'm sure Angela would love to give you all the gory details herself.'

'I can't wait,' Bridget said, jokily rubbing her hands together. 'Well, apart from Angela and her romance, how were Shay and Tessie and your Uncle Mick and everybody?'

'Grand,' Tara replied, but as she said it, she realised that her voice sounded very flat, even to her own ears. 'Well, actually, my father hasn't been too well.' She went on to tell her friend about the episodes Shay had been having.

'And how did he look?' Bridget said, concerned. She had always been fond of Shay, and found it hard to imagine that the devil-may-care man she had known since she was a young girl was getting older and inevitably more vulnerable.

'Actually, he didn't look that bad,' Tara told her. 'I don't know if I would have noticed anything if Kitty and Tessie hadn't told me.' She bit her lip. 'I suppose that when you're aware there's something amiss you're on the lookout for things. He's just that little bit slower, but that's only natural.'

'I'm sorry to hear it,' Bridget said. 'Is there anything I can do? Should I maybe send him something?'

'No, no,' Tara said, smiling gratefully. 'It's good of you, but I never even got the chance to broach the subject with him myself. He just acted the same as always, and didn't even mention his health.' She gave a little shrug. 'You know what he's like.'

Bridget nodded. 'Well,' she said, 'maybe it was just a one-off thing and he's back on an even keel now. He could be grand for the next ten or twenty years and never have another turn.'

'True,' Tara said.

'And did William enjoy himself?' Bridget asked. 'Was he out and about all over the place?'

'He was. Joe came up for a few days after the Easter weekend, but before that we went up to Dublin to visit the Museum, and to Athlone for a classical music evening. That kind of thing.'

'It sounds lovely,' Bridget said, nodding appreciatively, although museums and concert halls were not the sort of places in which she felt too comfortable. Conversations like this suddenly made her aware of the differences between Tara and herself. It reawakened the feelings of being less than her friend, who had married into 'the quality' and whose brother was a priest.

'Oh, and another thing.' Tara's face suddenly brightened. 'You'll be delighted to know that William has become a very proficient darts player.'

'Darts?' Bridget echoed, her face a picture of incredulity.

'Joe bought him a dartboard and they hung it in the old stables. He was out there practising any time he had a spare minute, so Fred will have to watch out now.'

Bridget's hand came up to cover her mouth. 'I can just imagine Mrs Fitzgerald's face when he tells her that one. I don't imagine she'll be too pleased to have a darts player in the family. She'd be happier with rugby or tennis.' Her eyes twinkled. 'You'll have to be careful, Tara, or she'll be thinking you and Joe are a bad influence on him.'

Tara rolled her eyes and laughed. 'I think I might already be in trouble with Elisha,' she confessed, and went on to explain William's plans to train in hotel management and eventually own his own hotel.

'Good for him!' Bridget stated. 'The lad knows his own mind, and Fred has told me that he's a natural behind the bar and in the kitchen.'

'Well, as long as his mother and Harry don't think I encouraged it,' Tara said ruefully. 'I'm not going to worry about it. It's early days for him to be making decisions about his future.'

'Any other news?' Bridget asked. 'How's your old Auntie Molly? Is she still in the home with the nuns?' Bridget felt much more comfortable chatting about the Flynn side of Tarn's family, which wasn't so grand.

Tara nodded. 'I think there are times when she drives Tessie and my father mad. Her memory comes and goes.'

'Did she know you at all?' Bridget asked. 'Or Joe?'

Tara shrugged. 'Not really. She mixes us up with other people. At first she thought I was one of the nurses or a cleaner, but she seems happy enough in her own way, and I think the company in the home is good for her. It's sad that she's ended up there, but it's taken a weight off Joe and, of course, Tessie and my father as well.'

'God love her. I suppose that it's all ahead for every one of us,' Bridget said, a faraway look on her face. 'We don't know where we'll end up, but at least she's had a good innings. You don't feel so bad when it's somebody that's lived a long life, especially when they reach the point they don't know where they are or who people are.'

'I think it'll still hit Joe hard when it eventually happens,' Tara mused.

'Naturally enough,' Bridget agreed. 'The two aunties more or less brought him up, and it was always to their house he went when he was home from the seminary.' She paused. 'Was there any other news around Ballygrace? Anybody died or just had a baby?'

There was a silence.

Tara took a deep breath. She couldn't keep silent about it any longer. 'There was a bit of bad news while I was over.'

'What about?' Bridget asked, then, when she saw the look on her friend's face, she sat up straight in the chair.

'Nora ...' Tara began.

'Nora?' Bridget looked confused. 'Do you mean Lizzie Lawless's Nora?'

Tara nodded, desperately trying to find the right words. But there were no right words for what she was about to tell her friend. 'She was found ... She's dead, Bridget ...'

Bridget's mouth moved, as though she were about to say something, but then she just sat there in a shocked silence. 'God rest her poor soul ...' she eventually said. She looked up at Tara, her eyes cloudy. 'She was only young. What happened to her? Was she sick or something?'

'Nobody really knows,' Tara said, her voice low. 'Some workmen from Bord na Mona found her body up the bog a few weeks ago, and it was just identified over the Easter weekend.'

'Up the bog?' Bridget gasped. Her eyes narrowed as she tried to make sense of the information, then eventually moved back to meet Tara's anxious gaze. 'How did she come to be up the bog?' she asked. 'Do they know why she was there?'

Tara shrugged helplessly. She found the whole, awful situation frightening herself, and knew what she felt was bound to be only a fraction of her friend's emotions. 'I think they're trying to discover that sort of information. They'll probably have to do all kinds of tests.'

Bridget swallowed hard. 'Poor Nora,' she whispered. 'She never did anybody a bit of harm. Imagine her ending up on a horrible, cold, dark bog.'

Tara clasped her hands on her knees, feeling uneasy about the effect this was having on her friend. She wondered if Bridget was up to talking further about the situation, or whether she should let it rest for the time being.

'How long was she there?' Bridget asked now, a deep furrow in her brow. 'Has it just happened, or was it a while ago?'

'Nobody seems to know anything as yet.'

'The ones that saw her must have had *some* idea,' Bridget said, her voice rising now. 'Surely they could tell if it was ten years ago or ten weeks? They must have been able to make a guess?'

'I think it's to do with the bog,' Tara explained, trying to pick her words very carefully. 'The turf can preserve things.'

'I know the teachers used to tell us at school about the bog pre-servin' things like blocks of butter, but I never knew it could preserve a human being,' Bridget said. She paused for a few moments, think-ing. 'You know that Nora just disappeared one day? Around the same time that I went up to Dublin to the nuns ...' There was another silence now as they both remembered the adopted baby, but neither of them referred to it. 'Lizzie Lawless said she had run away with a lad or something, but nobody ever knew for certain.' She shook her head. Then, her eyes suddenly widened as she had a thought. 'They don't think she was *murdered* or anything, do they?'

'I would think it will be a good while before they arrive at any conclusions,' Tara said, trying to keep her own voice calm in the hope it would have the same effect on her friend. 'It's not even official as to who the body actually belongs to. Somebody heard it from the Guards in Ballygrace, and it's got around the place that it was Nora.'

'Do you know if she was ever seen again after we left Ballygrace?'

'Kitty asked me the same question,' Tara told her. 'According to local talk, the girl hasn't been seen for years.'

'That means she *could* have been killed at the time she went miss-ing.' Bridget shook her head now, the thought horrifying her. 'Oh, dear God ... the poor, poor soul.'

Tara nodded. 'That could well be the case, but she might not have been killed. Anything could have happened to her.'

Bridget stared at Tara. 'Are you saying she might have had an accident or something like that?'

Tara shrugged, unwilling to put the word 'suicide' to her thoughts. 'Maybe she had had enough of her hard life ...'

Bridget's eyes widened. 'You mean she might have killed herself?'

Tara's voice dropped. 'It's terrible to think about it, but I suppose it's one possibility they might have to consider.'

Bridget's hands flew to cover her mouth. She shook her head. 'If she did kill herself,' she said, tears welling up in her eyes, 'then there are people who will have to answer for it. Lizzie Lawless or that evil old priest must have driven her to it.'

'Joe said he thought there would probably be an inquest into the death,' Tara said. 'It should all come out then.'

'Let's hope it does,' Bridget said bitterly. 'Let's hope that those that have done her any harm are made to pay for it.'

Chapter 31

A short while later, Tara left Bridget and walked slowly back towards her own house. To anyone watching her, she looked as though she were taking a casual stroll in the relative warmth of a spring afternoon. But there was no easy feeling within her. A deep-seated feeling of weariness was beginning to take hold of her now.

Tara knew the long journey back from Ireland had contributed, but a part went deeper than that. It was a weariness that went all the way back to her childhood. It was a weariness born out of sadness for her friend and the bitter past from which Bridget was always trying to escape. Even though she had avoided travelling back to Ballygrace, apart from the occasion of Gabriel's funeral, the place still somehow managed to creep into her life in Stockport.

Tara felt bad leaving Bridget to deal with this dark news on her own, but she knew there was not a single thing she could do to help her. And the fact that she was pregnant made Tara feel more sorry for her and all the more helpless. She decided that she would give Bridget a few days to come to terms with it all, and then, Tara thought, she might suggest that they have a day shopping in Manchester, or maybe she would drive them both over to Buxton or Macclesfield for dinner one evening.

Something to take Bridget out of herself.

As she neared her house, Tara debated whether to carry on to the Cale Green Hotel or to take an hour for herself in the house. She turned into the gateway. It would do no harm to leave William down at the hotel for a little longer. They'd had over a week together between Ireland and Stockport, and it would do him good to mix with other people for a while. William always enjoyed helping around the bar, but if he got bored he could always go out into the hotel garden and kick a football on the grass for a while, or even help old Mr Jackson, who came for an hour or two in the afternoons to keep the gardens neat and tidy.

There was an echoing silence in the house, as all the women who boarded there were either out or still at work. Tara went up to her bedroom and mindlessly set about unpacking her case, separating items for hanging up and the rest for washing or the dry-cleaners. That done, she lay down on the bed and closed her eyes.

The next thing she knew it was six o'clock.

The front door banging closed heralded the arrival of Vera Marshall, Tara's longest-serving boarder. The spinster teacher had just returned from Bramhall where she had spent two hours briskly walking around the park.

Tara quickly tidied herself up and brushed out her long red hair, then went downstairs.

'Ah, Tara,' Vera Marshall said in a delighted voice, 'you're back!'

'I am,' Tara said, smiling warmly at her old-fashioned but thoroughly decent lodger. 'And I'm just heading down to the hotel to pick up young William.' She checked her watch. 'We'll probably eat there. It will be easier than starting to cook at this stage.'

'Unless you have arranged to meet someone else,' the teacher said, 'would you mind if I joined you both?'

Tara was taken aback but covered her surprise. 'We'd be delighted to have you join us,' she said.

Vera took off her anorak and stood holding it by the hood. 'If you want to go on ahead, I'll be ready in ten minutes and will follow you down.'

'Lovely,' Tara said, suddenly thinking that Vera's polite, pleasant chat might just help to lift her own spirits a bit, and that the teacher would keep William occupied with school chatter and the like. 'I can't guarantee what time they'll have a table for us at this short notice, so we might have to wait until one is free.'

'That's not a problem,' Vera said, smiling brightly. 'In fact, I'd welcome the time on our own to have a little chat with you. There's something I would like your advice about.'

'Really?' Tara said, suddenly intrigued as to why the very self-contained spinster could possibly want her advice.

'I'll save it until we're having dinner.' She paused. 'Mr Kennedy rang twice looking for you. He said could you ring as soon as you arrived home, that it was fairly urgent.'

Tara's brow creased in annoyance. It was probably about the Grosvenor. Well, he could wait. She wasn't in any great rush to start discussing business with him again. 'Thanks for letting me know,' she said. 'I'll get back to him later.'

'There are a number of messages for you, Mrs Fitzgerald,' Carol the receptionist told Tara as she passed the desk. She handed the notes to her employer.

There was another message from Frank Kennedy and one from Gerry McShane, the fellow who had given her the Grosvenor business proposal, which she hadn't even glanced at. She would have to return his call tomorrow. She felt a pang of guilt now as she remembered how polite and nice Gerry McShane had been, and decided she would at least glance over the papers to familiarise herself with their plans, so that she could hold some kind of a conversation with him.

Then, as she stood looking down at the list of people who had called her, the phone rang. Carol answered it.

'She's actually here at the moment,' she said. 'I'll put you through.' She looked at Tara now. 'It's Mr Kennedy. He said he would be grateful if he could have a quick word.'

It was too late to say she wasn't available to take his call. 'Thank you, Carol,' she said. 'I'll take it in the office.'

'Hello, Tara,' he said when she picked up, 'I know you're probably up to your neck in things having just got back, but I wanted to catch you before you planned anything else for tomorrow night.'

'Sunday night? Why? What's on?' Tara asked.

'It's Kate's birthday,' he told her, 'and I'm holding a small dinner party out at my house for her. Just a dozen or so people. I know she would like you to be there.'

Tara held her breath for a few moments, her mind ticking over quickly. It was a difficult one, but she knew it would look very bad if she refused. She had nothing else planned, so she really had no excuse. Besides, she had a present for Kate, and had planned to call out to her sometime tomorrow in any case.

'What time?' she asked.

'The meal will be served around eight o'clock, with drinks beforehand?'

'Lovely,' Tara said. She paused. 'Will I know anyone else there?'

'You might,' Frank said. 'Kate's brother and wife, and her friend Liz who owns the boutique.'

'Lovely,' Tara said again. Then she thought. 'I'd better take your address and directions to the house.'

'You won't need them, I'll send a taxi to pick you up for quarter past seven.'

'I'm quite happy to drive,' Tara said quickly, not wishing to be beholden to him.

'We'll be having a few drinks, so I'm ordering taxis for everyone,' he said. 'And I'll organise the return journey as well.'

'Well, thank you,' Tara said, knowing it would have been churlish to say anything else.

After hanging up, Tara sat in the office for a few minutes thinking, and came to the conclusion that maybe it wasn't such a bad idea after all. It was obvious that Frank and Kate were getting closer if he was hosting a party in her honour. It suddenly crossed Tara's mind that maybe it was going to be more than a birthday celebration, and she wondered if Kate and Frank might announce their engagement. It was certainly within the realms of possibility. They had been going out together for a few years now, and she supposed it was about time for them to formalise their relationship in some way. She knew, from what Kate had told her, that her friend often stayed at Frank's house, so it would only be another step or two forward for them to get married.

She shrugged. Why should she care what they did? It would be nice for Kate to get married, if that's what she wanted, and it would certainly get Frank Kennedy well and truly out of her own hair if he were formally linked to another woman. She looked at her watch now, then got up and headed to the bar.

Tara found William very much at home there, chatting to Fred and one of the waitresses. She apologised for taking longer than she had planned down at Bridget's, then asked, 'Are you starving?'

'Not too bad,' he answered diplomatically, 'I had a packet of crisps and a glass of lemonade to keep me going until dinner.'

'Would you mind very much if Vera Marshall from the house joined us? You know, the older teacher.'

'No, I wouldn't mind in the slightest,' he replied. 'She's a very nice woman and was always kind to me when I was younger, giving me crosswords to do and listening to me play the piano.'

'Yes, she is nice,' Tara agreed. She turned to the waitress. 'Maria, would you mind popping into the restaurant to check if they have a table for three available?'

Fred gestured to Tara to come to the other end of the bar, out of William's hearing.

'What is it?' she said anxiously, sensing that something was wrong. 'Is there a problem with William?'

Fred's face broke into a cheery smile. 'No, not a thing – he's a great young lad. There's nowt wrong with William.' He paused. 'It was actually Bridget I wanted to have a word about.'

'Go on,' Tara said.

'Well, I feel that things have been getting on top of her a bit,' he said, slightly awkwardly. Personal conversations did not come too easily to him, especially when it was any kind of problem to do with Bridget. And although a lot of the staff would have been intimidated approaching Tara, Fred knew she was the one person who would understand. 'I feel she could do with a bit of a break, so I thought I might take her to Blackpool, or somewhere like that, to a nice boarding house or hotel. Just on our own, to get her away from the house and running after everybody else.' He halted. 'I was wondering when would be a good time for me to take a few days off?'

Tara nodded. 'I think you're right, Fred,' she told him in a low voice. 'I think taking her away is a great idea; it's exactly what she needs. I'd even thought of suggesting something like that myself.' She put her hand on his arm. 'You just sort out what dates suit you down in the boarding house and I'll make sure that we're covered here in the bar. Don't give it another thought.'

'You're a belter,' Fred said. 'None better. I knew you'd help me out.'

'No problem, Fred,' Tara said, smiling fondly at her friend's husband. God knows what Bridget would be like if she hadn't met such a good, kind man, she thought. She looked up at the clock behind the bar. 'Shouldn't you be finished now?'

'I'll just sort out the till and then I'll be heading off,' he told her. 'If I get the chance, I'll mention our little trip to her tonight.'

The waitress came back then and said that they were clearing a table now and would have it ready shortly. After telling William that she would meet him in the restaurant in ten minutes, Tara went back to the office and checked her filing cabinet where she found the documents about the Grosvenor Hotel in the unopened envelope. Then she went to her desk, deciding to take a few minutes now to read through them while waiting for Vera.

Tara was shocked by the price of the hotel and the projected costs of the expansion work. The hotel would cost over £50,000 to buy, before adding conference halls, bathrooms to the older bedrooms, and a general renovation programme.

Tara couldn't believe the figures. Frank Kennedy's company had done major work on the Grosvenor only a few years back. But, she supposed, time moved on, people demanded higher standards and costs invariably rose.

There was a vast difference between The Grosvenor's costs and the amount she had paid for her own small hotel. The £20,000 that she would be required to come up with, as a fifth member of the group, was completely out of the question. She was managing to meet the mortgages on the Cale Green Hotel and the two houses without any difficulty, but, after paying her hotel staff wages and all the running costs, it took every penny of what was left to cover expenses such as running the car, paying her housekeeper and running her houses.

Tara tossed the sheets of paper onto her desk, shaking her head. There was no way she could even think of borrowing and trying to pay back the money.

She decided that she would phone Gerry McShane tomorrow and put him quite clearly in the picture. She slotted the papers back in the filing-cabinet, then went back out to the bar.

Vera Marshall arrived a short while later, dressed in a dove-grey suit, blue blouse and pearls. Within moments Fred appeared at the table with the two pre-dinner sherries that Tara had ordered.

'Can you keep William occupied for a few more minutes while we chat?' Tara asked him.

'No problem,' Fred replied.

'Tara,' the older woman started,' I want to ask your advice on a private matter.'

Tara took a sip from her glass. 'Fire away.'

'I've decided that I want to *buy* my own house.'

'Really?' Tara said, hoping that her voice did not betray the fact that she felt rather let down by the news.

'I've been looking into the matter thoroughly and I've been assured by the bank that there will be no problem with a mortgage on a decent house.' The teacher gave a little smile now. 'It would only be a small mortgage as I have a reasonable amount saved and I've more invested in stocks and shares. I intend to follow your own example and rent out rooms to professional women, which should more than cover the mortgage, and make me a bit of a profit, too.'

'It doesn't sound as if you need any advice from me at all,' Tara told her. 'You seem to have everything worked out.'

'Ah, but getting the mortgage is only the start,' Vera said. 'I need your advice on what sort of house I should buy and where. I've no experience in that area at all, as I've always rented rooms.'

'Have you been to any estate agents yet?' Tara asked.

'No, no,' Vera said. 'I haven't got as far as that yet.' She halted. 'Basically, I'm looking for something very similar to your own two houses. I'm looking for something with two good reception rooms downstairs plus a decent-sized kitchen and three to four bedrooms upstairs, but I'm aware that they are difficult to come by.'

Tara nodded, knowing that Vera had done her homework. 'You might have to go a bit further afield,' she told the older woman. 'The bottom end of Edgeley or maybe even out towards Heaton Chapel or Heaton Moor.'

Vera took another sip of her sherry. 'That's what I didn't want to do. Both would be that bit further away from school, and I don't really want to add more travelling to my day.'

Tara thought. 'It would be worth introducing you to my old boss, Mr Pickford. He gave me all the help and advice I needed when I first started buying property.' As soon as she said it, Tara felt a small tinge of guilt at denying the fundamental part that Frank Kennedy had played in encouraging her to buy property, but she quickly put it aside, having never discussed her private life with her boarders. 'I'll give Mr Pickford a ring on Monday,' Tara told her lodger, 'and I'll get back to you when I've spoken to him.'

Chapter 32

Bridget got another shock on the Sunday evening.

All the lodgers had been fed and were otherwise occupied. Fred was outside washing the car – Michael and Helen ostensibly helping him with buckets of soapy water and chamois leather cloths. After ten minutes of serious work, all three had eased up and started messing around, splashing water and flicking cloths at each other, when a small green van pulled up alongside. The driver rolled the window down, his arm leaning casually on the ledge.

'Hi there, Freddie boy!' a familiar voice with a London accent called out.

Fred look puzzled for a few moments, then the penny dropped. 'Lloyd!' he said, his face breaking into a beaming smile. He squeezed the water out of his chamois and went to look in the van window. 'Long time no see. Where have you been hiding yourself, lad?'

'Oh, here and there. You know how it is,' Lloyd said, turning the van engine off. 'I'm doin' a big job out in Manchester and I thought I'd look you and the missus up again. See how you were both goin' on.' He halted. 'Last time I was around these parts, you were in hospital. You doin' OK now?'

'Beltin'!' Fred said, nodding vigorously. 'Got a lucky escape that time – bad bang on the head – but I'm back to me old self.' He thumbed back towards the car. 'Got my licence back last summer, so I'm mobile again and everything. We were lost without the car.' He reached his hand in through the van window, and Lloyd shook it.

'You're lookin' good, mate. You'd never know you'd had anythin' wrong at all.'

Fred gave him a big, grateful smile. 'Ah, I'm not so bad now …' He was glad that Lloyd had said that, because he knew that some people still thought he hadn't quite got back to where he was before his accident. There were sometimes little silences in conversations where he felt people were looking at him strangely, as though he'd said the wrong thing. 'You're looking well yourself, Lloyd,' he said. 'Bridget will be delighted to see you. It must be a couple of years or more since you were in this area.'

168

A deep furrow appeared on Lloyd's brow as he tried to work it out. 'Yeah, yeah. I suppose it could be that long.'

But he knew perfectly well how long it was. He hadn't been back at the house since that drunken night with Bridget over three years ago. He had vague, dark memories about that night, and even thinking about it made him break out into a sweat.

In truth, Lloyd had planned never to come back to this part of Stockport again, but fate had other plans. After the Manchester job, he was contracted to work for six months on a new office block on the A6, which was just down the road from Maple Terrace. He was bound to run into Fred or Bridget at some point, and he would definitely come across some of Fred's mates in the local pubs.

Lloyd reckoned it would be better to get things over and done with – and the first part had gone well so far. It was obvious from Fred's reaction that he knew nothing about the little indiscretion, and Lloyd was more than a bit grateful for that.

Michael and Helen came to stand beside their father now, curious as to who he was. There were very few people around who looked like Lloyd, with his dark skin and curly hair.

'Hi, kids,' he said, winking at them and grinning. 'You've both shot up since I last saw you.' He saw their hesitation and stopped. 'Now don't say you don't remember me? Good old Lloyd?'

'I remember you, I remember you!' Michael said, suddenly grinning. 'But you look different from last time.'

Lloyd patted his thinning head of hair. 'I suppose I have lost a bit of the old barnet since I last saw you.'

'I noticed the bald spot straight away,' Fred joked, 'but I was too polite to mention it.' He gestured with his chamois towards the house. 'You go on inside and see Bridget and the little one. I'll just finish the car.'

'Don't say you've had another nipper since I last saw you?' Lloyd said, getting out of the van now. He was still dressed in his paint-splattered working overalls, donkey jacket and heavy, steel-capped boots.

'Another little girl, just three years old,' Fred told him. 'Lucinda, but everyone shortens it to Lucy.' He gave a proud grin. 'And we've another one on the way.'

'I've got to hand it to you, mate,' Lloyd laughed. 'You don't waste time, do you?' He put a hand on Fred's shoulder. 'You've got a fine set-up here,' he said sincerely. 'Lovely house and business, and a lovely wife and family.'

'Cheers, Lloyd,' Fred said, suddenly feeling a little choked. Of course, he knew that the boarding house was really down to Bridget, since she had inherited it from Ruby Sweeney, the original landlady. But Fred knew that since he and Bridget had got married, they had worked together to maintain and build up everything that Ruby had started.

Lloyd climbed the front stairs up to the house, a little knot of apprehension forming in his chest. Then he steeled himself to knock on the half-open door before stepping into the hallway. 'Hi there,' he called, still rapping on the door and glancing first towards the sitting-room and then down the hallway towards the large kitchen. 'Anybody at home?' He heard a noise from upstairs and, when he stepped back to look up, he saw Bridget Roberts looking back down at him, her younger daughter held tightly in her arms.

'Lloyd!' she said, her voice high with surprise. 'Oh, my God …'

'Bridget …' he said, taking a deep breath and smiling warmly at her. Then, as she started to move down the stairs towards him, Lloyd's gaze moved to the dark-haired child with the coffee and cream skin, and his eyes widened.

He stared wordlessly at her and then back at Bridget.

Chapter 33

❧

'I was just changing her upstairs in the bedroom,' Bridget said, struggling to sound normal. As though this were just an ordinary occasion where an old friend had called out to the house. Only Lloyd wasn't just an ordinary friend, and the look in his eyes now told Bridget that he was feeling exactly the same.

'I was chatting to Fred outside,' he said quickly. 'I was tellin' him that I've not been up this part of the world for some time … must be three or four years.'

'We'll go into the kitchen,' Bridget said, aware that she was cutting him off, but not being able to stop herself. She led the way down the hall. 'I'll make us a cup of tea or a coffee.'

'As I said,' Lloyd went on, babbling now, 'I've been doing a job in Manchester this week, and I thought I'd drop in and see how you all were. It seems ages since I was in these parts. Time goes on so quick …' He followed her down to the kitchen now, halting to lean against the jamb of the door as though afraid to come any further. Even if he decided to make an escape now, he knew that Fred would meet him outside again and try to make him stay.

Bridget put Lucy in the high chair at the table and gave her a brightly-coloured rattle, then she turned to the worktop to switch on the kettle. 'Well, any big news since we last saw you?' Then, attempting to lighten the situation, she said, 'You didn't get yourself married or anything like that?' She lifted three mugs from the hooks on the wall, then reached into the cupboard above to get a packet of sugar to top up the already well-filled bowl. Her heart was beating like a drum, her head whirling with myriad thoughts.

'No,' Lloyd said, clearing his throat, 'no major changes in that department as yet.' He straightened up and moved a few steps into the kitchen, then closed the door behind him. Then he went over to the high chair and, very gently, ran a hand over Lucy's black loose curls.

Bridget lifted the tea caddy down from the shelf, then turned and caught sight of Lloyd with Lucy. She froze.

'She's beautiful, isn't she?' Lloyd said in a low voice.

Bridget nodded. She couldn't speak.

'How old did you say she was?'

'She just turned three,' Bridget whispered, her eyes flitting nervously towards the door.

Lloyd looked directly at her now. 'That's just what I was working out, calculating …'

There was a long, anguished pause. 'I'm right, aren't I?' he said eventually, in a hoarse voice.

Bridget's heart dropped to the bottom of her stomach, but she made her brow furrow as though she didn't understand his question.

'She's mine, isn't she?' He tipped the back of Lucy's dark curls. 'That night …'

'She's Fred's!' Bridget stated, her voice firm and clear. 'I don't know what you're goin' on about.'

Lloyd stared at Bridget, 'But she's half-caste,' he said in a barely audible voice. 'She can't be Fred's ... and she's a dead ringer for my sister.'

Bridget moved across the floor and lifted Lucy out of her chair. She hugged the child close to her chest. 'You're totally out of order, Lloyd. You've no business comin' here causing trouble,' she hissed.

'I came here for a friendly visit,' he told her, 'and I wish that's all it had turned out to be, but you can't expect me to pretend that the child is the same as the other two.'

'Nobody else has *ever* made any comments on how she looks.' This, of course, wasn't true. Tara had immediately voiced similar thoughts when Lucy was born, and her old friend Elsie had quite obviously had reservations about the child's appearance. And there had been that tactless Cub Leader. Bridget knew perfectly well that people were often surprised when they saw Lucy, but when her husband hadn't voiced any serious concerns, she had blanked the others out.

'Everybody else knows she's Fred's. Her skin's just a bit tanned, that's all.'

Lloyd shook his head. 'And Fred's gone along with it?' His voice was full of disbelief. 'Hasn't he ever questioned how she looks so different from the other two kids? Hasn't he ever wondered how her hair's so dark and curly and her skin is definitely more than just a bit tanned?'

'We both think there must be some kind of a throwback thing in my family,' she said now, trying to sound convincing. 'I told you I was fostered, so I don't know anythin' about my real family. They could have had any kind of blood in them, Spanish or Italian or anything at all ...'

'Don't talk daft,' Lloyd said, but his voice was gentle. He touched Lucy's hand now. 'She's definitely not from Spain or Italy. A blind man on a galloping horse can see that she's got West Indian blood. You can tell by the hair and the eyes.' He stopped, seeing the hurt in Bridget's eyes. 'I'd like to say different,' He shook his head. 'It's just too coincidental after that night ...'

'I honestly can't remember anythin' about what happened,' she told him in a choked voice. 'I was in a bit of a state at the time over Fred being ill and everything ... and because of it all, I have to admit I was drinking too much.' She actually looked up into Lloyd's face now. 'I've never been able to think clearly about what happened, and that's why I never really thought about Lucy being different. I just couldn't be sure that anything really happened at all.'

Lloyd's gaze shifted upwards and he gave a small sigh. 'I wish I could say the same ... it took me a long time to get it out of my mind. I felt so guilty. I've never done anything like that before. No matter what, I would never have looked at another man's wife. Especially someone I regarded as a friend.'

A cold fear gripped Bridget's heart and her legs suddenly felt weak. She sank down into one of the kitchen chairs and tightened her hold on Lucy. 'You're not going to say anything to Fred, are you, Lloyd?'

He stared at her for a moment. 'No, course not. I don't want any trouble, and I like Fred a lot. He's a decent old stick. One of the nicest men I know.' His voice dropped lower now. 'And I don't want to go causin' trouble for you, either, Bridget. We always got on well. But ... I'm still in a state of shock about Lucy ... I don't know what to feel about it all. I ain't never had a kid before, and it's something I never really thought about.'

'But you don't have to think about it,' she told him. 'It shouldn't make any difference to you. Nothing has changed. Me and Fred and the kids are just getting on with things the same way we always did.' She gave a watery smile. 'He's nearly back to his old self. You'd hardly know there was anything wrong with him. It's just little things that catch him out now and again.'

There was a little silence. 'Can I hold her?' Lloyd suddenly asked. 'Just for a minute.'

Bridget hesitated. *What if Fred were to come in?* She thought. *What if he noticed the similarity between Lloyd and Lucy?* This was now turning into a nightmare scenario she had never reckoned would happen. Recently she had almost convinced herself that Lucy was actually her husband's child. But Lloyd's visit here today had well and truly shattered that illusion, and quite apart from facing that stark fact, she now had to think on her feet and hope she didn't make any more mistakes. 'OK,' she agreed. 'You can hold her for a few minutes while I make the tea.' She handed the child over, then, hearing the front door open noisily, her hand flew to her mouth. Not Fred, she thought.

'Mum!' Michael was in the hall. 'The ice-cream van is on the street; can you give me and Helen some money?'

A wave of relief washed over her when she realised it was only her son. Bridget turned back towards the teapot and kettle, her whole body shaking now, and concentrated on putting the three scoops of tea leaves into the pot to make it strong the way Fred liked it.

Lloyd moved the smiling Lucy high up in the crook of his left arm, then reached with his other hand into his trouser pocket and came out with a handful of coins, just as the kitchen door opened. 'Here you are, mate,' he said, handing the lot over to the boy.

Michael cupped his hands together to make sure he didn't lose any of the coins. 'Oh, brilliant!' he said, when he noticed the half-crown and the two-shilling piece amongst the pile of coppers.

He looked up at his mother, his eyes dancing with delight. 'We've loads here, Mum. Can I buy us some crisps and a bottle of Tizer as well?'

'Go on,' Bridget said, her throat tight.

'Thanks, Lloyd,' Michael said, giving him a thumbs-up sign.

When they were on their own again, Bridget turned to Lloyd, her face pale and strained. 'I'm going to take Lucy upstairs and get her into bed before Fred comes in. I just haven't got the nerve to sit in this kitchen while the two of you are here with Lucy.'

'I promise I won't say a word ...' The child started to squirm about now in his arms, so Lloyd reached back to the high chair to get the rattle.

Bridget shook her head. 'Fred would know there was something wrong.' She bit her lip. 'I can't face the thought of him seeing you and Lucy together. You see, I hadn't realised that she looked so like you. I'd convinced myself that she was like me, and a bit like Fred with her dark hair...' Lloyd could see by Bridget's face that she was telling the truth as she actually saw it, however muddled and confused her thinking was. 'If you want, I'll go now,' he offered. 'I'll tell Fred that I only just remembered I had to meet a bloke down the pub.'

'No,' Bridget told him, shaking her head vigorously. 'It would look fierce strange if you suddenly disappeared as he came. It would only make him wonder what was going on.' She put a jug of milk and the sugar bowl in the centre of the table, then she went to the cupboard and lifted down the tin that held the fancy chocolate biscuits and put that on the table, too. 'The tea is all ready for you an' Fred,' she said, 'so I'll take Lucy upstairs now.'

Reluctantly, Lloyd handed his new found daughter back to her mother. 'What are we going to do now?' he said quietly.

'Nothing,' Bridget told him, straightening the collar on Lucy's dress with a shaky hand. 'Nothing at all. I made a terrible, terrible mistake and I have to live with it. We have to keep this to ourselves. I'm not going to make Lucy or poor Fred pay for it.' She looked at Lloyd now. 'What good would it do?'

Lloyd shrugged. 'As I've said, I don't want to go causin' trouble for anybody ...' He reached out a finger to touch his daughter's little hand. 'But it's gonna be very hard on me now that I've met her, and I know my mother would be over the moon to know she had a lovely little granddaughter.'

Bridget stared at him with wide, horrified eyes. 'Promise me you won't breathe a word about this to *anybody*.'

Lloyd's gaze shifted downwards. 'I promise,' he told her. 'But you and me will have to meet on our own to sort something out.'

Bridget's heart lurched. 'No!' she hissed. 'That can't ever happen. If we're seen, people will put two and two together. I can't take a chance on Fred findin' out.' Anxious tears welled up in her eyes. 'Don't do this to me, Lloyd. I'm expectin' another baby and it's not been easy this time.' Her voice suddenly became choked. 'Things are difficult ... and I can't take any more pressure.'

PART TWO

One may not
reach the dawn
save by the path
of the night.

KAHLIL GIBRAN

Chapter 34

❧❧❧

Tara came downstairs carrying Kate's small, beautifully wrapped birthday present. It was a gold charm, a cherub, for her already heavily laden bracelet. She knew her friend would love it. She had dressed carefully in a short-sleeved cream dress with blue piping that came just above her knee, with a matching double-breasted evening coat, and navy bag and shoes. It was an outfit she had bought in a boutique in Manchester, and she felt it was up to the minute enough for socialising with Kate's fashionable friends, like Liz, the owner of Mersey Style. Tara was early for the taxi, so she went into the sitting-room to watch for it from the big bay window. As she passed her black baby grand piano, she stopped. She lifted the lid on the piano stool and looked through the selection of music books. After a minute or so, she settled on a Romantic collection. She put the lid back down, perched on the stool and started to play an old favourite, one of Chopin's etudes. It was a practice piece she had played many, many times when she was learning the piano back in Ireland. She threw herself entirely into her playing and felt relaxed, almost breathless, when she came to the end of the piece. Smiling, she flicked through the book until she came to one of Beethoven's piano sonatas. A few minutes later she was just finishing the final bars in her old favourite, the *Moonlight Sonata*, when the black cab sounded at the gate.

As she sat in the back of the taxi, heading towards Frank Kennedy's house, Tara once again made the decision that she would set aside a regular period of time for her music. When she had a break from playing, the feeling she got when she returned to it was akin to being welcomed back by an old and dear friend.

When they had left the lights of the town behind and were heading out along the country lanes towards Alderley Edge, Tara's thoughts shifted to the evening ahead. A small knot of anxiety formed in her stomach at the thought of a whole night trying to appear relaxed and sociable in Frank Kennedy's house. She felt like asking the taxi driver to turn around and take her back home. Take her anywhere. But she knew that wasn't an option. Kate was her friend and she would have to endure the party for that reason alone.

Although she had vaguely wondered what sort of place Frank Kennedy would live in – and presumed it would be something fairly impressive – Tara was more than a little taken aback when they turned down a residential road where all the houses were hidden behind high hedges and tall trees. The driver slowed then turned into a wide drive, which led up to a well-lit, substantial, Tudor-style detached house. From what Tara could see, it was set in a couple of acres of beautifully kept grounds. Towards the back was a double garage and to the left side of the house an ornate, wrought-iron Victorian conservatory.

It immediately struck her that the property was similar in size to Ballygrace House and, as she glanced at the neat lawns and flower beds, which were orderly and full of spring flowers, she was acutely aware that her old house back in Ireland looked neglected by comparison.

When she thought about it, she shouldn't really be surprised that Frank Kennedy should live in a place like this. He had always been ambitious and she knew he had amassed a significant amount of money from all his building and business ventures over the years. And, she thought wryly, he would have no difficulties getting workmen and gardeners to do anything that needed doing to the building and gardens. He wouldn't have an awkward middle-man like Shay Flynn to contend with.

Tara alighted from the taxi, recognising a couple of the half-dozen or so expensive cars already in the drive, then she tilted her chin at a confident angle and walked towards the imposing dark wood door, which was flanked on either side by two ornate trees in plain stone tubs. She paused for a moment, deciding whether to press the bell or bang on the heavy iron knocker.

She rang the bell, then turned to look back at the lovely garden and breathe in the damp evening scent of the cut grass and flowers. A few moments later she heard quick female footsteps approaching and she turned back towards the entrance.

The heavy wooden door was swept open.

'Mrs Fitzgerald?' It was a young, bright-eyed girl with curly fair hair and a strong Dublin accent. She was wearing a plain black, long-sleeved dress, with starched white collar and cuffs, and a neat string of pearls.

'It is,' Tara confirmed.

The girl put out her hand. 'Welcome to Mr Kennedy's home.' She had enunciated every word carefully, obviously aware of her accent.

Tara had to stop herself from smiling at the formality of the greeting. 'You're obviously from my own home country,' she said, stepping into the panelled hallway. She looked around, amazed at the space and the height of it. Her eyes came to rest on the huge fireplace in the centre of the hall. A circular antique table with four, deep-buttoned leather chairs stood around it. There was an elaborate white floral arrangement in the centre of the table, which added a feminine touch to a very masculine area.

'Oh, you're Irish, too!' The girl glanced around, checking there was no one listening. 'Ballyfermot,' she told her in a low, conspiratorial voice. 'I've only been over here a month. Me name's Annie Kelly.'

Tara smiled warmly at the girl, seeing a resemblance to Bridget when she was a young girl. 'And how are you settling in, Annie?' she asked.

'Grand,' Annie said, nodding her head enthusiastically. 'I got married to a lad from Galway called Donal Kelly just before Christmas. He got work here first and I followed over after him. He's actually doing a bit of building work for Mr Kennedy, along with his brothers, and Donal was tellin' him all about me comin' over and that's how I got the job here.' Her words tumbled out.

'It sounds as though things are working out well for you,' Tara said.

'Oh, Mr Kennedy's been brilliant to us, so he has.' Annie rushed on. 'He got me some part-time work cleaning in his offices in Manchester and he's filled the rest of me hours doin' a bit of ironin' and cleaning for him in the house.' She beamed now. 'I was delighted when he asked me to help him out tonight, because we're savin' up to get the deposit together for a house, and every little bit helps.'

Tara heard a door opening further along where the hallway narrowed. 'Well, Annie,' she told the young girl, 'I really hope it all works out for you and Donal, and I wish you both the best of luck.'

'Thanks, Mrs Fitzgerald.'

'Tara!' Kate Thornley's tinkling voice sounded full of excitement. 'I was delighted when Frank told me you were coming.' She came rushing down the hallway, wearing a striped lime-green and dark-blue dress with a matching short jacket that had four big green buttons. Her blue eyes were fashionably accentuated with heavy shadow and mascara.

'Look at you!' Tara exclaimed, her eyes wide in admiration at the unusual but very flattering outfit. 'What an amazing suit.'

Kate did a twirl. 'From one of the top Parisian designers, my dear!' she said, in an imitation of a snooty fashion commentator. 'I got it at a knock-down price from one of my friends in the business.' She gave Tara a hug. 'And your own outfit looks equally fashionable and fabulous.'

'It's slightly tamer, like myself,' Tara said, laughing. She held out her gift and birthday card. 'They say that good things come in small parcels.'

'You shouldn't have,' Kate said, taking the gift and giving her a kiss on the cheek. Then she put her arm through Tara's. 'Come on in,' she said. 'Most of the others have arrived already.'

'This is a lovely house,' Tara said, as their heels tapped along the tiled floor. 'If the rest of it is half as nice as the hallway it will be amazing.'

Kate stopped dead. 'Surely you've been here before?'

'No,' Tara said, shrugging. She felt a warm blush start over her neck. They both usually skirted very carefully around the history between herself and Frank Kennedy.

'Oh.' Kate raised her eyebrows in surprise. 'Frank's had the house for a few years, so I just presumed you had seen it before …' She hugged Tara's arm closer and they started slowly walking down the hallway again. 'But you're right. It really is beautiful. I must give you a tour later.'

'That would be lovely,' Tara said, although something in Kate's attitude made her think she was relieved that Tara had never been to the house before.

'We're in the main reception room for drinks,' Kate continued on, 'and then we're having dinner served in the dining-room.' She leaned in closer to Tara and said in a low voice, 'He has a table that seats *twelve*. Can you believe it?'

'That's certainly impressive,' Tara said, smiling back at her. She could hear low and easy jazz music playing as they came towards the sitting-room.

'Frank has hired a catering company for the night,' Kate said, 'so we won't have to lift a finger at all.' Her eyes widened. 'I can't believe he's gone to all this trouble for my birthday. Isn't it just lovely of him?'

'It certainly is,' Tara replied. 'He obviously feels you're worth it.'

Kate halted just outside the door of the sitting-room. 'It's a big step forward in our relationship ...' She bit her lip, then gave an excited smile. 'There have been times when I didn't think we'd ever reach this stage.'

'Well,' Tara said, 'I'm delighted for you, if that's what you want.'

Kate's face was suddenly serious. 'Oh, it is, Tara. It really is.'

Tara followed Kate into the subtly-lit room and, within minutes, had been kissed and hugged by those she already knew and introduced to those she hadn't met before. But in the midst of all the hubbub it dawned on her that there was no sign of Frank Kennedy.

Tara glanced around the large room. The wood panelling in the room had been painted cream, which gave a light and airy feel, and there was an elegant white marble fireplace burning logs and coal. Traditional dark wood furniture and solid, well-padded sofas mixed well with a modern radiogram and a television.

'Tara, what will you have to drink?' Kate asked, going across to a glass-fronted mahogany cabinet.

Before Tara had a chance to think, Frank Kennedy came into the room carrying several bottles of champagne, followed by Annie Kelly, who was carrying a tinkling tray of tall crystal flutes.

'Lovely to see you, Tara,' he said as he passed her. 'We're delighted you could make it.'

'Thank you,' she replied, moving to allow him access to the drinks cabinet. She was grateful that he didn't make any attempt to greet her with a kiss or a hug.

The glasses were filled with the bubbly champagne and passed around, then Frank gave a birthday toast to Kate. Tara watched as Kate walked over to him and wrapped her arms around his neck in a kiss of thanks. Tara looked away, feeling mildly uncomfortable with the display of affection.

When everyone started chatting again, Tara went to talk to Kate's sister-in-law, Stella, and Liz from Mersey Style. Stella was a small, well-rounded woman a few years older than Kate, with a quick wit and a confident manner. She was dressed in a discreet navy suit with a wide swinging jacket, teamed with pearls, while Liz looked every inch the boutique owner in a short purple suede dress, cut in the latest smock-style.

After a few minutes, Frank encouraged everyone to finish their glasses, then he came around re-filling them with more champagne.

'I have a feeling we might have a surprise announcement later in the night,' Stella whispered to Tara and Liz.

'Really?' Liz said, her dark eyebrows arched dramatically.

Stella glanced over her shoulder to check no one else was listening. 'An *engagement*, if I'm not mistaken.'

Tara smiled, but said nothing. She was not the only one who had guessed the occasion was more than just an ordinary birthday party. No wonder Kate was in such high spirits.

'Oh, my God,' Liz said, trying not to look too obviously excited. 'Are you sure?'

Stella leaned forward and tapped her nose in a conspiratorial manner. 'I think it's been on the cards for a while, and Kate told me that he's dropped a few hints recently. Nothing outright, but why else would Frank throw such a lavish party for her?'

'He's a very generous guy,' Liz ventured. Then her eyes lit up. 'Oh, wouldn't it be fantastic? Can you just imagine the glamorous wedding they would have?' She looked at Tara. 'They make the most gorgeous couple, don't they?'

Tara felt her throat tighten. She wondered if the two women knew about her own past with Frank Kennedy. 'Yes,' said, 'they certainly look very well together.'

Liz put the back of her hand to her forehead and gave a little swooning sigh. 'Frank Kennedy is the most handsome man, and he never puts a foot wrong fashion-wise. He might not be interested in the more outlandish clothes, but he always manages to look just right whatever the occasion. Don't you think he's gorgeous, Tara?'

Tara smiled and gave a casual shrug, then let her gaze wonder around the room. Quite obviously Liz didn't know about her and Frank.

Then Frank moved to the centre of the room. 'Could I just ask everyone to move into the dining-room,' he called, bringing their conversation to a halt. Tara picked up her drink, grateful for the diversion.

The food was impeccable, cooked by a well-respected chef from one of the restaurants in Manchester that Frank had done specialised building work for. He had promised Frank that he would come and cook for him for a special occasion, and had kept his word. He had brought his own waitress, and Annie Kelly had helped wherever it was necessary, whether it was in the kitchen or carrying things through to the dining-room.

The guests sat down to a menu of pâté and melba toast, or melon with prawns to start, followed by a beautifully presented roast crown of lamb, or chicken breasts in a light lemon sauce. There were three puddings accompanied by a large dish of thick cream, and, as the guests took their pick, a large cheeseboard with a variety of crackers was deposited on a side table with a bottle of port and glasses.

Tara was amazed by how easily Frank Kennedy handled the evening. He went back and forward to the kitchen checking all was well there, made sure there was always a suitable easy-listening record on the turntable, and that everyone had plenty to drink.

Halfway through her main course, Tara could feel the two glasses of champagne and the glass of white wine she had with her meal beginning to affect her, so she discreetly filled her water glass and switched to drinking from that for a while. The other guests were happy enough to allow young Annie to re-fill their wine glasses, but the last thing Tara wanted was to end up in any way inebriated and perhaps saying something indiscreet at Frank Kennedy's house.

So far she had said all the right things and smiled at all the right times. But really, in all conscience, she could not find a single thing to complain about. Frank had been the perfect host, and, although he had been attentive to all his guests, he had been unobtrusive where Tara was concerned.

As the night wore on and the guests returned to the sitting-room, Kate opened her presents to a lot of cheering and clapping. She came rushing across, her eyes sparkling from the champagne and wine to thank Tara for the lovely cherub charm. Then she continued to open packages containing bottles of perfume, a brightly-coloured scarf and several LPs.

She paused when she came to the last present, which was from Frank. It was a small box wrapped in white paper and tied with a black ribbon. A small jeweller's box, just the right size for a ring. There was a hush as she removed the ribbon and then the paper. She glanced across the room at Stella, then opened the lid.

There was a moment's hesitation as everyone watched Kate's bent head, and Tara noticed that her friend's hands were actually trembling.

Then Kate gave a little gasp and lifted her head, and everyone could see her smiling now as she held the small box aloft, to reveal a beautiful pair of diamond earrings. 'Oh, my God,' she said in a hushed voice. 'Real diamonds. They are absolutely beautiful, Frank.'

Tara could see that the smile did not reach her friend's eyes.

Kate moved over to where Frank was sitting and wrapped her arms around his neck. 'Thank you. They are just gorgeous,' she said, kissing him on the lips.

'You can change them if they're not exactly what you want,' he offered. 'The jeweller said there would be no problem.'

'No,' Kate said, shaking her head. 'They're just perfect.'

There was a small, slightly awkward silence, and all eyes were on the couple.

'Why don't you put on one of your new LPs?' Liz suddenly suggested.

'What a good idea!' Kate said in a high, excited voice. She rushed back to the table where her presents were and lifted up the first record that came to hand. 'This is perfect,' she announced, holding it aloft. 'A nineteen sixty-five hits medley with all the best songs on it!'

Frank went over to Kate and took the record sleeve from her. They both stood studying it together, then Frank went over to the radiogram to put it on.

As soon as he moved away, Kate turned back towards the drinks cabinet and lifted a large wine glass from the shelf above, filled it halfway up with champagne, stopping for a few seconds to let the bubbles settle, then filled it to the brim. Without turning around, she drank a good half of the glass in one go.

Tara's heart sank, but not in the way it would have done had she seen Bridget do the same thing. Kate wasn't a big drinker. She and Tara had the same attitude to alcohol, that it was something to enjoy on an occasion and in moderation. It was rarely that she saw Kate drink too much. It was obvious that she was trying to drown her disappointment.

The opening bars to Georgie Fame's 'Yeh Yeh' sounded across the room, and Tara shifted her gaze in case her friend spotted her, and started chatting to a couple who were sitting on a sofa opposite.

The man was a keen golfer and an even keener talker, so Tara sat alongside his wife and listened as he discussed his finest moments on the golf course.

'Of course,' he elaborated, 'Ireland has some of the finest golf courses in the world, along with Scotland. You do know that, don't you?' He then gave the two women a potted history of all the places in which he had played golf.

When Tom Jones's 'It's Not Unusual' inspired several of the guests to get up and dance, the wife dragged her husband to join them. Before Tara had a chance to look around, Frank Kennedy appeared with a fresh glass of champagne for her and pulled a chair up.

'I noticed you hadn't had a drink for a while,' he told her quietly, 'so I thought I'd rescue you a glass from the last bottle of champagne.'

'Thank you,' Tara said, glancing around to see where Kate was, then saw her standing by the window, arms crossed and in deep conversation with Liz.

'About the Grosvenor,' Frank said. He held his hands up. 'I know this isn't the place to be talking business, and we've all had a few drinks and everything, but I just wanted to say that I hope you will give it some thought. It really is a golden opportunity.'

Tara took a deep breath. 'I've been very busy since I got back from Ireland,' she told him, a slight frostiness in her tone, 'and I've not had a chance even to think about it.' Then, knowing it would make him feel uncomfortable, she added, 'I have Gabriel's young brother staying with me as well, so I've had a lot more on my mind than schemes about buying a hotel.'

Frank merely nodded. 'Of course you're very busy,' he agreed, sounding awkward now. 'It's just that I'd hate you to miss the boat on this. I doubt if we'll ever get this kind of chance again. Hotels like the Grosvenor just don't come on the market that often.'

Tara moved her gaze away from him towards the fireplace. 'I appreciate you asking me, and I don't want to sound rude, but I don't think you should concern yourself with my business interests. I'm happy enough the way things are. I think I've taken on as much as I can.'

'But Tara,' he persisted, 'you're the most capable woman I've ever met in my life.'

Tara turned towards him now and looked him in the eye. 'I'm sure Kate wouldn't be too impressed if she heard you saying that.'

'What would I not be impressed about?'

Kate was suddenly beside them. Her normally pale face was flushed, and although she was smiling, it was obviously forced. She took a good drink from her glass.

'Oh, it's just business talk,' Frank said casually.

Kate leaned forward now, her free arm coming to rest around his shoulder. 'It didn't sound like business talk to me, darling,' she said; shaking her head. 'Maybe you would prefer it if I left you both to finish talking – about whatever it is that you don't want me to hear.' Her voice was louder than usual and had a definite slur. 'Perhaps I should leave you both to your private conversation.'

Several people glanced over at them.

Tara swallowed hard and felt her own cheeks start to redden, as if she'd been caught out saying or doing something wrong. But of course she hadn't. It was Frank who had instigated the conversation. Why should she feel guilty about that? And besides, the conversation had only been about business. 'Don't be silly, Kate,' she said lightly. 'We weren't talking about anything private. It's this Grosvenor thing again.' She sighed. 'I have absolutely no interest in buying it, and I was just telling Frank that. I'm sure you understand.'

Kate's eyebrows shot up. 'Buying *the Grosvenor?*' she said in a shocked voice. 'This is the first *I've* heard about it.' She removed her arm from around Frank's neck. 'And are *you* interested in buying it, Frank?'

Tara sat silently, suddenly realising that she had put her foot in it and remembering that Frank hadn't initially told Kate about his plans for the hotel. Even so, she presumed that Kate would know all about it by now.

Frank took a deep breath. 'I've been to a few meetings about a group takeover. It's still in the early days. I didn't think it was worth mentioning at this stage.'

'Ah,' Kate said, nodding. 'You mean you didn't think it was worth mentioning to *me* at this stage.' She pointed her glass in Tara's direction, the liquid swishing dangerously. '*You*, on the other hand, were obviously worthy of the news, being an intelligent businesswoman, while I'm only an airy-fairy type who dabbles in fashion and silly, arty things.'

'Oh, Kate,' Tara said, reaching out to touch her friend's arm. How had this awful, embarrassing situation suddenly flared up? 'Nobody thinks that. You're very successful. You have a really exciting career travelling all over Europe with the magazine, and meeting famous people. Anyone would be proud to have a career like that.'

Kate took another swig from her drink. 'Yes, but I'm not a self-made woman like *you*, Tara.' Her voice was higher now, slightly hysterical. 'I've had all the advantages of money and family contacts and a top-class education.' She paused, and Tara saw the glint of tears in her eyes now. 'Success doesn't mean the same when you haven't had to work hard for it – according to Frank.'

'Of course you've worked hard,' Tara told her, hoping people couldn't hear exactly what was being said.

Frank pursed his lips. 'You've taken that out of context, Kate,' he said in a wounded voice. 'And you know it. I've supported you in everything you've done over the last few years, and I've never said a bad word about your family background. The conversation you're referring to was a light-hearted one with a group of *your* friends who were teasing you. That's not my style.'

'I'm not saying you haven't supported me,' Kate argued, a catch in her voice now. 'I'm just saying that you chose to confide in Tara about the Grosvenor before telling me. I didn't even know you'd seen each other recently . . .' She halted, then turned her attention back to Tara. 'But then Frank obviously feels he has more in common with you than me. Your Irish connections are obviously stronger than I thought.'

Tara's green eyes suddenly blazed. 'Frank and I have absolutely *no* connections,' she said, 'Irish or otherwise. And I'm every bit as surprised as you are that he hasn't told you.' She swung round to Frank now. 'If you know anything about relationships, then surely you should have told your girlfriend about your plans before anyone else?'

Frank's face tightened. 'Kate has never been interested in my business dealings before.'

'Well,' Tara snapped, 'it seems you still have a lot to learn about women.' She was amazed to hear her own voice sound so brittle and defensive, and again hoped that no one else had heard. She looked at her watch now. 'I think maybe it's time for me to call a taxi.'

'No ... no, Tara,' Kate said, 'you're taking it all wrong. I didn't mean to offend you ...' She put her hand up to her mouth in distress.

Frank stood up and put his arm around Kate. 'Look,' he said in a warm, easy tone, 'this has all been a silly misunderstanding. Surely we're not going to let it spoil a lovely evening?'

Tara immediately caught herself. How rude of her to think of walking out on Kate's birthday party, especially after all the planning, effort and money that had obviously gone into it. She took a deep breath. 'Of course not. You're perfectly correct, Frank; it has been a really, really lovely night, with beautifully cooked food and in such a lovely house. I'm grateful to you both for asking me.'

Kate nodded. 'Yes. I'm grateful, too, Frank.'

'Enough!' he said, clapping her on the back in a slightly forced, hearty manner.

Any further awkwardness was spared when Kate's sister-in-law, Stella – who had been dancing – came half-walking, half-dancing towards the threesome now as Roy Orbison's 'Pretty Woman' struck up. She took Kate by one hand and Frank by the other. 'Come on, birthday girl – up on the dance floor!'

Tara felt a wave of relief wash over her as they moved away. Thank goodness that little fracas had been stopped sooner rather than later. She sipped on the remainder of her drink, watching as the three of them danced to the lively tune.

Then, when a slower number came on, Stella joined Kate's and Frank's hands and left them to dance on their own.

'Is Kate all right?' Stella said, flopping into the chair next to Tara. 'I could see her getting a little fraught there. She's had too much to drink, of course, the poor thing.'

Tara looked over at Frank and Kate dancing cheek to cheek. 'I think she's grand now.'

'She's trying to hide it, but she's devastated about the engagement business,' Stella stated. 'I'm amazed myself. He could have bought her a decent-sized diamond for what he paid for those damned earrings.'

'Maybe it's not the right time,' Tara ventured. She picked up her handbag and held it in her lap, wondering when she could make a decent escape. So far, no one was showing any signs of leaving and she didn't want to be the first. As soon as someone else looked as though they were ready to go, she would discreetly ask for a taxi then locate her coat.

Stella sighed. 'Perhaps it will never be the right time.' She bent forward and whispered, 'Regardless of his good looks and all his money, maybe Frank Kennedy's not the right man for her.'

Chapter 35

Tara hadn't been in the hotel long the following morning when a call from Kate came through. Immediately, she knew the conversation could go one way or the other. She decided the decision would be Kate's.

'Hi, Kate,' she began. 'I was planning on ringing you later to thank you for a lovely, lovely night.'

'I am so sorry, Tara,' Kate said without any preamble. 'I don't know what came over me last night. I have no excuse. I simply drank too much and I can hardly remember half of what I said.'

Tara was very relieved. The last thing she wanted was an awkward situation with her friend. 'Don't worry about it,' she said in a comforting tone. 'My main feeling after the night was that I had a great time. Frank really pushed the boat out with the chef and the staff. I think it was one of the most elegant dinner parties I've ever been to.'

There was a pause, then Kate said, 'I'm afraid I must have seemed very ungrateful, making such a scene about the Grosvenor. Again, I can't remember all the details. Frank has been very gracious about it all.'

'We all do things like that from time to time,' Tara said reassuringly. 'And I'm sure Frank isn't the slightest bit bothered.' She gave a little exaggerated sigh. 'And anyway, between you and me, it might have wakened his ideas up a little. You know what men can be like about remembering to tell us things.'

There was a little silence. 'Thank you, Tara,' Kate said, 'I really appreciate you being so nice. And once again, I apologise for anything untoward I said. It won't happen again.'

Tara hung up and sat for a few moments, mulling the conversation over in her mind. Kate hadn't mentioned anything about not getting an engagement ring. But then, maybe that wasn't too surprising. She obviously felt embarrassed and awkward about the whole situation, and, in any case, perhaps an ex-girlfriend of Frank Kennedy's was not the person to open her heart to.

Later in the morning, Tara and William drove down to Maple Terrace to see Bridget.

After a few minutes, Tara began to get an uneasy feeling that all was not well. Apart from the fact she was quieter than usual, Bridget was pale, and there were dark shadows around her eyes.

Tara looked closely at her. 'Are you sure you don't mind me leaving William with you?' she checked.

'Sure, he'll be no trouble at all,' Bridget said. 'Michael and Helen were badgering me to let them take Lucky down to Alexander Park for a walk, so I'd feel better if William went with them. He's older and more sensible than those two, and he'll stop them arguing with each other.' She paused. 'To be honest, I could do with them getting out of the house for an hour or two, especially when the weather is sunny for a change. I'll be glad when they go back to school next week. It's hard to keep them occupied all the time when they're on holidays.'

'That's grand,' Tara said. She touched Bridget's arm. 'If you don't mind me saying, you look a bit washed-out this morning. Is everything OK?'

Bridget nodded wearily. 'It's just that I didn't sleep very well last night.' Then, before her friend could ask why, she quickly said, 'I'll try to get an hour's rest later, and let June carry on with the work on her own.'

'Is the business back home on your mind?' Tara asked, instinctively knowing how things like that worried her friend.

Bridget's mouth tightened. How could she tell Tara that Nora was only one of several things that were on her mind? How could she say that one of her worst nightmares looked as though it might actually come true? She already knew Tara's view on what had happened between herself and Lloyd, and there was no point in bringing her friend's disapproval down on her head by resurrecting the subject again.

'What good is worrying going to do?' she said quietly. 'It's not going to bring poor Nora back now, is it?'

'That's true,' Tara agreed, 'but I don't want you to let the whole thing get you down.' She looked down at Bridget's stomach. 'You need to take care of yourself, especially now.'

'I know.' She managed a weak smile. 'And don't be worrying about leaving William here; he'll be more of a help than a hindrance.'

As she drove through Davenport towards Mr Pickford's estate agency in Bramhall, Tara felt very unsettled. She had seen Bridget like this before, just after her old friend Ruby had died, and she didn't want to see her so low again. Then Tara reminded herself how bad she had felt when she lost Gabriel, and remembered how no one could comfort her. Things had to take their own course. And this tragic thing that had happened in Ballygrace was bound to affect her friend, bringing up feelings about her childhood and everything that went with it.

Tara would just have to be there to help pick up the pieces.

'Tara! Lovely to see you!' Mr Pickford said, coming around from his side of the desk to give her a slightly awkward kiss on the cheek. 'And what can I do to for you on this bright and sunny morning?'

Tara smiled back at the older man. She had grown very fond of him over the years, and there was no one else she felt she could trust so implicitly with all her financial dealings.

'I've actually come on behalf of a friend,' Tara told him, when they were both seated on either side of his desk. 'But if you don't mind, I thought I might just pick your brains on a couple of other matters while I'm here.'

'Fire away,' he said.

Tara went on to explain about Vera and the kind of property she was looking for. As soon as she was finished, Mr Pickford went out into the main office and, a few minutes later, came back with several sheets of house descriptions and photographs.

'These might just be of interest to your friend,' he told Tara. 'They are of a similar size to yours, but more modern.'

'I'm sure she'll be delighted to have something to start on,' Tara replied, putting the papers into her handbag. She looked at her old boss now. 'Have you heard anything about the Grosvenor Hotel going up for sale?'

'Of course,' Mr Pickford said, nodding vigorously. 'It caused quite a stir when the news was first announced. I only wish we were the estate agents representing the sale. I think it will fetch a tidy sum.' He paused, then leaned forward on his desk. 'Have you an interest in the hotel, Tara?'

Tara raised her eyebrows. 'I used to work on the reception desk in the Grosvenor some years back, so I suppose I have an onlooker's interest.'

'It's a fine hotel,' Mr Pickford said. Then an amused look came into his eyes. 'I don't suppose you were approached by any local businessmen who might be interested in forming a group to buy the hotel?'

Tara looked back at him in surprise, then she smiled. 'I should have known you would have heard. Don't tell me – has Mr Kennedy been in chatting to you again?'

'Ah, Tara,' the estate agent said, shaking his head, 'I'll never know what you have against Frank Kennedy. Your own countryman, *and* a gentleman, too.'

Tara took a deep breath and held it. She had never explained the extent of their relationship to her old boss, as she was sure it would only embarrass him. She also felt that it would be wrong to paint such a black, albeit truthful, picture of Frank to someone who thought so highly of him.

'To have such an astute businessman in your corner is a very valuable thing,' the estate agent went on. 'And never forget that if it hadn't been for his encouragement with your earlier property, you might never have progressed to buy your own hotel.'

'Yes,' Tara said, nodding, 'you're quite correct. Frank was indeed helpful to me at the time, but I can't keep being grateful to him for ever. And I can't have him constantly involved in all my business dealings.'

'Surely you wouldn't miss such a wonderful opportunity because of personal feelings?' he asked, an incredulous look on his face.

Tara was starting to feel uncomfortable. 'Taking Frank Kennedy out of the equation,' she stated, 'I'm just not in the same league as any of those men, both financially and in the world of business.'

'Well,' Mr Pickford said now, 'you are quite a bit younger than most of them, apart from Gerry McShane, of course.'

'Do you know him?' Tara asked, suddenly curious.

'I know all who are involved in the group,' he said, 'and they are decent, solid men.' He paused. 'Gerry McShane has legally represented a number of my clients, and he's straightforward and honest.'

Tara bent down to her handbag again and lifted out the envelope enclosing the documents about the Grosvenor. She slid the papers out and passed them across to Mr Pickford. 'What do you think of these figures?' she asked in a low, serious voice.

Mr Pickford leafed through the documents for a few minutes, then he sat back in his chair. 'It's a golden opportunity.'

'I know you'll be honest with me,' Tara said. 'Isn't it way, way out of my league?'

There was a small silence. 'At the time you bought the Cale Green Hotel, I wouldn't have recommended you aiming any higher, *but things have changed considerably since.*'

'In what way?' Tara asked.

'Well,' he said, 'you've now cut your teeth well in the property business. The hotel was a real challenge and you've risen to it admirably.'

'It came at the right time, and filled a terrible gap in my life,' she told him honestly.

'I know that, my dear,' he said kindly.

She paused. 'It's an awful lot of money. I just don't feel I'm brave enough to take the risk.'

'Oh, I think you could,' he stated. 'You have money tied up that you could release. I'm sure you mentioned substantial stocks and shares that you own.'

'They were Gabriel's,' Tara said. 'I've never touched them, and, to be honest, I don't even know what they're worth.' She gave a shrug. 'I've never needed to think about them, and when they were passed over to me, the bank in Ireland suggested I just leave them, for the time being.'

'I would check them out,' Mr Pickford advised. 'Your money might be worth much more invested in property like the Grosvenor.' He rubbed a finger on his chin, thinking. 'Perhaps you should also look at releasing capital from other properties ...'

Tara's face darkened. 'Not Ballygrace House?' she said. He had obviously been talking with Frank Kennedy about it already. 'You're not going to suggest I sell my home in Ireland?'

'Not at all,' he said quickly. 'I wouldn't dream of suggesting such a thing.'

Her features softened a little. 'Well, what are you suggesting?'

'I'm suggesting that you sell your houses in Cale Green to your friend.'

'Sell *both* houses?' Tara said in a surprised tone. She had briefly considered selling the semi-detached house next door, but felt it wouldn't bring in nearly enough to make any difference.

'You could solve two problems at one stroke.'

Tara sat back in her chair, a bemused look on her face. 'I would have a major problem selling *both* houses,' She said eventually. 'It would leave me with nowhere to live.'

Mr Pickford raised his eyebrows and there was a slight twinkle in his eyes. 'You could always rent your old room.' He paused. 'Think about it, Tara. This opportunity is unlikely to come around again.'

'But it would be a complete gamble,' Tara argued. 'Risking everything else I own, everything I've worked for …'

'Not *everything*,' the older man said pointedly. 'And it would be a very calculated risk.' He smiled. 'Do you really think that men like Frank Kennedy and Gerry McShane would involve themselves in a reckless business venture?'

There was a silence, then Tara suddenly said, 'I'm really not sure about all this … There's a part of me that feels it's just being greedy.' Her eyes flickered towards the window now. 'If the truth be told, I have more than enough money now, and I don't know if I want to put myself in an uncomfortable position just to make more.'

'But it's not just the money, my dear,' the estate agent said. 'The hotel trade is something you've made a career of. It's almost a way of life.' He paused, searching for the right words. 'You're an intelligent, capable young woman, and that particular group have asked you to join them for that very reason. They're not in it for charity. They know you have skills that would really benefit the whole venture.'

'But they could buy those skills in from interior decorating companies and the like,' Tara pointed out. 'And they could easily get another man to put in the fifth share. They don't need me.'

His eyes narrowed in thought. 'You know, they may well have more plans for you than you realise.'

'Such as?'

'Talk to them, Tara,' Mr Pickford advised, glancing at his watch.

Tara got to her feet. 'I really appreciate your time and your advice.'

'It's always there, Tara,' he told her with a warm, paternal smile. 'I've had great satisfaction from charting your business progress so far. From the houses to the hotel ...' He paused. 'And I shall enjoy watching your progress to the next venture, whenever and whatever that might be.'

Chapter 36

When Tara arrived back at the hotel, she was told that there was another message from Gerry McShane. Without waiting to think about it, she went into her office and dialled his number.

'Mrs Fitzgerald.' His tone was warm and very friendly. 'Thank you for returning my call.'

'I'm sorry I didn't get back to you sooner,' she told him, 'but I had a meeting that went on a little longer than I expected.'

'Of course, I know you're a very busy lady. I just wondered if you'd had a chance to read the proposal about the Grosvenor yet.'

'Yes,' she told him, 'I have looked at it.'

There was a short pause. 'I would really be interested in hearing your thoughts. I don't suppose you're free for dinner tonight?'

'*Tonight?*' Tara thought. She had planned to have a chat with Vera Marshall tonight, and then there was William to consider. Since coming back from Ireland she hadn't spent as much time with him as usual. But he was quite happy going up and down to Bridget's and the hotel, and she knew he would easily occupy his time.

'I thought we could perhaps eat at the restaurant in the Grosvenor,' he suggested. 'It wouldn't be too far for you to travel.'

'Actually, tonight's just fine,' Tara heard herself say. 'What time do you suggest?'

'I'm delighted you can make it,' he said. 'Would eight o'clock be all right? I can pick you up at the hotel or at your house at about quarter to.'

'I'll be at home,' she told him, and gave him the address.

When she put the phone down, Tara sat thinking for a few

moments. Had she made the right decision in accepting his offer? A little warning voice at the back of her head told her to be careful – to be *very* careful. It told her that she hadn't checked out Gerry McShane's marital situation. She had already been badly burned before, assuming that Frank Kennedy was a free man when he wasn't. She couldn't ever allow herself to walk into that particular lion's den again. And she wouldn't.

Perhaps she should have made enquiries about him, but how? She could hardly ring Mr Pickford, for example, to ask whether Gerry McShane was married or not. No, she reasoned, it wasn't the right way to go about it, and anyway, since she was having dinner with him tonight, it was too late now. She would deal with it in her own way and in her own time.

She picked the receiver up again and dialled Bridget's number.

'Sure, that's no trouble at all,' her friend told her when she asked if William could spend the evening at the boarding house. 'In fact, Fred was thinking of taking the lads to a football match tonight – just a local schoolboys match – and I was going to give you a ring to say that William could stay the night if he wanted.'

'I could pick him up on my way home,' Tara said.

'Oh, leave him for the night,' Bridget told her. 'By the time they get out from the match and walk up for a bag of chips it'll be late enough.'

'That would be great,' Tara agreed. They chatted for a few more minutes, and then just as she went to hang up, something in her friend's voice made her hold on. 'Bridget ... how are things? How are you feeling?'

There was a hesitation, which immediately warned her. 'I'm OK,' Bridget finally said. 'But I suppose I'm just that bit more tired than usual and a bit more ...'

'What?' Tara prompted. 'Are you still feeling down?'

'I suppose at times I am.'

Tara glanced at her watch. It was nearly one o'clock. 'Do you want me to come down to the house for a chat? I could take an hour or so off just now.'

'Not at all,' Bridget told her, her voice suddenly brighter. 'Sure, I'll be fine. Anyway, I have June coming in shortly to help me with the washing and ironing, so that'll keep me occupied and stop me brooding.'

'OK,' Tara said, 'I'll leave you to it then, but you will let me know if you're not feeling the best? Don't keep it to yourself. You know I'm always here if you need me for anything.'

'Of course I'll tell you,' Bridget said now. 'And thanks, Tara …'

Vera Marshall sat across from Tara at the dining-room table, scrutinising the house details on each sheet of paper. 'Interesting,' she commented every now and again. 'Very interesting.'

Tara smiled at her. 'Can I ask you something, Vera? Just out of curiosity …'

'Of course,' the teacher said, looking intrigued.

'If I offered to sell you *this* house, would you be interested?'

Vera's mouth opened in an 'O' of shock. 'Are you serious? Would you really consider selling it to me?'

Tara leaned her elbows on the table now and clasped her hands together. 'To tell you the truth, I'm not at all sure.' She paused, picking her words carefully. 'I've been offered a proposition myself – a business proposition and I would need to release some of my assets. At this stage, it's only a vague idea. I'm afraid I can't promise you anything definite.' Tara looked at her watch. 'I have a dinner appointment tonight, so I must go and get ready. I'll know more in a day or two, and I'll come back to you about it then.'

Tara went upstairs and ran a bath. Just as she went to step into the steaming water, she halted for a moment, then quickly wrapped a towel around herself and padded along to her bedroom. On a shelf in her wardrobe she located a bottle of expensive bath oil that Kate had brought her back from France, along with a matching perfume spray, which she would use when dressed. Then she went back in the bathroom and poured a generous measure of the oil into the hot water and spent the next half an hour luxuriating in the comforting, scented bath. It suddenly occurred to Tara, as she finished drying herself and applied body lotion, that she hadn't taken such care before going out for an evening since Gabriel had died, and the thought gave her a sudden jolt.

The fact was she had lived like a nun since she had become a widow.

She had buried everything that was feminine and vulnerable deep inside herself, and had thrown herself headlong into her work seven days a week. And the Cale Green Hotel had benefited from all the attention she had lavished on it, from the initial rebuild and renovation, to finding just the right furniture, curtains and cushions. And now, with all the right staff in place, an excellent chef in the kitchen and a good reputation established, Tara supposed that the time had come for her to take a few steps back and see how the business could manage with her in the background.

Whether it was the chat with Mr Pickford this morning about new ventures, she didn't know. But somehow, in a matter of a few hours, she had begun to feel that there was a small but very important part of her life that she had neglected for too long.

She moved towards the window and stood staring into the distance, her thoughts back in Ballygrace with the man who had been the centre of her world, whom she'd loved since she was a young girl. The man who was dead now. He would never return.

Tara stood silently for a good ten minutes, then she gave a huge, shuddering sigh and made herself move to her wardrobe to pick an outfit for her evening out.

Chapter 37

G erry McShane's Mercedes pulled up outside Tara's house at exactly quarter to eight. On hearing the car engine, she moved to the side of the bedroom window and watched him step from the car and make his way to the front door.

Vera answered it. 'Tara's just on her way down,' she said in a light tone, which Tara immediately knew was the result of their earlier conversation.

The door widened and, as Tara came down the staircase, she was suddenly aware of Gerry McShane's eyes firmly fixed on her. She felt herself start to blush.

'Lovely to see you again, Tara,' he said in a warm, friendly voice. He stretched out his hand to take hers in a firm, warm handshake. 'It's good of you to meet with me.'

*

The Grosvenor was much busier than Tara expected, with functions on in one of the cocktail bars and a golden wedding celebration in the main room. They were asked to wait in the lounge until their table was ready.

'I have to admit I suggested us having a meal on the spur of the moment,' Gerry McShane said as he guided her towards the lounge, 'but if I had planned it carefully in order to impress on you what a gold mine the hotel is, I couldn't have picked a better night.'

Tara looked up at him and caught a glint in his eye which made her smile. 'I'm not at all sure why I agreed to come,' she told him truthfully. 'And I still don't think it was one of my better judgements.'

'Nonsense,' he said, grinning at her now. 'How can you say that when they do the best food in town?' Then he clapped a hand over his mouth. 'Except for the Cale Green Hotel, of course.'

Tara found herself laughing along with his boyish sense of humour. As they turned into the lounge bar, she caught sight of them both in the large gilt mirror at the door and was immediately taken aback at the reflection that presented itself at that precise moment. A well-dressed, handsome couple who looked perfectly at ease. A couple who were obviously enjoying each other's company. A couple who were out on a date.

A wave of guilt washed over her that she could actually feel so light-hearted in another man's company. The smile disappeared and her face became stiff and serious, as they walked across the bar to a quiet corner table. When Gerry McShane went to the bar to order their drinks Tara found herself feeling self-conscious in case she met anyone she knew, who might think she was behaving like a merry widow.

And yet, a little voice inside argued, she could no longer live the sterile, cloistered life she had become so used to. She had to move back into the world, and that included mixing socially with men.

Gerry McShane came back to the table now with a long gin and tonic for Tara and a brandy for himself. If he noticed any change in her mood, he did not refer to it, and instead launched straight into a discussion about Tara's previous involvement with the hotel.

'I was only an employee,' she told him, lest he have any misconceptions about her very mundane role. 'A receptionist.'

The surprise was evident in his eyes. 'Well, you have to start somewhere,' he said, smiling. 'Although it's hard to imagine you in such a ... well, *ordinary* position. Everything about you speaks of elegance and good breeding.'

Tara smiled and said nothing. Her background was her own business and she wasn't about to reveal it to a total stranger.

'Going in at the ground level must have given you a good insight into what works in the hotel and what doesn't.'

Tara shrugged and took a sip of her drink. 'It gave me a good enough grounding to build up a small place like the Cale Green Hotel, and I'm thankful for that.'

He studied her for a moment. 'Have you given any real thought to joining our takeover group?'

'I have,' Tara said, avoiding his gaze. 'And I still don't think I have anything to offer you. Even if I could come up with the money, I'm not sure if it would all be worth it in the end. It's a very big gamble, and I don't think I'm brave enough for it. Maybe in five years' time, when I know how my own hotel has shaped up financially.'

'But you can't lose,' he reassured her. 'Whatever happens with the business itself, the price of the property will surely increase over the next few years. Even if you just sit it out, you'll reap the financial rewards.' He lifted his brandy glass and took a sip from it.

Tara looked at him now. 'I wouldn't be in the same financial position as the other members of the group. Even if I freed up any assets I have to come up with the investment price, I would still have to use money that is set aside as a safety net for the Cale Green Hotel.' She paused, frowning deeply. 'And while I'm not exactly a spendthrift, I've been used to having money available for travelling and maintaining the houses and car and so on.'

Gerry McShane put his drink back on the table and looked squarely at her. 'Of course you have. We all have a certain lifestyle to maintain, and that needn't change.'

'But it will,' she said adamantly, 'if I don't have the same money available.'

'I have a proposal to put to you,' he told her. 'How would it be if the rest of the group were to offer you a salaried position in the hotel?'

'In what capacity?' she asked, suddenly curious.

'A managerial position, to oversee the refurbishment,' he explained, 'and to ensure that the high standard we need is achieved, then a day-to-day job when we have the hotel up and running.' He smiled.

'It would be a good salary, Tara, and it would easily cover all your needs.'

'But I still have my own hotel to run,' she countered, her voice rising in surprise. 'I couldn't possibly manage two businesses at the same time.'

'Put a part-time manager in place at the Cale Green,' Gerry told her. 'It would only be half the wages and you wouldn't need anyone full-time if you're in and out of the place on a regular basis.'

Tara looked at him for a few moments without speaking. 'You seem to have all the answers already worked out.'

He gave a broad smile. 'I can't take all the credit for the suggestion,' he told her. 'I had a chat with the others when you were away. We anticipated some of your reasoning and came up with the idea of you taking the managerial post.' He spread his hands wide on the table. 'If you can raise your share of the investment money, then we can move things on very quickly. It's just a case of drawing up the final papers.' He looked directly at her now. 'We've delayed things for the last few weeks to give you time to sort things out.'

'And if I decide not to join you,' Tara said, 'presumably you have someone else lined up to take my place?'

'No,' Gerry McShane said, shaking his head. 'We were going ahead with four members until you were suggested, so that would still be the case.' He raised his eyebrows. 'We decided we needed your particular talents, and if we can't have them, then I suppose, sadly, we'll have to go ahead without you.'

Tara nodded. 'I'll have a decision for you by tomorrow,' she told him, a note in her voice indicating that the conversation was now closed.

A few moments later, the restaurant manager came through to tell them that their table was ready.

Seated in a quiet corner, Tara found herself chatting easily with Gerry, as they looked at the wine list and the menu. An hour later they had just finished their main course and were still chatting. Gerry told her all about his late father who came from Athlone. 'I have uncles and cousins still living in Ireland,' he explained, 'and I'm always promising myself that I'll go over sometime.'

'It's a nice town,' Tara told him, 'built on the banks of the Shannon river. It has a lot of history – there's a Norman Castle in the centre of the town.'

'It sounds very impressive,' he said. 'Maybe I should combine a trip to Dublin with one to Athlone.' He paused. 'Do you go back to Ireland often yourself?'

'Not as often as I should.' Tara felt her throat tighten, then she suddenly heard herself ask, 'Do you have children?' Having asked the question that had been burning at the back of her mind, she then tried to cover up her motive by babbling on. 'The castle is always very popular with them, as well as Clonmacnoise, an old monastic place on the river.'

He looked at her for a moment, then gave a small laugh. 'I've no children that I'm aware of ... or a wife for that matter.'

Tara suddenly blushed, knowing that she had approached the subject with all the tact of a bull at a gate. But it had achieved her objective and that was better than the alternative of not knowing. 'Oh, I'm sorry, that came out wrong ... I didn't mean to sound as if I was asking your personal business. I only meant that Athlone was an interesting place for all ages, and I know that children often go there on school tours and that sort of thing.'

He leaned across and lightly touched the back of her hand with his fingers. 'What you said was perfectly fine,' he said, grinning at her. 'I suppose most men my age are married with families.'

Tara slid her hand away. 'But that's not my business,' she said, rolling her eyes in embarrassment. 'I shouldn't have said it or presumed—'

'I would feel a bit strange having dinner with you if I were a married man.'

'Well, it's only a *business* dinner, isn't it?' Tara said lightly.

'We have indeed been discussing business.' He lowered his voice now. 'But if it had been purely business we could have discussed it during the day in an office.' He smiled again. 'Looking across the table at a beautiful, sophisticated woman certainly adds another dimension to the evening – and that was the reason I suggested it.'

Tara looked back at him and felt herself starting to relax. 'Thank you,' she said, inclining her head and smiling. 'I shall take that as a very nice compliment.'

Later that night, after being dropped off at her front door by Gerry McShane, Tara was mounting the stairs when Vera came rushing out of the kitchen.

'Tara,' she said, slightly breathless, "you had a call from your mother-in-law."

Tara's heart gave a little start. 'Is there anything wrong?' The memory of the phone call from Elisha telling her that Gabriel had died was still deeply ingrained.

'She said to tell you that all was very well at her end, and that she was just enquiring how things were with you and William.'

'Grand,' Tara said, heaving a little sigh of relief. 'I'll ring her in the morning when William's back from Bridget's and she can chat to him then.'

There was a pause. 'I know we only spoke today,' the older woman said, 'but I'm really very excited about the house.'

Tara nodded slowly. 'I've been thinking about it a lot. As I said, I should have a decision for you very soon.'

She continued up the stairs, spent a short while on her usual nightly ablutions, then switched on her bedside lamp and got into bed. She lifted a magazine from the small bedside cabinet and started flicking through it, but her mind was only half on the pictures and the features.

Unable to concentrate, she gave up reading and switched off the lamp, then lay in the dark thinking about the Grosvenor, trying to look at it from every possible angle.

Soon, her thoughts moved on to Gerry McShane. Was she ready to start seeing another man? She closed her eyes and willed herself to sleep.

Chapter 38

Tara woke early the following morning, feeling unusually light and positive, and full of anticipation about the day ahead.

The fact that the businessmen involved in buying the Grosvenor Hotel were prepared to offer her a job, to go out on a limb to have her join them, had definitely made her feel good about herself and her business skills. She instinctively knew that this was nothing to do with Frank Kennedy, because the whole venture was much too big and expensive for personal feelings to hold any sway. She had achieved the respect of these men solely by her hard work and business reputation.

The night out with Gerry McShane had confirmed that. The way he had talked to her as a business equal, and had implied that the other men of the group thought of her in the same way, had suddenly hit home. She realised that she was being paid a great compliment, and it pleased her because she had never really stopped to wonder how other people viewed her before.

Of course, her female friends, like Bridget and Kate, had always been effusive in their praise of her property dealings, and had been amazed and delighted when she bought the Cale Green Hotel, but it meant that bit more when the praise came from seasoned business-men.

She threw back the bedcovers, deciding to get into the bathroom before the other women in the house were up and about. She bathed, washed her hair and was out of the bathroom before she heard Angela move around.

Tara had a busy day ahead. She had a lot of paperwork and phone calls to catch up with at work, and she wanted to check out Gabriel's stocks and shares with her accountant. Then, when she had all the relevant information, she was going to have another chat to Mr Pickford.

It was also William's last full day in Stockport before heading back to London, so she wanted to do something special with him. He would wander up from Bridget's late morning, and then they would have lunch in the hotel, which he always enjoyed. Angela was on a split shift and said she would take him for a game of tennis in Davenport in the afternoon, and then they would go into Manchester to the theatre or cinema in the evening.

As soon as Tara got into work, she decided to ring Elisha Fitzgerald. Normally, she would have waited so that she could speak to William, but something made her ring her mother-in-law before he arrived at the hotel.

'Tara, dear,' Elisha said, in her quiet, reserved tone. 'How are things with you? Did the trip to Ireland go well?'

'Perfectly,' Tara replied. There was no point in going into the details about the discovery of Nora's body, as Elisha was unlikely to know or remember any local people. 'William has had a very nice, very busy time. He's up at Bridget's boarding house this morning, and we're hoping to go to a show tonight.'

'Wonderful,' Elisha said. 'You're so good to have him.' She paused. 'Now that he's older, it's not always easy to find things to occupy him, but you seem to cope admirably. I have to admit there are times when Harry and I don't quite know what to do with him. We try to keep him busy with tennis and swimming and that sort of thing.'

'He is getting older,' Tara agreed. 'But luckily he enjoys helping around the hotel and he's actually going off for a game of tennis this afternoon with my younger sister.'

'How is the hotel going, dear?' Elisha asked. She had been surprised and more than a little cautious when Tara initially suggested buying the Cale Green Hotel, but had come around when she recognised that it filled a void in her daughter-in-law's life. And lately she had been positively effusive when she saw what a success Tara had made of it.

'Very well,' Tara replied, then, something made her suddenly say, 'Actually, Elisha, there's something I wouldn't mind your advice on – and maybe Harry's opinion, too.'

'Certainly, if I can be of any help,' her mother-in-law said.

'I've been asked to join a business consortium to take over the Grosvenor Hotel in Stockport,' Tara explained. 'It the biggest and busiest hotel in the area, and my share in it would be in the region of twenty thousand pounds.'

'My goodness!' Elisha said, seemingly lost for words for a moment. 'That's an awful lot of money ...' Her voice trailed away, revealing her concern.

'It will cover buying the hotel and the cost of a complete renovation and refurbishment,' Tara went on. 'It's a very imposing building and the work has to be of the highest standard.'

'I see,' Elisha said, sounding very hesitant again. 'I'm not quite sure what to say to you, Tara, because, in all honesty, I was concerned when you bought your own small hotel, and, of course, it's turned out to be a wonderful investment. I'm not really the person to give advice or encouragement on these matters.' She paused for a moment, then she said, 'Can I put Harry on to you for a moment? He's been listening to my side of the conversation, and looks very eager to chat to you.'

207

'Hello, my dear.' Harry's warm voice was good to hear. 'Your conversation with Elisha sounded most intriguing. I'd love to hear all about it.'

Tara sat back comfortably in her office chair and related the whole story, including possibly selling both her houses to Vera Marshall.

'My word!' Harry exclaimed. 'You don't go in for things by halves, do you? What an exciting project to be part of.'

'I haven't made any decisions yet,' she said, laughing. 'I'm still counting the pennies and adding up the figures.'

'Selling the houses will certainly give you a good start,' he told her, 'and presumably your portfolio of shares will be worth even more than that?'

Tara frowned. 'I don't know about that. I'm meeting with my accountant this afternoon.'

'But, Tara,' Harry said, 'didn't you check out how much you made on the Woolcott takeover last year?'

'Harry,' Tara interrupted, 'I'm afraid I haven't the faintest notion about shares.'

'My dear girl,' Harry sounded almost breathless, 'Gabriel was left a large number of those shares by his aunt, so you should have made a killing when Woolcott was taken over. The shares absolutely zoomed up. Elisha had some, and a number were signed over to young William, and I know she was absolutely delighted when she realised how much they were worth last year. I believe they've gone up more since then.'

Tara sat up straight in her chair now. 'Gabriel dealt with all those things. And after he ... well, later, I passed everything on to our accountant.'

'Tara, check it all out with him this afternoon,' Harry advised. 'I have a feeling that you're going to be very pleasantly surprised.'

Chapter 39

❧❧❧

William arrived at the hotel mid-morning, full of the great football match he, Fred and Michael had been to the night before. After she had caught up on some of the backlog of work in the office, Tara suggested that he have a look at yesterday's issue of the *Manchester Evening News* to see what was on in the cinema or theatre. 'It will be in the bar or the kitchen,' Tara said. 'They usually save the newspapers for the cleaner to put on the floor when it's just been washed.'

William went off into the bar in search of the newspaper. A few minutes later he came rushing back. 'Tara, there's a Beatles film on in the cinema in Stockport – *A Hard Day's Night*.'

Tara looked at him quizzically. 'Didn't you see it down in London when it came out?'

He shook his head. 'I never got the chance. Mother said it was a load of rubbish and not suitable for younger people. She thinks bands like the Beatles are a bad influence.' He looked downcast. 'I feel a bit of a baby in school when I say I haven't seen it yet, and I'd feel really stupid if the other boys knew it's because I'm not allowed to go. Even boys who are younger than me have seen it.'

Tara took a deep breath, immediately wondering what Gabriel would have done. 'OK,' she told him, deciding to go with her instincts. 'Let's go and see it tonight.' She smiled at him. 'It came out nearly two years ago, so I reckon you're old enough to see it now.'

'Oh, brilliant ...' William said, hardly able to believe his luck.

Tara nodded towards reception. 'Why don't you ask Angela if she'd like to join us? It's the sort of thing she really likes.'

'I'll go and ask her now,' William said.

As she mulled over the situation, Tara decided that if Elisha found out about their outing to the cinema, then she would just have to stand her ground and say that she felt William was almost an adult and needed to be treated as such. She would say that all the boys in his class had probably seen these films and it was only normal for him to want to be the same.

Whether Angela would be interested in going to the film with her

209

older sister and a younger boy was another matter, but there was no harm in asking. She knew William liked Angela and she was much nearer his age, so more likely to know all the Beatles music and any interesting information about them.

From the scant snatches she had heard on the radio and television, Tara liked the music very much, but she just didn't have the time to sit down and listen properly to the Beatles, the Rolling Stones or any other band. Even Bridget was more up to date on things like that, and could chat to younger girls about all the new hits in the Top Ten.

Tara gave a little sigh now, suddenly feeling old, and yet, deep down, she knew she wasn't that different from how she was at Angela's age.

A short while later William came back again, grinning from ear to ear. 'She said she'd love to come,' he told Tara. 'She's already seen it twice but said it's one of her favourite films.'

'Well, that's good news,' Tara said. She checked the newspaper. 'The film is on at eight o'clock, so if we book into the restaurant for six, that should give us plenty of time to get there for the start of the film.'

'I can't wait,' William said, adding, 'I'm really, really grateful, Tara, for all the things you've planned for me. I've had a fantastic holiday with you – here and in Ireland. I always do completely different things with you than I do with my mother and Harry. I feel so much more grown up here.'

'I'm glad you've enjoyed yourself, William,' she said warmly.

After a sandwich lunch in the bar, Tara suggested she and William take a quick drive down to Stockport, as William wanted to buy some small gifts for his mother and Harry. Tara had already bought a bottle of Tullamore Dew whiskey for Harry and a bottle of an Irish liqueur for Elisha for him to take back, but he wanted to pick something himself.

They walked around the town looking in different shops and eventually, with Tara's guidance, William settled on a lovely silk scarf in soft spring colours for Elisha and a nice tie for Harry.

'Practical and easy to carry,' Tara said approvingly. She checked her watch. 'I'm afraid I'm going to have to get back to the office. I've a few calls to make and then I have a meeting.'

'Do you mind if I stay in Stockport for a bit longer?' William asked. 'I'd like to get Bridget and the children something for having me to stay.'

'There's no need for that,' Tara told him, although she was pleased that he was mature enough to have thought of it. 'But if you want a bit of time on your own, then I'll meet you back at the hotel later on.'

Tara dashed off then, conscious of all the things she had to do. While she had enjoyed her time with William, she knew it was now time for her to catch up with her own life.

As she drove past Bridget's road, Tara was tempted to pull in for a quick chat, but decided against it. She went straight on to the hotel and into her office. She picked up the phone and dialled Mr Pickford's number.

'It's Tara,' she said, in a low, slightly anxious voice when she was put through to his office. 'I'm sorry for disturbing you again, but I needed to check something with you ...' She swallowed hard. 'Do you really, really think that the Grosvenor Hotel is worth investing in?'

'Definitely,' he told her, without a moment's hesitation. 'You won't get a chance like this again.'

Later that afternoon, Tara came out of her accountant's office, her mind reeling with information about stocks and shares.

But she knew one thing for certain.

If she wanted to be a part of the Grosvenor Hotel takeover, the money was there.

As she drove up through Shaw Heath, Tara decided to pull in at Bridget's for a few minutes, even though she was tight for time. She caught her friend having a break after clearing up from lunch.

'You're sure I'm not disturbing you?' Tara asked, following her into the sitting-room.

'Not a bit of it,' Bridget said. 'I was only half-watching a television programme. June went out to the greengrocer's to give our vegetable order in for the week, and she took Lucy and the dog with her to give them a bit of a walk.'

She walked over to the television now and switched it off, then sat down on the sofa while Tara chose an armchair opposite.

'I'm pleased you're having a break,' Tara told her. 'And I definitely think you're looking better. You're not as tired around the eyes.'

'I feel better,' Bridget said. 'June's coming in more often and I'm sleeping better, too, so it all helps.' She smiled, hoping that she sounded more convincing than she actually felt, because the image of Lloyd holding Lucy in her arms was still haunting her when she went to bed at night and when she woke in the middle of the night. 'And I've got next weekend to look forward to.'

'Blackpool? Is it next weekend already?' Tara said. 'Gosh, that's come up fairly quick. It seemed ages away when Fred first mentioned it.'

Bridget nodded. 'I feel exactly the same, but I'm really looking forward to it now. It'll get me away from everything for a few days – a change of scenery, like. And at this time of the year it shouldn't be too rowdy. They won't be into the full summer season yet.' She suddenly halted. 'I'm very bad-mannered, Tara – I never even asked if you'd like a cup of tea.'

'No, no,' Tara said, waving away her friend's offer. 'I've really only stopped to ask your advice about something ...'

'Go on,' Bridget prompted, all ears now. She loved it when Angela, June and especially Tara asked her opinion. It made her feel valued and trusted, and helped to take the edge off the horrible way she felt about herself at times.

Tara clasped her hands together and took a deep breath. 'The Grosvenor Hotel ...'

Bridget's eyes widened. 'You don't mean ...' She put her hands over her mouth and gave a high-pitched giggle, the way she used to do when she and Tara were young girls starting out in the world and everything new was an adventure. 'You don't mean you're actually thinking of buying into it?'

Tara nodded her head. 'I've just been to see my accountant,' she said, 'and, with a bit of juggling around, it would seem I can afford a fifth share in it.'

'Oh, my God ...' Bridget said. 'I don't believe it.'

'It means selling both houses and working as a manageress in the Grosvenor.' Tara gazed at her friend for a few moments, scrutinising her face for any negative reaction. 'It's taking a big chance.'

'Where will you live?' Bridget asked.

'Vera Marshall is buying both houses,' Tara explained, 'and she has said that I can continue living there, have my usual bedroom et cetera. The only change is that I will be a boarder there instead of the owner.'

Bridget nodded, trying to take in this astounding information. 'And how will you manage to run your own hotel and work in the Grosvenor?'

'I would have to employ a part-time manager in the Cale Green Hotel,' she explained, 'and I would just catch up with things in the evenings and weekends.'

Bridget shook her head. 'Won't you kill yourself running back-wards and forwards? You'll hardly have time to call your own.'

'What else do I have to do with my time?' Tara said quietly. 'And it would only be for a few years, until the Grosvenor is up and running under the new ownership.' She suddenly smiled. 'When you think of it, you're on the go from morning until night in Maple Terrace, and you have a husband and children to take care of as well.' She gave a little shrug. 'I've only myself to look after.'

Bridget knew that Tara would love to have children of her own. She nodded. 'I can understand ... when you put it like that.' She suddenly grinned. 'Oh, Tara! Can you imagine yourself waltzing around in the Grosvenor Hotel knowing that you own the place? A huge, posh place like that?' She shook her head, laughing. 'Can you just *imagine* it?'

Tara rang Harry with the news about the shares. 'I knew it!' he said, thoroughly delighted. He paused. 'Do you have the money you need now?'

'Yes,' she told him, 'but I'm still not sure.'

'Tara,' he said, 'it sounds a wise investment to me. If I were younger and asked to join the group, I would jump at the chance.'

'Really?' Tara said.

'Definitely, and so would Gabriel Fitzgerald.'

There was a small silence.

'I'm afraid I might regret it,' Tara said eventually.

'Don't be afraid,' Harry told her. 'The biggest regrets that people have in life are the things that they *don't* have the courage to do.' He gave a chuckle. 'You've never struck me as a quitter, Tara.'

'But I've never been in this kind of position before,' she argued. 'It's much bigger than anything I ever contemplated.'

'Go for it,' he told her. 'That's what Gabriel would want.'

Chapter 40

W hen Vera returned home from school, Tara sat down with her in the privacy of the dining-room and told her that she was prepared to sell the house in Cale Green to her, and that, if she were interested, the house next door was going up for sale as well.

There was a few moments' silence.

'Yes, Tara … I'm going to say *yes*.' She looked up at Tara with determined eyes. 'I've never taken a chance in the whole of my life, and this time I'm going to do it. I have enough to buy this one outright, and a mortgage will cover the other one. If I don't buy them, someone else will snatch them up.'

'When you do buy the house, will you allow me one thing?' Tara said.

'Of course. What is it?'

'That I can still have my piano here.'

The older woman laughed, too. 'I was actually going to make that a condition of the sale. I shouldn't imagine I'll have any money left over to buy one of my own.'

Tara dialled the number, her hand trembling.

'Tara,' Gerry McShane said as soon as he heard her voice. 'I was hoping to hear from you.'

'I've decided to accept the group's offer' she said, 'I'd be delighted to buy a share in the Grosvenor Hotel.'

'That's wonderful news,' he said, his voice warm. 'And I know the other members will feel the same.'

'I have my full share,' Tara said, 'but, having thought about it, I'm still interested in the managerial post you suggested. Is that offer still open?'

'It certainly is,' he replied. 'It's a two-way thing. It means we have someone working for us who has the same vested interest in the business as we have ourselves.'

'Good,' Tara said. She paused, all sots of things running through her mind. 'So, what do I have to do now?' she asked, trying to not sound anxious or show that she felt out of her depth. 'How long do I have to sort out the finances?'

'That, I think, will require another night out to dinner with copious amounts of champagne to celebrate,' he said light-heartedly. 'But unfortunately for me, we will not be alone on this occasion. The other three members will insist on being there, so we'll all have to share your charms.'

'May I remind you,' Tara said lightly, 'that this is all strictly business.'

He gave a little chuckle. 'I'll get back to you shortly with arrangements for our next meeting.'

After she put the phone down, Tara walked into the dining-room and went to stand by the window, her arms folded across her chest and a thoughtful look on her face. She remembered quite clearly how she had felt when she bought this house. The feeling of excitement and anticipation. The sense that she'd achieved something huge all on her own.

She thought back to the hard work she had put in. Working days in the estate agency, giving piano lessons in the evenings, and then working on reception in the Grosvenor Hotel at the weekends. Hour after hour of hard work. But it had paid great dividends. Saving up for the houses had given her a goal, a reason to get up every morning, and to keep going when things were hard. Then later, more hard work and careful planning had paid for the Cale Green Hotel. And that had been her saviour when Gabriel died. It had got her through the long, dark, empty days and even longer nights.

And now the Grosvenor Hotel would fill the gap that a husband and family filled for most women. And although it was only a substitute, Tara knew it was as good a substitute as she could ever hope to find.

She moved away from the window now and her gaze fell on the polished baby grand piano. Inevitably her thoughts turned to Frank Kennedy, since he had bought it for her.

He had been part of her life when she had moved into this house, and had played a major role in the purchase of it and the house next door. And although she hated to admit it, even to herself, there was always the question of whether or not she would have been brave enough to buy the houses if it had not been for his encouragement and support.

She looked at the piano now and bit her lip. She had taken some time to decide about the Grosvenor, and although finance had been the main obstacle, if she were completely honest with herself, Frank Kennedy had been another.

Being involved with him in a business venture seriously rankled with her. But she knew that to have turned down this opportunity would have been cutting off her nose to spite her face, although her worst instincts would have made her do exactly that. But something had made her rise above the connection with Frank, and, whatever happened, she would continue to do that.

As always, business would come first.

Fortuitously, Tara thought, she now had a connection with one of the other members that would help to keep Frank at a good arm's length. Gerry McShane had made it obvious that he liked her, and if she were careful in her handling of the situation, he could be a good ally.

Tara had also noted that the other two members of the group had been very serious businessmen, and she instinctively knew that they would not be happy if Frank caused any kind of friction between himself and her. All in all, she felt it was a safe enough risk, and it might just show him that she didn't regard him as being any different from the other men in the group. That he was just another business-man.

That he was nothing special.

Chapter 41

Although she felt a little wave of relief when she'd put William on the train back to London, in the days following his depar-ture Tara found she missed having him around. He had filled the weeks over the Easter period, and she had got into a routine with their outings to the cinema and into town.

After she had spoken to Joe about the incident in Dublin – and felt reassured by his take on it – she had put aside any awkward feel-ings and settled back into her old, comfortable way with her young brother-in-law. Tara had been surprised and very touched by a lovely thank you gift of a Parker pen engraved with her name, which he'd bought for her on his shopping trip into town. 'You shouldn't have spent your money on me,' she had told him, but her delight was evident.

After William had gone, Tara knew it was time to focus all her attention on her forthcoming business venture. Her future, and most of what she owned, would certainly depend upon it.

As she was leaving for work one morning, Tara bumped into the postman at the gate and he gave her two letters with Irish stamps. One for her and one for Angela. A quick glance told her that her own letter was from Kitty. She put the other letter in her handbag to give to Angela when she arrived at the hotel. Her sister had been on the early reception shift and had left for work an hour before.

Tara hesitated at the door for a few moments, then she quickly walked back into the empty sitting-room and opened her letter. It was only two pages long and contained one piece of news, but it told her all she needed to know.

The police reports back in Ireland showed that Nora had committed suicide. Her well-preserved remains, thanks to the peaty bog, showed that her wrists had been repeatedly slashed and that a large quantity of aspirin mixed with alcohol had been taken.

The one piece of good news about the affair was that Bridget would not have to attend an inquest, as the verdict had been open.

Tara paced up and down for a few minutes, wondering what to do. Bridget was due to go away for her little break soon. She had improved recently, but if Tara told her this news, it might set her back.

She would have to think about it very carefully.

Angela's eyes lit up when Tara handed her the letter. She took it from her, scanning the postmark and the handwriting.

'No need to ask who it's from,' Tara said, giving her a wry little smile. She put her handbag on the reception desk.

'I've had one nearly every day since I've got back,' Angela said, a blush rising to her cheeks. 'Aiden's a great writer. He tells me everything he's been doing all day, and all that's going on in Offaly.'

'He's certainly keen,' Tara said, lingering at the desk. Since Angela had told her all about Aiden Byrne on the boat, the relationship between the half-sisters had been the warmest it had ever been. Whether it was her new romance or something else, Angela seemed suddenly to have matured, and Tara found she could now talk to her in a way she'd never been able to before. 'Have you heard anything from home?' Tara asked now. 'Any news about my father and Tessie?'

Angela shrugged. 'No,' she said, shaking her head. 'But that's not unusual. My mother only writes every few weeks. The last letter said that Dad was on new tablets and seemed a lot better.'

Tara decided to confide in Angela. 'I had a letter from Kitty this morning about Nora ...'

Angela's eyes widened. 'That girl that was found in the bog in Ballygrace?'

Tara nodded. 'It seems she committed suicide.'

Angela's hands flew to her mouth. 'Oh, my God ...'

'I'm worried about how Bridget will react to it.'

'Don't tell her until she comes back from Blackpool,' Angela said instinctively. 'You don't know what she might do – she could decide not to go at all.'

Tara slowly nodded. 'I was thinking the very same thing myself.'

'Oh, the poor girl,' Angela said. 'Her mind must have been tormented to do such a terrible thing.'

'Obviously I'm very sad about it, but I didn't really know her,' Tara explained. 'It doesn't have the same effect on me as it will have on Bridget. She was more or less brought up with Nora.'

'It's shocking news all right,' Angela said. She turned her letter over in her hands, then put it down flat on the reception desk and ran her fingers lightly across the address, as though she were reading in Braille.

Tara noticed the little gesture and realised that, while she had shown interest in the depressing news, Angela was desperate to read her letter. She lifted her handbag. 'If any of the girls are passing the desk,' she said, 'would you ask them to drop me in a cup of coffee, please?'

Angela lifted the phone receiver. 'I'll do better,' she said, smiling. 'I'll ring the kitchen and ask them to do it straight away.'

Tara realised she had moved into a much higher league when she sat down for a lunchtime meeting in the Grosvenor Hotel with her four business colleagues. A large round table had been set for them in a private room off the main dining area, so that they would not be disturbed, nor their conversation overheard.

There was none of the light-hearted banter that had been present on the previous occasion, and Gerry McShane, who was sitting in the chair to the right of her, had the demeanour of a much more sober, serious man than the one she had dined with the week before.

Eric Simmons, the balding architect and the quietest in the group, was sitting to Tara's left, while John Burns and Frank Kennedy sat opposite her. The men were all dressed in their usual dark business suits, and Tara had carefully selected a conservative dark grey coat for the meeting, which she had teamed with a fine-wool, grey sweater dress and pearls. She had tied her curly hair back with a large pearl clasp, and kept her make-up light enough to be natural, highlighting her green eyes with a subtle grey eye-shadow and mascara, and using a slick of pale lipstick on her full lips. She had finished with a very light spray of Madame Rochas, feeling that the flowery fragrance was just enough to impress her feminine difference upon the men.

'Gerry has gone over all the legal documents that have been drawn up,' John Burns told the group without any preamble. 'We've hammered out any points that weren't clear or satisfactory, and Gerry reckons that everything is now as it should be, and that we can go ahead and sign.' The older man paused now, his eyes serious as he looked over his half-rimmed reading glasses. 'Has anyone any points they want to raise at this stage?'

Tara felt a knot in the pit of her stomach, a physical acknowledgement of the enormity of the step she was about to take by signing these papers. It was the biggest financial step she had ever taken in her life. And, as she glanced around the group, she remembered that it wasn't the same for the others. Gerry McShane had told her that they had all been involved in big financial deals before. The Grosvenor might be her first rung on the major business ladder, but it certainly wasn't theirs.

From the first time she met Frank Kennedy she knew that he was a naturally skilled and shrewd businessman. Over the years, despite her personal feelings about him, she had been deeply impressed by his talent for spotting a good investment, as well as his ability to keep his nerve when things looked as though they were heading in the wrong direction.

A few years ago he had bought a dance hall in Manchester, only to find that it had been a front for an illegal gambling den. He had spent a good many nights, over a period of months, turning the whole venture around. He had refused to give into the thugs that were running the place, and, after hiring the right doormen, had joined them weekend after weekend in turning the undesirables away until they eventually gave up and moved on. That was Frank Kennedy's way. When he made up his mind to do something, he saw it through to the end.

As Tara glanced at Frank from under her lowered eyelashes now, she realised that she probably wouldn't have considered this venture if he hadn't been a part of it. And while Gerry McShane had been the one who had encouraged and coaxed her in the end, it had been Frank who had initially suggested that she join the business group.

For all she didn't want anything to do with him on a personal basis, she knew that he would not be involved in a venture of this enormity if it were not a solid investment. Subconsciously, she realised, she had probably been swayed by that very fact.

As John Burns handed around the individual business contracts, Tara told herself that once the hotel was up and running under the new ownership, there would be no need for any contact with Frank Kennedy. She would keep him at the same arm's length she had always done, only discussing business with him when there was a group meeting. And if he tried to ingratiate himself any further, Tara would very quickly put him in his place. It was the way she had learned to handle him, and it worked.

When Tara's contract was placed in front of her, she reached down to the side of her chair for her handbag and found William's pen. She had brought it with her for this very purpose, feeling that the gift, which had been so warmly given, might bring familiarity to a serious situation.

When the business of signing the contracts was over, the serious mood prevailed until all the issues pertaining to the takeover were discussed, including Tara's managerial role in the day-to-day running of the hotel.

'Tara, we'll have a starting date for you as soon as the contracts have been cleared and the deeds passed into our keeping,' Gerry McShane told her. 'Which should be within the next week or so.'

'Grand. I'm ready to start as soon as I'm given the go-ahead,' she replied in a confident, steady voice, which belied the trepidation she felt at now being responsible for the prestigious hotel in which she had worked as a young girl. She had already decided to appoint a manager in the Cale Green Hotel.

Gerry McShane looked around the group. 'And presumably Tara can get going with any refurbishment that's necessary for the main part of the hotel, which will stay open for business, while the building work commences on the new extension?'

Frank Kennedy studied the solicitor. 'How are *you* proposing that we handle the refurbishment if *we're* open for business?' he said, with an edge to his voice.

She glanced around the other members to see if they had picked upon the unspoken challenge, which quite clearly objected to Gerry McShane's right to make unilateral decisions. But Tara knew that he was also questioning the solicitor's right to decide what Tara would or would not be doing in her management capacity.

'Presumably,' Gerry stated, unflinching under Frank's scrutiny, 'we'll have a meeting to decide all that as soon as we have the deeds.'

Frank raised his dark eyebrows then nodded, satisfied that he'd made his point.

'Right,' John Burns said, clapping his hands and then rubbing them together. 'That's the business part of the lunch over and done with, so we can now relax and celebrate the fact that the contracts are all duly signed, sealed and about to be delivered!' He took off his glasses then reached behind him to the ice-bucket and lifted out a bottle of Bollinger champagne. He held the bottle aloft and popped the cork. Then, as the froth started to erupt from the top of the bottle, he stood up and began to pour the bubbly drink into the champagne flutes in front of each member of the group. When all the glasses were full, John Burns held his out and said, 'To the Grosvenor Hotel and its new ownership.' Then, in a very cheery and hearty manner, he touched his glass against Tara's, and the other members of the group reached across the table to clink their glasses together and repeat the toast.

Frank Kennedy came around the table to touch his glass first to Eric Simmons's and then Tara's, and, as he did so, he stared straight into her eyes. 'Well done, Tara,' he said in a low voice. 'You've made the right decision.'

Tara looked back at him and, for a brief moment, their eyes locked – but she said nothing.

Chapter 42

❧❧❧

Bridget looked at herself in the mirror and smiled. She was delighted with her new purchases. Her new spotted, empire-line dress and short matching jacket looked lovely on her. The navy dress skimmed over her small pregnancy bump, which was only starting to become visible. She decided immediately that she'd wear the outfit for going dancing in Blackpool on the Saturday night and again for Mass on Sunday morning. For travelling she'd wear her comfortable jersey skirt and matching top with a pink diamond pattern, which Fred loved.

She felt better than she'd felt in weeks, and was glad she'd listened to Tara's advice about trying a new hairstyle. She'd asked the hairdresser to trim then flick out her bob instead of turning it under, and it made a lovely change. June and Angela had both said it made her look years younger, and although Bridget had told them to go on with themselves, she was delighted by their compliments.

She had gone shopping with Angela in Manchester the previous weekend at Fred's insistence, to buy some new outfits for their weekend away. 'Spoil yourself for a change,' he had told her, giving her a wad of notes. 'You work yourself to the bone in this place, and we're not doing badly at all, so we can afford to treat ourselves now and again.'

Even the day out shopping had done her good. Angela was a good laugh, and they'd spent two full hours in the café in British Home Stores eating fish and chips, and bread and butter, and drinking several cups of tea. Bridget loved days out like that, where she could totally relax and not have to mind her p's and q's the way she did when she went shopping with Tara. They usually ended up in some posh hotel or restaurant where Bridget was always glancing over her shoulder to see if she was as well-dressed as the other women in the place.

And while she enjoyed going to the more up-market shops for weddings and special occasions, Bridget was happy to have a day getting bargains in the cheaper shops like C&A or British Home Stores, as was her younger companion.

As they relaxed over their fish and chips, Angela brought Bridget up to date on the new boyfriend she'd met in Tullamore at Easter.

222

'You sound very keen on him,' Bridget had said, feeling young herself again, and a touch envious, as she listened to Angela describing the romantic walks and drives she'd had up to Dublin and around Offaly with her new man.

Angela gave a little sigh and looked off in the distance. 'I still can't believe that someone like Aiden would be interested in me. And d'you know something, Bridget? I never, ever thought that I'd be interested in an older man.'

'Love is blind to all these things,' Bridget told her, picking up a chip with her fingers and popping it into her mouth. She was thoroughly enjoying eating a meal that she hadn't had to cook. 'Age doesn't matter as long as you have feelings for each other.'

'Have you ever gone with an older man?' Angela asked. She'd heard so many of Bridget's stories over the last few years that she couldn't always remember the details.

A memory of when she was a very young girl and had an illicit and illegal romance with her foster-carer's lodger, suddenly sprung to Bridget's mind, but she very quickly blocked the image, knowing instinctively that it was not the sort of thing she should tell Angela. 'Not really,' she said vaguely. 'My proper romances were all with fellas around the same age as myself.' She hesitated for a few seconds then ploughed on, enjoying the gossip. 'But there was a few years between Tara and Frank Kennedy. She was younger than you when she first met him. And, of course, Frank's a bit older than Kate Thornley as well.'

'I hadn't thought about Tara being so young when she met him.' Angela's eyes lit up. 'I'm not sure if you've ever told me all the details about how she met Frank.'

'Two minutes,' Bridget said, grinning at her young friend, then she quickly finished her fish and chips and spent the next half an hour giving Angela a blow-by-blow account of Tara's ill-fated romance. She had made sure that Angela understood that Tara had no idea she was dating a married man, but she wound up the story by saying that if Tara Flynn could be fooled, then the same could happen to any woman.

Since the day out in Manchester, Bridget had perked up, and the thought of the weekend Fred had organised in Blackpool had kept her in good spirits. It was the first time they'd been away on their own for years and she was really looking forward to it. They were to stay in a nice boarding house on the seafront that a friend of June's had highly recommended, and Fred had booked both the Friday and the Monday off work to make it a long weekend.

Bridget would get up at her usual time and cook breakfast for the seven lodgers they presently had in the house, then she would do a quick tidy before having breakfast with Fred and the three children. June was due in later in the afternoon to cook the evening meal for the men, and she and Angela would then take over until Monday.

'It shouldn't be too busy in Blackpool at this time of the year,' Fred said as they lay in bed on the Friday morning, Bridget in his arms. 'So we'll get plenty of attention in the boarding house.'

Bridget stared up at the ceiling, thinking that it could do with a fresh coat of white paint in the very near future. There were a few odd jobs that needed doing before the baby came. 'I suppose you can't compare seaside boarding houses with this place,' she mused, 'but it'll be interesting to see how many tables they have and what kind of food they serve.'

Fred tapped her lightly on the head. 'Don't forget you're going there for a break, not to be thinking about work.'

'I know, I know,' Bridget murmured.

'Are you sure you don't want me to drive?'

'I'd prefer the train for a change,' she told him. 'And it'll let you relax as well. You do enough driving at home.'

'I don't mind taking the car,' he said, 'if it makes things easier for you.'

'There's no need,' Bridget insisted. 'June said her friend told her that the station is only a few minutes' walk from the boarding house, and we won't need the car when we get there. We'll be walking up and down the beach and to the shops and all that.'

'OK, love,' Fred finally agreed. 'If you're happy gettin' the train, then that's what we'll do.'

Bridget heaved a small sigh of relief, as she had dreaded the thought of Fred trying to negotiate a map to get them to Blackpool and then drive through the busy town. Since his accident, he wasn't so clever at driving to strange places, and although he wouldn't admit it, Bridget knew he got very anxious at times.

They'd just finished breakfast when Fred's parents arrived to collect the children. Michael and Helen were beside themselves with excitement, as they were having two, unauthorised days off school to stay with their grandparents, who indulged them. They weren't actually supposed to come until eleven o'clock, but Fred's father explained that his wife had insisted on setting off early in case the roads were busy.

'You know what she's like,' he told Fred, rolling his eyes to the heavens. 'When she gets an idea in her head there's no changing it.'

Bridget stopped washing up the family's breakfast dishes to make the elderly couple a cup of tea, and sent Michael and Helen along to Pilkington's baker's shop to get some fresh rolls and the iced, vanilla slices that Mrs Roberts loved.

'They're all ready and packed,' Bridget told her mother-in-law. 'And I've put a few extra pairs of knickers in with Lucy's things in case she has a little accident. She's been dry for months during the night now, but you never know when she's in a strange place.' She rattled about now, lifting cups, saucers and side-plates down for her visitors.

Lucy came into the kitchen now, clutching her favourite teddy-bear, which she took everywhere with her. She was dressed in a pink checked dress with a net underskirt, white ankle socks trimmed with pink, white leather sandals and a matching pink cardigan that Bridget had knitted for her.

'C'mon, love,' Mrs Roberts said, beckoning the child to sit up on her knee. 'She'll be as right as rain,' she told Bridget, 'and if she has an accident, so what?' She ran her hand over the checked dress. 'She's like a little doll in that outfit, isn't she? All the neighbours are always commenting on her clothes. You keep her so lovely, like.'

Bridget smiled gratefully at her. Her children's appearance was a source of pride to her, especially after the way she'd been brought up in Ireland with hand-me-down clothes that were totally inadequate for the cold, damp climate. Long before she'd ever become a mother, Bridget Hart had vowed that no child of hers would ever go without decent shoes and clothes. 'I've put ribbons and a few clasps in the case as well,' she told Fred's mother,' and a good strong brush.'

Mrs Roberts ruffled the child's curly dark hair, which had recently developed unusual but attractive lighter streaks running through it. 'I usually just tie her hair up in a ponytail. I'm not as good as doing it as you are, Bridget.' She raised her eyebrows. 'Now Helen is a different kettle of fish. Her hair is easy to manage as it's so soft and straight.' She jiggled Lucy up and down on her knee. 'Goodness knows where you got that head of hair from, Lucy, eh? You've got the thickest, curliest hair I've ever seen.' The child giggled now and her granny tickled her under the arms, her face close to the Lucy's. 'Wherever you got it from, it's definitely not from the Roberts side of the family.'

Bridget's heart suddenly leapt into her mouth. She stared, stricken, at her mother-in-law for a few moments, but the older woman's attention was still concentrated on the child. She turned back to the cupboard, fiddling amongst the crockery, waiting for someone to say something else. Waiting for something terrible to happen.

Then the front door opened and Michael came striding down the hallway and into the kitchen, followed by a slower and out-of-breath Helen. 'Baker's delivery!' he said in an important voice, putting the carrier bag down on the table.

'Good man!' Fred said, winking at him. 'Your granny couldn't come to Stockport and not have one of her bloomin' vanilla slices, could she?'

'We'll have less of that,' Mrs Roberts said, smiling indulgently at her son. 'I'm glad that Bridget knows how to look after her guests, even if some people don't.'

'Shall I put the cakes out on a plate, Mum?' Helen asked.

'Good girl,' Bridget said, her voice breathless with relief. 'I'll get you a big plate now.' As she reached into the cupboard, she blinked back the tears that had suddenly filled her eyes, and wished that she could be a normal mother with normal, everyday problems, instead of a mother filled with dark, dreadful secrets that constantly threatened to spill out and drown her.

Chapter 43

The boarding house was a longer walk from the station than June's friend had described.

'We'll get a taxi,' Fred said, when they'd got directions from the station porter. He glanced up at the grey sky. 'It might be best, just in case.'

'We can walk,' Bridget replied. 'That way we will know how to get back to the station when we're going back home.' She glanced at the holdall that Fred was carrying. 'The bag's not too heavy for you, is it?'

'Not at all,' he reassured her.

The rain came on when they were still a few streets away from Seaview House. 'Oh, damn it!' Bridget exclaimed. 'My bloody hair will be ruined, after I had it set yesterday.' She stopped and started frantically searching in her handbag for a Rainmate, which she always carried for occasions just like this.

'You're OK, love,' Fred said, looking anxiously at her. 'We'll find you another hairdresser's and you can have it done again.'

Bridget gave a deep, shuddering sigh and continued to rummage through her bag, irritation mounting at Fred, even though she knew, rationally, that the rain wasn't his fault. She eventually located the plastic head-cover and, after dramatically dropping her handbag onto the ground with a thud, proceeded to unfold the Rainmate, put it carefully over her flicked-out hair and tie it under her chin. 'I hate these feckin' oul' things,' she muttered. 'It makes me look like a granny.'

'You always look beltin',' Fred said, putting an arm around her.

Bridget shrugged him off and bent down for her handbag. 'Let's get moving,' she told him, 'or we'll be totally drowned. I don't know why on earth we didn't get a taxi like normal folk.'

Fred bit back the retort that was on his lips, which would have caused a bigger row. He had learned over the years – and more recently, since she had become awkward to the point there was no reasoning with her – that it was better to stay quiet.

Eventually, just as the shower eased off, they rounded a corner and there, in the middle of a yellow-and-blue building, stood the sparkling white Seaview House.

'Thank God,' Bridget stated, taking the Rainmate off.

'It looks all right, doesn't it?' Fred said with some relief. All they needed now was to find the place was an absolute dump and that would just put the tin hat on the day before it even started. 'In fact, it looks quite nice, as though it's well-maintained.'

'Let's get inside first,' she said, 'and then we'll know.'

They walked up the white steps, through the heavy, blue doors and into the reception area of the boarding-house. Bridget stood silently, taking in the intricately patterned blue, white and rust-coloured Victorian tiles, the ornate, marble-topped consul table and matching mirror with its tasteful display of flowers. Immediately she knew that Seaview House was exactly what she needed at this difficult time in her life.

'It's gorgeous,' she said, her whole face lighting up. 'Much better than I expected. I wouldn't have thought that any of June's friends knew anywhere like this.'

'I think she said it was someone she worked for,' Fred said vaguely.

'Well, we're lucky she knew about it,' Bridget said. 'I don't think we could have picked a better place ourselves.'

Fred put the holdall down on the floor and went to the desk, afraid to agree with his wife in case the bedroom or restaurant or any other part of the building might not live up to the expectation promised by the entrance. There was a half-glazed door, which led to another room behind the desk. 'I'll just give this a ring,' he said, indicating the old-fashioned press bell, 'and let them know we're here.'

Bridget nodded, walking across the hallway to look through the glass door with 'Dining-room' etched on it, then stood gazing at the round tables covered with starched white linen cloths and carefully folded napkins. There was a gleaming wooden floor, the walls were papered in a peaceful blue and cream William Morris design, and on each table stood a tall vase filled with luxurious white lilies.

'It's really, really lovely,' she said, suddenly choked. The sight of the calm, peaceful room made her realise that she was temporarily free from responsibility and hard work, which she had used to drown out the disquieting thoughts that had recently threatened to engulf her. She felt strangely emotional.

The door behind the desk opened and a small, curvaceous woman in her forties with red-tinted hair swept up in a bouffant-style came out. She was wearing a green floral dress with a short, matching jacket.

Fred glanced over at Bridget, expecting her to take charge, but when she made no move from the dining-room door he stepped forward, clearing his throat. 'We have a room booked.'

The woman stretched out a well-manicured hand, the nails painted the same red as her hair. 'Delighted to meet you. I'm Thelma Stevens,' she said, smiling warmly. 'The landlady.'

'Nice to meet you, too,' Fred said, returning her smile.

'And you're?' she enquired, looking from Fred to Bridget. She stopped herself from adding 'Mr and Mrs', as she had made up her mind some time ago not to put people on the spot regarding their marital status. In the long run, she had come to realise, it made no difference. People were people, and they would argue or behave properly whether they were married or not. She'd had plenty of warring couples in her boarding house, and, in her experience, the worst ones were married.

'Mr and Mrs Fred Roberts,' Fred said, 'from Stockport.'

'Near Manchester, isn't it?' Thelma Stevens said, opening the hotel register. 'I've heard of it often, but it's a place I've never been to.'

Bridget came over to join Fred at the reception desk. 'It looks lovely,' she said. 'Everything here looks lovely.'

'Thank you, that's very kind of you to say so,' the older woman said, looking delighted. 'I just had it re-decorated from top to bottom before Easter.' She hesitated, then held out her hand. 'And you're Mrs Roberts?'

'Bridget,' she said, shaking the woman's hand.

A door further along the corridor opened and a couple around Bridget and Fred's age came out, each holding a young child by the hand. The landlady gave them a cheery greeting as they dropped their room key in, commenting on how wise they were to have brought raincoats and umbrellas.

Thelma Stevens chatted away as she sorted out the key to their room, then gave them printed details about breakfast times, as well as evening meals if they wanted to eat in. 'We do a three-course dinner for a reasonable price,' she said. 'And we change the menu every evening. You're welcome to eat in or out, but it would be helpful if you could let the desk know before five o'clock.'

'If it's OK,' Bridget said, glancing at Fred, 'we'll let you know as soon as we've had time to settle in and decide what we're doing.'

'That's fine by me,' the landlady said. She pointed to a room on the left. 'We have a comfortable sitting-room with a television and radio, and you can order teas and coffees throughout the afternoon and up until ten o'clock at night.'

'Oh, that's lovely,' Bridget said, really beginning to relax now.

'And if you want to go out for a drink later in the evening,' the landlady went on, 'there's a nice pub just down the road. You turn left and it's there in front of you. It's called The Lantern. It's cosy and very handy, especially if it's raining, and the fella that runs it is a good friend of mine.'

Fred's face lit up. 'That sounds like just the kind of place we're looking for – not too far to stagger back home.'

Thelma Stevens leaned forward in a conspiratorial manner. 'That's exactly why I recommend it, and I often go there myself!'

All three laughed heartily.

'Unfortunately, I can't go too mad,' Bridget confided. 'I'm expecting at the minute.'

The landlady's eyes lit up. 'Oh, congratulations, love,' she said. 'And a few drinks won't do you a bit of harm. I always found that it helped me to sleep. In fact, a couple of milk stouts will do you and the baby the world of good.'

'D'you think so?' Bridget said, feeling cheered by this piece of information.

'Of course,' the landlady said. 'It's full of iron and vitamins and that kind of thing.'

She handed Fred the key and the hotel information, along with a few brochures about the town. 'If there's anything I can do, just call down to the desk.'

The bedroom was very comfortable and nicely decorated. 'Just how I'd like to do ours next time around,' Bridget said wistfully, looking at the teak fitted wardrobes with the mirrored doors, and the matching bedside tables with the floral lampshades. She hung up her coat in the wardrobe alongside Fred's jacket, then she sat down on the bed and gave a weary sigh.

'Why don't you have a little rest, love?' Fred suggested, putting the case down on a small stand by the window.

'Won't it look terrible, me lying down in the middle of the afternoon?'

'Who's going to know?' he said. 'And anyway, you're expecting a baby. We've paid for the room and we can do whatever we like. Nobody's going to bother us. It's a big place, so people will be coming and going all day. The landlady's a nice woman, isn't she?'

'She's lovely and friendly,' Bridget said. 'Makes you really feel at home considering it's such a big place. I wonder how many rooms there are?'

'I'd say there could be twenty or more,' Fred calculated. 'There's a good few on the ground floor and then there's two more flights going up to more rooms.'

'Will you lie down beside me?' Bridget asked, patting the bed. 'We could both have a sleep.'

Fred looked out at the rain-splattered window. 'Might as well,' he said. 'I don't fancy wandering up and down the beach while the weather's like this.' He went to the holdall and took a newspaper from the zipped part at the front. 'If I can't sleep, I'll just read through this while you're having a doze.'

'D'you think we should let her know about the evening meal now?' Bridget paused, thinking. 'It might not be a bad idea to eat in the first night, you know. It would give us a chance to meet the other residents. What d'you think?'

Fred shrugged, 'You know me; I'm happy if you're happy.'

Bridget looked at her big, gentle husband and felt a sudden surge of affection for him. How lucky she was to have such a nice, agreeable man. There wasn't anything that he wouldn't do for her, and he'd always been that way since they got married. Ruby Sweeney had told her to grab him with both hands, and her advice had been right. He might not be the most exciting or dynamic man in the world, but he more than made up for it in other ways. And how many men would have put up with her moods recently? 'What would I do without you?' she said, a little catch in her voice and her eyes big and watery.

Fred sat down on the bed beside her, and pulled her close into his chest.

'And what would I do without you?' he said. 'Takin' care of me when I'd that stupid accident, and making sure I got back to my old self.'

'Don't be talkin' like that,' Bridget chided. 'What else would you expect me to do? Didn't we say in our weddin' vows that we'd stick by each other in sickness and in health?'

Fred's face became serious now as he tried to recall the traditional wedding vows. 'And for richer and poorer,' he suddenly said. 'I don't know about you, but I never expected to do as well as we've done. Who would believe that Maple Terrace would have been such a little gold mine?'

Bridget closed her eyes for a few seconds. 'Ruby,' she said, thinking of her old landlady, who had set them up by leaving Bridget the boarding house in her will. 'Ruby knew what she was doing. She was a clever, clever lady.'

'No doubt about it,' Fred agreed, rubbing her shoulder affectionately. 'And she knew she was leaving it to an equally clever young woman.'

Bridget buried her face in her husband's chest now. 'Oh, Fred,' she whispered. 'Hold me really, really tight.'

Chapter 44

❧

'I'd love to ask the cook for the recipe,' Bridget whispered, as she finished her last mouthful of fish pie, which had been accompanied by creamy duchess potatoes and garden peas mixed with runner beans.

'A bit fancy for the lads back home,' Fred said, grinning at her. 'Your efforts would be wasted on them.'

'I wasn't thinking of the lads,' Bridget commented. 'I was thinking of when I have Tara around for a meal. If she wasn't so touchy I'd ask Frank Kennedy at the same time, but you can't even mention his name without her getting all uppity and awkward.'

The waitress came to take their plates and check which dessert they were having.

'Apple tart and ice cream for me,' Bridget said, smiling gratefully at the young girl.

'And I'll have the trifle,' Fred decided.

When the waitress left, Fred said. 'D'you fancy tryin' the Lantern after we've finished here?'

'We might as well,' she agreed, 'since we're all dressed up.'

It was just going on for nine o'clock when they stepped out into the fresh night air.

'It's better now than it's been all day,' Fred said, glancing up at the clear sky. He pointed across the road towards the pier and the shimmering, grey-green sea. 'That's a nice sky way over in the distance. Red or orange means it's going to be nice in the morning.'

'Why don't we have a walk along the promenade?' Bridget

suggested. 'It'll do us good after that big dinner.'

'You seem more like your old self this evening,' Fred told her as they strolled along, arm in arm. 'I think that bit of a rest this after-noon must have done you good.'

Bridget looked up at him now, a little blush creeping over her neck and face. 'I think our little kiss and cuddle afterwards might have helped, too.' She giggled. 'I can't remember the last time we got up to anything like that in the middle of the afternoon.'

'We wouldn't dare,' Fred said, winking at her, 'what with the kids and the lodgers.'

He shook his head, laughing now. 'You can't even go to the jaxie without somebody looking for you in our house, so fat chance we'd have of gettin' up to a bit of hanky-panky in the afternoons.'

After a half an hour walk down towards the Pleasure Beach and back, they headed for the Lantern. It was already busy, a juke-box adding to the buzz of the place, but they were lucky enough to find two seats at the end of a long table.

'You park yourself down and I'll get us a drink,' Fred said. 'What d'you fancy?'

'I think I'll go mad and have a sherry,' Bridget said, looking around. The pub was typically Old English with low black beams. It was dimly lit with pink-tinted lamps, and there was a big fireplace at the back with lots of candles on the mantelpiece giving out a lovely glow. Then, as Sonny and Cher came on the jukebox singing 'I Got You Babe' – one of Bridget's favourite songs – she became aware that, for the first time in ages, she felt relaxed and content.

'It'll soon be throwing-out time,' Fred said, standing up and feeling for his wallet in his back pocket. 'Will you chance another one?' he said nodding to her empty milk stout bottle.

Bridget looked down at the glass now, knowing she'd had quite enough for an expectant mother. But it was the first time in weeks she'd felt like her old self, and that made such a difference. 'Oh, go on,' she said, 'you've twisted my arm. I'll have a brandy and lemon-ade.' Brandy, as everybody knew, had medicinal qualities, so Bridget reasoned that it would probably be just as good for the baby as the milk stout.

Fred was just returning from the bar with the drinks when the pub door opened and Thelma Stevens came in. The landlady entered so quietly and discreetly that Bridget wouldn't have noticed her if it hadn't been for her red hair, which was unmissable.

She came straight over to their table. 'You found it, then?' she said, beaming.

'Yeah, and it's a beltin' little place,' Fred told her. 'What you having to drink?'

'You might have to check,' Thelma said, sitting down. She patted her piled-up hair to check that the lacquer was still holding it all in place. 'Jim often has one already poured behind the bar for me. It's a whiskey and dry ginger.'

A few minutes later Fred came back with her drink. 'He says to tell you that's a large one, and he'll be over to join you as soon as it quietens down.'

'Oh, he's a love,' the landlady said, lifting her glass and taking a good swallow.

'Are things quiet back at the boarding house?' Bridget said, sipping her drink.

'All settled down,' Thelma told her with a relieved smile. 'There's a nice crowd in this weekend; no riff-raff, thank God. I get more than enough of them at the height of the summer to last me the whole year round.'

Bridget raised her eyebrows. 'You wouldn't think that a lovely place like yours would attract the rougher ones.'

'Ah, but it's the drink,' Thelma said, taking another mouthful of her whiskey and ginger. 'They might have decent jobs and decent money coming in, but their true natures come to the fore when they have alcohol inside them. They let themselves go.' She nodded her head ominously. 'That's when you see the real people.'

'We have a small boarding house ourselves,' Fred told her. 'Nowt like yours, of course, it's only for working lads, but it keeps us busy enough.'

'Really?' Thelma said, sounding most impressed. 'I could tell you were business types the minute I clapped eyes on you.'

Bridget glowed with pride. 'As Fred says, it's nothing like your lovely place, but it's clean and decent and we only take the right types.'

They chatted on the same theme for a while, then, when the last orders bell came, Fred went up to the bar and got another round.

Some time later the bell rang again to warn everyone to finish up. Fred looked at his watch. 'I suppose we'd better be drinkin' up,' he said ruefully. 'Being a barman myself, I don't like to take advantage.'

'Hold your horses,' Thelma told him in a low whisper. 'You're with me, and I'm not goin' anywhere.' She gestured to the bald-headed man behind the bar. 'Jim'll lock the door and we'll all have a few more drinks in peace.'

'Are you sure?' Fred checked, looking across at the bar.

'Definitely,' she said. 'Any friends of mine are friends of Jim's.' She knocked back the dregs of her second large whiskey.

Bridget looked over at Fred, but he just shrugged, as though to say they should wait and see.

A short while later the landlord saw the last few drinkers out, then he bolted the top and the bottom of the door, before coming across to their table, wiping his brow with the back of his hand.

'Jim,' Thelma said, 'this is Fred Roberts and his wife, Bridget. They're from Stockport.'

'The home of the Hatters,' Jim said, grinning. He stuck his hand out to Fred and then to Bridget. 'Nice to meet you. What will you have to drink now? On the house, like.' When they were all sorted out with another round of drinks, the men settled into talking about football, while Bridget and Thelma got into a cosy chat about their home lives.

'I'm divorced, love, these past twelve years,' Thelma said, nodding her head gravely. 'Got a lucky escape.' She lowered her voice so the men couldn't hear. 'When he started knocking me about, I knew it was time to call it a day. You can't put up with that carry-on when you've got children depending on you, no matter how much you think you love the man.'

Bridget's heart lifted. This was exactly the sort of thing she needed to hear to take her mind off her own problems. To remind herself that other people made mistakes, too, and that she wasn't the only one. And it was especially heartening to hear that someone as capable and glamorous as Thelma Stevens had made bad choices in her life. 'And how old are your children now?' she asked.

'Sarah is twenty-three and Neville has just turned twenty,' Thelma said. 'Neville is at college up in Newcastle training to be a teacher,' she said with more than a hint of pride in her voice. 'Oh, he's a very clever lad, is my Neville. Very clever indeed. And Sarah is ...' she hesitated. 'Well, she *was* training to be a nurse ...' Her hand rested on Bridget's arm. 'To be honest with you, Bridget, she had a little bit of trouble with her nerves and she had to drop out.'

Bridget's face immediately softened. 'Oh, the poor girl ...' she said, her voice heavy with sympathy.

Thelma's eyes suddenly filled with tears. She turned to the side now, making sure Jim and Fred couldn't see she was upset. 'I blame her father,' she whispered. 'All the trouble that bastard caused us – it's scarred her. Ruined her life.' She shook her head. 'She's a good girl underneath it all.'

'Don't go upsettin' yourself,' Bridget told her, reaching for her handbag to find a hanky.

'It's OK,' Thelma told her. 'I always get like this when I think of Sarah ... I suppose it's the way we mothers are.' She took the hanky from Bridget now and dabbed at her eyes. 'Oh, please excuse me,' she said, sniffing hard, blinking and trying to compose herself. 'I'm going through an emotional time at the moment, with one thing and another. My father died a couple of months ago, and I'm start-ing to get these hot flushes ... I suppose it's only to be expected. My time of life and all that.'

Bridget reached out and took Thelma's hand. 'Well, I think you're a wonderful person,' she said, suddenly feeling all upset herself now, 'and you look wonderful, too. Your lovely red hair and your lovely clothes – you look immaculate and nowhere near old enough to be goin' through the change of life.'

'Thank you, Bridget, you're very, very kind.' Thelma was smiling now.

She went on to relate how she had gone into partnership with her cousin to buy the boarding house eight years ago. 'And then she took ill a couple of years ago and wanted to retire down to Bournemouth, so I got a big bank loan and bought her out. I took a bit extra and did the whole place out at the same time – new carpets, curtains, beds, the lot.'

'That was very brave of you,' Bridget said, 'being on your own.'

'Ah well,' the landlady said, 'I'm not entirely on my own these days.' She gestured in Jim's direction. 'I suppose you could say we're an item – have been for five years.'

'Oh,' Bridget said, looking at the balding, slightly paunchy man engrossed in a conversation with Fred about boxing now. 'That's nice for you. And is he …?' She halted, waiting for Thelma to carry on.

'Divorced?' Thelma said, nodding. Her voice dropped again. 'Same situation as me, but no kids, thank God.' Her voice was so low now she was almost mouthing the words. 'They were living in a small village outside Leeds, and his wife ran off with the local butcher.' She shook her head and rolled her eyes. 'It was terrible for Jim, because the whole place knew all about it before him. The worst bit was the shop closed down when the butcher and Jim's wife disappeared, and people had to travel to the next village for their meat, so everyone was inconvenienced on account of their carry-on.'

'Disgraceful,' Bridget tutted, really enjoying all the gory details and thinking what a lovely, lovely evening it had turned out to be. She felt that the brandy had done her a power of good, even though she was feeling a bit light-headed from it.

'And what about yourself, love?' Thelma asked now. 'Have you and Fred any other children or is it your first?'

Bridget lifted her brandy glass and took a mouthful of her drink. 'This is actually our fourth,' she said, and was delighted when Thelma didn't believe her, saying she didn't look old enough to have that many kids. Then she launched into her own story about coming over to Stockport at eighteen with her friend, omitting the real reasons for their escape from Ireland, as well as the fact that she was orphaned young and fostered out.

'Amazing,' Thelma said, when Bridget told her that Ruby Sweeney had left the boarding house to her. 'You landed on your feet, and no doubt about it.'

'Oh, and don't I know it,' Bridget told her, her voice sounding a little thick now from that last brandy. 'I thank God every single day for sending me to Maple Terrace.' Tears sprung into her eyes as they often did when she mixed her drinks. 'Although I'd rather have nothing if I could bring Ruby back – she was like a mother to me …'

The older woman's face softened. 'And you were obviously like a daughter to her, love. I can tell by the way you're talking about her – you loved her just like she was your very own.'

Bridget nodded, starting to sniffle a little now.

'And what about your own mother?' Thelma asked. 'Is she still back in Ireland?'

Bridget took a deep breath. 'I wasn't going to tell you all this, because it's a bit depressing, but I never really knew my family …'

And then she went on to fill in certain bits of her life that she'd missed out earlier.

As she listened, Thelma nodded encouragingly, completely enthralled. 'It's like something out of a book,' she said. 'Rags to riches …'

'Well, we're not really *that* well off,' Bridget said, wondering if she'd told the landlady a bit too much about her background, 'but it's a good little business and we have a nice home.'

'But you're such a wonderful, wonderful couple,' Thelma gushed now, the whiskey adding extra emotion to her words. 'And so well-suited to each other.'

Bridget suddenly thought of another untapped source of conversation. She dragged her chair that bit closer to Thelma's and lowered her voice. 'Poor Fred's not always had it easy, either. He had a terrible accident a few years ago and we're lucky to have him alive.'

Thelma's eyes widened. 'Go on,' she said. 'I'm all ears.'

Bridget launched into her new story now, delighted to have made a new friend in whom she could confide. At long last, she had met an older woman who might just be a replacement for Ruby Sweeney.

Chapter 45

June walked to Maple Terrace more slowly than usual on account of a hangover. As she stepped in the front door she could hear someone flushing the toilet upstairs, so she scooted down the hallway and into the kitchen as fast as she could. Thankfully, there were no signs of any life, so she quickly filled the kettle and put it on to boil, then went to the fridge to find sausages and bacon for the breakfasts.

By the time two of the lads appeared, the table was set and the breakfast was well on its way. June had sat down at the kitchen table and taken five minutes to apply her make-up with a slow, shaky hand, which made her look passable by the time the men came downstairs, and no one was any the wiser about her late start to the morning.

As she was clearing up after breakfast, Lucky started yelping out in the yard, making June's hangover headache even worse, and it dawned on her that she would have to take him for his usual walk otherwise he would mess the place up. She gave a deep sigh, as it was one of the jobs she hadn't bargained on when she agreed to keep house. She tried to ignore him for a bit, but there was no getting away from the subsequent crying and whining, so she eventually decided it was easier to take him for a quick run in the park than listen to the noise.

She took the lead from the back of the door, then stopped by the cupboard where Bridget kept the medicines to take two aspirins on her way out. She still felt so bad that she hadn't even had a cigarette this morning, which was a very unusual state of affairs.

She walked only half the distance she usually did in the park, then picked up a few bits and pieces from the baker's and headed back to the boarding house.

As she turned towards Maple Terrace a van came alongside her and pulled up at the kerb outside the boarding house. She glanced at the van but didn't recognise the driver, so she continued on up the stairs and into the house, Lucky straining at the lead. She dropped the baker's bag on the kitchen table and took the lively dog back to his pen in the yard.

She planned to have a sit-down in the kitchen for a half-an-hour with a fresh cup of tea, a cigarette and Fred's *Daily Mirror* before starting on the lunches. But, as she returned to the kitchen, the front door bell sounded. Swearing to herself, June strode along the hallway to answer it.

'Hi.' It was a dark-skinned, curly-headed fellow, leaning casually on the doorjamb. 'Is Bridget or Fred around?'

June studied him for a few moments longer than normal; the alcohol had slowed her reactions. You didn't often see foreign fellows around Stockport, especially ones with a cockney accent. 'They've gone away for a few days,' she told him. 'To Blackpool, actually.'

He nodded. 'OK, gotcha.' He smiled at her, a warm friendly smile, then prepared to head back down the steps. 'It don't matter. Just took a chance since I was in the area.'

'Have you travelled far?' June asked.

'Up from London,' he said. 'I've been doin' a job out in Chester and thought I'd call in. I'm headin' back home after this.'

'Do you know them well?' she asked, her eyes narrowing.

'Yeah,' he said, grinning broadly now. He could tell that this peroxide-blonde was sceptical as to who he was and what he wanted. 'I was one of Ruby's old lodgers when Bridget first came over from Ireland.' He held his hand out. 'Lloyd's my name.'

'Oh, right,' she said, shaking his hand. 'An' I'm June. I give Bridget a hand here with the cooking and things. They've left me in charge while they're away.' She was sure she had heard the name before. She opened the door wide now, and smiled back at him. He was one of those foreign but handsome types, and even though she had long given up any physical interest in men, she could see that he was the sort a lot of women would go for. As far as she was concerned, men were more bleedin' trouble than they were worth. She'd far rather cuddle up in bed with an electric blanket, a good thriller and a cup of cocoa any night. 'You'd better come in and have a cup of tea or something,' she told him, 'or I could be in big trouble for sending you off to London with a flea in your ear.'

Lloyd laughed. 'Well,' he said, 'if you're gonna twist my arm so nicely, I can't really say no, can I?'

A short while later June and Lloyd were chatting away as if they'd known each other all their lives. She made him two oven-bottoms with ham and tomato, while he told her how things used to be in Maple Terrace back in Ruby Sweeney's days.

'Bridget and Fred talk about her often,' June said, putting the sandwich plate down beside her guest.

'Aw, Ruby was a great character,' Lloyd said, picking up one of the oven-bottoms, 'a real little livewire. A small, dainty blonde, always dressed to the nines. Good-lookin' woman, the sort that never seemed to age.'

'Bridget absolutely worshipped her, by the sounds of it.' June put two mugs of tea on the table, then sat down opposite him, reaching for her packet of cigarettes and lighter.

'They were like mother and daughter,' Lloyd said. 'And it stands to reason that Ruby thought of Bridget as a daughter when she left her this place.'

'Amazing,' June said, lighting up her cigarette and taking a deep, satisfying drag.

Lloyd was halfway through his second sandwich when he looked up at June. 'It's very quiet in here today, isn't it? I've never known it to be so quiet.'

As her gaze met his dark, deep eyes, something in them hit a chord of familiarity, yet she knew that couldn't be – she was positive that she had never met him before. And in any case, he was so different from any of the other lads in the house that June would have easily remembered him. It would be impossible to miss that dark skin and those big dark eyes. 'The house is quiet because the lodgers are all out,' she told him. 'There's nobody else in.'

'What about the kids?' he asked casually. 'I suppose they've gone off to Blackpool, too, with all their buckets and spades and everything?'

'No,' June said, blowing a long stream of smoke high into the air. 'Bridget and Fred went on their own.' She leaned towards him now. 'To tell you the truth, Bridget hasn't been too bright recently, and Fred reckoned she needed a bit of a break. You know she's expectin' again, of course?'

'Yeah, brilliant news.' His eyes flickered towards the back door. 'So where are the kids, then? Playing outside or what?'

'They've gone off to Fred's parents' house for the weekend.'

Lloyd nodded. 'I was just reckoning, it must be the youngest one's birthday around now. Am I right?'

'Lucy? It was a few weeks ago,' June said. 'They had a little party for her.' She paused for a moment. 'Actually, they took some lovely pictures of all the kids that day.'

Lloyd's face brightened. 'Have you got them? I'd love to see them.'

'Yeah,' she said, 'I'm sure they're in the pull-down part of the sideboard.' She balanced her cigarette on the side of the glass ashtray and got up from the table, returning a few moments later with the folder containing the photographs. Then she slid them out one by one, and handed them to him, giving a little commentary on each photograph.

Lloyd looked closely at them, then he came to a complete halt, mesmerised by one particular photo. 'She's a gorgeous kid, isn't she?' he said, his voice almost a sigh.

'Which one is that?' June said, leaning across the table to get a look at it.

'Lucy,' he said, his voice hoarse. He was holding a close-up picture of Lucy pausing to smile just before blowing out the three birthday candles on her cake. Whether it was the tone of his voice, the look on his face or his general demeanour, June didn't know, but something suddenly struck her as she looked from the picture of the Roberts' young daughter and back to Lloyd, something she had never considered or thought about before: Lucy Roberts was not a Roberts at all.

Without a shadow of a doubt, June realised that Lucy's father was sitting opposite her. She sat back in her chair now, smoking her cigarette, and watching Lloyd as he went through the pile of photographs again, studying each one very carefully.

Then the phone rang in the hall. June stubbed out her cigarette and ran to get it.

It was Bridget.

'Hello, June,' she said. 'How are things back home?'

June's pulse quickened. 'Everything's fine,' she replied. 'I'm just about to make the sandwiches for the lads' lunch, and I'll be back later to cook their tea.'

'Has anybody called or anything like that?'

June hesitated. Some instinct told her to say nothing about the visitor sitting in the kitchen. She didn't want him to hear her discussing him, and, knowing what she did, she wasn't at all sure how Bridget would receive the news. It was best to save it until she came home and they were both on their own with Fred well out of earshot. 'No,' she said, 'it's been very quiet, like.' Then, for something to say, and to prove she hadn't shirked on any duties, she added, 'I gave Lucky a good run in the park this mornin', then bought some nice baps and things for the lads.'

'Oh, June,' Bridget said, 'you're great. Fred said I'd nothin' to worry about leaving you in charge, and he was right.'

'Go on with you,' June said. 'It's only doin' what we usually do. Anyroad, how's Blackpool? Are you havin' a good time? Is the boarding house as nice as I was told?'

'We're havin' a great time,' Bridget told her. 'And the boarding house is first class – the room, the food, everythin'. We found a terrific little pub last night, and we got after-hours on account of our landlady being the girlfriend of the landlord.'

'Oooh,' June said, sounding most impressed. 'I wish I were there with you. It sounds right nice. I can't wait to hear all about it when you get home.'

They chatted for a few minutes longer, then Bridget said she'd have to go as Fred was waiting outside for her.

June went back into the kitchen to find Lloyd out in the yard messing around with Lucky. 'I'm just headin' off now,' he said, coming back up the steps. 'You can tell Fred and Bridget that I'm sorry I missed them. I'm not sure when I'll be back this way again.' He lifted his jacket from the back of the chair.

'I'll tell them,' June said, as they walked along the hallway. She saw him out with a smile and a wave.

A few minutes later she came back into the hall, checking her watch. It was after one o'clock. She was running late now for her own weekend shopping, and she had to be home with it and back here again for five o'clock to make the evening meal. Once again, she rued the fact she'd got carried away last night; no doubt she would be running after herself for the rest of the day to make up for it.

She went quickly back into the kitchen to clear up the table and make the sandwiches for the lads, who would be due in any time now. She rushed backwards and forwards, putting the used crockery into the sink, then she wrung a dishcloth under the hot tap and began wiping down the table. She lifted the packet of photographs that Lloyd had left on the table, to wipe underneath, but something made her pause. She put the dishcloth on the table and took the photographs out of the folder. She went through them one by one, and when she had gone through them all, she put them back into the packet. He'd done exactly what she'd suspected.

The photograph of Lucy Roberts and her birthday cake was missing.

Chapter 46

On the Saturday evening, Tara paused to look at her reflection in the dressing-table mirror, trying to decide whether or not she preferred her new hairstyle. She had been to the hairdresser's in Davenport earlier that afternoon and, as she sat in the salon with the towel wrapped around her curly red hair, she had suddenly decided to have a change of style.

'You know you suggested a few weeks ago that you'd like to try blowing my hair straighter?' she said to the girl. 'Well, I've decided to give it a go.'

'Great,' the young hairdresser said, grinning. 'I'm dying to see what you look like with it in a looser style.' She gave Tara's hair a quick, vigorous dry with the towel, then proceeded to brush it all out, taking care not to pull too hard on the tighter curls.

Tara had been going to the same salon for the last few years, always asking for a shampoo and a trim. She had never allowed the hairdresser to do anything different, presuming there was little that could be done with her long, spiral curls. But recently she'd noticed in magazines, and in the new books of hairstyles in the salon, that curled hair could be blow-dried into the more fashionable, straighter styles.

Half an hour later Tara emerged from the salon with a very different look. Her striking red hair now fell in long, soft waves past her shoulders.

As she looked in the large salon mirror, Tara had been immediately struck by the fact that, with her hair straighter, she looked very like Angela. It was a resemblance she'd never noticed before, but with her hair in a similar style to the younger girl's, there was no doubting that they were sisters.

When she arrived back at the house, Tara had gone upstairs to her bedroom to check her hairstyle again, and she now sat on the dressing-table stool, unable to make up her mind about the stranger with the soft auburn waves who looked back at her. She moved across her room now and went out into the hallway to knock on Angela's bedroom door to get her opinion, but there was no reply. Then Tara remembered that she had gone down to Maple Terrace to help June out with the evening meal since Bridget was away.

On the spur of the moment, she decided to drive the short distance down to the boarding house. And as she drove, she made up her mind that if both Angela and June hated it, she would quickly wash her hair and dry it back into its usually curly style before her date tonight.

She was going with Gerry McShane to the Palace Theatre in Manchester to see the musical *Oliver!* They had fallen into a discussion about music and shows the afternoon they had celebrated the signing of the contracts. A few days later Gerry had rung Tara to say he had two tickets for Saturday night, if she'd like to accompany him. With only a moment's hesitation, Tara had said yes. What else was she going to do? She had no exciting plans for the weekend, so she might as well. She knew she would only end up going down to the Cale Green Hotel and finding work for herself.

After pulling up outside the boarding house, she got out of the car and ran up the steps. The door was ajar so she gave a quick knock and stepped inside. She could hear female chatter coming from the kitchen, so she walked straight down the hallway towards it. She recognised both June and Angela's voices in the animated conversation and smiled. Bridget's house was always a hive of activity, and she knew the two women would enjoy examining her new hairstyle and giving their verdicts on it.

She had just placed her hand on the doorknob and was ready to walk into the kitchen when she heard June say something that stopped her in her tracks. She stood rooted to the spot, listening to make sure she had heard right.

'You think this Lloyd is Lucy's father?' Angela said, in a shocked tone.

'I'm positive,' June said. 'And when I saw the way he looked at the photo of her, there wasn't a shadow of a doubt. They're the bleedin' double of each other.'

Tara's stomach did a somersault. The subject of Lucy's parentage had never arisen since the child was born. Apart from a heated conversation with Bridget shortly after the birth, and a fleeting comment made by Frank Kennedy to Tara, there had been no other discussion. As far as Tara knew, everyone had accepted Bridget's version of events, that there must have been dark-skinned Irish-Spaniards in her family at some point.

But as she listened, Tara realised that obviously wasn't the case any more.

'Has Bridget ever said anything to you about Lucy being different from the others?' Angela asked.

'No, no,' Tara could hear June saying. 'She's never said a thing. She's always acted as though Fred was the kid's father, the same as the other two.'

Angela's voice dropped a fraction lower, but it was still loud enough for Tara to hear. 'And you're sure he took the photograph away with him?'

'Positive,' June said. 'I had the funniest feeling he'd do something like that, so I checked the photos the minute he'd gone, and the one of Lucy was missing. There was only the two of us here looking

245

at them, so it had to be him.' There was a pause. 'Honest to God, Angela,' June said, her voice shaky now, 'I nearly died when I realised who he was. You could have knocked me down with a bloody feather.'

Tara had heard enough. She turned the door handle now and walked into the kitchen.

'Tara!' Angela exclaimed, her eyes wide. 'What have you done to your hair?'

Tara put her handbag down on the table. 'Never mind my hair,' she said, looking from one to the other, her face tight and grim. 'I overheard all that you were saying about Bridget, and it sounds as though we have a very serious problem on our hands.'

By the time she arrived back at her own house to get ready for her night out, Tara felt flustered and knocked off her stride. But, she reasoned with herself as she searched through her wardrobe, there was nothing that could be done about it tonight. She had sworn both June and Angela to secrecy about Lloyd's visit and the missing photograph, and she had made them promise not to discuss it with anyone else until she had time to think about it.

'You know Bridget hasn't been feeling too well,' Tara had reminded them. 'That's why she's gone away for a few days, and the last thing she needs is to hear vicious gossip like this when she gets back. Especially from her closest friends.'

'But you know we think the world of Bridget,' June stated, not as afraid to voice her opinion to Tara as Angela was. 'And nobody's going to go making accusations or owt like that. But it isn't just gossip ...' She looked doleful. 'I've seen the evidence before my own eyes.' 'Lucy is the exact double of that Lloyd fella ... the spittin' image of him.'

'You have to admit that Lucy looks different from Michael and Helen,' Angela said in a quiet voice. 'Her skin is much darker and she has that funny curly hair.' She would never have dared say anything like this to Tara before, but she now felt that June had only confirmed her own suspicions.

'Well, *I've* never had any reason to think that Lucy isn't Fred's daughter,' Tara snapped. She had no qualms about keeping Bridget's secret – there was far too much at stake to trust anyone with the real facts. Tara instinctively felt that, whatever happened, she had to keep this situation under control for the time being until she decided on the right course of action. 'And I don't think any of us have the right to speculate about it. It's simply not our business.'

June had folded her arms across her chest. 'Are you sayin' that we shouldn't tell Bridget he was at the house lookin' for her? D'you not think we should warn her?' She looked at Angela for moral support. 'If he's that desperate to take the photo of Lucy, he obviously wants to see her.'

Tara bit her lip. If there was no chance of Lloyd coming back to the house, then Tara's inclination would have been to say nothing, to let sleeping dogs lie. Bridget had enough on her plate just now. But if he started calling at the house more regularly, then other people, including Fred, were bound to start putting two and two together. She wished she knew what Lloyd's intentions were.

'I'll call back down here tomorrow evening,' she said finally, lifting her handbag. 'And then we'll have a chat about whether we should say anything or not.' She turned towards the kitchen door.

'Tara,' Angela said, as they walked along the hallway, 'your hair.'

Tara came to a halt. She'd forgotten all about it. 'Is it terrible?' she asked.

'Not at all,' Angela said, smiling at her. 'It's lovely. A really nice change.'

Chapter 47

◈

Back at the house, Tara quickly freshened up and went to the wardrobe to pick her outfit for the evening. Usually, she would have decided in advance what to wear, but her mind had been focused on her hair earlier on, then she had been further distracted by the situation at Maple Terrace.

She lifted out a new shift dress she'd bought the previous week, studying the brown and gold geometric print. Was it the right thing to wear for an evening out with Gerry McShane? The colour suited her hair perfectly, but it was the cutaway armholes and the length that bothered her. It was shorter than anything she'd ever worn before

– a couple of inches above her knee – but she reminded herself that it wasn't as daring as the lengths a lot of girls were wearing at the moment.

All in all, the dress was undoubtedly modern, but suitable for a woman of her age. Tara decided that she'd wear it, with a gold cardigan thrown over her shoulders.

Although she wasn't an avid fashion follower, Tara was conscious of keeping reasonably up to date with both her clothes and her hair. She tended to dress classically, but kept an eye on newer trends that suited her tall, slim figure. And although she loved clothes and accessories, she had recently become wary of trying new fads that might look too young for a woman in her thirties.

As she looked in her dressing-table mirror now, she decided that she liked her hair straight. As Angela had said, it was a nice change. Then a feeling of uncertainty crept over her as she stared at her reflection. She scrutinised her face for wrinkles, which would confirm the fact that she was too old for the shorter dress and the new hairstyle.

But she didn't look that different. Maybe she had just got used to looking at herself and thinking she was ok. She wished that Bridget had been around to give her opinion on her hair and outfit. She also wished that she'd been in a better mood when she'd been down at Maple Terrace earlier and could have asked Angela for a serious opinion about her hair. The way things had been, her half-sister would have said anything to keep on her good side.

Then she wished that Gabriel were there, because he had always told her the truth about how she looked. He had always told her the truth about everything.

Tara gave a little sigh and started to apply her make-up.

Twenty minutes later she had the answer to all her questions when Gerry McShane arrived.

'Wow!' His eyes lit up as Tara walked down the path towards his car. 'What have you done to yourself, Tara? You always look gorgeous, but tonight you look absolutely amazing.'

Although they were in plenty of time, the Palace Theatre was already busy.

'I suppose *Oliver!* is a show that appeals to all ages,' Tara mused, as they made their way through the busy foyer, with Gerry's arm gently around her waist, guiding her along. 'I know I loved the story when

I was a child, and I'm sure a musical about it is even more appealing to the children today.'

Gerry bent his head towards her, his lips almost brushing the side of her head. 'You must have been a very serious child to like Charles Dickens,' he joked.

Tara looked surprised for a moment. 'Yes,' she said, laughing. 'I think I was rather serious.'

His arm tightened around her waist, and, as he pulled her towards him, Tara suddenly felt a little tingle in the pit of her stomach. A pleasurable tingle she had not felt for a long time.

'Shall we go for a drink?' he suggested, motioning towards the bar. 'We've already got our tickets and we've over half an hour before we need to be in our seats.'

'Grand,' Tara said, trying to sound relaxed, but aware that Gerry McShane's hands had hardly left her since they got out of the car. When they parked, he had rushed around to help her out taking her hand in his. Then, as they walked along, he had either taken her hand, or held her gently around the waist or under her elbow.

They found a small empty table by the window. Tara put her bag on the floor and sat down in the deep leather chair. As she did so, her tightly fitted dress rode up, revealing several inches of her slim thighs. Immediately, she moved both her hands towards the hem to pull the dress down, terrified that she would reveal the tops of her stockings.

'Don't,' Gerry said, smiling at her. He leaned forward, and his hand covered the one nearest to him. 'There's not many women who look as good in a short skirt.'

'It's the first time I've worn this particular dress,' Tara said, blushing with embarrassment, 'and I really didn't expect it to be quite so short.'

Gerry kept a hold on her hand and brought it up to his lips. 'You really are a stunner, Mrs Fitzgerald,' he told her, looking deep into her eyes. 'And I'm very much looking forward to being both a business colleague – and perhaps more than just a good friend.'

Once again Tara felt a warm tingle at the unfamiliar feel of a man's touch. Of course she had known that there was bound to be some sort of physical contact during their night together, but she hadn't really been prepared for the constant closeness. And neither had she prepared herself for the pleasure she would feel. Gradually, as they sat together chatting and drinking white wine, Tara felt herself relaxing.

Gerry McShane had a good sense of humour and wasn't afraid to tease her – usually about being a strict boss or a driven workaholic. The few times he said something that made her react in a touchy way, he squeezed her arm affectionately and she found herself laughing along with him.

When the five-minute bell rang, they finished their drinks and made their way into the auditorium.

Afterwards, Gerry drove out of Manchester and into the country. Their conversation was mainly about the show, which they had both enjoyed immensely.

'You seem to have a great understanding about music,' Gerry commented. 'And I noticed that you had a very smart-looking piano in your house.' When he saw the quizzical look on Tara's face he laughed. 'I haven't been breaking into your house in the dead of night to look around – the blinds were open in the front room when I called for you, and a piano does tend to stand out.'

'I suppose it does,' Tara said, smiling.

'Do you play yourself?'

'Yes,' she told him. 'Not as much as I'd like to do these days, but I still have odd little outbursts on the piano now and again.'

'I'd like to hear you play sometime, if I may,' he said.

'Oh, I'm very much out of practice,' Tara told him. 'I haven't played in front of an audience for a long time.'

'But it's something you never forget,' he said lightly. 'I should imagine it would all come back to you very quickly. A bit like riding a bike.'

Tara laughed. 'Oh, I could do that in my time as well. I used to cycle everywhere when I was growing up in Ireland, but then everyone did. In the country it was a way of life.'

'You have a very different sort of life here, I would imagine. Moving from the country to the town, even within England, is very different, so coming from Ireland must require more changes.' He raised his eyebrows. 'I know that moving from York to Manchester was a big change for me, although it's amazing how quickly you adapt.' He paused. 'Did you know Frank Kennedy back in Ireland or did you meet him over here?'

Tara stiffened. 'I met him over here.'

'Through business?'

Tara suddenly felt uncomfortable, yet she knew that it was a perfectly ordinary conversation to have when they both knew him. 'I can't quite remember the circumstances,' she hedged. 'It was shortly after I moved here, when I was looking at property.'

'Ah, property.' Gerry said. 'Frank Kennedy is certainly the man when it comes to property. He has his finger in many pies, the Grosvenor being but one of them.' He pulled up at traffic lights now. 'I believe you and he had a romantic connection a few years back?'

Tara took a deep breath. It was bound to have come out. He must have heard it from Frank or someone else. 'A long time ago,' she said, with a sigh in her voice, 'when I was a young girl.' She looked out of the car window. 'A lot of water has passed under the bridge in both our lives since then.'

'Of course,' Gerry said. 'When you reach a certain age we all have that.'

Then, just in case he had any illusions about her romance with Frank Kennedy, Tara added, 'Now it's very hard to imagine how I could have been involved with someone like Frank, but when you're young, you don't always see the differences.'

'That's very true,' he replied.

There was an easy silence for a few minutes as they drove through Didsbury. Then, as they came into a quieter part of the village, Gerry drew the car to a halt and switched the engine off. 'I live here,' he said, indicating the big house just in front of them. 'And if you don't feel it's too late ... I wondered if you might like to come in for a coffee or a drink or something?'

Tara glanced up at him, totally taken aback.

He saw the hesitation on her face. 'It was only a suggestion ... because we were passing this way.' He reached for the ignition key to turn the engine on again.

'OK,' Tara said quietly. 'A drink would be very nice.'

Chapter 48

❧

Bridget woke with a slightly fuzzy head early on Saturday morning, and, as she looked around the dimly lit bedroom, she wasn't quite sure where she was. It took her a minute or so to work out that she was in Thelma Stevens's boarding house in Blackpool. She lay back and closed her eyes again, going over the events of the night before. As she recollected the grand evening out she and Fred had had in the Lantern pub with Thelma and Jim the landlord, she smiled. Thank God there was nothing she had done or said that she might regret.

Her memory of the whole night was quite clear now. Thankfully, she had stopped drinking just as it was beginning to affect her. But, just as Thelma had said, the few drinks had made her relax. And wasn't that exactly why Fred had brought her away? To relax and enjoy herself, and have a break from all the hard work she did back home. Well, she had certainly enjoyed herself last night and was looking forward to the two full days they still had to go.

She turned over now and cuddled into Fred's broad back. In a few minutes she was asleep again.

It was nine o'clock when Fred woke and checked his watch. He gently shook Bridget and reminded her that breakfast finished at ten. 'If you want, love,' he told her, 'I can go down and bring your breakfast up to you.'

'Indeed you will not,' Bridget told him. 'You're on holiday, too. We'll get dressed and go down to the dining-room for breakfast together.'

Bridget felt at ease as she sat at the beautifully-set dining table with the tall white lilies, and she enjoyed looking at the other guests and occasionally whispering the odd comment about them. She and Fred took their time over their full English breakfast, savouring the luxury of it all.

'Imagine having Danish pastries for breakfast,' Bridget commented as she took a bite of her cinnamon and raisin iced pastry. 'They're absolutely lovely. I must get them to have at home now and again.' She smiled. 'It's the little touches that make the difference, you know.'

'You have to hand it to her, she's a good businesswoman, that ...' Fred halted, his brow furrowed as he tried to remember the landlady's name.

'Thelma,' Bridget said quietly to him. 'Thelma Stevens.' She was used to filling in names of people and places for him, and did it automatically.

'She's not around this morning,' Fred said. 'It were a young girl on the desk.'

'I suppose she needs a long lie-in now and again,' Bridget mused, 'just like other people.' She lifted the teapot and filled Fred's cup again for him, then poured her own. She put milk and sugar in both cups, then sat back to finish her Danish pastry. 'D'you know something, Fred?' she said, a contemplative look on her face. 'I think we're the only young couple here on our own. It's all elderly people or couples with kids.' She smiled now. 'That just shows how romantic we still are, doesn't it? We're still happy enough to have a few days on our own.'

Fred's eyes suddenly became moist. 'I'm always happy when I'm with you, Bridget,' he said, sounding choked. 'I'm glad that we came away, and even gladder that you're lookin' a bit more like your old self.'

Bridget gave a little sigh. 'I've not exactly been the life and soul of the party recently, have I?'

Fred reached out and took her hand now. 'You've had a lot on your plate, love,' he told her, 'and you just needed a few days to yourself.' He squeezed her hand and winked at her. 'You'll be fine when we get back home.'

After breakfast they had a nice long walk around the gift shops, selecting presents for all the children. Bridget chose a Sindy for Helen, dressed in a stripy red-and-blue sweater and jeans, and Fred picked a fancy Swiss army knife for Michael.

Bridget's face clouded over when she saw the knife, her memory flashing back to the incident a few years ago when Fred had been stabbed. 'Don't you think that's a bit dangerous for a young boy? I don't think the Cubs let them have those things.'

'He's old enough,' Fred said, opening the knife up to reveal a number of handy implements like a bottle opener, small scissors, a screwdriver and nail clippers. 'He'll be joining the Scouts soon enough, and then he'll need things like this when he goes away camping.'

Bridget put her hand on Fred's arm. 'But what if it gets in the wrong hands?'

Fred turned to look at his wife. 'Idiots like that fella who went for me will always be able to find weapons. They don't have to buy a Swiss army knife, they can just as easily use a small vegetable knife or a Stanley knife if they want to injure somebody.' He put his hand over hers and squeezed it. 'Michael's a sensible lad; he'll only use the knife for what it was designed for.'

Bridget stared back at him, surprised that he had worked out what was bothering her so quickly. He was improving all the time. Just a year ago, he wouldn't have been able to do that. 'OK,' she said. 'If you think he'd like the knife then get it for him.'

They walked along the main row of shops, trying on cowboy hats with silly messages on the band, which made them laugh. Then they stopped at a newsagent's, bought a paper and had another laugh at the rude seaside postcards.

'What about Lucy?' Fred said, as they came out. 'We haven't bought anything for her yet.'

'Oh, I'll get her a doll or something,' Bridget said. 'I don't want to get her one of those small teenage dolls, because she puts all the little shoes and bags in her mouth.'

Fred pointed to a display just inside a gift shop door. 'There's some bigger dolls there in a basket. Why don't you have a look at them?'

Bridget stepped inside and went over to the basket. She picked up a blonde doll and examined it, checking that the hair was well stitched in and that the clothes had no little fiddly bits that could come loose and end up in her inquisitive daughter's mouth. She put the doll in the basket and reached down for another one, and when she brought it up to have a look at it, her whole body froze. It was a doll with dark skin and black curly hair. Very quickly, she threw the doll back into the basket.

'No good?' Fred said from the doorway.

'No,' Bridget said in a quivery voice. 'There's nothing there that would suit her.'

They walked back towards the boarding house now, Fred still suggesting things for Lucy every time they passed a shop, and Bridget terrified to go in, in case she saw another dark doll that looked like her daughter.

'Are you all right, love?' Fred asked every so often, clearly anxious at the change in his wife's temper.

'I'm fine,' Bridget lied. 'I'm just feeling a bit tired.'

'The sea air,' Fred told her. 'It can do that to you.'

They had lunch in a fish and chip shop on the pier, then walked up towards the Pleasure Beach, the cool sea air bringing a glow to Bridget's pale cheeks. The walk helped to lighten her mood, and she felt considerably better when they saw a lovely baby doll in a plastic carrycot for Lucy.

'That's a belter,' Fred laughed, as the lady put it into a large brown carrier bag. 'I can't wait to see her little face when we give her it.'

'How old is your little girl?' the shop assistant asked.

'She's just turned three,' he replied. He looked at Bridget. 'She's a proper little madam, isn't she?'

'She is indeed,' Bridget said.

'The cleverest out of the three of them, I reckon.' Fred winked at Bridget. 'Just like her mam.'

As they came out of the shop, Fred pointed to a wooden board outside advertising a fortune teller. 'Madame Marie-Rose. Why don't you go in?' he suggested, nodding towards the narrow doorway, which was shrouded with an exotic, Eastern-style curtain. 'You and June had a right laugh when you went to that woman down in Stockport.'

'I don't know...' Bridget said hesitantly. She had enjoyed her night out with June and some of June's friends, but it seemed somehow different going in on her own. God knows what the woman might tell her.

Fred fumbled in his pockets for change and came up with two half-crowns. 'There you are,' he said. 'That should be plenty.'

'What will you do?' Bridget asked, still unsure. 'You'll be left standing outside here like Piffin.'

'The bookies,' Fred grinned. 'There's a couple of good races on this afternoon. I wouldn't mind placin' a few bets.'

Bridget shook her head. 'There are no flies on you, Fred Roberts, are there?'

Chapter 49

❧❧❧

Bridget pushed back the exotic curtain and went inside the narrow doorway to a small, dimly lit corridor. Immediately, she was hit by the sickly-sweet smell of incense and joss sticks. She walked down the corridor, then turned into another doorway, this time through a multi-coloured, glass-beaded curtain. A young girl with brown curly hair sat at a desk, reading a magazine and filing her nails. Behind her was a red door with 'Madame Marie-Rose' in gold lettering on it, and to the side of the desk was a row of four pink, velvet-covered chairs. Various pictures and posters of zodiac signs and crystal balls adorned the purple walls.

'Is the fortune teller free?' Bridget asked, half hoping that she would be told to go away and come back later.

The girl looked up from her magazine and indicated the chairs. 'She'll only be five minutes,' she said in a strong Dublin accent.

'You're Irish!' Bridget said, smiling warmly at her. 'And I'd say from Dublin. Am I right?' She sat down on one of the chairs, immediately feeling more relaxed.

The girl beamed now. 'Yeah,' she said, nodding. 'I came over for the summer last year and I enjoyed meself so much tha' I decided to stay.'

'And are you doing this full time?' Bridget asked. 'Is this your job?'

'No,' the girl said, looking horrified. 'I only do this on a Saturday. I work in a factory during the week.' She paused. 'And you're Irish, too, by the sounds of it, and not from Dublin. Which part are you from?'

This was a question that Bridget always dreaded being asked. She hated the thought of running into people who might know anything about her background. But she had learned the best way to answer these kind of questions was to lead them off the subject. 'Offaly,' she said, then quickly added, 'but I've been over here for years. I'm livin' in Stockport now, near Manchester. Do you know it at all?'

Bridget had no problems with anyone knowing about her life since she left Ireland. In fact, she was proud of the fact that she was a landlady and loved talking about her business and her family to anyone she met. It was much safer territory than wandering back into the past.

'I was only in Stockport once,' the girl said. Then, before she could elaborate any further, the red door behind her opened and a woman came out.

'Thanks for that, love,' she called back to the fortune teller. 'I promise to come back an' let you know what happens.'

'You can go in now,' the girl told Bridget. 'And you give her the half-crown when she's finished.'

Madame Marie-Rose, a bird-like creature, sat in the small, candlelit room in a high carved chair. A small round table in front of her held a large crystal ball, several flickering candles and a small dish with a smoking joss stick in it. Her slanted eyes were outlined with black kohl and purple shadow, and she wore a sequinned, multi-coloured scarf tied gypsy-style around her long jet-black hair. Large earrings, like tiny chandeliers, dangled from her ears. She was dressed in vibrant robes topped with an embroidered black kimono decorated with beads and small mirrors. Her hands and fingers were heavily bejewelled, and Bridget's eyes were drawn to a large turquoise ring on her right middle finger. A silver chain, decorated with smaller turquoises, attached the ring to a bracelet. On her other arm was a variety of bangles and bracelets, which jingled loudly when she waved to Bridget to sit.

Bridget sank into a black chair appliquéd with silver moons and stars, her heart quickening at the thought of all the revelations that lay ahead. 'Lovely afternoon,' she heard herself say, immediately thinking that the exotic fortune teller would not have the slightest interest in a subject as mundane as the weather.

'My dear,' Madame Marie-Rose replied, giving a slow, serene smile, 'the weather is always lovely when it's lovely in our hearts.'

Bridget nodded earnestly.

The fortune teller handed her a pack of large tarot cards and asked her to shuffle them. 'This will transfer your own energy to the deck of cards,' she explained.

Bridget wondered what she was talking about, and how energy could transfer to cards, but thought it best to say nothing. She found the pictured cards bigger and more unwieldy to handle than normal playing cards, but she did her best to mix them up and, after a minute or so, she handed them back.

Madame Marie-Rose clasped the cards to her bosom and said, 'Now, I'd like you to think of a question you need answering or an area of your life where you need guidance.'

Bridget looked at her blankly. 'What sort of question?'

The fortune teller held her hands out. 'Perhaps you would like to know if a business venture is going to be successful? Perhaps you would like to know if there is a change of house awaiting you?' She then looked pointedly at Bridget's stomach. 'Perhaps you would like to know what lies ahead for your next child?'

A peculiar little feeling came into Bridget's throat. How had the fortune teller known she was pregnant? She hardly showed at this stage, and no one else had guessed until she told them. Immediately, Bridget decided that this woman was the genuine article.

'While you're thinking about your question or area of concern, I'm going to spread the cards into a past, present and future pattern,' Madame Marie-Rose went on, 'and then afterwards we'll do a horoscope spread.'

For the next half an hour, Bridget sat transfixed as the fortune teller picked up cards and told her details about her recent and distant past, during which she referred to people in her life with dark hair, fair hair and red hair. Then she went on to tell her about her present life, and Bridget held her breath when she mentioned children.

'I can see more than one child in this picture,' Madame Marie-Rose said, looking directly into Bridget's face. When she saw an expectant look appear, she quickly went on. 'I can see two ... three ... maybe four children?'

Bridget nodded confirmation.

'But I can see another child ...' the fortune-teller ventured.

Bridget's hands flew to her mouth.

'A very clever boy ... a boy who will make a difference to the world.'

Bridget closed her eyes now, reeling with the information. It was her child in Ireland. He must have his intelligence from his father's side and, regardless of the circumstances of his conception, would obviously go on to do something brilliant.

Madame Marie-Rose then went on to pick up various cards and talk about money that was coming to Bridget, which perhaps would be used for a car, or a change of car if they already had one.

Bridget nodded. 'It's about time Fred changed his car,' she said.

'He's a terrible man when it comes to spending money on himself – the family always comes first.'

'Someone he knows will try to sell him a car, but make sure he buys the car from a reputable garage,' the fortune teller advised. 'And tell him to avoid the colour green. A green car will only bring him bad luck.'

'I'll certainly tell him,' Bridget replied. 'We don't need any more accidents.'

Another card was pounced on. 'The man you have in your life is the one true love of your life,' the fortune teller pronounced. 'And you will both live to a great age.'

Bridget's heart soared. 'Thank God for that,' she said.

She went on lifting cards, which included weird pictures of men hanging upside down, magicians, lovers, fools, and skeletons.

Bridget's eyes widened when she saw Madame Marie-Rose pick up a card that showed a skeleton wielding a scythe. 'Does that mean I'm going to die?' she asked fearfully.

'No, no,' the fortune-teller said, smiling at her.

'But that's the grim reaper, isn't it? And that means death.'

'Not necessarily,' the colourful woman replied. 'In many cases it can mean an ending.' She picked up another card. 'This card shows that you've had a struggle in your life about something, and the first card means that struggle is coming to an end. That you're entering a new phase in your life where you can be free of worries, of secrets. That things will be fine.'

Bridget's face suddenly glowed. 'Are you saying that the secret or secrets won't be found out?'

Madame Marie-Rose nodded her head, her large earrings jingling as she did so. 'Your secret is safe,' she said.

'Well, what lies did she tell you?' Fred asked when they met up outside.

'Don't be saying that,' Bridget scolded. 'The woman was brilliant. She could tell me everything about my past, me growing up in the country and everything, and she described Tara down to a tee.'

'Did she?' Fred said, who wasn't the slightest bit interested in what the fortune teller had to say. But if it kept Bridget happy, that was all that mattered.

They started walking back towards the boarding house, Bridget taking Fred's arm. 'And you've got to get a new car soon, but not a green one,' she told him firmly.

Fred raised his eyebrows but said nothing.

'And the children will all do well, and we've to encourage them to stay on at school.'

'But that's only common sense,' Fred laughed, unable to stop himself. 'That's not fortune tellin'. I bet she tells everybody that. How much did she charge you for that load of rubbish? The bloody robber.'

'Shush,' Bridget said, gripping his arm tightly. 'She said you and me would live to a ripe old age and be very happy together.'

Fred was silent for a few moments. 'Oh, well,' he said in a softer voice. 'I suppose it was worth any amount of money for her to tell you that.'

Chapter 50

Tara sat back in the square black leather chair and looked around her at the collection of modern and traditional furniture, trying to get a feel for the sort of life that Gerry McShane led in this big house all on his own.

It was hard for her to imagine, because she had little experience of a single man's life. She had grown up knowing almost everything about Gabriel. Being his sister's close friend since a young age, she had known all there was to know about his daily routine in Ballygrace House. And when she was a teenager, she had spent a lot of time with the Fitzgeralds and seen their gracious, very refined home life at first hand.

And then, of course, there had been Frank Kennedy. The work-obsessed Frank had only used his house to sleep in. He had little time for a domestic home life, preferring restaurants and hotels for socialising, but of course that could all have changed by now. He was older and more mature, and, for all she knew, he might place more value on domesticity since he was in a long-term relationship.

And then there was the constant single male in her life – Joe. She smiled as she thought of him now. Joe's life could hardly be described as typical, living in a parochial house with only an elderly priest and an equally elderly housekeeper for company, at the beck and call of his parishioners around the clock.

As her eyes moved along the main wall, from one painting to another, Tara concluded that her experience of men was indeed fairly limited. Apart from her marriage, her main connection with them was through business. That was an area in which she felt both equal and comfortable with the opposite sex. And although she felt perfectly at ease discussing business with Gerry McShane, the situation in which she now found herself was entirely different.

She could hear him rattling about in the kitchen, organising ice-cubes and lemon for their gin and tonics. The house was spacious, the size of her two houses combined, and beautifully kept. There was not a speck of dust or a cushion out of place. He obviously had someone coming in to look after it. Tara couldn't imagine any man keeping it so clean on his own.

He came back into the room now, holding a glass full of ice, a small pair of tongs, and a little Spanish-patterned dish with slices of lemon.

'I'm very impressed,' Tara said, waving her hand around the room. 'You've got excellent taste; you've managed to mix the modern and the old very well.' She looked at the items in his hands. 'And I'm also impressed with your culinary skills. I'm going to give you ten out of ten so far.'

He caught the humour in her green eyes and they both started to laugh.

'I don't know what kind of men you're used to,' Gerry said, 'but it has to be a very useless one who can't come up with a few ice-cubes and a bit of lemon.'

He put the things down on the coffee table, then went to the sideboard and brought over the two tall gin and tonics he had poured earlier. He put one glass in front of her and left one sitting in the middle of the table for himself.

'What sort of music do you like?' he asked, going over to a large, well-polished radiogram. He switched on the lamp on top of it, then opened one of the doors and lifted out several albums. He went through them. 'The Beatles, Rolling Stones, Bob Dylan, the Seekers ...'

'Bob Dylan,' Tara decided, feeling that it would be the most relaxing at this time of night. She leaned forward now and spooned a couple of ice cubes into her drink followed by a chunk of lemon. Then she sat back, smoothing her dress down over her thighs with her free hand. She had been conscious of the shorter dress throughout the evening, but was much more so now, in this intimate situation with a man. A very handsome man.

'I've got a few of his albums,' he told her. 'Have you any preference?'

Tara shrugged. 'To be honest, I only know a few of the titles, so just put on the first one that comes to hand.' She took a sip of her long, cool drink, deciding that she really must make more time to listen to some of the new popular music. She rarely listened to the radio, as her mind was always on work-related matters in the mornings and evenings, and she never joined Angela or any of the other women in the house when they were watching pop programmes on television. She had always thought the music was trivial compared to the classical works she had always enjoyed.

But recently, she had realised there was a depth and quality to some of the music when she took the time to listen properly. And the lyrics of the songs related to the here and now, the modern sixties life that Tara was a part of.

Gerry lifted *Bringing It All Back Home* from the pile of albums and put it on top of the radiogram, then put the others back inside. He switched the record player on, took the album cover off and slid the black vinyl record from its white sleeve, then put it on the turntable.

As Bob Dylan's voice floated across the room, Gerry went over to the far corner to put on another lamp. He switched off the main light, which suddenly changed the whole atmosphere. The centre of the room was now dimly lit with small pools of lights in the corners. Then he came to sit down on the sofa opposite her.

'That's better,' he said, picking up his drink. 'A bit more of a late-night atmosphere as befits the late-night music.' He took a good slug of his drink, then stretched out, his head resting on the back of the sofa, looking very relaxed.

There was a small silence. 'You're extremely organised,' Tara told him, for something to say.

'I wasn't always,' he said, shaking his head and smiling at her. 'I had to be trained into this.'

Tara hesitated for a moment, unsure whether she should tread into personal territory. 'Well, whoever trained you,' she said carefully, 'did a very good job.'

'Actually, it was an older woman,' he volunteered. 'Well, older by a few years. We had a relationship for a while.' He patted the modern leather sofa. 'She was the one who encouraged me to be a bit more adventurous about things. She travelled abroad a lot, and I suppose she had a fairly sophisticated taste.' He lifted his glass and took another drink. 'Before her, I was your typical professional man who treated home as a base to eat and sleep.'

Tara nodded. 'To be honest,' she said wryly, 'I'm not much better myself.' She rolled her eyes, a slight feeling of embarrassment stealing over her. 'In effect, I'm now a lodger in the house I used to own, and I only really have one room I can call my own.'

'But that was a business decision,' he told her. 'And I'm sure it's only a temporary measure. When the new hotel starts to pay off, you can buy into the housing market again.'

'I don't really mind living like that at the moment,' she told him. 'And with the new job in the hotel coming up, I won't be spending that much time at home.'

'You can always have a room in the Grosvenor any night you want,' he reminded her. 'That's one of the perks of owning the hotel. And, unlike your smaller hotel, it's big enough for you to have a degree of anonymity.' He laughed now. 'In fact, if you sent for room service for all your meals, you could hide away completely and no one would even know you were there.'

Tara laughed, too. 'It's a good option to have if the going gets tough.' Then something suddenly prompted her to divulge her feelings further. Probably the fact that Gerry McShane was new to her life and didn't have the information to prejudge the situation. 'I suppose I am in a bit of a quandary regarding houses and homes ...'

Gerry's brow furrowed. 'In what way?'

'Well,' she started, unconsciously toying with a strand of her newly straightened hair, 'while I'm essentially living in one bedroom in someone else's house, I have a big house back in Ireland that I only visit a few times a year.' A little cloud passed over her face. 'It was my husband's family home.' She paused to take a mouthful of her drink. 'Apart from the fact that it's a beautiful Georgian house, it has everything I could possibly want or need in a home, but at the moment it just doesn't fit in with the way my life is going. My work and all my main business interests are over here in Stockport.' She shrugged. 'Several people have suggested that I should sell it, but I feel I can't even contemplate the thought of it. It just doesn't feel right.' Then, whether it was the effect of the gin and tonic, or the fact she needed to talk things over with somebody, she suddenly heard herself saying, 'Ballygrace House is a family house. It wasn't meant to be left empty. It has lovely gardens, grounds and stables. It was built for people with children who can use all those things.' She shrugged again. 'Maybe I *should* consider selling it at some point.'

'Maybe *you* and your family will live in it again some day,' Gerry said quietly. 'When the time is right, you could have a husband and children living there with you.'

Tara looked down into her glass, took another drink from it. It was funny how she'd been able to say such a thing to Gerry McShane, when she'd been unable to voice her thoughts even to Joe or Bridget. 'I'm happy enough with the way my life is at present,' she told him, 'and the future can take care of itself.'

He held up his glass and smiled. 'I'll drink to that,' he said. 'That's exactly how live *my* life.'

They finished their drinks, then Gerry went over to the sideboard and poured them each another.

'Make mine smaller this time, please,' Tara said. 'I'm afraid I don't have a very good head for strong drink.'

He brought the drinks over to the table, then stretched his hand out towards her. 'Why don't you come and sit beside me?' he suggested in a soft voice.

Tara looked at him and reached her hand out. He gently pulled her to her feet, then drew her straight into his arms. Before she had time to think about it – to analyse whether she was doing the right thing – his warm, sweet mouth was crushing down hard on hers, and the tingling feeling that had been within her all night suddenly intensified into a blaze.

After what seemed a long time, he drew away from her, holding her at arm's length. 'I've been wanting to do that since the first moment I set eyes on you.'

Tara met his gaze, and, when he saw his own feelings mirrored in her vivid green eyes, he moved back to the comfort of the big leather sofa, pulling her down beside him. 'You are the most beautiful woman I've seen in a long, long time,' he whispered into her hair. His lips moved now to trace a little path from her forehead down her cheek, then halted at the scented hollow in the base of her neck.

Tara closed her eyes, savouring the delicious feelings that were racing through her. Feelings that had not been ignited for a long time.

'The touch and the feel of your skin is a hundred times better than I imagined it would be,' he whispered, then his lips came to meet hers again in a longer, more exploratory kiss.

When her hands reached up to link behind his neck, ruffling his thick fair hair and pulling him closer, Gerry subtly manoeuvred them both again until they were lying entwined on the long leather sofa, limbs pressed tightly against each other as their kisses deepened and their tentative caresses grew more intense.

At one point Tara suddenly thought of her short dress and whether she might be showing the tops of her stockings, but, after a few moments, Gerry's burning kisses drove all such cares away. She felt herself yield as his hand came to cover and then gently circle her breasts. And then his mouth traced the route it had found earlier, pausing again at the little dip in her neck, but this time trailing down to the hollow between her breasts.

Tara lay back, her eyes closed, almost drowning in the feelings that were enveloping her. It was only when she felt his hand move along her thigh to touch the patch of naked skin above her stocking that she was suddenly jolted into the reality of what she was doing.

'No, Gerry,' she said, moving away from him, drawing her legs underneath her and pulling down the hem of her dress.

'What's wrong?' he said, a perplexed look on his face. 'What have I done?'

Tara's head drooped, and the heavy waves of red hair covered her face. 'It's not you,' she whispered. 'It's ... I'm not ready for this.' She fought back the tears that were prickling at the back of her eyes. 'I wasn't prepared to go this far ...'

'It's OK, Tara,' he said, putting his arm around her.

'I'm sorry, Gerry – it's just too soon.'

Chapter 51

❧

Bridget turned around to let Fred look at her navy polka-dot outfit. 'What do you think?' she asked. 'Is it fancy enough to go dancing in the Tower Ballroom?'

'It's absolutely gorgeous,' he told her, the sincerity shining in his eyes. 'And it's perfect for a dance.'

'Do I look very pregnant in it?' she asked.

Fred shook his head. 'You still wouldn't know you were expectin' at all.' He looked at his watch. 'We'd better get a move on,' he said, 'if we want to get a good seat. We can't have you standing all night; it wouldn't be good for you.'

Bridget lifted her light duster coat and bag from the end of the bed. 'I'm really excited,' she told him. 'I've always wanted to go to the Blackpool Tower.'

As they came down the stairs towards the reception desk, Fred said, 'I'll just hang onto the room key tonight, in case there's no one on reception when we get back.'

'Good idea,' Bridget replied. 'I wonder if Thelma's around? I'd like to let her know where we're going.'

'I think I hear her in the office,' Fred said. 'But it sounds as if she's busy – somebody is in there with her.'

Bridget craned her neck. The office door was slightly ajar and she could see Thelma's red jacket through the frosted glass and hear the murmur of low voices in conversation. Then the door opened a bit further and Tara saw a blonde-haired young woman leaning against the wall in the office. A very brassy, cheap-looking woman. Not the sort of person that she would have expected to see in Thelma's nice boarding-house. The girl was nodding at whatever the landlady was saying, while twirling a piece of chewing gum she was stretching from her red-painted mouth around her finger.

'Have you seen the girl that's in with Thelma?' Bridget whispered, frowning in disapproval.

'Come on,' Fred said, putting a hand under her elbow. 'We can't disturb them, and anyway, we're not going to get seats in the ball-room if we don't get a move on.' Then the office door opened and

Bridget heard the girl say, 'Look, I'll pass on your message, but you know what she's like. I've already warned her about him. He's bad news.' The girl turned her head now and, catching sight of Bridget and Fred, she moved back and quickly closed the door to continue her conversation with Thelma Stevens in private.

Bridget moved now, her husband almost propelling her out the front door.

'I hope Thelma didn't see us standing there gawping at them,' Fred grumbled. 'She'll think we're a right pair of nosy-parkers.'

'I'm surprised at her allowing anyone like that on the premises,' Bridget said. 'I hope she's not one of the guests.'

The Tower Ballroom lived up to all Bridget's expectations. While Fred was at the bar, she gazed around her at the ornate ceilings, the fancy chandeliers and the plush seating and decoration. She couldn't remember being in a place that was so nice. She must tell Tara about the décor, she thought. It was exactly the sort of thing that would look good in the Grosvenor Hotel. In fact, maybe she, Tara and Angela might take a drive over one Saturday to have a good look at it in the daylight.

Bridget was quite pleased with herself for thinking of that, but then she'd worked in the Grosvenor Hotel before Tara had. She knew exactly what she'd do to it if she had a free hand with the decorating. She reckoned that the big function room in the hotel would look brilliant with similar big gilt mirrors and the fancy wall-lighting. It needed a big room to show features like that to their best advantage.

'Excuse me, but is anyone sitting in those two chairs?'

Bridget looked up, momentarily startled out of her little daydream, and saw a middle-aged couple standing in front of her. 'No,' she replied, 'there's only myself and my husband sitting here, so you're welcome to sit down.'

The husband – a tall, thin man with strange, sandy hair – pulled out a chair for his equally thin wife, then sat down himself. 'We don't like to be too near the band,' he explained to Bridget. 'Otherwise you can't hear yourself speak.' He gave a little shrug. 'There's no point in coming out if you can't have a bit of a chat, is there?'

By the time Fred came back from the bar with their drinks, the couple had told Bridget all about themselves. They were Sam and Gladys Bennett and they'd lived in Blackpool all their lives. They said that they went dancing every Saturday night and gave her and Fred their opinions on the other dance halls in Blackpool.

'I like the Tower the best,' the more talkative Sam had explained, 'because they know how to keep a proper dance floor. Not too highly polished, in case people slip, you know, and not too ... otherwise you end up tripping over your feet.'

'It's a fine dance hall,' Fred agreed. 'No doubt about it.' He hailed a passing waitress now, and ordered another two drinks for him and Bridget and two for the couple.

Sam then went on to give Bridget and Fred a potted history of the Blackpool Tower. 'Have a guess when it was built?' he challenged them.

Fred looked at Bridget and shrugged. 'I haven't got clue.'

'Neither have I,' Bridget said. 'But I suppose it must be old enough.'

'Eighteen ninety-nine!' Sam said, delighted to have caught them out.

Bridget stifled a sigh of boredom. This was not the sort of evening she had envisaged, sitting with a know-it-all of a man and his mousy wife, who let her husband do all the talking. She'd also worked out the reason for Sam Bennett's odd hair: he was wearing a wig. She could tell by the tufts of grey hair that were showing at the back of his neck and the side of one ear.

'That's right nice of you, Fred,' Sam said, when the drinks were brought to the table. 'I'll get the next round for us.'

'Sam always likes to stand his round,' Gladys announced. 'He hates free-loaders, don't you, Sam?'

Sam nodded gravely, then took a drink of beer. 'Now, I'm going to ask you both a question,' he said, putting his pint back on the table, 'and we'll see if you know the answer this time.' He rubbed his hands together, enjoying himself immensely. 'What year did they have the terrible fire in the Tower Ballroom?' He pointed his finger like a gun now, first at Bridget then at Fred. 'Any idea?'

'I haven't a clue,' Bridget said again.

Gladys gave her a sympathetic smile. 'Sam's always trying to catch people out.'

Fred's brow furrowed in concentration. He'd known about the fire at the time, it had been on the news and in all the papers. He racked his brains now, then inspiration struck. 'Nineteen sixty,' he said.

'Wrong!' Sam Bennett stated, as quick as a flash. 'But close – you were a year out. The Tower Ballroom caught on fire in nineteen fifty-nine.'

Then, to Bridget's utter boredom, he went on to tell them, in great detail, how all the restoration work was carried out and how long it took. 'Eighteen months,' he stated, jabbing his finger on the table for emphasis, 'and they had it back to the way it was before. Can you believe it? An exact replica of the way it was.'

Eventually, the band came on and Bridget almost dragged Fred onto the floor when they struck up the first tune.

'We'll have to move, Fred,' she told him heatedly. 'I can't stand listening to that man for the rest of the night. He's driving me mad.'

'Aw, he's not too bad,' Fred replied, 'and he knows his stuff. He can tell you the history of all the main things in Blackpool. You should have heard all the things he was telling me about the wrestling matches they have here.'

'If I want to hear the history of bloody Blackpool,' Bridget hissed, 'I'll buy a flamin' book. I don't want to come out for the night and have to listen to all that claptrap.'

They had several more dances, but eventually had to return to the table, as there were no other spare seats available. Bridget gritted her teeth and endured another half an hour of Sam Bennett's revelations, and then, mercifully, another older couple came in who knew the Bennetts. They drew two spare chairs in at the end of the table, leaving Bridget and Fred to their own conversation.

Later that night, the Roberts walked along the seashore back to the boarding-house.

'Well,' Fred said, throwing an affectionate arm around his wife, 'did the Tower Ballroom live up to your expectations?'

'It did,' Bridget told him. 'Once we got rid of that boring pair, I thoroughly enjoyed my night. It's a beautiful place, and it gave me a few ideas to pass onto Tara for the ballroom in the Grosvenor.'

'Fair play to her for getting involved in that venture,' Fred commented. 'It's not many women who could hold their own with the crowd that have bought it. You'd have to be very strong to stand up to each and every one of them.'

'Frank Kennedy's not like that,' Bridget said. 'Frank's as nice and easy-going as you'll find.'

Fred gave his wife a sidelong look. 'Not when it comes to business he's not. He's as tough as the next man – and tougher than most. I've seen him in action on a number of occasions, and he won't let anyone talk him down.'

'Have you seen much of him recently?' Bridget asked. 'He hasn't been down at the house for ages.'

Fred shrugged. 'I've seen him occasionally at the Cale Green for business meetings or if there's a big match on in the Grosvenor, but he's not around as much as he used to be. He's been travelling to Ireland a lot recently. I think he said somebody in his family has been sick.'

'Who?' Bridget said, interested.

Fred's brows knitted together. 'He definitely said *somebody* was ill ... but I can't remember the details, or whether he said they were in hospital or anything like that.'

Bridget didn't press him. Although he was more or less back to his old self since his accident some years back, his memory still let him down on occasion.

'I wonder how things are going with the new hotel?' Bridget mused. 'Tara will have to be in meetings with Frank. She didn't look a bit happy about that when I mentioned it to her recently.'

'Tara's a great boss,' Fred said, 'but she can be very frosty with people when it suits her. I've seen her with Frank Kennedy and she cuts the nose off him at every opportunity.'

Bridget made a disapproving noise with her tongue. 'You'd be ashamed to be there when she has to talk to him. She can be down-right bloody rude, so she can. It's a trait in Tara that I don't like one little bit.'

'It's a pity she's like that with him,' Fred said, 'because they're both very nice people. Tara's a lovely lady and Frank's a sound bloke. When I was sick, he was in and out of the hospital all the time.'

Bridget gave a little shiver as she recalled those awful dark months when Fred was recovering from his accident. Fred could hardly re-member them. He talked about that time now as though he did, but Bridget knew he was only repeating all the things that people had told him.

'Frank Kennedy was a rock in my life then,' she said with passion in her voice. 'He offered to help in every way he could – even with money if it was needed. There's not many you can say that about.'

She let out a long, slow sigh. 'It's a pity things went so bad between him and Tara, for they were well suited.' She looked up at Fred now. 'Even better suited than her and Gabriel.'

Fred's brow furrowed. 'Was that the blondy fella from Ireland? The one that died?'

Bridget bit her lip. For some reason, he'd always had trouble remembering Gabriel. It was one of the little gaps he still had in his memory. 'That's him – Tara's husband,' she said, trying not to sound irritated.

There was a small silence then Fred suddenly said, 'Well, there's one thing for sure – Tara and Frank Kennedy will never get together again.' As they came towards the Lantern pub, Fred checked his watch. 'It's not closing time for another half an hour. D'you fancy a nightcap?' Then, when he saw the hesitation of Bridget's face, he said, 'It might help you to sleep.'

Bridget laughed. 'Go on then,' she said.

As soon as they walked into the crowded pub, Bridget spotted the blonde, cheap-looking girl she'd seen talking to Thelma Stevens in the office earlier on. She was sitting at a small corner table with another cheap-looking girl, who had very obviously dyed black hair.

They found a place at the end of a long table, and Bridget sat looking around her while her husband went to get the drinks. Fred had a few words at the bar with Thelma's landlord friend, then he brought their drinks back to the table.

'No sign of Thelma tonight?' Fred asked, handing Bridget her brandy and lemonade.

Bridget shook her head. 'To tell you the truth, I'm not too bothered about company tonight. I'm tired after all the walking we've done today, and I'm tired listening to people talking after that old bore back at the Tower Ballroom.'

Fred laughed. 'Well, we'll enjoy this drink and then we'll head back to bed.'

The reception desk and sitting-room were deserted when Fred and Bridget came back to the boarding house. They went quietly upstairs, Bridget using the bathroom on the landing first, followed by Fred. Within ten minutes of getting into bed, both of them were fast asleep.

Bridget woke with a start around three o'clock. She sat up in bed, listening, sure that something or somebody had wakened her. She lay back down again and tried to get back to sleep, but she was still awake a good five minutes later.

Then she decided she might feel more comfortable if she paid a visit to the lavatory. Very quietly, so as not to wake Fred, she crept out of bed and padded across the floor in her barefeet. She lifted her dressing-gown from the back of the door, then silently went out into the corridor and headed towards the bathroom.

She was on her way back again when she heard a noise downstairs. She halted, listening, then she heard it again. It was Thelma's voice – and it was raised. Loud enough for it to be heard on the floor above.

Bridget wondered now if she'd maybe brought Jim back. By the sounds of it, they were having some sort of row. Then she heard Thelma's voice again, this time more insistent, and something made her go towards the stairs. Quietly, she tip-toed down the top few steps, until she came to a bend in the staircase where she could see down to the reception desk. A figure was lying flat out on the floor. In a pool of blood.

Bridget clapped a hand over her mouth to stop herself from screaming. And then she recognised the figure. It was the girl from the Lantern. The girl with the dyed black hair.

Chapter 52

❧

B ridget stood motionless for a couple of minutes, not knowing what to do. Then she heard quick footsteps coming along the corridor and recognised the red hair of Thelma Stevens.

The landlady was carrying an armful of the boarding house's blue towels. She went straight to the girl and knelt down beside her, pressing a towel to the side of the girl's head, then putting a folded one under her head to serve as a pillow. She then put several more around the girl to mop up the trail of scarlet blood, which presumably was coming from a wound in her head.

Whether it was the heaving of Thelma's shoulders that alerted

Bridget to the fact she was very upset, or whether Bridget's natural instincts just automatically took over, she found herself making her way down the rest of the stairs.

'Thelma,' Bridget said, padding across the cold, tiled hallway. 'Are you OK? What's happened?'

Thelma's anguished face turned towards her. 'Oh, Bridget,' she said. 'We're in terrible trouble. What will I do if any of the other guests come out and see her?'

'Who is it?' Bridget looked down at the rough-looking girl in the dirty denim jacket.

There was a moment's silence. 'It's Sarah,' Thelma said. 'Sarah, my daughter. She collapsed and banged her head on the floor.'

Bridget's throat suddenly ran dry. How on earth could this cheap-looking tramp of a girl be the glamorous Thelma's daughter?

Quarter of an hour later, Bridget and Thelma were sitting in Thelma's bedroom, both staring at the girl, who was now lying on the land-lady's bed. They had managed to drag the girl in, and had done their best to clean her up with a basin of soapy water and some of the blue flannels that matched the towels. Bridget had felt a bit queasy as she wiped the blood away, but they had both been relieved to find that the worst of the blood had come from her nose when she had fallen, and not from the small cut on the side of her head.

'I can't thank you enough,' Thelma said, her eyes filling up again. 'I'd never have managed to carry her here on my own, even though it's only the ground floor. I would have had to call for an ambulance or something like that, and they'd have woken everybody with their sirens.'

'What are you going to do now?' Bridget asked, feeling winded from half-carrying, half-dragging the girl. 'You might still have to call an ambulance – she doesn't look a bit well to me.'

'I can't phone the ambulance,' Thelma whispered. 'They'll only phone the police.'

Bridget stared at her, not understanding.

'It's drugs,' Thelma said. 'I've seen her like this before. I know all the signs.'

Bridget looked back at the girl. 'D'you think she could die if we don't get her help?'

Thelma shook her head. 'No. She's taken something tonight that's made her go all weird, seeing things that aren't there … hallucinating.'

'LSD?' Bridget said fearfully. She'd read about it in papers and magazines.

'Probably.' Thelma bit her lip. 'It wasn't just that, though. When she got into a state, her friend gave her a sleeping tablet to calm her down. 'That's what's made her conk out.'

'Oh.' Bridget suddenly got the picture. 'Where's her friend now?'

'Buggered off,' Thelma replied. 'She wouldn't want to have to explain anything to me.'

'What will you do?' Bridget asked.

'I'll just have to leave her here and let her sleep it off.'

'What about you?' Bridget asked. 'Where will you sleep?'

'I'll be fine here in the chair.' Thelma sounded weary, like someone who had lost the fight too many times. 'I can have a lie-down in the afternoon tomorrow if it catches up with me.'

'If you need me,' Bridget said, 'just call up to the room. I probably won't sleep much.'

'Thanks,' Thelma said. She attempted a little smile. 'But do try to sleep. You need it when you're in the family way.'

Bridget went out of the room now and started to make her way back up to her bedroom, hardly able to believe what had happened in the last half an hour. Then, as she turned the bend in the stairs, she came to an abrupt halt, wondering whether she should wake Fred to tell him what had happened. Should she tell him at all? She usually told him everything. Well, apart from things that would hurt him.

She thought for a short while, then decided that she would speak to him before they went down for breakfast. Bridget felt herself suddenly shiver and started back up the last few stairs, but somehow, as she neared the top, her bare foot got tangled in the hem of her long nightdress. She put her left hand out to the wall to steady herself, but her hand slid along the smooth painted surface and she was propelled forwards, her stomach landing heavily on the edge of the top two stairs.

She heard herself call out as she fell, then she lay there silently for a few minutes. How unbelievable, she thought. Two dramas in one night. She stayed still, just breathing very carefully and gently, and trying to work out if she'd done herself any real damage. The only pain she could feel was in her left hand, which had landed awkwardly on the stairs. It felt numb and painful.

After a while, she moved her other arm and, very slowly, levered herself into a sitting position. Then she sat up straight and took stock. Apart from her left arm she didn't feel too bad. Just a bit winded and shaky, but she didn't appear to have broken any bones or suffered any serious injury.

Very gingerly, and leaning with her right hand on the banister she pulled herself into a standing position now. Again, she waited for a minute or so to check there was nothing amiss, then she continued to the top of the stairs and along the corridor to her room.

She slid quietly into bed beside her sleeping husband, pulling the blankets up under her chin for warmth and hugging her sore arm close to her chest to ease the dull ache. Eventually, she closed her eyes and said a few silent prayers asking God to help poor Thelma to cope with the problems that inevitably lay ahead for tomorrow and all the days afterwards.

But she knew she was asking a lot of God, because Sarah Stevens was not going to be an easy girl to sort out.

Chapter 53

When Bridget woke around eight o'clock the following morning, she lay quietly for a while, wondering if the strange events of the previous night had been some sort of weird nightmare. But when she went over it all again in her mind, she quickly realised that it had all actually happened. She turned on her side now to face Fred, who was still in a deep sleep, and placed a tentative hand on his shoulder.

'Fred?' she whispered. 'Are you awake?'

Fred grunted and opened one glazed eye. He looked at her for a few moments and then his eyelid slowly came down like a shutter – and stayed closed.

Bridget lay there for a little longer, then slipped out of bed. She stood for a minute, checking that she felt OK after the fall last night, before dressing. She put on the same jersey suit she had arrived in, and, satisfied that she looked decent enough to be seen by the other guests, dabbed a bit of Panstick on her face and applied pink lipstick.

She decided not to waste any time, and to brush her teeth and freshen up properly later. Lastly, she brushed her hair, tutting quietly at a wing of it that insisted on turning under instead of out.

Then she silently tip-toed out of the room.

Heedful of her minor accident the previous night, she placed her hand firmly on the handrail as she descended the stairs. The reception desk was deserted and, as far as Bridget could see through the frosted-glass door, there was no sign of Thelma Stevens in the small office, either.

She crossed the hallway to look into the dining-room and spotted the familiar red hair at a table by the window. Thelma's head was bent over her breakfast, but from what Bridget could see, she looked her usual smart, professional self.

Bridget stared for a few moments, wondering what to do, then Thelma lifted her head and caught sight of her helpful guest. She held her fork aloft and waved it, signalling Bridget to come and join her.

'Are you all right?' Bridget whispered, sliding into the seat opposite the landlady. 'I've been worried about you all night.'

Thelma nodded and gave a little sigh. 'I'm fine, love ... and thanks for all your help. I don't know what I'd have done without you.'

From a distance, dressed in a bright-green suit with a dark-green blouse and pearls, the landlady looked as pristine as ever, but Bridget could see that the night had definitely taken its toll. There were dark circles under her eyes that the double layer of foundation had not managed to conceal, and the rouge she had rubbed into her cheekbones only served to highlight her deathly pallor. And there was an obvious flatness about her whole demeanour.

'It was nothing at all,' Bridget told her. 'I'm only glad I was awake when it happened.' She leaned across the table now, not wishing any of the other diners to overhear. 'How is Sarah?'

'She came around from the sleeping tablet about six o'clock this morning, so I got her a pot of strong black coffee and made her drink the lot. I nearly poured it down her.' Thelma pursed her lips. 'She couldn't remember half of what had happened to her. Those bloody drugs, which I suppose she mixed with drink. That's her usual caper.'

'Actually,' Bridget suddenly remembered, 'I saw her and a friend in the Lantern last night.' Then, when she saw the alarmed look on the landlady's face, she said very quickly, 'They looked fine. They were just sitting in a corner by themselves, not doing anybody any harm.' How could she say otherwise? She couldn't say that they both looked like something the cat had dragged in off the street, could she?

'I bet they were trying to tap Jim for money. That's what they usually do.' Thelma let out a sigh of exasperation. 'That friend of hers, Shirley, has been the ruination of our Sarah. She was a good girl up until she got in with her and the crowd she hangs around with.' Tears suddenly filled her eyes. 'They'd do anything for drink and drugs at the weekend ... and I mean *anything*. No man is safe when that Shirley's around, and it's always her that suggests they go into the Lantern to see Jim. They know he's a soft touch and will give them free drinks.' Thelma lifted her starched white napkin and touched it to the inside corners of her eyes.

Bridget's eyes were wide with shock. 'It must be very hard on you,' she murmured.

'Indeed it is ... indeed it is.' Thelma's voice dropped to an anguished whisper. 'Can you imagine admitting all that about your own daughter?' She shook her head. 'Never in my wildest dreams did I ever think I'd be saying that about my lovely Sarah.'

Bridget nodded, giving a sidelong glance at the tables around to check that nobody had noticed Thelma's upset. 'It must be very hard on you,' she repeated, unable to think of anything more suitable to say.

'She was a beautiful little girl,' Thelma said now in a choked voice. 'I dressed her in the best of everything. I had her feet measured twice a year for Clarke's shoes, when I hadn't the money for a decent pair of shoes for my own feet.'

'Where is she now?' Bridget asked.

'She's gone home ... or back to that dump she calls home. She lives in a flat with Shirley.' Thelma took a deep breath. 'I sent for a taxi at seven o'clock this morning to collect her. Thank God I got her out of the place before any of the guests were up and about. Some of the older ones are inclined to get up early in the morning and go for a walk down by the shore, and there are others that like to go out to get the morning papers before breakfast.'

Bridget nodded. 'If Fred's up early, he often goes for the paper.'

Thelma's face suddenly dropped. 'What did Fred say when you told him what happened?'

'He doesn't know yet,' Bridget replied. 'He slept through it all, and he's still flat out this morning.'

'Thank God,' Thelma said. She shook her head and look down at her dish of grapefruit segments. 'I only hope you never go through anything like this with your children, Bridget. It's like carrying a cross on your back all the time. It never goes away. You're constantly wondering and waiting for something to happen.'

'Maybe you could get her some help,' Bridget suggested, 'send her to a doctor or something like that ...'

'I've tried. God knows I've tried.' Thelma reached for the teapot. 'You'll have a cup of tea, Bridget, won't you?' She indicated the cup and saucer in front of her. 'And maybe some toast? A slice of toast won't spoil your appetite for breakfast later.' Bridget checked her watch. 'Go on,' she said. 'A long lie-in won't do Fred a bit of harm.'

They sat chatting for a while longer, and when the subject turned to her son, Thelma brightened considerably. 'Neville is the light of my life,' she told Bridget. 'I don't know what I'd do without him. A clever, clever lad. He's the only thing that keeps me going.' She nodded to the ceiling. 'Him and this place. I don't know how I'd have managed without Neville and my business.' She paused before adding. 'And Jim, of course. He's a tower of strength, because he's been through tough times with his own wife.' She shook her red head. 'It's no joke when the whole village knows your wife has run off with the butcher. Poor Jim was the butt of their jokes after it all happened. He was glad to move out here where nobody knows him.'

Bridget nodded. 'Small places can be lethal for gossip.' She knew only too well what it was like to be talked about. Back in Ballygrace she had been the subject of much cruel chatter.

'Can you imagine what my life would be like with Sarah if I lived in a small place? I'd never be able to hold my head up or look anyone in the eye again.' She gave a small, watery smile. 'At least around here there's not that many people that really know you. I mean, I hardly know the people that live in the next street, and if there's anything in the newspaper about Sarah, then nobody's going to know that I'm her mother.' She leaned forward now. 'Some of my closest friends don't even know the problems I've been having, and I wouldn't dream of telling them.'

'If they're real friends, they'll understand,' Bridget said, taking a bite of her buttered toast.

A sceptical look crossed Thelma's face. 'Oh, you'd be surprised when it comes to friends. Not everyone is like you, Bridget. Not everyone is so kind and understanding.'

Bridget's heart lifted at the compliment.

'No, when it comes to Sarah, I'm careful who I talk to,' Thelma went on. 'I try to swing the conversation around to Neville. In fact, I end up boring them to tears about Neville, telling them all about his college exams and his teaching practices.' She laughed now, her whole face lighting up. 'I love repeating the funny stories that he tells me about the school. The things the innocent little kids say – they fairly warm your heart.' She took a sip of her tea. 'Of course, you're used to all that, having three young children of your own. Oh, you don't know how lucky you are, Bridget. When they're young like that you don't have a worry in the world.'

'I suppose not,' Bridget said, a thoughtful look on her face.

'Come on now,' Thelma said. 'What worries can a young child bring to you? Apart from their health and how they're doing at school, of course. But that aside, all they bring is joy and contentment. I remember it well from when my own were small.'

Bridget looked at Thelma now, wondering if she dared confide in her about Lucy. She would give anything to be able to sit down over a drink and spill it all out to someone who wouldn't judge her. There was no one she could ask advice from. Not even Tara, who disapproved so strongly about what had happened between her and Lloyd. But someone like Thelma might understand. After all, she was divorced and was having a relationship with a divorced man. She was obviously broad-minded about these things. It was always people who had been through a tough time themselves who understood the problems of others.

'Since it's our last night,' Bridget ventured, 'we might have a little drink together down in the Lantern?'

Thelma's eyes brightened. 'That would be lovely. I was going to suggest the same thing myself. Fred and Jim hit it off like a house on fire the other night, so we can leave them chatting together again.'

She finished the last of her cup of tea. 'I'll make sure I get a couple of hours' sleep this afternoon to make up for last night.'

'Grand,' Bridget said. 'I'll really look forward to it. I'll probably have a rest myself.'

Fred listened solemnly as Bridget related the whole sorry saga about Thelma's daughter over their full English breakfast. 'Bad stuff when it comes to drugs,' he said. 'And it can happen to any family.'

'Well, the poor girl went through a terrible time when her father was at home.' Bridget struggled to cut a piece of bacon, which wasn't as crispy as she liked. 'Mind you, it's harder on Thelma. She went through a terrible time with her horrible husband, and now she's suffering a second time with her daughter's carry-on.'

'It sounds like the daughter's as bad as the father,' Fred said, spearing a piece of black pudding with his fork. 'There's a saying about that ...' He put the pudding in his mouth and chewed it while he thought. 'Something about the sins of the fathers ...' He shrugged. 'Can't remember the rest.'

Bridget had heard the saying, too, and she couldn't remember the exact words, either. But she knew what it meant. 'It doesn't mean to say that Thelma's daughter is going to turn out the same as her father,' she said, with an edge to her voice. 'She could just as easily turn out like her mother – a decent, hard-working girl.'

'But she didn't,' Fred stated. 'It sounds as if she's taken on the sins of the father.'

'I don't know the stupid point you're makin',' Bridget said, suddenly all irate.

'I was only chatting,' Fred said, 'I wasn't really making any point.' He stared at his wife now, wondering what on earth had got into her. 'What d'you want to do this morning?' he asked, to change the subject.

'I'm going to go to Mass,' Bridget said. 'I saw a notice in the sitting-room yesterday giving the times of Sunday Masses and the directions to the church. There's one on at eleven, so I'm in plenty of time.'

'D'you want me to come with you?' Fred offered. Although he wasn't a Catholic himself, he had married Bridget in church, went along to christenings and First Communions, and always accompanied his wife at Christmas or any time she asked.

'Thanks,' she replied, 'but I'll be grand on my own. You can walk me as far as the nearest newsagent's and get the papers for yourself. You'll be happy enough reading in the sitting-room until I come back.'

'Are you sure?' Fred checked. 'You don't seem so bright this morning.'

'It's because I had a disturbed night,' she told him. 'I'll be grand. A walk out will do me good.'

Bridget's own relationship with the Catholic Church was sporadic and very much depended on her moods. The abusive experiences she'd suffered at the hands of an elderly priest back in Ireland had tainted her view on religion, but her early Catholic upbringing had made it hard for her to break away from it entirely.

She had had the children baptised because she was afraid of them dying and going to Limbo. And when the time came for them to go to school, she had wrestled with her conscience about sending them to a non-denominational school, but her early indoctrination had won the day again, and Michael and Helen ended up attending the local Catholic primary school. And she attended Mass with the children every Sunday because she didn't want them to get into trouble for missing it.

In truth, Bridget didn't really know where she stood with religion. When she was worried or upset, she found herself seeking the comfort of her Rosary beads or a Novena prayer, which had to be said for nine days in front of a candle. And occasionally, she found herself stealing into Our Lady's Church in Shaw Heath when it was empty, to light a few candles and say prayers for whatever was on her mind.

And this particular Sunday morning was one of the occasions when she felt that going to Mass might just help to soothe the nerves that had been jangled the night before.

Within a few minutes of walking out in the fresh morning sea air, Bridget felt her spirits start to lift again. She had thoroughly enjoyed her few days away, and Fred had done everything and anything that she wanted. She felt a bit guilty, thinking of the way she'd snapped at him at breakfast, and decided she'd make it up to him later.

She slid her hand into Fred's bigger one now as they walked along the footpath at the side of the beach. 'I was just thinking,' she said, squeezing his hand, 'that we might just have another little lie-down after lunch. What d'you think?'

281

'Are you tired, love?' he said, his tone full of concern. 'Of course we'll have a lie-down if you feel you need a bit of a sleep.'

'I wasn't really thinking of sleep.'

Fred looked at her blankly. 'I'm not with you, love.'

She glanced shyly at him and smiled. 'I thought we might have a bit more of that romance that we had on Friday afternoon.'

Fred beamed. 'You mean I'm on a promise, like?'

She laughed. 'I mean we're both on a promise.'

Bridget found the old grey-stone church on the corner of a street. She went inside, stopping to dip her hand into the holy water font and bless herself, and sat in one of the pews at the back.

By the time Mass started, every seat in the church was packed, and Bridget found herself crushed in the middle of the pew. The church was warm and airless, and she found all the standing up, sitting down and kneeling difficult and uncomfortable, as the people at either side of her kept jostling for more space.

As she walked back down the aisle from Communion, Bridget was debating with herself whether to continue walking all the way down and straight out of the church. Then, as she neared her pew, she remembered that she wanted to light some candles, so ended up back in the squashed-up pew again.

When the final hymn – 'I'll Sing a Hymn to Mary' – was finished, Bridget stifled a little sigh of relief. She sat back in the uncomfortable wooden bench and waited until all the other worshippers had gone, then she made her way to the front of the church to light her candles.

She felt the first stab of pain as she was reaching into her handbag for her purse. She bent over double with the ferocity of it, clutching onto the end of the candle-stand to steady herself. When it passed, she slowly straightened up and walked over to sit on the nearest pew, beads of sweat standing out on her forehead. Then the second wave of pain hit her, hard enough this time to make her cry out.

When the third, red-hot pain came, Bridget felt a contraction worse than any she'd felt giving birth, and when she tried to stand up a darkness suddenly enveloped her.

She barely had time to call Fred's name before her head hit the holy floor.

Chapter 54

❧

Since it was a dry, clear morning, Tara and Angela walked down to ten o'clock Mass at Our Lady's Church in Shaw Heath. As the priest and the congregation went through the usual rituals, Tara found herself going over the events of the past week – one of the busiest she could remember. Although she hadn't officially started work there, she had spent a lot of time in the Grosvenor.

At some stage, she knew she would have to relinquish a lot of the responsibility in the Cale Green, something she found hard to do. But she knew she would have to start delegating work sooner rather than later, because she couldn't work two jobs at the same time.

The other night she found herself lying awake, thinking about the work she'd done the previous day and planning work for the following day. But she had been through all that before when she bought the Cale Green Hotel and had worn herself out, which she had no intention of doing again. She needed all her energy and skills to do her new, prestigious job well. Besides, she had reliable staff in place – especially Angela – and she knew that things would be well looked after in the smaller place in her absence.

Tara found work at the Grosvenor Hotel exciting and almost exhilarating at times, but in the short time she had been working there she was well aware that she was now in a very different league. Even though no one checked her decisions, there was a subtle but definite pressure on her to get things right from the start. And when she analysed it, usually in the early hours of the morning, she knew that she was putting pressure on herself.

She wanted to prove to the other group members that she could live up to their expectations. And privately, she wanted to prove to herself that she could do the job as well as any man. She also knew that she had been given a chance that few women got in the hotel business, or any other business, and whatever happened, she was determined to succeed. It was imperative both to her reputation and her self-respect.

'I hope Bridget and Fred are having a great time in Blackpool,'

Angela said, as they came out of the church. 'I'm sure the break will do her the world of good.'

'She might have to start taking a break more often,' Tara replied, 'especially when she has the new baby. Hopefully, she'll feel the benefit of this weekend and see it for herself.'

Half an hour later, the two sisters were in the kitchen, drinking coffee and eating toast, when Kate Thornley rang.

'Tara,' Kate said, 'I know this is very short notice, but is there any chance of us meeting up for lunch today?'

'No problem,' Tara said. 'I was just going to go down to the hotel for lunch myself, so we can go together.'

'I was actually thinking of the Midland in Manchester,' Kate said. 'We've often had Sunday lunch there before, and, to be honest, it would suit me better for us to meet there than in Stockport where I might run into people I know.'

Tara felt a little pang of alarm. 'Is there anything wrong?'

There was a small silence. 'I suppose I've come to a decision,' Kate said, 'and I want to talk to you about it.'

After a short discussion, they agreed to meet up at one o'clock in the Midland Hotel in the city centre.

It had been a while since Tara had heard from her friend, but that wasn't unusual. They were both busy, professional women, and, understandably, Kate's romance with Frank Kennedy took precedence over any friendship.

Tara parked her car at the side of the Midland Hotel. She walked briskly around to the front steps, then went up and straight through the wooden revolving doors. As she crossed the thick carpet in the hotel foyer, her eyes flickered to left and right, before focussing on a table up on the terrace bar where Kate was already waiting. Even before she reached the table and greeted and embraced her friend, Tara sensed that there was something wrong.

Kate Thornley looked impeccably stylish as always. Today she was wearing one of her casually belted sweater dresses that suited her pencil-slim figure so well, with a green-stoned necklace and matching earrings that looked striking against her strawberry-blonde bob.

But in spite of her bright outfit, her face was pale and her eyes showed a lack of sleep. Tara decided to say nothing until Kate was ready. She put her navy bag on one of the spare seats, took off her grey woollen coat and scarf, and sat down opposite her friend.

Kate took a deep breath. 'I'm really grateful to you for coming into Manchester. I know it was short notice.'

Tara reached over and touched her hand. 'I'm always delighted to catch up with you, Kate, and it doesn't take long in the car.' She smiled and raised her eyebrows meaningfully. 'And coming into nice places like the Midland always gives me ideas for the hotels.' She laughed, trying to sound casual. 'Not that I'm ever likely to have the Cale Green, of course ...' Then, seeing the look on her friend's face, she suddenly stopped.

'Tara, I wanted to see you because I have a new job in Paris and I'm leaving soon.'

Tara caught her breath. 'When?'

'I start the week after next.'

'How long is it for?' Tara joined her hands together and leaned her elbows on the table. 'I presume it's with the magazine?'

'No, it's not with the magazine,' Kate told her. 'And I'm moving there indefinitely.'

Just at that point, a waiter appeared beside them. 'Your table is ready now,' he told Kate.

The two women stood up, gathered their belongings and followed him into the half-full restaurant where they were shown to a corner table. Tara's mind was in whirl, as she tried to take in the ramifications of a permanent move to France.

After they had settled at their table and chosen from the menu, Tara quickly resumed their conversation. 'Are you saying that you're going to be living in Paris full-time?'

'Yes,' Kate confirmed. 'I'm going to be living and working there.'

Tara's brow creased in confusion. 'And what about Frank? How does he feel about you being so far away?'

Kate lifted her white linen napkin from the table and spread it out over her lap, carefully patting it flat. 'It's all over between us, Tara,' she said, looking up through lowered lashes. 'I finished with him last night.'

'Why?' Tara asked, shock written all over her face. 'What's happened?'

'I suppose I finally woke up,' Kate said, her voice sounding thin and weary. 'Woke up to the fact that he would never feel the same way about me I do about him.'

A tight little knot formed in Tara's stomach. 'But Kate ...' she started, searching for the right words.

Kate shook her head. 'I would *always* have been second-best.' She took a deep breath. 'All three of us know that.'

There was a deathly silence, then Tara reached for her friend's hand again. 'But Kate, I thought you were getting on so well ... You've been going out for a long time now.' She halted, her throat suddenly feeling dry. 'I know there was that awkward incident at your birthday party, but apart from that you've always seemed so happy and relaxed together.'

'You're perfectly right,' Kate said, her voice tight and strained. 'He was always happy when *you* saw us.' Her hand gripped Tara's tightly. 'He was only ever happy when you were around. He was never that happy when he was alone with *me*. I was only another way of getting close to you ...' Then, abruptly, she let go of her friend's hand, almost shrugging it off, her face pale and her eyes filling with tears.

Tara sat upright in her chair now, wounded and confused by her friend's anger and rejection. 'I have never, *ever* encouraged Frank Kennedy in any way,' she said, hearing herself sound defensive. 'And you, of all people, know that, Kate. You and Bridget were the people I confided in about Frank, and you both knew what happened between us. You know I had nothing to do with him after we parted, and I hardly saw or spoke to him when I was married. I squashed any ideas he had about me long ago, and he certainly hasn't made any approaches physically or verbally to me since you two have been together.' She paused, and her voice softened. 'I really thought things were going well for you both.'

Kate nodded. 'There was a time when I thought that, too.' She gave a little, shuddering sigh. 'Of course I knew he was still in love with you when we started going out,' she said matter-of-factly, 'but I was sure it would change. I was giving it time, thinking he would eventually get over you.'

Tara cut in. 'Has something happened recently? Has Frank said or done something that's made you decide to give up entirely?'

'It's what he *doesn't* say that's the biggest problem,' Kate said sadly. 'Oh, he tells me he loves me, and that we make a great team. He says things that sound fine on the surface, but I know he doesn't have the right feelings for me. He's an entirely different person when you're around. There's a light in his eyes that's never there with me.' With a slightly shaking hand, she tucked a wing of her hair behind her ear. 'I know in my heart and soul that if you said you would have him back, he'd be gone tomorrow. And I just can't live with that uncertainty any longer.'

'That will *never* happen,' Tara said adamantly.

'That's as far as *you're* concerned,' Kate countered, 'but I think Frank will always keep hoping. It's you he wants, Tara – it's always been *you*.'

'If that's true,' Tara said, 'then he's the biggest fool of a man I've ever met in my life.' She felt a hot rush of anger at Frank Kennedy for once again causing havoc in her life, even when she wasn't directly involved. He had managed to cause friction between herself and Bridget a year or two ago, because Bridget kept standing up for him. And now he had caused *real* hurt to her friend Kate.

Tara knew she was naive for being surprised that this had happened, because she knew, as clearly as night follows day, that Frank had always loved her and always would. She looked across the table at her friend, trying desperately to think of something that would make her feel even a tiny bit better – but she knew that nothing she could say would help.

The waiter came across to the table now and placed a glass of white wine in front of each of the women. When he had gone, Tara leaned across the table again.

'Have you definitely made up your mind?' she asked in a low voice. 'Is it what you really want?'

'It's the only way,' Kate replied. 'I can't keep torturing myself like this. I don't want to accept second-best. I want someone who loves me passionately – the way Frank loves you.' She looked Tara directly in the eye. 'And that's exactly what I told him.' She picked up her wine glass now and took a sip from it.

Tara's heart sank. 'How did he respond?'

Kate shrugged. 'What could he say? He just blustered around a bit, saying he loved me enough in his own way for us to stay together and work things out. He said we got on better than most couples, but I said I wanted more than that. After going round and round in circles, we eventually agreed that it was for the best that we call it a day.'

'Kate,' Tara said softly, 'I don't want this to spoil our friendship.'

Kate nodded. 'I don't want it to, either; that's why I wanted us to meet up before I go.' She took another sip of wine. 'It's my own fault anyway. I can't blame you, or anyone else, for this mess. I nearly ruined our friendship by going out with Frank in the first place.'

Tara clasped her hands around her wine glass. 'It was just awkward in the beginning because I was hardly speaking to him, and I wasn't in great shape after losing Gabriel anyway. But that soon passed, and I had got used to you as a couple.'

Kate's misery was etched on her face. 'You were very good, Tara, after all you'd been through, and I really don't want you to feel bad about any of this. You're not to blame in any way. It's not your fault that he can't love me or anyone else the way he loves you.'

'I sincerely hope you're proved wrong about that,' Tara said.

The conversation drew to a halt as the waiter arrived with their meals – they had both ordered steak and salad – and for a while they concentrated on eating. When they resumed talking it was about more practical issues.

'So tell me all about the new job in Paris,' Tara said.

Kate put her knife and fork down, her meal barely touched. 'It's with a fashion house,' she explained. 'It's not terribly well paid, but it's something I've always been interested in doing.'

'It will be a totally different direction for you,' Tara said, impressed that her friend was trying something so adventurous.

Kate gave a little shrug. 'It's what I originally trained for. It will broaden my horizons and give me more background experience if I ever go back into covering the fashion events in magazines.' She gave a little smile that didn't quite reach her eyes. 'It'll give me a chance to brush up on my schoolgirl French, too – and it will put a good distance between myself and Frank.'

'You seem to have it all thought out.'

'Well,' Kate said, 'things seemed to happen at the same time. I was offered the job a few weeks ago and I initially turned it down.' She sucked her breath in. 'But ... I've been thinking a lot about it since the birthday party, and I decided that it would be the ideal solution.'

'Even if it only gives you a break for a while,' Tara agreed. She paused to finish her glass of wine. 'Although I'll really miss you. I love our get-togethers.'

'You can come and visit me in Paris,' Kate suggested, brightening a little. 'It's only a few hours on the plane.'

Tara suddenly thought of the trip to Paris that Gabriel had planned for them both just before he died, the trip they never made. She wondered now if she were brave enough to do it on her own and visit all the places that Gabriel had suggested. 'Yes,' she said, nodding. 'I will. I'll come and visit you when you're settled.'

'I'll look forward to it,' Kate said, a hint of her old enthusiasm evident in her voice now. 'By the time summer comes, I'll know Paris really well and I can take you around all the sights.'

'It sounds wonderful,' Tara said, smiling warmly at her friend.

As she was driving back to Stockport, Tara replayed the conversation that she had had with Kate over and over in her mind. She could still hardly believe that things had taken such an unexpected turn. She had presumed that Kate's relationship with Frank would just carry on and that eventually they would get married. Frank and his estranged wife had divorced some time ago, and his children were more or less grown up. There was nothing to stop him re-marrying if he wanted to. But that was obviously not going to happen with Kate now.

The whole situation left Tara feeling very, very unsettled. She wasn't at all comfortable with the thought of Frank Kennedy being a single man again, especially after what Kate had said about his feelings for her.

If he made the slightest move towards her, she would be more than ready for him.

Chapter 55

The baby was gone, of course. When she woke up in the ambulance that the elderly priest had sent for, Bridget was devastated. Her suit and underclothes were covered in blood, and she knew it could only mean one thing.

As soon as she arrived at the hospital, her details were taken and they contacted Thelma Stevens, who in turn sent out a small search-party of guests, plus her friend, Jim, to look for Fred. He had bought his Sunday papers and had decided to walk down to the beach to read them on a bench in the sunshine.

The minute he saw Jim running towards him, Fred knew that something terrible had happened to his wife.

Jim drove him and Thelma straight to the hospital, and they all waited in a small room while Bridget was in theatre.

Eventually, it was all over and she was brought to a small private room until she had recovered from the anaesthetic.

Fred was at her side the minute he saw her eyes flutter open. 'Are you all right, love?' he whispered.

'The baby ...' Bridget muttered. 'The baby ...' Then she had lapsed back into a troubled sleep.

'You'll have to stay on for a few more days,' Thelma told Fred, when they were down in the hospital café. 'There's no problem with your room,' she assured him. 'And me and Jim will take turns driving you over to the hospital.'

Bridget gradually came round, and by evening visiting she was sitting up in bed, wearing a frilly, fuchsia-coloured nightdress and matching dressing-gown that Thelma had brought in for her. The pink only served to highlight her pallor.

'I hope it wasn't to do with Sarah and all that carry-on last night,' Thelma had said, her eyes filling with tears. 'You were running up and down the stairs and helping me to carry her.' She put her hanky to her mouth. 'I was so distracted with it all that I never thought of what it might do to you.'

'It's OK,' Bridget told her in a dull, flat voice. 'The doctors said it can just happen.' She didn't tell Thelma or Fred that one of the doctors had told her off for being so upset about losing the baby, saying that she should be grateful to have three healthy children already.

Thankfully, the nurses had all been kinder and more understanding about her loss, and she had been well looked after until she was released from hospital. Fred had rung home and arranged for June and Angela to look after the children and the boarding house for a few more days until they got back.

'Don't worry about a thing,' June had said. 'If it's OK, I'll just move into your bedroom until you come home. I'll change the bed and have it fresh for when you and Bridget get back.'

'Great,' Fred had said, although he couldn't have cared less if twenty people slept in the bed as long as the kids were looked after and Bridget recovered.

When she finished talking to Fred, June went into the kitchen to find a cigarette to calm her nerves. She was trying to give up, but on occasions like this she desperately needed one. As far as she could see, things were going from bad to worse for Bridget. She'd been jumpy and uptight before going to Blackpool, so God alone knew what she'd be like when she got back.

June made up her mind that she wouldn't breathe a word to her about the visit from Lloyd. The last thing she needed was to hear about that.

Fred phoned Tara and told her the sad news, and she and Angela drove over to see Bridget in hospital on the Monday evening.

The minute she clapped eyes on Tara, Bridget started crying inconsolably, telling Tara that she was being paid back for all the bad things she'd done in her life.

Tara shooed Fred and Angela out of the room, then tried to comfort and reason with her.

She sat at the top of the bed with her arms around her friend. 'It is *not* your fault or anybody else's fault,' she said. 'These things just happen, and you have to cry it out of your system for a while and then pull yourself together for your own sake, and for Fred and the children.'

'I can't,' Bridget sobbed. 'I just keep thinking about the little baby back in Ireland, and then I start to think about Nora again ...'

Tara felt a cold shiver run through her. She had been so busy recently that she just presumed a weekend in Blackpool would sort out her friend's problems. But obviously they ran much deeper that she had imagined. Tara rubbed her friend's arm. 'You will just have to make yourself forget about all those things,' she told her, 'or you're going to make yourself really ill. You haven't been feeling too well recently, and if you let all this get on top of you, you're going to find it harder to get back to normal.' She kissed Bridget on the side of the head. 'I know how it feels when things get on top of you. I remember how bad I felt after Gabriel died.'

Bridget was quiet for a few moments as she digested Tara's words. 'Oh, I'm sorry for goin' on so much, Tara. I know you've had your own terrible problems. I'm just a selfish person ...'

'No, no, you're not,' Tara said soothingly. 'You're a kind, good person and it's not fair what's happened to you. I'm just saying that you need to try to get over things, so that you don't make yourself very ill.'

Bridget looked up at her friend with wide, tear-filled eyes. 'I will try, Tara. I will try.'

After she was let out of hospital, Bridget spend another two nights recuperating and taking it easy at the boarding house with Fred. Thelma had insisted that they stay as her private guests, and waved away Fred's offer of money.

'You will not pay a single penny,' she told him in a stern, uncompromising tone. 'It's the least I can do after all the help Bridget gave me with my daughter. A lot of other people would have turned away when they realised Sarah had brought all the trouble on herself.' She shook her head, tears coming into her eyes. 'Imagine Bridget falling on the stairs that night and not telling any of us. If the nurse hadn't mentioned it, we'd never have known.' She looked up at Fred. 'Your wife is a very special lady – you don't meet many like her.'

'Oh, I know she's special,' Fred sighed. 'I only wish she knew it herself.'

Chapter 56

❧

Tara waited for a couple of days after Bridget came home to make sure she was well on the road to recovery, then she went down to spend an evening at Maple Terrace, with the intention of telling her about Nora.

Bridget was still pale and drawn, but she was doing bits and pieces around the house, and sounded more like her old self. She had just put the children to bed, and Fred had gone out for a few drinks with some of his wrestling mates, since he knew that Bridget had company.

The two women sat opposite each other by the fire, drinking tea and picking at a bowl of grapes and a box of Cadbury's Roses that June had bought to welcome Bridget back home.

Tara thought she'd start with information that would lift Bridget. 'Are you up to hearing a bit of gossip about some mutual friends?'

Bridget looked intrigued. 'Of course I am. Go on.' She reached forward for a purple-covered sweet, then sat back to unwrap it.

'Well,' Tara said, deliberately drawing it out as she knew Bridget loved hearing news of this sort, 'Kate phoned me on Sunday to ask if I would meet her for lunch in Manchester, as she had something she wanted to tell me.'

Bridget's eyes widened. 'They're not getting married, are they?'

'No,' Tara said, shaking her head.

There was a few seconds pause. 'Is she pregnant?' Bridget ventured.

Tara hid her relief at the fact that Bridget was able to mention the word 'pregnant'. It was a real step forward, and she felt it justified making a drama out of poor Kate's misery.

'She and Frank have finished.'

'You are codding!' Bridget's eyes were wide with surprise and interest. 'Is it serious or just a bit of an argument?'

'It's deadly serious,' Tara told her. 'Kate's got a job in Paris and is leaving this weekend to look for an apartment.'

'I don't believe it. When did this all happen?'

'On the weekend, apparently.' She glanced at the door leading to the hallway, to make sure they weren't overheard. 'And do you know why they've broken up?'

Bridget looked even more intrigued. 'Go on,' she said again.

'*Me*,' Tara said, pursing her lips. 'Can you believe it?'

Bridget put her hands up to her mouth. 'Oh, my God!'

'Kate decided that as far as Frank is concerned she will always be second-best,' Tara continued in a low voice. 'She said she suddenly realised that things would never change and there was no point in carrying on.'

'And how did Frank take it?'

Tara shrugged. 'I think he tried to talk her round, but she had made up her mind.'

'But what about *you*? Did she confront him with her suspicions?' Bridget asked.

Tara nodded, her face flushing at the thought of the awful situation she'd been dragged into. 'He just said that they got on well enough to make a go of the relationship.'

'And what did she say?' Bridget asked, trying not to look as though she were enjoying the drama too much.

'She told him that she wanted him to love her the way that he loved me ...' Tara shook her head, mortified even thinking about it.

'Oh, my God!' Bridget repeated. 'And what did Frank say to that?'

'Nothing, apparently.'

'Well, he's hanged himself, so,' Bridget stated emphatically. 'Nothing surer. There's no woman who is going to take that.' She popped the chocolate she had been holding into her mouth.

'Exactly,' Tara said. 'So she's heading off to Paris to a new job to get away from him.'

Bridget chewed on her sweet for a moment then swallowed it. 'Well,' she said, 'if you want my opinion ...'

'I might as well hear it,' Tara said, 'although I'm not sure whether it's going to make me feel better or not.'

Bridget looked at her with raised eyebrows. 'Now you know I'm always on your side.'

Tara smiled. 'Ye-es,' she said.

'Well, it was obvious from the start that Kate was only a time-filler for Frank. Everything about them told you that. He didn't care that she spent a lot of her time away in London and travelling around with that magazine job of hers.' She shrugged. 'It never bothered Frank. As long as he could bring her to dances and fancy functions, that was enough.' She paused. 'And of course, it suited him to bring her to bed on a regular basis.'

'Bridget!' Tara acted more shocked than she felt to keep her friend's high spirits up. 'That's a terrible thing to say.'

'It's the truth, Tara, and you know it.' Bridget gave a guilty little laugh, half-enjoying Tara's discomfort. 'You know fine well that Frank Kennedy has that hot-blooded look about him – he's not the type to go without. And if Kate's not been obliging him, there are plenty of other girls out there who will.'

'Well, that's something I know nothing about,' Tara said, a touch indignantly.

'Surely Kate's told you the sleeping arrangements when they go off for weekends to fancy hotels and all that kind of thing?' Bridget persisted.

'No, she hasn't,' Tara said. 'She's never confided in me over Frank, and I certainly wouldn't ask her. It's not the sort of thing I've ever thought about. Anyway, you know there's always been an awkwardness between us when it comes to him.'

'True,' Bridget said. She lifted her cup of tea and took a tiny sip.

'It's an all-round disaster,' Tara mused, 'and I don't know how I'm going to react to Frank Kennedy the next time I see him.'

'Don't let on you know anything, unless he mentions it first,' Bridget advised. 'Wait and see what he tells you.' She leaned across the table and took another chocolate. 'I haven't seen him for a few weeks.'

'I'll miss Kate,' Tara said truthfully, 'and I could kill Frank for being the cause of her moving away.'

Bridget raised her eyebrows and smiled. 'No more boutique openings with George Best for us. Nobody will invite us now that Kate is leaving.'

Tara smiled and shook her head. 'You never change, do you, Bridget Hart?'

They sat chatting for a while, then Bridget went out and made them both a cup of Camp Coffee, with warm milk, and a ham sandwich.

When they'd finished their supper, Tara put her cup down on the coffee table and sat forward in her chair with her hands clasped.

'Bridget,' she said, 'I have more news to tell you.'

Bridget saw the serious expression on her friend's face. 'I'd a feeling there was something else,' she said.

'It's about Nora.'

Bridget's face tightened. She clasped her own hands together and waited.

'I'm sorry to say that the post-mortem showed she had taken her own life.'

Bridget closed her eyes. 'Oh, dear God,' she whispered.

To Tara's great relief, Bridget took the tragic news fairly well. 'Thank God she wasn't murdered,' she kept repeating. 'Thank God nobody had harmed her. I was terrified it would turn out that somebody like Father Daly had done it. Because, lookin' back on it, I'm sure he was doing the same filthy things to Nora as he was to me.'

'But to commit suicide ... the poor soul.' Tara said, feeling suddenly choked. 'She must have been desperate to do such a thing.'

Bridget had looked at her in surprise. 'But it was *her* choice, Tara,' she said. 'Don't you see the difference?'

'I don't understand what you mean,' Tara said, an uncomfortable feeling beginning to gnaw at her stomach.

'I'm just grateful that it was Nora's decision,' Bridget said simply. 'At least nobody else did that terrible thing to her.'

Chapter 57

❦

T he French stamp immediately caught Tara eyes. When she recognised Kate's small, neat handwriting, she felt a little pang of alarm. One part of her wanted to rip the envelope open to check that Kate was well and settled in her new job in Paris, while the other half was more reserved and wary in case the letter was full of recriminations about the situation with Frank Kennedy. She decided to wait. She put the letter into her handbag to read properly when she got to the office.

As she walked the short distance to the Grosvenor Hotel in the fresh morning air, Tara found herself going back over the last time she'd met Kate in the Midland Hotel, and she was filled with a sense of guilt and awkwardness over what had happened. But, she reasoned with herself, there was nothing she could do to change things. She could not help the fact that her friend had got involved so deeply with Frank. Kate was a grown woman and had been fully aware of Frank and Tara's past relationship. She had walked into it with her eyes wide open. She had known all there was to know about Frank and, just like Tara, had ended up being badly hurt.

Sitting at her desk, Tara opened the envelope to reveal fine, tissue-like, pink writing paper. Her heart was beating quickly as she scanned the first page. Then she started to relax.

Kate was fine. There were no recriminations. The letter was cheery and friendly. She turned the page, and continued to read her friend's news, which was all about her work, her new life in the beautiful, romantic city, and, to Tara's relief and delight, a new relationship.

... Guess what? I've met a wonderful French artist called André. Penniless, of course – as is usually the way! He is amazingly talented

and is just beginning to establish a reputation in the city. He usually sells his paintings in the artists' quarter in Montmartre, but he is due to exhibit some of his work in one of the main studios in the city along with more renowned artists. He lives in a tiny but beautifully furnished apartment across the street from where I'm living, and in the morning we can wave to each other from our small balconies.

I'm not going to say that it's anything more than a lovely friendship at the moment, but it definitely has all the possibilities of turning into a full-blown romance. He asked me to go to a party with him the other night and we spent the whole night chatting about every subject under the sun – André speaking in broken English and me in broken French!

A knock came on the door and one of the women who worked in the kitchen came in with a large cup of freshly made coffee. After thanking her, Tara continued to read her letter, digesting all the information about the concerts that Kate had been to and the marvellous restaurants with unbelievable food and wine.

When she reached the end, Tara put the letter down on her desk, a thoughtful look on her face. Kate had asked her to come over for a visit very soon, and had described all the places they would visit and the things they would do. *Just the two of us,* she'd written. *Just two good friends, on our own, catching up with each other's news!*

If Kate could rebuild her life in a short time, then surely Tara could face a trip over to see her on her own? She took a deep breath, then nodded. She had taken the decision about the Cale Green Hotel all on her own. She had done the same for the Grosvenor. The time had come for Tara to visit Paris on her own.

To face the rest of her life on her own.

PART THREE

*Of all the music
that reached farthest
into heaven,
it is the beating
of a loving heart.*

HENRY WARD BEECHER

Chapter 58

❧❦❧

From the minute she arrived in the bustling Manchester airport, Tara was happy that she had decided to make the trip to Paris to see her friend. And it wasn't just the idea of visiting such a beautiful city, but the fact that she and Kate would get the chance to spend valuable time together and make sure that any awkwardness over Frank Kennedy was well and truly buried.

Tara was also glad of the few days' break. Both her business and home life had been busier than she could ever remember.

In addition, the house sales had not been as straightforward as they should have been. The deeds of both houses in Cale Green had gone missing in the solicitor's office, causing a frantic search. A week later they turned up in the wrong file. A simple mistake, but one which had caused Tara several sleepless nights.

And then, of course, there had been the worry over Bridget's health following her miscarriage in Blackpool. For the first few weeks after she came out things seemed to be improving. And then Bridget suddenly became very quiet. She seemed to have withdrawn into herself, which worried Tara. All she could do was watch and wait, and be there to help if things didn't improve.

A short break in Paris was definitely a welcome diversion from all the various problems at home.

Apart from the things that Kate had lined up for her over the five-day visit, Tara had a list of places she wanted to see. The places she and Gabriel had planned on visiting.

'Tara!' Kate called waving enthusiastically as she recognised her red-haired friend in the arrivals hall at Orly airport.

Tara, dressed in a cream sweater and brown trousers, came towards her with a wide smile. 'Kate! You look absolutely wonderful.' She dropped her case on the floor and they hugged each other, then Tara held Kate at arm's length. 'I love the new hairstyle.' Kate's strawberry-blonde hair, usually classically bobbed, was now in a longer, more casual, layered style. Tara studied her from head to toe, her gaze full of admiration. 'You look so chic! You're going to have to take me to the boutiques that you frequent and bring me up to date.'

Kate threw her head back and laughed, delighted by the compliments. And in that moment, Tara knew her friend had got over Frank Kennedy.

'It was one of those things in life that you feel was meant to happen,' Kate said, as the taxi took them into the city. 'I had to get away from England to see things more clearly, and this new job was the push I needed to move on in my life. To move away from Frank.' Then she raised her eyebrows and smiled. 'And to let me find a more deserving man – like André.'

'So you really have no regrets?' Tara said, feeling intensely grateful that the situation seemed to have ironed itself out.

'"*Je ne regrette rien*", as Edith Piaf would say.' Kate and Tara laughed together.

Kate then chatted in French to the taxi driver.

'What was all that about?' Tara said, who had no French whatsoever, apart from the few words she had picked up in her phrase book.

'I've asked him to give us a quick tour of the city,' Kate told her, 'so I can point out some highlights as we go. I want you to see as much of Paris as possible on this trip.'

'Oh, that's so thoughtful of you,' Tara said, leaning over to give her friend a hug. Then she sat glued to the window, entranced by the beautiful old French buildings and breathless with delight when she saw the Arc de Triomphe, the Eiffel Tower and the Champs-Elysées. As the taxi came to a halt in traffic outside Notre Dame cathedral, she turned to her friend. 'This has been worth waiting for. I'm going to make the most of every minute.'

Soon they arrived at Kate's apartment in the Latin Quarter. It was a bustling university area, with cafés, restaurants and hotels, and the apartment was very different to the places in which Kate had previously lived. Like Kate herself, it was very chic, with an individual twist.

'As you can see, Tara, I've completely fallen in love with everything French,' she laughed, as she opened doors which led into high-ceilinged rooms with dangling chandeliers and tall, elegant windows, each with its own traditional iron balcony. She had mixed antique French furniture with more modern pieces, and an eclectic mix of prints and paintings hung on every wall. Jugs and vases filled with pastel-coloured flowers were dotted around the rooms on tables, fireplaces and window-sills.

Her bedroom was decorated in a pale, washed green, and her antique iron bed was a high, cream-painted ornate affair, covered in layers of white and cream sheets and a mountain of lace-edged pillow-cases. Coordinating cotton and lace curtains were tied back with thick cream ropes.

'Kate … it's so beautiful. I'm lost for words.' Tara said, gazing around the unashamedly romantic room. 'How have you put all this together in such a short time?'

'I've enjoyed searching out every little piece,' Kate told her, 'and it filled the empty hours when I first arrived in Paris, before I made proper friends.' She laughed. 'And I'm glad I did it when I had the time, because I never seem to have a spare minute now.'

The rest of Kate's bedroom furniture was darker wood, and much more serious than the frivolous bed. 'The dressing-table is a Louis the Sixteenth style in walnut,' she told Tara, grinning with delight. She ran her hand over the floral decoration at the top. 'I've really enjoyed learning about the different furniture styles since I got here. It's got to me in the same way as the French fashions.' She shrugged and held her hands out. 'I didn't know one wood from another when I was back home, and now I'm buying books about it. How I'll get everything over to England if I ever move back, I do not know.'

'You have a real eye for furnishings and decoration,' Tara told her. She pulled a face and laughed. 'I was asked to choose the furniture and oversee the decoration of the Grosvenor Hotel, and I'm delighted with what I've done, but when I look at this …' She waved her hand around the room. 'It's in another league.'

'No,' Kate said, 'the difference it that it's in another *country*. And don't forget, I've only had to furnish a comparatively small space for my own individual taste. What you've chosen will be a style that's absolutely perfect for the people who will be staying there. Picking stuff for a business is a very different matter from choosing things for a home.' She stopped. 'I've rattled on enough about what's happening to me, when I really want to hear all your news about the Grosvenor. Imagine you being involved in such a huge business venture. It's wonderful.'

Tara felt a little pang of anxiety at the thought of going over all the details with Kate, wondering how she would manoeuvre the conversation around the very sensitive subject that was Frank Kennedy. 'To be honest,' she said, looking out of one of the windows, 'I've been so busy with the hotel that I'm just happy to be away from it for a bit.'

She had already written a long letter to Kate, explaining how she had come to be involved, and laying a lot of the credit at Mr Pickford's door. Kate had known the estate agent since she was a child.

'You know, Tara, I can hardly believe how both our lives have changed so much since the beginning of the year,' Kate said. 'Who would have guessed that I'd be living here in Paris and that you would own one of the biggest and most prestigious hotels in Stockport?'

'Part-owner,' Tara reminded her friend with a wry smile. 'A one-fifth owner.'

Kate showed Tara to the guest bedroom, a spacious room with simple muslin drapes, a polished wooden floor and a cream carved bed with a matching armoire and an old wash-stand with a marble top. A pale-pink table by Tara's bedside held a delicate, floral-shaped lamp and a small copper jug filled with delicate flowers.

'I'll go and run you a bath,' Kate said, leaving Tara to unpack. She paused at the doorway of the bedroom. 'I've left you towels in the wardrobe. Do you think you have you everything you need?'

Tara hesitated, a serious frown on her face. 'There's only one problem ...'

'What?' Kate asked, looking concerned.

'Everything is so lovely, I might never want to go back home.'

'I really, really don't care about Frank any more,' Kate told Tara over dinner in a nearby restaurant that night. 'And, in a way, I blame myself for hanging onto him for so long.' She bit her lip. 'I'm almost embarrassed when I think about it now. He always talked about us just enjoying each other's company and taking one day at a time and seeing what the future might bring. That kind of thing ...' Kate's voice trailed off. 'He was always kind and generous, but when I look back on it, he never really promised me anything, and he never lied. If I'm painfully truthful, I lied to myself. I believed he loved me and wanted to marry me, because that's what I desperately wanted. But in retrospect, it would never, never have worked.' Her eyes lit up. 'It's completely different with André.'

'I'm dying to hear all about this André,' Tara said. 'Am I going to get the chance to meet him while I'm here?'

'Tomorrow,' Kate said, glowing. 'He's going to take us on a guided tour of the Louvre. Apart from his own painting, he's a real art buff and just loves a captive audience, so he can show off his knowledge about the exhibits.' She lifted the white wine from the ice-bucket and poured them each another glass.

'That sounds wonderful,' Tara said, taking a sip of her wine. 'I was going to say that I have a list of places I want to visit, and the Louvre is near the top.' She smiled. 'And it will be great to be with an expert who knows what they're talking about.'

'He's very entertaining, not a bit pompous,' Kate said, a light blush stealing over her face. She lifted her glass and sipped her wine. 'Now, Tara, tell me all that's been happening since our last letter. What's the situation with *your* new man?'

'Gerry?' Tara said, nodding. 'Yes, well … it's going OK.' She tucked a ringlet of hair behind her ear. 'I've been seeing him on a regular basis over the last month or two.'

'And?' Kate raised her eyebrows questioningly.

'Like I say,' Tara hedged. 'It's all going grand.'

'Is it serious?'

Tara shrugged. 'It's early days.'

Kate looked around her in a funny, over-dramatic way, then she lowered her voice. 'Have you done the deed yet?'

Tara's green eyes opened wide with surprise, then she started to laugh. 'Don't beat about the bush, Kate. Just come straight out with the personal questions.'

'Come on,' Kate giggled. 'We're modern women, women of the world.'

'Actually, we haven't … not as yet.' She cradled her wine glass between both hands now, staring down into it.

Kate suddenly looked serious. 'Not yet?' she asked. 'Is it still too soon for you … after Gabriel?'

Tara took a few moments, considering her friend's question. 'I don't know if it's that … It just doesn't feel right at the moment.' She gave a little shrug.

'Is it the morality of it, because you're not married to him?'

Tara shook her head. 'No. I've been in that situation before.' She stopped, feeling awkward.

Kate raised her eyebrows. 'Frank?'

Tara swallowed hard. 'Yes, well, you know all that ... and it's definitely something I don't like to be reminded of.' She took tiny sip from her glass for something to do.

Kate put her head to the side in a studied fashion. 'I think it's the greatest pity that things went so wrong with you and Frank ...'

'What do you mean?' Tara looked stunned.

Kate spoke quickly now, trying to clarify what she'd said. 'I don't mean any disrespect to Gabriel's memory or anything like that, but I can't think of anyone else more suited to you *now* than Frank. You both have the same business interests, you're both from similar backgrounds, and you look so right together – his brooding, dark good looks and your gorgeous, wild, Irish red hair.' She gave a small sigh. 'I always thought that. He and I never looked quite so suited.'

Tara gave a bitter little laugh. 'No, Kate,' she said, shaking her head, 'you're very wrong there. How we look together means absolutely nothing.' She put her glass down on the table. 'Now, I don't mean to be rude, but that's the subject of men closed for the remainder of my holiday.' She smiled, her eyes crinkling at the corners. 'I'd much rather discuss all the wonderful things I'm going to see while I'm in your beautiful city.'

The sun shining through the light muslin curtains woke Tara early the next morning, and, over cups of dark, strong French coffee, she and Kate planned their day.

They started with a trip around the main shops in the morning, then lunched in a lovely restaurant, and met up with André for their tour around the Louvre.

Tara found him as handsome and talented as Kate had described, and, watching them together, she knew that her friend had made the right decision about moving to Paris. Whether it was a short-term or a long-term move, it had turned Kate in a new, more positive direction.

The next few days flew by, with more sightseeing and shopping, and Tara enjoyed exploring some of the city on her own. From Kate's apartment on the Left Bank she found her way to Notre Dame where she spent a quiet half-hour thinking and praying and remembering all the happy times she had had with her husband. Then she came out into the summer sunlight and took a leisurely stroll down by the Seine. She arrived back at her friend's apartment tired but content now that she had seen most of the places that Gabriel had wanted her to see.

Later that evening she and Kate met up with a crowd of Kate's arty friends in a rosy-lit, smoky wine bar in Montmartre where they were entertained by an eclectic group of musicians. Tara wore an unusual bohemian kaftan that she had bought in one of Kate's friend's boutiques, and let her hair curl down over her shoulders. She had also let Kate experiment with some dark-green eyeliner and an olive shadow on her lids, coupled with heavy black mascara which had made her eyes look like smouldering emeralds. It was a look that pleasantly surprised her, but she knew it was only for the holiday, and that she would return to the safety of her formal, professional outfits when she returned home.

During the evening, much to Kate's amusement, Tara had been approached by several handsome musicians and artists, and had firmly but politely turned down their obvious advances. One of the young men had even pleaded with Tara to allow him to paint her, and although she had been firm in her refusal, she had been secretly very flattered.

As each day of her long weekend progressed, Tara felt herself relaxing and unwinding in Kate's beautiful apartment and in the fascinating French capital, to which she knew she would return again and again.

Chapter 59

Bridget stared at the one o'clock news on television as a picture of a young girl who had been murdered came up on the screen. Why on earth were they allowed to show such things in the middle of the day? She got up and switched the television off.

The sitting-room door opened and June's peroxide-blonde head appeared. 'I've finished hooverin' the upstairs rooms,' she said. 'Do you want me to do in here?'

Bridget gazed at her for a few moments, as if not quite understanding.

'The hooverin'?' June repeated. 'Will I do in here?'

Bridget slowly nodded. 'I'll get out of your way.'

'After I've done this, do you want me to walk down and collect the fish for dinner?'

'Oh ... it's Friday, isn't it?' Bridget said. 'I never thought about the fish.'

'Is Lucy still playing out in the yard?'

Bridget nodded again, her eyes dull and heavy. 'She's been walking up and down the back entry with her doll's pram. I checked on her a short while ago.'

'If you like, I can take her out with me when I'm going. The poor little thing could do with a proper walk out in the fresh air. She's not been out of the yard this last few days.' June paused. 'Is Angela comin' in to help you with the dinner or do you want me to stay on?'

'I'm not sure what she said,' Bridget said, biting her lip. 'I don't know whether she's working late at the hotel tonight or if she said she would come straight here.' She gave a weary little sigh. 'Sometimes the days go so fast that I can't keep track of them. I hardly know what day of the week it is ... they all seem to roll into one ...'

June pulled the vacuum-cleaner in behind her, knowing exactly what Bridget meant. But the problem was that the housework was rolling along with the days, and they were getting noticeably behind.

Bridget wasn't doing half the amount of work she normally did. Over the last few weeks June had noticed things going steadily downhill in the boarding house. In fact, two of the men had moved out at the weekend, leaving only three boarders at the moment, the lowest number they'd had in for a long time. The men had said something about their jobs being moved nearer Manchester, and that they needed to find lodgings closer to work, but June knew it was only an excuse. She'd overheard them complaining that their breakfast hadn't been ready at the right time in the morning, that there hadn't been hot water for baths when they wanted them, and just yesterday morning there had been a shortage of clean towels.

And it wasn't as though the men were fussy. After all, they were *men*. Things like clean towels and bedding would only occur to them if standards had suddenly dropped, which they obviously had.

June was trying her best to fill any gaps, but it was difficult because Bridget didn't seem to be able to think even far enough ahead to the very next day. And she was getting mixed up about things – saying she'd cleaned the toilets when she hadn't, or that the meat for the evening meal had been picked up when it hadn't. Only the other week June had had to rush out before the baker's closed and buy ready-made pies for the lodgers, or they would have had nothing to eat.

June had tried to tell Bridget that things weren't up to scratch, but she had only got upset and said she felt things were starting to get on top of her again. Since the two lodgers had gone, June had tried to keep on top of things herself, and was checking and double-checking her work so they didn't lose any more. The boarding house in Maple Terrace had always had a good reputation, particularly with the Irish building trade, but if word got out that men were going to work without a decent breakfast and there was no hot water after work, then business would inevitably suffer.

'I'll go and make a start on the potatoes,' Bridget said, 'and check we've enough tins of peas to go with the fish.'

She went into the kitchen now, leaving June to get on with the hoovering. Looking out of the back door, she expected to see Lucy in the yard. But there was only Lucky, asleep in his kennel, and the doll's pram in the corner. Then she saw the back gate was wide open.

Bridget came down the few steps from the house into the yard. The pram was as neat and tidy as usual, with Lucy's baby doll carefully tucked up with a little matching yellow pillow and blanket. For a young child, Lucy was very particular, and she liked her dolls to be dressed neatly, with their hair well-brushed and covered with a bonnet. She kept her doll's cot and pram in pristine condition, just as a new mother might.

Bridget went over to the open gate and looked out into the cobble-stoned back entry – but there was no sight or sign of her younger daughter. Then, with her arms folded over her chest and her brow furrowed in concern, she turned left and walked down past several other houses to the end of the entry. She came to a stop, looked left and right, but could see no sign of Lucy. Then she came all the way back, past her own house again, to look at the other end of the alleyway. When she realised there was no sign of the little girl, her legs suddenly started to feel weak and her heart began to thump against her ribs.

She turned and went back to the house as quickly as her wobbly legs would allow. She started up the steps towards the open back door, calling loudly for June.

June had just finished hoovering the sitting-room and was pushing the vacuum-cleaner back out into the hall when she heard Bridget's voice. She turned towards the kitchen and caught sight of Bridget's white, anguished face.

'It's Lucy,' she said, her hand flattened against her chest to still the pounding in it. 'She's gone out of the yard – she's not anywhere to be seen.'

'Don't worry, she'll be fine. She's probably just wandered off,' June said reassumingly.

They both went through the kitchen and outside again. On hearing their voices, Lucky suddenly woke and came out of his kennel, yelping loudly.

'Get in, you!' June shouted at him. 'And you can stop that bleedin' well barkin'!'

Chastened, his ears flat against his head, the Yorkshire terrier scuttled back into his kennel.

'Maybe she's gone into one of the other houses,' June said.

Bridget went quickly towards the gate and out into the entry, followed closely by her friend. They both stood, hands on hips, looking one way then the other.

'What are we going to do?' Bridget said, her voice quivery and distressed now. 'Where could she be? What if somebody's taken her?' Her shoulders started to shake and then tears came streaming down her face. She knew something terrible was going to happen – she'd felt it for ages, nearly every day when she woke up.

'She won't be far,' June said, beginning to feel a panicky sensation in her stomach. Then a thought came to her. 'Maybe she came into the house while we were chatting in the sitting-room. Maybe she's upstairs in the toilet or in the bedroom.'

Bridget's crying instantly stopped. 'Right,' she said, quickly moving towards the house. 'We'll check every single room, one by one.'

As they rushed past the kennel, Lucky started yelping again, and they were just going in the back door when they heard a little voice calling, 'Mummy!' Both women stopped in their tracks and whirled around to see Lucy peeping out of the dog's kennel.

'What on earth are you doing in there?' Bridget exclaimed, rushing down the stairs to scoop Lucy up in her arms.

'I was sleeping,' Lucy told her, rubbing her eyes. 'Me and Lucky were having a little sleep.'

'Thank God you're all right!' Bridget said, holding her tightly. She pressed her damp face into the child's thick curly hair, breathing in the scent of the Johnson's baby shampoo.

While June and Lucy were out at the shops, Bridget went upstairs and into her bedroom. She went over to her dressing-table drawer and opened it, then looked inside for a few moments before lifting out a flat, square jewellery box. She opened the lid and took out a small white envelope, then slid the two-page letter out from it.

The letter was surprisingly well-written. She read it for the sixth time since receiving it yesterday morning:

Dear Bridget,
I hope this letter finds you well.
I have been thinking about you and Lucy a lot recently, and I was sorry that I missed the two of you when I called at the house back in May. I was talking to the woman who helps you out and she showed me some pictures of Lucy's birthday. I hope you don't mind, but I took one of the photographs, as I wanted to let my mother see what her granddaughter looks like. She's not been very well recently, and she loves to hear all about Lucy. I didn't tell her that you were married with other children when it all happened; I thought it was best just to say it was a romance that never worked out, and I didn't know about Lucy until you'd got married to someone else.
I'm due up in Manchester again soon, and I wondered if maybe I could take Lucy out for the afternoon. I wouldn't take her far, maybe to the cinema or to a nice park or for a walk around the shops.
I can understand if you feel it's not a good idea for a strange man to take her out on her own, and I'd be more than happy for the three of us to go out together.
I realise you don't want Fred to know anything about this, so I thought it might be better if I wrote to you privately, to give you time to think about it.

You can write to me at the address above or phone me anytime you want to make arrangements. It's still the same number as before.
  Lloyd

Bridget stared down at the finely-written letter, then she folded it and slid it back into the envelope again, before putting it back in the jewellery box and the drawer.

She hadn't been surprised to receive it. Ever since Lloyd had turned up at the house that day and saw Lucy, she knew in her heart that he would come back again. It had just been a question of time. And it had hung over Bridget's head like the Sword of Damocles until yesterday, when it had finally fallen on her.

Bridget now knew that June must have guessed about Lloyd and Lucy, and that was why she hadn't mentioned his visit. She must have been too afraid to say anything about it in case she gave away her suspicions about him. A little shiver ran through Bridget now. What if Lloyd had actually told June that he was Lucy's father? What if June had sat listening to the whole terrible story, with Lloyd telling her that Bridget had thrown herself at him when her husband was lying sick in hospital, and ended up pregnant with their child? And what if June had felt so sorry for him that she had given him the photograph of Lucy?

Then common sense would prevail for a while and Bridget would tell herself that Lloyd had said nothing at all about her and Lucy. That he'd just come in and had a cup of tea, politely looked at the photographs that June had innocently showed him, then left again. And that the explanation of June's silence was that she had quite simply forgotten to mention it. It wasn't too hard to believe, given the weekend that Lloyd had turned up. The Blackpool weekend. The weekend of the baby.

But that was all water under the bridge. Nothing could change it. Nothing could bring the baby back. And there were more than enough problems to be dealt with without digging over that still-fresh wound.

What was to be done about Lloyd? Bridget asked herself. If she gave in and agreed to meet him in secret, then God knows where it would lead.

And yet, if she didn't, he might tell Fred.

Maybe she could talk to Lloyd. Explain about Blackpool. Maybe he would understand.

Bridget suddenly felt very, very tired. She needed to lie down for an hour, try to make up for the sleep she missed last night.

She would think about Lloyd and his letter tomorrow.

When June returned from the shops with Lucy, she found Bridget fast asleep upstairs. She tip-toed quietly back down, made a sandwich and a drink for Lucy, then went to the phone. She dialled the Cale Green Hotel number and asked to speak to Angela.

'Bridget's not too great,' June said, when Angela came on the line. 'And I was just wondering if you're able to come down to get the tea ready for the lads this evening.' There was a silence as Angela checked her diary. Just as she thought, she had the evening already marked with Bridget's name.

'I can be finished for around five,' she said, 'so that should be just enough time to get things ready for the lads coming in from work. I'm sure I already told Bridget that I would come down.'

'She couldn't remember,' June said in a quiet, resigned voice. She paused. 'She's in bed at the minute, so I'm going to hang on here with Lucy and try to catch up on a bit of cleaning and ironing. I can wait until you come in.'

'Are things no better?' Angela asked.

'Not really. She doesn't seem to be able to keep to any kind of a routine. It's hit and miss. Fred's doing his best to help when he comes in from work, and he's very good with the kids, getting them ready for bed and everything. But she's falling behind with the sort of things that a man wouldn't notice. Clean towels and the ironing – that kind of thing.'

'You're officially doing extra hours now, aren't you?' Angela checked. 'Fred is paying you to help out more?'

'Yes,' June confirmed. 'He's very good. When he found out I'd been comin' in for extra hours here and there, he gave me a few pounds to cover it, then he said he'd like me to come in every day, and do regular hours, like. So I've given in me notice at the other houses I was cleaning, and I should be able to do proper hours from next week on.'

'Oh, that's great,' Angela said, relief evident in her voice. 'I hope it wasn't too awkward for you, giving up your other work?'

'No,' June reassured her. 'I always preferred being down in Maple

Terrace compared to the other places. It's a better laugh working with you and Bridget.'

'We've not had too many laughs recently,' Angela said wryly. 'Poor old Bridget.'

Angela had been up and down to Maple Terrace a lot recently. She didn't mind in the slightest, because she always felt she owed Bridget for all the help she'd given her over the years. When she'd been younger, she'd been glad of the extra money to boost her hotel wages and to help with trips back home. Now her finances were much improved, but she was happy to help out for a few hours here and there, whether she was paid or not. It was different for June, because she relied solely on her cleaning work to pay her rent and bills.

'What do you think yourself?' June asked. 'I'm tryin' me best to help out – talk to her, like – but I don't feel I'm makin' much head-way. She's very quiet in herself, not her usual chatty self. And the slightest thing sets her off in tears.' She then went on to relate the story of Lucy and the dog's kennel.

'I'll have a word with Tara,' Angela said decisively after listening. She'd also noticed that Bridget was treating every little incident as though it were a major drama. 'Tara said that she was going to try to get Bridget to the doctor's if things didn't improve soon.' She gave a little sigh. 'I suppose it's only natural that she would feel down after what happened, but she wasn't exactly herself before the miscarriage.'

'All we can do is keep trying to help out,' June said, 'until she finally turns the corner.'

'The thing that worries me,' Angela said, 'is the corner she might decide to take.'

Chapter 60

❦

It was a lovely September morning as Tara parked the car in her own space and walked around to the front entrance of the Grosvenor Hotel. Slim and elegant as always, she was dressed in a classic black suit with an emerald-green blouse, sheer black stockings and black leather court shoes.

She went through the swing doors, across the thickly carpeted foyer and headed towards her office. It was at least four times the size of her small office in the Cale Green Hotel, with a large, modern desk and high-backed leather chair, as well as a small conference table for six people.

Tara had been working in the Grosvenor for three months now. It had been hard work initially, trying to keep the hotel running while parts of it were being renovated, but it had eventually fallen into a routine. At least she didn't have to worry about her own small hotel as Angela was now in place as manager. She had been by far the best candidate Tara interviewed, and got the job fair and square.

So far, the foyer of the Grosvenor, the main ballroom and two cocktail bars had been completely redecorated with new curtains and furniture, and work on the function rooms and bedrooms was well underway. The decorating contractors had kept to a tight schedule and working areas, using the side door while the foyer and downstairs corridor were redecorated. It had been hard but satisfying work, and the other members of the group had played a supportive role while leaving all the main decorative and furnishing decisions to their manageress.

So far, everything had gone to plan. Tara had ensured that delivery of the new furniture and soft fittings had been timed exactly, so that they could move straight in to the finished rooms while the workers moved onto the next. Any hold-ups had been minor and Tara had dealt with them immediately. And if the refurbishment had caused any problems with the guests, she had made sure they were well looked after and compensated to prevent any loss of custom. Within a few weeks it became apparent that Tara had handled it so well they already had more bookings for the newly refurbished function rooms than they had had the previous year.

Due to Frank Kennedy's experience in the building trade, he had hired the contractors for both the new extension and for the refurbishment work. Consequently, he was in and out of the hotel on a more regular basis than the other group members.

John Burns kept in touch with Tara by telephoning regularly, offering encouragement and support when necessary, while Eric Simmons used one of the small offices a couple of times a week while he was setting up the company accounts. He was a quiet man who came and did his work without any fuss, then left equally quietly.

Off all the group members, Gerry McShane had the least contact with the hotel and with Tara – during the day. The night was a different matter.

At first Frank had kept his dealings strictly with the foreman, and was on the site early in the morning, checking plans and confirming that everything was strictly in line with building regulations before going off to deal with his other business. He had run into enough problems with other ventures where breaches of regulations had completely halted work or held it up for months, and he was ensuring that all the work on the Grosvenor went completely by the book.

But as the weeks went on, Tara noticed that Frank was arriving later. He would come just after ten o'clock with a special jacket covering his bespoke suit, his working boots and his hard hat on, and spend some time checking things with the foreman and the builders, then he would remove his work things, change into his highly polished shoes, and come into the hotel to check the interior work.

Inevitably, he would end up in Tara's office, bringing her up to date on what was happening, then one of the staff would appear with a tray of coffee and biscuits for them.

'How are you finding things yourself?' he asked her once, sitting back in one of the comfortable leather armchairs in her office. 'Are things working out here as you hoped? You're not finding things too much – running this place and then going back to check on the Cale Green?'

'I'm grand, thanks,' Tara told him, making sure she kept a polite, if cool, façade. 'I knew exactly what was entailed when I took on the job, and so far it's all working out well.' Then she had said pointedly, 'If I have any problems I'll be in touch with you *and* the other members about it. John Burns keeps close tabs on things, too.' Then, to press the point even further, she added, 'The staff that were already here are all very competent, and bookings are excellent for the time of year. Really, there's nothing more to add to what I told you last week.'

But Frank Kennedy hadn't been easy to put off, and it had made her feel especially uncomfortable when he attempted to get things on a more personal level. He had asked her how she thought Bridget was, and whether Tara felt there was anything he could do to help.

'I'm very fond of Bridget and Fred and the children,' he had said last week, as he said on numerous occasions. 'They've been through a lot with one thing and another, but they always seemed to get back on an even keel.' He pursed his lips. 'This time things are not looking so good. She's not a well woman in many ways.'

'Hopefully things will improve,' Tara had said.

After several conversations along the same lines, Tara found herself resorting to different ploys to avoid him. She arranged meetings with other people when she thought he might be about. When she saw him outside with the builders, she would time it so that she was in the kitchen working on menus with the catering staff or having a meeting with the head housekeeper, or she would take herself out of the hotel to discuss wallpapers and fabrics with local suppliers. In short, she did everything to make it plain to him that she wasn't available for cosy chats or one-to-one meetings.

One night she did something she had never done before: she discussed her personal life with Angela over dinner in the Cale Green Hotel. It was Angela's last shift before going off on holiday and they were having a handover meeting in the restaurant.

Whether it was the fact that Bridget had enough problems on her plate, and still hadn't got back to the way she was before she lost the baby, or whether Angela had suddenly matured into someone she could trust, Tara didn't know. But the time had seemed right – and the fact was, Tara didn't have anyone else she could confide in about the situation.

'Do you think Frank still has feelings for you?' Angela said, secretly thrilled to have her older sister ask her opinion. She was very careful not to let Tara know that Bridget had filled her in on certain aspects of the affair with Frank, and adopted an innocent air.

Tara had given a wry smile. 'Unfortunately, yes.'

Angela nodded, considering the situation carefully. 'And how does Gerry feel about that? Isn't he jealous?'

Tara looked at her younger sister for a few moments. 'I haven't actually told him about it. It's a bit awkward with them both being in the same group.'

'Does Gerry know that you used to go out with Frank?'

'Yes,' Tara said, 'but I didn't go into any great detail about our relationship.' A slight darkness passed over her face. 'I think he's probably more curious about the fact I've been married.'

The conversation came to a halt as the waitress arrived at the table with their main courses – steak for Angela and a fish dish for Tara – and then, a minute or so later, came trotting along with their potatoes and vegetables. They both thanked the young girl, who had only been in her job for a week, and then Angela had looked up at her.

'That all looks lovely, Ursula, and you've served it very efficiently.'

'Thanks, Miss Flynn,' the girl had said, blushing, but grateful for the compliment.

Then Angela had lowered her voice. 'Don't be putting too much pressure on yourself to go quickly, especially when you're carrying hot food. Just go that little bit easier.'

'You handled that very well,' Tara said when the girl had gone back into the kitchen. 'You very gently pointed her in the right direction without making her feel she was being told off.'

'Thanks,' Angela said. 'I'm learning all the time – at least, I hope I am. It's not always easy to get it right, especially when some of the staff are quite a bit older than me.' She pulled a face. 'I'm also conscious that they all know we're sisters, and I don't want anyone to think I got the job just because of that. I know I'm very lucky to have got the chance you've given me and I want to be as professional as I possibly can.' She passed the dish of potatoes to Tara.

'I don't think you should have fears of people thinking that I gave you the job for any reason other than you were the best person,' Tara told her. 'And you're one of the most popular members of staff.' She gave a little knowing smile. 'You have a very good way with people, and I'm sure they all think you're easier to work for than me.'

'Oh, no, not at all. No one would even think of that,' Angela protested, but she was delighted to hear Tara say it.

They both helped themselves from the dish of vegetables and were quiet as they ate.

After a while Angela put her knife and fork down on her almost empty plate. 'What you said about Frank Kennedy . . .'

Tara quickly finished the last forkful of her fish. 'Go on,' she said. 'I'm listening.'

'I think that you should arrange to have Gerry call at the hotel one of the mornings that Frank's there.'

Tara frowned, not quite sure what Angela was getting at. 'And what would he do?'

Angel leaned forward, her elbows resting on the table and her hands clasped under her chin. 'Have a chat to Gerry and explain that you're beginning to feel uncomfortable about the amount of time Frank is spending at the hotel, and that you think he needs to be made more aware of your relationship.' She shrugged. 'He doesn't need to be too heavy-handed or anything. Maybe if you also mention something that the two of you have planned, or already done together. I don't know ... like a film you've been to see or a show.'

Tara raised her eyebrows, pondering the suggestion. 'Maybe that would make the point ...'

The following night Tara and Gerry met up for a drink in Bramhall. Gerry looked troubled when she explained how often Frank called into her office.

'Do you want me to speak to him?' Gerry said quietly. 'He shouldn't be bothering you, Tara ... I'm sure he knows perfectly well that you and I are seeing each other.'

'I'd prefer it if we could do it as subtly as possible,' Tara told him. She chose her words carefully. 'I knew when I got involved with the Grosvenor that it would mean closer contact with him than I would normally have considered – and that was my choice. But I've made it perfectly clear to him that any connection we have, or are likely to have in the future, will be strictly business.'

'And do you think he is refusing to accept that?' he said, sounding surprised. 'Frank Kennedy is the type that likes to call all the shots. I've never thought of him as the type of man who would put himself in such an embarrassing position.'

Tara lowered her gaze now, feeling awkward at having to open up her personal life in such a way. 'Perhaps I should explain the reason I feel so uncomfortable. He was going out with a lovely girl for the last couple of years – a very good friend of mine – and she broke up with him because he made her feel second-best – to me. She's gone to Paris to get away from him.' She shook her head. 'I've honestly never encouraged him. Over the years I've made it plain that I have no feelings for him.'

'He sounds obsessed by you, Tara.' Gerry had leaned across the table and put his hand over hers. 'I think it's time we sorted it out.'

The next morning Tara went over to one of the windows in her spacious office, and lifted a slat on the grey Venetian blind. She looked out onto the building area where work had obviously been well underway for the last hour or so. She watched for a few minutes as men in protective headgear and big boots went up and down the scaffolding, carrying bricks and timber. There was no sign of Frank Kennedy, so she put the blind back in place and went to her desk to start her morning's work.

Half an hour later she crossed the floor to the window again, and there, parked just outside the building area, was Frank's distinctive maroon Jaguar.

Tara dialled Gerry McShane's number. 'He's here,' she told him.

Within a quarter of an hour, Gerry was at Tara's office door. 'I parked in a corner of the guest car park,' he said, 'so that Frank won't see the car.'

Sure enough, ten minutes later a knock came on Tara's door and Frank came in. He looked taken aback when he saw Gerry McShane sitting in the chair opposite Tara's, but he quickly covered it.

'Ah,' he said, lifting one of the conference chairs to join them, 'I see we're having an impromptu group meeting.'

Gerry looked him straight in the eye. 'No, Frank,' he told him, 'I have to confess my motives are not as professional as yours. I've come on a purely selfish basis.' He reached into his inside pocket and brought out a long brown envelope, which he placed on the desk in front of Tara.

She picked it up, a quizzical look on her face. 'What is it?'

'Open it,' he said, winking at Frank.

Tara slid a long white folder out with British Airways stamped on the front. Inside were tickets. '*Paris?*' she said, her voice high with surprise.

'Paris,' he confirmed. 'In a couple of weeks' time. We're going there when Angela gets back from Ireland.'

She looked down at the tickets again, wondering if she was taking the information in properly. They had never been away anywhere together, nor had they even discussed it. 'You've really surprised me,' she said, giving him a bemused smile.

'You said you had a wonderful weekend with your friend recently, but it was spoiled by being too short. I thought that a few days away might just suit us and let you see all the bits you missed.' He turned to look at Frank. 'I don't think there will be any problem giving her the time off before the extension opens. What do you think?'

'Do you think the Grosvenor and the Cale Green Hotel will still be standing when she comes back?'

Tara glanced at him now, and saw that Frank's face stiffened. Something about the way he looked, his sudden pallor, made her catch her breath, and in that second she was shocked to realise that she actually felt sorry for him. She had dealt him a devastatingly low blow. Her arguments with him had always been done in private, but Tara now knew that this little set-up between herself and Gerry McShane had wounded and humiliated him. And the link with Kate in Paris had just twisted the knife that little bit too far.

Frank looked from one to the other, nodding. 'I'll leave you both to it,' he said in a slightly hoarse voice, 'and my apologies for interrupting.' He turned towards the door.

Gerry stood up now. 'No, no,' he protested. He waved his hands expansively. 'You came to discuss something with Tara, so please don't let me hold you back.'

Tara felt herself cringe a little. Surely Gerry knew that the point had been made? Frank Kennedy wasn't a stupid man. She had asked that they handle this sensitively; after all, they were still going to have to work closely with him and the others when it came to matters relating to the hotel. It wouldn't do if things suddenly became awkward between the group members all because of her romantic associations with two of the men. ·

Frank's eyes narrowed. 'I was just checking things with the foreman, and I thought I'd call up and see how the work was progressing in the bedrooms.' He checked his watch. 'I think I'll leave it for today. I have another meeting in Manchester.'

'But it will only take five minutes,' Gerry stated, a slightly smug look on his face. 'The three of us can go and have a look at them now, can't we, Tara?'

Tara felt herself colouring up. 'Fine,' she said. 'I'm available to show you them now or another time.'

'Another time,' Frank said, walking towards the office door.

After the door closed behind him, Gerry turned towards Tara. 'I think that little scene has quickly sorted out our problem with Mr Kennedy, don't you?'

Tara looked back at him. 'I'm not quite sure how I feel about it,' she said, a serious look on her face. 'I think the Paris thing might have been too much.'

'I don't think so at all,' Gerry said, sweeping aside her reservations. 'And much as I admire Frank's business sense, I feel he's rather lacking in certain skills when it comes to people – and especially when it comes to you. Underneath his suave sophistication, our Mr Kennedy is a bit of a rough diamond.' He gave a little laugh. 'He won't have any doubts as to how the land lies now.'

'Regarding Paris—'

'I thought it killed two birds with one stone,' Gerry said quickly. 'It sorted Frank out and it means we've made concrete plans to spend some time together *properly* on our own.' He came over and put his arms around her. 'Don't you think we're ready to spend some time on our own, Tara? We've been seeing each other for a few months now and ...' He paused, then kissed her forehead. 'We're grown-up people, and we have grown-up needs.'

Tara looked up at him and, when their eyes connected, she felt the usual physical quiver she got when she was near him. The feeling that made her suppose he was right. She couldn't go on rejecting Gerry for ever. After all, he was the type of fellow who would never be short of female company. He was good-looking, financially well off, witty and entertaining. There were plenty of women who would be only too glad to jump into her shoes and be whisked away for a trip to Paris.

As he bent his head to kiss her on the lips, Tara knew she would have to commit herself or he would move on.

Chapter 61

Summer came late to Ballygrace. Angela was delighted that it had waited for her trip back home in September. Aiden Byrne had been to see her twice in Stockport since her Easter visit, and they had written to each other and phoned on a very regular basis. She had decided that this fortnight home would be the make or break for their romance. For one thing, it would be the longest period of time they had spent together, but another, more important reason was that Aiden was going to introduce Angela to his family, including his little daughter, Clare.

On his last visit, Aiden had told Angela that he was in love with her and wanted her to think seriously about their future together. One half of her was excited and delighted about the way the romance was going; the other half was fearful of all the changes that would be wrought in her life because of it.

There was her job. Angela had discovered that not only could she do the work, but she actually enjoyed it. And that, of course, was yet another complication to be considered when she thought of where her romance was leading.

The night she arrived home, Angela had taken the bull by the horns and told Shay that she had met an older, widowed man with a child when home at Easter, had continued to see him throughout that holiday, and that he had visited her in Stockport.

'You've taken your time to tell me,' he had said accusingly. 'It seems I'm the only one that was left out of the picture.' He turned to Tessie, who was sitting on the sofa beside him. 'Even your mother never saw fit to tell me.'

'It wasn't my place,' Tessie had protested. 'How was I to know it was going to last this long? I thought it would all fizzle out when Angela went back to England. I didn't know how keen he was, nor did I know Angela's feelings about him for that matter.'

'Weren't you writing letters to her and getting them back every other week?' Shay demanded. 'Don't tell me you weren't askin' how the big romance was goin'? What else would you be writing about? A lot of women's nonsense, no doubt.'

'It might surprise you to know what I have to write about,' Tessie told him, trying to keep her voice even. Her eyes narrowed now, knowing the tack that her husband could take on these matters. She didn't want him getting all heated up about things, as the doctor at the hospital had warned him that the calmer he kept, the lower his blood pressure would remain. And there had been an improvement in him over the summer, which in turn had relaxed Tessie. 'Anyway, you know all about the romance now, so isn't that enough?'

Shay wasn't about to give up so easily. 'And what did Tara have to say about it?' he wanted to know.

'She thinks he's a grand fellow; they got on like a house on fire.' Thankfully, Angela had Tara on her side, the best ally she could possibly have when it came to dealing with their father.

'And where did this Aiden fella stay when he was over in Stockport?' Shay was determined to show his authority now, given the fact that it had been flouted so easily by his wife and daughter. 'I hope he wasn't kipping down in that fine house of Tara's with all them professional women there, and giving them plenty to talk about.'

'Shay …' Tessie shot her husband a warning look. 'Would you stop goin' on?'

'Indeed he was not!' Angela said, her voice high with indignation. Even if she had wanted him to stay in the house, there was little chance of anything illicit going on with the likes of Vera Marshall around. Since she'd taken over the ownership of the house, Vera had taken her responsibilities very seriously, and kept a close watch on the younger women.

'Ah, don't tell me,' Shay said now, 'you landed him down on poor oul' Bridget and Fred. Taking advantage of their good natures.'

'For your information,' Angela said, 'Aiden was actually staying in the Cale Green Hotel.'

'Oh, so he has a few bob, then?' Shay said as quick as a flash. His eyes lit up. 'What kind of work does he do? Don't tell me,' he repeated. 'A farmer. A big oul' farmer from Birr.'

Angela sighed and rolled her eyes. There were times when her father drove her round the bend. 'He's an accountant, if you must know.'

'An accountant, begod!' Shay was flabbergasted. 'No shortage of money there. And what would a fella like that see in you?'

'Shay!' Tessie warned, leaning across to poke him on the arm. 'That's your own daughter you're talking about. Don't be going in-sulting her like that. She's a fine-looking girl, and she has a good job. Why shouldn't a man be interested in her?'

'Well, of course, he has the child,' Shay said, tightening his lips and giving a knowing half-wink. 'He'll be lookin' for a housekeeper, no doubt.'

Tessie got to her feet. 'Angela,' she said in a heated tone, 'take yourself off to bed and don't be wastin' your time talking to this *amadán*.' She shook her head, sighing deeply. 'There are times when I wonder is he the full shilling at all? Talking about a widower with a child, as if he hadn't done the exact same thing himself. And havin' the nerve to be talking about it to me and you!' She gave Shay a good prod on the shoulder. '*You* were the very man that came cap in hand asking me to marry you, and you a widower with two children and not a penny to your name.'

Shay moved further back on the sofa. 'That's a nice thing to be sayin' in front of Angela,' he said in a wounded tone. He shook his head. 'Ah, you know how to hit below the belt when it suits you, Tessie.'

'Never mind all that,' Tessie said. 'Would you just tell Angela now that you're delighted for her that she's met a nice fella, and one from home as well.' She gave Angela an encouraging smile. 'Who knows? If it carries on the way it's going, we might have her back home before too long.'

Angela raised her eyebrows and smiled. 'I wouldn't get *too* carried away,' she said.

Shay rubbed his chin thoughtfully now. 'Well, when are we going to get to get a look at this fella?' he asked.

Angela ran a hand through her blonde hair. 'I don't know. I'll have to see how things are going. Sure, I'm only back today, and I haven't even seen him myself yet.'

'Make sure you take him out to Ballygrace House,' Shay said, standing up to give the fire a poke. 'Show him around the place and let him see that you come off of decent people.' He rattled the poker around the glowing sods of turf. 'Don't let him think he's dealin' with a bunch of *amadáns*. And you can let him know we have a priest in the family as well while you're at it.' He lifted the empty bucket by the side of the fire and headed out to the turf-shed to refill it.

'Would you credit it?' Tessie said, as he disappeared. 'I never thought I'd see the day when he was bragging about Tara and Joe.' She shook her head incredulously. 'There was a time he was so touchy about them, always making comments about the rich relations and how uppity Tara was. You never know what's going through that mind of his.'

Angela stood up now and went over to the sideboard to get her handbag. 'I let it in one ear and out the other,' she said coolly. 'And I'll warn Aiden well in advance what to expect when he meets him.'

Tessie's face softened. 'Whatever rubbish he talks, he's proud of ye all in his own way.'

'I know,' Angela said. 'I know.'

Later that night, after Angela had gone to bed, Tessie and Shay sat drinking their last cup of tea before the dying embers of the fire.

'She's looking well,' Tessie said, holding her mug of tea between both hands.

'She is,' Shay agreed. 'And growing up fast. I see a big difference in her now, even from Easter.' He prodded the arm of his chair. 'And she's not as crabby as she used to be. Before, if we'd said a word, she'd have been yelpin' and giving out to us that it was none of our business.'

'She's matured,' Tessie said. 'I think that manager's job at the hotel has suited her well. She's lucky that Tara has given her such a good chance. She's young to be in a responsible position like that.'

'What d'you think about this Byrne fella?' Shay said now. 'Do you think it could be serious?'

Tessie thought for a moment. 'I honestly don't know. I've never seen her serious with a lad before, and he's a mature man.' Tessie was relieved to have Shay back to his more relaxed self, the way he was most of the time when they were on their own. It annoyed her when he got awkward over things, when she knew he could just as easily be reasonable. She could never understand why, when he had an audience, he felt that he had to play to the gallery, to show he was the head of the family.

He was the same when any of the other family members were around, or their husbands or wives. It was as if he had to flex his muscles to keep them all in check and remind everyone who was the boss. He seemed to have no idea that it just got people's backs up and made them fight against him – especially Angela.

'It's all this not knowing that worries me,' Shay confessed. 'What is his actual age? Is he that much older than her?'

'I think he's in his thirties or thereabouts.'

Shay took a drink of his tea. 'Maybe ten years' difference,' he mused. 'There's plenty of decent-looking girls been married off to oul' farmers twice and three times their age. But nobody's forcin' her to go out with him. I suppose it doesn't make a damn bit of difference – if she likes him, she likes him. As long as he's treating her well, there's no point us standing in her way.' He gave a small sigh. 'And if we're both honest, we'd like to have her back home, wouldn't we?'

Tessie stared into the fire, a faraway look on her face. 'Definitely. I like having all the family around us, the little grandchildren and everything. The older you get, the more you appreciate your family.'

Shay suddenly said, 'Did you phone the nursin' home about Molly this evening? I never thought to ask, with Angela here and everything.'

'I did, of course,' Tessie told him. 'There's no great change in her.

They just said that she was only picking at her food and is sleeping a lot of the day now.'

'I think I might give Joe a ring and let him know,' Shay decided. 'He's fierce fond of her, and would hate to think that she'd slipped away without him seeing her.'

'That's a good idea,' Tessie agreed. 'One of these times she'll just go. She's not going to keep rallying round. She's well into her eighties now, so we can't expect her to go on for ever.'

'She's had a good innings,' Shay stated. 'And had us running up and down to Mullingar for years. It would be a blessing for us all if she went soon.'

Tessie took a deep breath and closed her eyes. There were times, she thought, when Shay Flynn could be the most insensitive man that God ever put breath into. How was it that just when you saw a reasonable, kind side to him, he always managed to pull the rug out from under your feet?

'The poor oul' devil will go when she's ready,' she said, 'and not a minute before.'

Chapter 62

It was a Monday night and Tara had left the Grosvenor Hotel early since it was quiet. She'd found the Cale Green Hotel equally quiet. Since Fred was busy in the bar, Tara decided to take a walk down to Bridget's, knowing she would catch her on her own for a chat.

The children were still up so Tara sat for a while in the sitting-room, checking young Michael's homework and listening to Helen reading while Bridget washed Lucy and got her into her pyjamas.

Tara had then taken Lucy up to bed to read her a story, while Bridget supervised the two eldest in their bedtime preparations. By nine o'clock the two women were on their own in the kitchen.

'I wonder how Angela's getting on back home?' Bridget said, as she rolled out a large piece of pastry for the apple tart she was baking for tomorrow evening's dessert.

'She sounded fine when she rang the hotel last night,' Tara said, taking a sip of coffee. 'She said the weather is lovely.'

'And is the romance still going strong?'

'Seemingly it is,' Tara replied. 'They've been out and about, and I believe she's going out to meet Aiden's little daughter at the weekend.'

Bridget wiped the back of her floury hand across her forehead. 'I hope it all goes well for her. He seems a fine fella – a bit quiet, like, but I suppose it's only to be expected when he's only just met us.'

'He's actually very nice,' Tara said. She gave a wry smile. 'Although, if it becomes serious, I don't know what she's going to do. She'll have to make some serious decisions.'

Bridget took a tablespoon of caster sugar, liberally coated the rectangular dish of sliced apples, then placed the piece of flattened pastry on top. She did it very mechanically, as she seemed to do everything these days. 'Do you think she'll go back to Ireland?' she asked.

'I think it's a real possibility,' Tara said, giving a little sigh.

'God, we'd miss her if she went away now.' Bridget shook her head.

'We certainly would,' Tara agreed, a wistful look on her face. 'She's matured into a lovely young woman, and she's doing a great job of managing the hotel. Everybody likes working with her and for her, but I'd much rather she went back to Ireland if it means she has a decent fellow like Aiden Byrne.' She smiled at her friend. 'And of course I can't complain – I did the same thing myself when Gabriel and I decided to get married. I upped and left everything here and moved back to Ballygrace House. It's the thing people do when they're in love.'

Bridget glanced over at her friend now, surprised again by how Tara was able to refer to Gabriel more easily these days. She'd said something at the weekend in a similar vein, referring to his funeral. Just a few months ago she could hardly mention his name without getting upset, but now she could speak about him in the midst of a conversation then move on to something else.

And the funny thing was, although she seemed less upset, she was speaking about him much more often, and telling Bridget things about him that she had never said before. And Bridget knew exactly when the change had come about in Tara: it was around the time she met Gerry McShane. It was as if becoming close to another man had somehow unlocked a door to all the happy memories she ... of Gabriel.

Another turn-up for the books had been when Tara told her s... was going away for a weekend to Paris with this Gerry fellow. Bridget had been delighted, and told her widowed friend that it was about time she got a bit of romance back in her life. Tara had just smiled and said it was still very early days, and not to get too carried away.

Bridget wondered now if Tara could ever love anyone again, if she would ever get married again, if she could ever replace Gabriel.

These were all things that Bridget wondered more about these days. She often lay awake in the middle of the night – in the silence and the darkness – thinking about them. Thinking about the child she had lost that Sunday morning back in Blackpool. Wondering if it had been a boy or a girl, and whether it would have looked like her or Fred. It would have been due to be born in the next month or so, had things gone the way they should have. Bridget kept going over and over the weekend in her mind, replaying the events of those few days, trying to pinpoint what she'd done wrong to make it happen.

There was the fall of course – when she'd tripped on her night-dress, going up the stairs in the boarding house. Even in her darkest moments, she knew that the fall on her stomach had been the most likely cause. And then she would go back over the incident with Thelma's daughter, and how she had helped Thelma to lift and drag her all the way along the corridor to the landlady's bedroom. Either of those incidents could have caused a miscarriage.

And yet she was still haunted by her own selfishness and careless-ness, the fact that she had been drinking the night it had happened. She'd had several brandies and milk stouts in the Tower Ballroom, and then another couple in the Lantern. She hadn't felt drunk as such, but she knew, in her hearts of hearts, that she'd drunk more than she should have done, and had had even more the night before.

She was so ashamed of herself that she couldn't describe her feelings to anyone. She had promised Tara that she wouldn't drink heavily again after that night with Lloyd. And until that weekend in Blackpool she had kept her promise. Since then, it had been very hard. She'd tried to keep away from alcohol when she was out in public, but she often found that the only way she could sleep was to have a tumbler of sherry or a few brandies. But she had been careful only to have it late at night when everyone was in bed.

ankfully, Fred understood. He didn't mind her having a drink ong as she didn't have too much, or make a fool of herself, or start ying over nothing. And, so far, she had been very, very careful not to let Fred or Tara down.

Bridget took the apple tart over to the oven now.

As Tara looked at her friend, the little anxious feeling she'd had about her suddenly intensified. There was a kind of flatness about her that Tara had only seen a few times before, including just after Lucy's birth. It worried her to see it again. 'How are you finding the new medication the doctor gave you last week, Bridget? Is it starting to help you yet?'

Bridget shrugged as she slid the tart into the oven. 'Oh, I don't know. I can't really tell. The doctor said it could take a few weeks before it has any great effect.'

'You'll go back to the doctor if it doesn't work,' Tara said in a quiet voice, 'won't you?'

'I will,' Bridget said, nodding.

'Is June still coming in to help you every day?'

'Yes,' Bridget confirmed.

Tara looked at her watch. It was time to head home. She went to lift her bag off the table, then something stopped her. She sat back in her chair again.

'Bridget,' Tara ventured, 'is there something still worrying you, apart from the baby? I know that must still be upsetting you, but I feel there's something else that you're not telling me.' When she saw Bridget's shoulders stiffen, she carefully softened her voice. 'If there's anything on your mind, please, please tell me. You'll feel a lot better if you speak about it.' She went over to where Bridget was standing and put her arms around her. 'I know there are times when you think I'm hard on you and haven't understood, but if I've ever been like that I only meant to help you.' Tara swallowed hard. 'When I found out about Lloyd, I know I was angry, but it was only because I was petrified of what you might lose with Fred, of you losing all you'd worked for. It wasn't because I didn't care about you.' She hugged her friend tighter now. 'Whatever you want to tell me, I'm not going to be like that now, I promise. I know you don't feel too strong, and I wouldn't dream of making you feel worse.'

Bridget looked up at her with big, watery eyes. 'What if it's something I've brought on myself?'

'I don't care,' Tara said in a low voice. 'I promise I'll do everything and anything I can to help. You're my oldest and dearest friend, and I want to make you feel better.'

She took Bridget's hand now and guided her over to the table. 'Sit down,' she said, 'and tell me all about it.'

Bridget took a deep breath. 'It's Lloyd again,' she said.

Tara's heart plunged but she managed to conceal her feelings. 'What's happened? Has he come back up to Stockport to see you?'

Bridget nodded her head. 'Twice,' she said. 'Once when I was here and once when I wasn't.' She bowed her head. 'He knows about Lucy. The minute he saw her he said he knew she was his. And then he came back the weekend I was in Blackpool.'

Tara thought for a moment, then decided to come clean. 'I know about it,' she said quietly. 'June and Angela told me.'

Bridget was startled, her eyes suddenly brighter and more alert. 'When?' she asked. 'What did they say?' She still had no idea what Lloyd had said or done that weekend, because June had never referred to it. But she knew now that *something* must have been said, or suspected, if Angela and Tara knew, too.

Tara quickly tried to decide which way to go with the conversation. She didn't want to risk frightening Bridget, but at the same time she wanted her to know that she had good friends who would help and protect her if they could. 'June just said that Lloyd had called when you were away, and that he had started asking a lot of questions about Lucy, so, while they were having a cup of tea, June showed him the photographs of Lucy's birthday.' She paused. 'I'm afraid that when she looked at the photograph and then at Lloyd she suddenly saw a resemblance.'

'Well, she never said anything to me,' Bridget said quietly.

'She wouldn't,' Tara said simply. 'She's your friend and she thinks the world of you. She would just feel that it wasn't her business, that if you wanted her to know you would tell her.' She reached out and covered Bridget's hand with her own. 'Even though she guessed about Lucy and Lloyd, June hasn't judged you or treated you any differently, has she?' When there was no reply, Tara continued. 'She hasn't judged you, and neither has Angela. They both love you, Bridget, and they would never say or do anything to hurt you. You know that, don't you?'

Bridget lifted her head now and looked directly at Tara. 'I'm just terrified, Tara. I'm terrified of everything.' Her voice rose. 'I'm terri-fied of Lloyd causing more trouble and I'm terrified of Fred finding out. The more people that know, the more chance there is of it all coming out.'

'The people who know are not going to say a word,' Tara reassured her, 'so you can stop worrying about that.' Her eyes narrowed in thought. 'Has Lloyd been in touch again since that weekend you were in Blackpool?'

Bridget nodded. 'He sent me a letter.' She stood up. 'I'll show you.' She had nothing to lose now, and if Tara could help her she would be grateful.

What a mess, Tara thought as her friend went upstairs to get the letter. What a terrible mess. She only hoped that there was something she could do or say to make things better. She had already elicited from June and Angela that they would never breathe a word about their suspicions to anyone else, and she believed them. She knew that Frank Kennedy would never say a word. He was honourable and decent when it came to Bridget and Fred. He, like Tara, would do everything he could to protect his old friends.

Tara looked at Bridget when she came to the end of the letter. 'Have you been back in touch with him?'

Bridget nodded. 'I phoned him the week after I got the letter and I told him ...' Her eyes filled up. 'I told him about the baby.'

'What did he say?'

Bridget's shoulders shuddered as she sighed deeply. 'He said he was very sorry, and that he would leave things for a while. He said he didn't want to cause any trouble and that he would wait until I felt better.'

'And you haven't heard from him since?' Tara checked.

'No.'

'Maybe he won't get back to you at all,' Tara suggested. 'He might decide to forget all about it.' She shook her head. 'Even though I'm annoyed at the mess he's got you into, I always thought Lloyd was a decent fellow. Out of all the lads in Ruby's boarding house, Lloyd was way and above the best. He was the most intelligent and man-nerly. And I'm sure if you explained what this would do to you and Lucy if Fred found out, then he might understand and drop the whole thing.'

'I've already said all that,' Bridget sniffed. 'But he still wrote the letter, and he's said that when I'm better he still wants to meet up. He keeps going on about his mother wanting to hear about Lucy.' She gave a little shrug. 'I don't think she has any other grandchildren.'

'Let's leave it for the time being,' Tara told her. 'He might never get in touch again.'

Bridget bit her lip. 'Let's hope he doesn't.'

Chapter 63

On the day she was due to visit Aiden Byrne's house, Angela arranged to meet him at the top of the town, as she didn't want Shay or her mother to see them together. If things carried on the way they were going, they would meet him soon enough, but today wasn't the day for it. Angela was much too nervous and anxious to have to cope with her parents, on top of worrying about meeting Aiden's little girl.

Angela had dressed very carefully, conscious of not wanting to appear too smart or too casual. The day was a bit cooler than previous ones, so she settled for a short-sleeved grey sweater dress with a big black belt, black shoes and long black beads. The dress was fashionably short – a couple of inches above her knee – but not as short as some of the dresses that were appearing in the shops. But it was the sort of outfit that made Angela feel more grown-up and confident, which was exactly the impression she wanted to give.

She checked her appearance just before she left the house, then rushed back into her bedroom and changed the black beads for the gold locket that Aiden had bought her when they first met.

Aiden was relaxed and smiling as he reached to open the car door for her. 'You look gorgeous as usual,' he told her. When she was settled in the car he leaned across and gave her a warm kiss on the lips.

'You don't look too bad yourself,' Angela told him, smiling. She glanced into the back seat. 'I thought you were bringing Clare with you?'

'The road out to Tullamore is very bumpy and full of pot-holes at the minute,' he explained, 'and I didn't want her falling all over the car when I was driving, so I decided to leave her with my mother until we got back.'

Angela's heart quickened. 'We're not going out to your family's house today?'

'No,' he said, 'we'll leave that until next weekend. My mother will be in Birr shopping in the afternoon, so I'll just drop down and meet them, then bring Clare back with me.'

Angela felt a wave of relief. 'That's grand,' she said quietly. She knew she would eventually have to meet his family, but she wasn't ready for it just yet. Meeting his little daughter would be enough of an ordeal for the time being.

Three-quarters of an hour later they pulled up outside Aiden Byrne's large, imposing Georgian house set in a square of similar properties just off the town centre in Birr. Angela's heartbeat had quickened as they turned down the road, and she realised that he lived in one of these fine big houses, which could only be owned by people of quality.

Of course, she had known that he would have a nice house, being an accountant, but seeing the reality was a different matter. And even though she tried to remind herself that her sister owned Ballygrace House, which was every bit as grand and also had a good bit of land, she still felt more than a little overwhelmed at entering such an imposing place.

As they mounted the steps at the front of the house, Angela was thankful for the showery weather, which meant that there was no one about to see her going in. She followed Aiden into a large hall. Light streamed in from the stained-glass windows surrounding the arch-shaped door, and a huge window on the facing wall gave more light and reflected on the black and white marble tiles. An ornate, marble table with a high matching mirror stood centre-stage.

Aiden opened a door just off the hall, which revealed a good-sized cloakroom and downstairs toilet. He had brought both their coats from the car and stopped now to put them on wooden hangers. As he did so, Angela took in the gleaming, white-painted staircase with its dark polished banister, obviously part of the recent refurbishment that Aiden had been describing to Carmel's mother that afternoon back in the farmhouse. Then her eye caught the delicate yet dramatic cut-glass chandelier hanging centre-stage over the staircase. Immediately Angela thought of the woman who had lived here and probably helped choose the tasteful decorations.

She followed him through the hall now and down a few steps, then along a low-ceilinged corridor until they came into a large, bright and airy kitchen.

'I'll put the kettle on,' Aiden said. 'I'm sure you're ready for some tea or coffee?'

'That would be lovely,' Angela replied, wondering now if she had made a mistake coming here. She suddenly felt out of her depth. The huge house somehow made her feel young and inexperienced, as if she had no business being there. And she knew that was exactly how Aiden Byrne's in-laws would feel if they knew she was visiting him at home. Angela presumed that Aiden hadn't told his wife's family, or anyone else, about his visits over to Stockport.

She went to sit at the circular wooden table. A vase in the centre was filled with a mixture of red and yellow roses. Definitely a female touch. Surely Aiden hadn't arranged them himself?

As though he had read her thoughts, Aiden said, 'I have a nice woman who comes in a couple of days a week to keep things in order, and she also bakes the most beautiful fruitcakes and tarts.' He laughed. 'I think she's terrified that Clare and I will go hungry if we're left to fend for ourselves.' He lifted down two large cake tins. 'She was in yesterday and left me a few nice things. Have a look and see if there's anything that you fancy.'

Angela lifted the top off one of the tins, and the smell of sweet coconut and cinnamon drifted out. 'She's obviously a wonderful baker,' she said appreciatively.

Then the front doorbell sounded. Angela's heart gave a little flip of alarm as Aiden went to answer it. She heard voices. A few moments later, several pairs of footsteps sounded in the hall, then down the steps, and approached the kitchen.

Angela felt her breath quicken and looked up to see Aiden in the doorway, holding a blonde, curly-haired child in his arms.

'Clare,' Aiden said, 'this is Angela. She's come to the house today because she wanted to meet you.'

Then, as he moved forward into the room, Angela noticed a woman behind him and her face suddenly flushed. She didn't know quite what to do, whether to speak to the child first or to the woman.

Since neither Aiden nor the woman spoke, she decided to go for the child.

'Hello, Clare,' she said, standing up and forcing a bright smile. 'It's lovely to meet you.' As she went towards her, the child suddenly buried her face in her father's chest, making a little noise, which was either a sob or a giggle.

'Oh, look at her,' the woman said in a cheery tone, 'pretending she's all shy now.' She came into the middle of the room now and looked directly at Angela. She was a small stocky woman, with brown hair the same colour as Aiden's, but lightly streaked with grey. She wore a cream Arran-style cardigan over a flowery blouse and a pair of casual dark trousers. 'Don't be fooled for a minute by that little lady. She's not a bit shy. She's been chatting about meeting you all morning.'

Aiden came towards Angela now and put his free arm around her shoulder. 'Angela, since my daughter is too busy hiding from us, I'd like you to meet my mother – Catherine Byrne.'

The woman immediately came towards Angela, her hand out-stretched. 'Pleased to meet you at long last, my dear,' she said, smiling broadly. 'We've all heard so much about you, and I'll be delighted to tell them that I'm the first to meet you.' She shook Angela's hand briskly then stepped back. 'He did a good job of describing you, anyway – blonde and beautiful.'

Angela blushed to the roots of her hair. 'Oh, I'm not that ... I think he's been codding you,' she blustered, but inside she was delighted by the compliment, as she could tell Aiden's mother was being sincere.

Clare suddenly twisted around. 'Let me down, Daddy,' she said, struggling out of his arms. Aiden put her down on the floor and she walked over and stood in front of Angela. 'Will you take me to the bathroom?' she asked, her shyness having disappeared.

'Of course,' Angela said, 'but you'll have to show me where it is. I haven't been there yet.'

Clare took her by the hand and led her out of the kitchen and down to the small toilet off the hall.

By the time she returned, Aiden and his mother had the tea and cakes organised, the radio was playing in the background and the atmosphere was suddenly very homely. Aiden lifted the large teapot and poured tea for all three of them in pale-green, gold-rimmed china teacups with matching saucers.

'Tell me all about yourself, Angela,' Catherine Byrne said, handing her a side-plate with a slice of the coconut cake on it, and a pink linen napkin. Then she smiled warmly. 'I believe you know our relations from Tullamore?'

'I've known the Malone family for years,' Angela told her, suddenly conscious that she was speaking a bit too fast, 'and I've been great friends with Carmel since we were at school together.'

'Oh, they're a great crowd, aren't they, Aiden?' She went on to relate a funny story about when the Malone lads were young and went off fishing for the day. They came back with four terrible-looking fish that they wanted their mother to cook for the dinner, and she had to sneak out to buy fish from the shop and pretend it was what they had caught.

They all laughed over this, and several other stories that Catherine Byrne related, with Aiden chiming in good-naturedly. He moved around the kitchen, checking they all had enough tea and cake, and constantly catching Angela's eye to make sure that she was OK with his mother's constant chat and interest in her.

Mrs Byrne then asked Angela all about her work, and, as she explained about how she had been promoted to manageress of the Cale Green Hotel, Angela felt a little surge of pride. Even to her own ears, her job sounded very responsible and interesting.

'They're a very dynamic pair,' Aiden commented. 'And apart from owning the Cale Green Hotel, Tara has recently become part-owner of one of the biggest hotels outside of Manchester.'

Angela felt herself blushing, knowing that she was nowhere near as brave or successful as her half-sister. In fact, there was no comparison between them. Tara was a sophisticated, wealthy businesswoman, while she was only a paid worker, who owned nothing of any significance.

'Amazing for a woman to achieve all that,' Catherine Byrne mused, 'even in this day and age. Men still seem to hold all the reins when it comes to business in this part of the world.' She reached over and touched Angela's arm. 'Especially in the farming world, which is definitely a *man's* world.'

'I have to admit I'm very proud of Tara,' Angela said quickly, anxious to set the record straight, 'but I don't want you to run away with the idea that I'm in the same league. As I've explained, I *manage* Tara's hotel. I don't own it. I'm only a paid worker.' But having said that, she had told the truth when she said how much she enjoyed running the small hotel. She was surprised by how easily she had taken on the new responsibility, in fact. And she had recently started saving to buy a little car, had actually booked herself in for driving lessons when she got back home.

'Don't put yourself down, my dear,' Catherine Byrne told her. 'However you wish to describe yourself, you sound as though you are a hard-working businesswoman.'

Then Clare announced that she wanted to go upstairs to get her toy monkey, and Aiden took her off to find it, leaving the two women to chat. As soon as he was out of earshot, Catherine Byrne said, 'I believe your sister is married into the Fitzgerald family from Ballygrace.'

Angela's face was suddenly serious. 'She's actually a widow now. She was married to Gabriel Fitzgerald, but he died a few years ago.'

'So I believe,' Mrs Byrne said, nodding her head sympathetically. 'Poor man. It was very sudden, wasn't it?' She leaned her elbows on the table. 'You know, of course, that Aiden has been through a similar ordeal with Clare's mother?' She made a little clucking noise with her tongue. 'It was a terrible shock. Poor Aiden didn't know what hit him. It's only this past year that he's come around to being anything like himself.'

Angela swallowed hard. 'Tara, my sister, was the same.'

'She had no children, did she?'

'No,' Angela said, and just stopped herself from saying, *thank God*, which would certainly have been putting one foot in it, if not two.

Catherine Byrne reached for the teapot again to top up both their cups. 'I don't know whether these things are better happening in a sudden way. I know it's better for the poor person, than to be suffering slowly, but it can be very hard on the people left behind.'

Angela reached for the milk jug, then caught the older woman staring at her and suddenly felt very self-conscious again. She offered the milk, which Mrs Byrne declined, then she poured a drop in her own tea, acutely aware of being closely studied.

'Angela,' Mrs Byrne said in a low voice, 'I'm not one for interfering in my family's lives, but I just want you to know that we've seen a great difference in Aiden since he met you. He's happier than he's been in years.'

Angela looked back at Mrs Byrne and smiled. 'Thank you,' she said, in a voice that was almost a whisper. 'I've been very happy since I met him.'

Catherine Byrne glanced over at the doorway now, checking that there was no sign of her son. 'It's just a pity that you both live so far away,' she said very quickly. 'Aiden has told me that you write and phone regularly, but it's hard keeping a romance going from a distance.' She put her hand out now and covered Angela's. 'Do you see yourself coming back to live in Ireland at any time soon?'

Angela felt herself flushing. This was something that Aiden had hinted about on several occasions this week, but he hadn't directly asked her if she would consider moving back. 'Not *soon*,' she said quietly. 'I don't know what might happen in the future, but at the moment there's no reason for me to come back.'

For all the silly day-dreams she had, where he would get down on one knee and propose, she knew it was probably far too early for anything like that to happen yet. Aiden Byrne was a practical and sensible man. He wasn't the type to take such a big decision lightly. And there was little Clare to think of. Angela wasn't at all sure if she was ready to take on the responsibility of a child. Especially another woman's child.

'When do you go back to England, Angela?' Catherine Byrne asked now.

'At the end of the week.'

'And do you think you'll miss Aiden?'

Angela took a deep breath. 'Very much.'

Catherine glanced at the door again, an anxious frown on her face. 'I don't want you to think I'm prying or anything, but I just wondered if Aiden had mentioned anything to you about the ... about an incident that happened some time ago?'

Angela looked at her quizzically. 'He hasn't mentioned anything about an incident to me.'

There was a noise from out in the hallway.

'Leave him to tell you in his own time.' The older woman reached out and grasped Angela's hand again. 'When he does tell you, please don't judge him too harshly. It's not as bad as it sounds, and it was very out of character for Aiden to be involved in anything like that.'

A little bell rang at the back of Angela's mind and her hand came up to finger the gold locket. That day down in Galway, in the jewellery shop, Aiden's mother-in-law had said something about him making

339

a show of himself in a local hotel. She had presumed it was just a silly drunken incident, and had forgotten it had ever been mentioned. But now, as she saw the strained look on Catherine Byrne's face, Angela knew there was obviously a lot more to it.

She decided that she would put it to the back of her mind until Aiden decided to tell her.

Chapter 64

Angela felt a little warm glow inside as she watched Aiden eating the lamb chops, potatoes and mixed vegetables that Tessie had put in front of him. He had called over to take her out to Athlone for the afternoon, and Tessie had been well prepared. She had called in at the butcher's first thing in the morning, and made sure that there was more than enough food for the four of them. If it didn't suit him, the food wouldn't go to waste as it would be used up the following day.

'It's very good of you to include me in your lunch. I really wasn't expecting this,' Aiden had said when Tessie insisted that he stay.

'Sure, you're not in any great rush, are you?' Tessie poured him a glass of milk to have with his meal. 'And it'll save you cooking yourself something, or having to go out to buy it.' She went on to pour milk for the others and a glass of water for herself.

Shay had leaned over and tipped Aiden's elbow with his own. 'Take it while you're gettin' it handed to you,' he advised, cutting into one of his lamb chops. 'Because you could be waitin' a while on Angela ever cooking you anything. A few slices of bread and butter would be her stretch.'

'Daddy!' Angela said, tutting indignantly. Trust her father to go putting his foot in it, giving Aiden the impression that she wasn't able to do the simplest of domestic tasks. And, even worse, making it sound as though she had her feet so well under Aiden's table that she was all ready to take over his housekeeping for him. 'I'm well able to cook for myself. How do you think I've survived over in England for so long?'

'I'd say that you have most of your meals in the hotel,' Shay quipped, winking at Aiden and Tessie, 'and that you survive on toast and biscuits the rest of the time.'

'I'd like to see how you would survive without Mammy to cook for you and pick up things after you,' Angela retorted, flicking her blonde hair. 'I don't recall you organising many meals or making the beds or anything like that.'

'Pay no heed to that fella,' Tessie said, glancing anxiously at Aiden. She was amazed that her daughter had got such a good-looking, decent fellow for herself, and she certainly didn't want him to think badly of their family because of Shay's banter. 'He doesn't mean a word that he's saying – he's only trying to rise her. I'm afraid that's the usual way in this house.'

Aiden raised his eyebrows and smiled. 'We were the very same in our own house when we were growing up, so I'm not hearing anything I'm not used to.'

'Thank God,' Angela said, looking across at him. 'There's many a fellow would run away hearing things like that.'

Aiden held her gaze for a few moments then shook his head. 'Oh, I wouldn't be put off that easy ...'

As they drove out to Athlone, Angela thanked Aiden for being so tolerant of Shay and his caustic sense of humour. 'He drives me mad at times,' she said, 'but he doesn't mean it the way it sounds.'

'Your parents are the finest, Angela,' he said, 'and as long as they have no problem with me and Clare, then I'm absolutely delighted with them. They made me as welcome as anyone could, and that's what matters.'

Angela took a deep breath. 'There's a big difference between our family house and yours. You could fit our house into yours about four times. Does it bother you?'

He looked at her incredulously. 'Of course it doesn't,' he told her. 'The house is grand – it's in the middle of the town and it's big enough for their needs. Why should it bother me?'

Angela shrugged. 'I just want you to know that I'm aware there is a bit of a difference between us ...'

'If you're going to look at it like that,' he said, 'then I would have to say that no one in our family owns a hotel like Tara's, nor do we have a priest in the family. Our family are mainly farmers, although

341

I have one brother who is a teacher.' He reached across and took Angela's hand. 'There's no big difference between us at all.'

Angela held onto his hand until he had to place it back onto the driving wheel to negotiate a winding stretch of the road. She sat contentedly, looking out of the car window and thinking how lucky she was. Things were turning out well for them. The problem she had anticipated between their families had not materialised. Catherine Byrne had made it quite clear that she would be welcomed into their family, little Clare had taken to her immediately, and her father and mother had got on with Aiden like a house on fire. They hadn't even mentioned the age difference, and were totally understanding – as far as Shay could be understanding – about how hard it was for a man to be widowed and left on his own with a young child.

She smiled when she thought of Aiden's lovely big house. A few years ago it would have overwhelmed her, but now she knew that she could adapt to live in it. She supposed that the years of going in and out of Ballygrace House had got her used to the way things were done in grander circles, and her experience of dealing with all kinds of people in the Cale Green Hotel had made her much more confident.

Yes, Angela thought, this has come at the right time. A year ago I wouldn't have been ready for it.

Now it was just a case of waiting until he made his intentions quite clear. When that happened, Angela was ready to make any changes in her life so that they could be together.

Since it was quite warm and sunny, they took a walk through Athlone town and down by the Shannon river. Then, just as they were about to turn back for the car, Aiden took Angela gently by the arm and guided her over to an empty bench.

'You're going back to England in a day or two,' he told her, his face suddenly solemn, 'and there are still a few things I need to talk to you about before you go.'

Angela's heart skipped a beat. 'What sort of things?' she asked, for want of a better thing to say. She clasped her hands together in her lap and waited.

'I think you already know,' he said, looking earnestly at her.

Angela's hands tightened around each other as she waited for him to get to the point, to tell her exactly where she stood.

Then he tilted his head to the side so that he wasn't looking at her any more, and she noticed his jaw tighten. 'There's something I need to tell you,' he said, his voice now low and slightly hoarse. 'Something that happened ... something that I'm very ashamed of.' He put his head in his hands.

Angela's throat immediately ran dry. She now had no idea what he was going to tell her. It could be something trivial, or truly awful. And it suddenly crossed her mind that she couldn't know Aiden that well if she couldn't even hazard a guess at the sort of thing he might be ashamed about.

'You're going to have to tell me at some point, Aiden,' she said quietly. 'So you might as well get it over with.'

He took a deep breath. 'A short while before you and I met,' he said, staring straight ahead, 'when I was out with my partner and the office staff at a local hotel, there was an awkward situation.' He swallowed hard. 'We'd all had a nice meal with a few drinks and everything was going fine. Then we left the restaurant and went into the main function room where there was dancing. Anyway ... James, the other fellow, and I took the women in the office out on the floor for a dance – the sort of thing you have to do on those occasions. The sort of thing I never thought twice about when Elizabeth was with me.' He paused for a moment, collecting his thoughts. 'There was a group at another table. James knew them, and he brought me over to be introduced. Two of the girls asked us on the floor to dance ...' He shook his head. 'It was the first night out I'd had since Elizabeth died and I really didn't want to be there. I wasn't ready to be mixing and carrying on with crowds of younger people, and I suppose that didn't help.'

Angela felt her stomach sinking. 'What happened?' She looked straight at him, but his gaze was still directed somewhere far in front of him.

'I didn't realise it until I got on the floor, but the girl I was dancing with was very drunk. She was literally hanging on to me. Then she asked me to take her outside to get a bit of air. We walked outside into the hotel grounds and she seemed to have sobered up a bit, but then, as I went to walk back inside with her, she suddenly put her arms around me and started kissing me.' He shook his head and shuddered. 'It seems she works in one of the banks in town and had seen me around. Apparently she—'

'She had her eye on you,' Angela said in a flat voice. There was a pause, then she said in a low voice, 'Was she very attractive?'

Aiden turned his head now and looked at her incredulously. 'It was nothing like that,' he said, sounding wounded. 'She was just an ordinary-looking, nice enough girl. But I certainly wasn't interested in her – or any other girl for that matter.' She could see the hurt in his eyes now. 'I told you the truth when I met you, Angela. You're the first girl I've had the slightest interest in since Elizabeth.'

'Please, Aiden,' she whispered, 'finish your story.'

He cleared his throat. 'She was very embarrassed and annoyed when I moved away from her, said I obviously thought I was too good for her ... and then she went on to say the most hurtful things about Elizabeth. Saying that she had always thought herself a cut above everyone else, too, and did I know that she had shared a flat with a lad when she was only eighteen, when she was at university in Dublin ...' His voice broke off now.

Angela stared at him silently, not quite knowing what to say.

'Anyway,' he continued, 'after she'd thrown all that information at me, she staggered back into the dance, and I went into the gents. Just to splash a bit of water on my face and compose myself before going back into the hall.' He sighed and lifted his eyes to the clear blue sky. 'The next thing I knew, two of the fellows she had been sitting with burst through the door and started hitting and kicking me. God knows what she'd told them. Naturally, I defended myself as best I could, and since they were both very drunk, it was easier to handle them than it normally would have been.' He let out a long, painful sigh. 'It descended into a complete brawl, and only ended when I threw one of the fellows against the wall. He fell into the cubicle and broke his leg in a very awkward place. To make matters worse, he was a prominent Gaelic football player. Apparently he hasn't been able to play since.'

'Oh, dear God,' Angela said, putting her hand over his. 'It sounds terrible.'

'It was,' he said simply, 'and I feel very bad about it. I've never been involved in any kind of a fight since I left school.' He squeezed her hand now. 'I wish I'd been able to walk away, but it all happened so fast, and, if I'm honest, I was still raging with anger at what the girl had said to me. If things had been different I might have tried to talk them round, or try to dodge away from them.'

Angela hated herself for asking, but she had to know. 'Was it true?' she said in a hesitant voice. 'What the girl said about Elizabeth?'

Aiden gave a big, deep sigh. 'Apparently.' He rubbed his hands over his face. 'She was only a young girl when it happened.'

Angela couldn't stop herself. She needed to know more about the woman Aiden had shared his life with. The woman who was the mother of his daughter. 'Did you know about it? Had Elizabeth told you?'

'She had mentioned something about it, but I never pressed her.' He shrugged. 'She was embarrassed. It was one of those stupid mistakes that can be easily made when you're young.' There was an awkward silence. 'It's something I had more or less forgotten about, and it was a shock to have it thrown at me by a total stranger.'

Angela sat for a few moments, digesting all this unexpected information. In her own mind, ever since she had met Aiden, she had pictured Elizabeth as a holy saint. She had imagined her as the perfect partner, a woman without stain or sin. To hear that she had shared a flat – and very probably a *bed* – with a lad when she was only eighteen, made Angela feel almost elated. It freed her from the notion that she had to try to live up to the high standard that Elizabeth Byrne had set.

Even more importantly, it freed her from the worry of Aiden's reaction if he ever found out about her teenage misdemeanours. Listening to what Elizabeth had got up to made her realise that her own experiences were trivial by comparison. When she looked back on it, Angela realised she had learned from her early mistakes, and since then she hadn't let her guard down. She was now in her mid-twenties and still a virgin. She had been determined to wait for the right man.

And, as she looked at Aiden Byrne now, Angela knew she had found him.

'Look,' she said firmly, 'what happened wasn't your fault. You did nothing wrong. You were an innocent victim and you only defended yourself.' She put her arm through his. 'I don't know why you were so worried about telling me. I completely understand.' She looked up at him. 'It's all in the past. It's behind you now.'

Aiden looked at her. 'Angela,' he said quietly, 'you don't understand. It's not in the past at all. The worst is still to come. I've got to go to court again soon, on a charge of serious assault.' He gave a weary sigh. 'It should have been over and done with by now, but one of the main witnesses was sick at the last hearing and it was postponed, so I'm waiting for another date to come through any day.'

Aiden's news hung over them like a black cloud for the remainder of Angela's holiday. An awkwardness seemed to have grown between them, and Angela was unable to do anything about it.

The whole situation made her feel both sad and angry, because everything else had gone so well. She had spent two afternoons with little Clare and grown very fond of her in that short time. She had also spent an evening at Aiden's home, meeting his father, two brothers and sister, and it had been lovely. The men had been jovial and friendly, and Aiden's sister, Fiona, had repeated her mother's observation that she had not seen Aiden look so content in the last few years.

Of course, they were all aware of the impending court case, and Catherine Byrne had been very relieved when Aiden told her that Angela knew all about it. She was even more relieved that it hadn't made any difference to their relationship.

Aiden had been apologetic on their last night together. 'I can't see anything or plan anything until it's all over,' he told her. 'All I can do is ask you to wait and see what happens.'

Chapter 65

❦

Tara could just hear Kate's elegant old French clock in the hallway chime three times as she stood on the bedroom balcony in her friend's apartment. She glanced back at the high, antique bed where Gerry lay lightly snoring, then turned to look down at the Parisian street where Kate lived. It was all silent now – apart from the odd late-night car or cyclist – a very different scene to the bustling city street of four or five hours ago.

If she leaned out over the balcony, Tara could see the café bar where she, Gerry, Kate and André had dined earlier in the evening, and stayed drinking wine until almost midnight. Several of André's

friends who lived nearby – and whom Tara had met on her previous trip – had turned up unexpectedly and joined them for an hour or so. It had been another vibrant, colourful Paris evening, which Tara had enjoyed immensely. So much so that in another, different kind of life, she could almost imagine herself living in the atmospheric Latin Quarter and enjoying the carefree, artistic lifestyle.

She had actually said as much to Gerry on one occasion, when she felt slightly carried away by the traditional music and the carnival atmosphere. 'I think it's wonderful. If I can ever afford it, I'd love to buy a small place on the banks of the Seine.'

Gerry had shaken his head and laughed. 'Even though you look very fetching in your French kaftan and beads, you could no more exist here amongst all these arty, beatnik types than the Queen of England.' He'd waved his hand around the chic little café. 'This isn't the real world, Tara. After a while you'd find it very shallow and boring. You're much more suited to the cut and thrust of the business world, just like myself.'

Tara had pulled a face at him and given his elbow a little friendly push. But it was when they'd got back to Kate's apartment, after he'd drunk several glasses of wine, that she realised Gerry wasn't enjoying the trip as much as she had assumed.

'It's not Paris,' he had explained, as she lay in his arms amongst the white lace pillows, 'it's the company we've been keeping. I love the city – it's a beautiful, elegant place – but I wouldn't have minded spending some time on our own. I think we might have been wiser to book into a hotel than stay with a friend.'

'But I thought you liked Kate,' Tara said, feeling very confused. 'You said she was a lovely, talented, bubbly girl.'

'*Woman*,' Gerry corrected. He lightly kissed her on the top of her head. 'I agree she's very fashionable-looking, vivacious and talented – but she's still a grown woman. A woman in her thirties.' He had nuzzled his face into the warm hollow of Tara's neck. 'And that's the problem. She's living the life of a starry-eyed teenager here in Paris amongst a crowd of no-hoper, arty types who will never have a penny or a French franc to their names.'

'But Kate says that André's paintings are starting to sell in city art shops and exhibitions for a very good price,' Tara argued. She had taken a deep breath, trying not to show her disappointment. 'I think he's an excellent artist and very original. In fact, I liked the abstract

347

ones he showed us in his studio this afternoon so much that I've ordered one to take home with me. I'm going to hang it in my office at the Grosvenor.'

'Oh, Tara,' Gerry had said, in a highly amused voice, 'you are impossible.' Tara could feel his shoulders gently quivering with laughter, and she moved out of his arms to look at him.

'I don't see what's so funny,' she whispered heatedly, her brow wrinkled with annoyance. 'I really do think he's a good artist.'

'Well, that's fine,' Gerry said, shrugging. 'But personally, I think you've thrown your money away. The Parisian scenes are reasonable enough, but the abstract stuff could have been done by an enthusiastic child.'

'Well, I totally disagree!' Tara said, very indignantly. 'And not only are you insulting André's talent, but you're insulting my taste.'

Gerry looked back at her, his eyes filled with amusement. 'My, my,' he said playfully, 'I didn't realise you had such a temper.' Then, as she turned her head away from him, he had suddenly reached out and pulled her into his arms. 'I'm only teasing you, Tara,' he said. He paused and his hands came up to cup her face, then he kissed her deeply on the lips. 'You look even more ravishing than usual when you are angry,' he whispered. 'That fiery Irish temper reminds me of Maureen O'Hara in *The Quiet Man*.'

Then, when Tara had made to protest, he had covered her face and hair with kisses, then drew her tighter towards him. 'You really are the most gorgeous, sexy woman,' he said, moving his lips over her face and then down to her throat.

Tara felt herself shiver at his touch, just as she had done the previous night when they had made love for the very first time. His hands came up to her shoulders and he slipped the light straps of her gold satin nightdress downwards, allowing his lips to travel down between her voluptuous breasts. Then, as his mouth came back up to kiss and explore hers with his tongue, any further protestations were forgotten, as Gerry McShane expertly manoeuvred himself and Tara around until she was beneath him.

They kissed and caressed each other, desire rushing through Tara like a red-hot fire, and then, when she thought she couldn't stand it any longer, he arched his body over hers and moved inside her, taking her passion to a higher level.

As they lay back in the bed afterwards, Gerry sinking into a deep, sated sleep, Tara stared into the darkness, thinking how pleasant yet how strange it felt to have a man lying in the bed beside her. She had thought it even stranger the previous night, when it had been her first experience for such a long time.

Although she felt tired, sleep was just eluding her. Every time she felt herself slip down into it, she found her mind stirring again. And in that half-sleep state, Tara found herself remembering the intimate nights she had spent with Gabriel. They had been lovely, tender, safe nights, when she knew she had found the love of a good and decent man. A love that had matured between them through childhood and adolescence. A love that had given Tara the self-esteem and respect she had sought all her life.

Those few years of being physically close to Gabriel had been precious, but had passed so fleetingly. The fact that he had been tired, and gradually becoming weaker, had made them put any sexual needs on the back-burner, presuming that when he recovered they would resume their intimacy. But of course, he never did. Not knowing what lay ahead, they had given up on their intimacy much too soon.

Then, her eyelashes damp from holding back the tears, her sleepy mind travelled further back, before her marriage, to the passionate nights she had shared with Frank Kennedy. The man she had first trusted with her all her ambitions and most of her secrets. The man she had first trusted to make love to her.

Whether it was the fact that she was in a strange city, or the fact that she had drunk those few glasses of wine, Tara's mind refused to let go of the old memories it had conjured up. She was careful not to wake Gerry as she turned around in the bed, trying to escape from the uncomfortable, unwelcome thoughts.

No matter how hard she fought it, memories of the nights she had spent with Frank Kennedy in the Lake District floated back into her head, forcing Tara to get out of bed and walk across to the window. She had quietly opened the shutters and the French windows, then stepped out onto the small balcony, and into the cool night air, in an attempt to break free of her thoughts.

Three men, she thought now as she looked out into the early-morning Parisian street. Three men who had been trusted to share the intimacies of her life. Compared with some women in this day and age, it wasn't a huge number. Compared with other, more traditional women, it was a lot. There were still plenty of women who didn't have sex until they were married, and then remained faithful to that same man for the rest of their lives.

And then there were women like Bridget, who had always needed the physical comfort of a man, someone to put their arms around her and tell her she was safe, rather than for sexual reasons. But that was often a difficult distinction for a man to make – and definitely in the case of the males that Bridget had encountered from an early age. Because of that great need, she had suffered, and paid a high price.

Tara was lucky, because, being more self-contained, she was able to put that part of her life to one side and just get on with things. And, in her more recent years, she had done so quite ably, until last night, when she had allowed a third man – Gerry McShane – into her bed.

She turned away from the balcony and looked back into the room again, to the sleeping Gerry. Whatever happened between them, she didn't regret this trip away. On the contrary. She had enjoyed it very much. Apart from making up a foursome with Kate and her lover, it had given Tara back an important part of herself. It had reminded her that she was an attractive, sexual woman who had normal, healthy needs. Thankfully, they were needs she could ignore when it suited her, but they were were there to be re-awakened when she met the right man. The man that, hopefully, she would spend the rest of her life with.

Whether the handsome, clever Gerry was that man she didn't know. But she was definitely going to enjoy finding out.

It was the last night of Tara and Gerry's three-day trip to Paris, and, as she looked across the rosy, candle-lit table at Kate, Tara almost envied the starry, adoring look in her friend's eyes. She looked glowing and in love as she listened to André relate another of his amusing stories about his Bohemian artist friends. Kate, her elbow leaning on the table and her chin resting casually on her hand, caught her looking and winked. She then pointed in the direction of the ladies' and gestured for Tara to come with her.

'How do you think it has gone?' Kate asked anxiously, her hand touching her friend's arm. 'Has Gerry enjoyed the restaurant and the meal tonight?'

'Of course he has,' Tara said, giving her a big, reassuring smile.

'How could anyone *not* enjoy it? It's one of the top places in Paris, and the food and wine were spectacular.'

'I'm glad,' Kate said, smiling with relief. 'I know the smaller café bars are more André's scene, but it's nice to be in a more sophisticated atmosphere now and again.' She paused. 'I still feel bad about you booking into a hotel for your last night.'

'Kate, please don't take it like that.' Tara said, looking and sounding awkward. She felt bad herself about the situation because it did look rude, but Gerry had refused to be put off, saying they deserved one night on their own. 'Gerry just fancied it because it was more central and easier for us to get to the airport in the morning.' She shrugged. 'You know how men can be more practical about these things. I much preferred staying in your gorgeous apartment.'

'You will come again soon, won't you?' Kate asked.

Tara nodded her head. 'Of course I will. I'll come because I want to see Paris, but especially to see you.'

Chapter 66

❧

STOCKPORT

On her first free evening back in Stockport, Angela had gone down to Maple Terrace. Over several cups of tea, she poured out the whole story about Aiden and the court case to Bridget and June. She had waited until Tara was in Paris to tell anyone, as she hadn't wanted anything to spoil her sister's badly needed break.

Angela was also afraid that Tara might wonder if she were capable of keeping her mind on her work when she had such a serious worry. In actual fact, Angela found herself grateful that she had such a busy, interesting job, as it occupied her mind for most of the day.

'Have Aiden's lawyers said what they think might happen?' Bridget asked, clearly worried for Angela. Although the new medication had now started to make a difference – had taken away the worst of her depression – she still wasn't back to her old self, and the smallest worries kept her awake at night. But, with June's help, she had got the lodging house back into its old routine. There weren't too many lads in at the minute, as Fred had said he was happier having just four or five lodgers, to give her a bit more time to herself.

'They really don't know,' Angela said. 'It all depends on what happens in court. He said they're fully prepared, and have witnesses they can use if necessary, but I think they're hoping that Aiden's good reputation and clean record will speak for itself.' She shook her head. 'It's the waiting that's the worst thing. It should all have been over and done with, but it's been adjourned twice now for various reasons.'

'That's the worst things about court cases,' Bridget mused, 'they just hang over your head.'

'So, what do you think to Tara and this fella, Gerry McShane?' June said, lighting up a cigarette. 'Do you think it's serious or what?'

Bridget smiled and gave a little shrug. 'It's hard to know,' she said. 'Believe it or not, I haven't even met him yet, so I can't really give an opinion until I see them together. Tara says he's not one for mixing with crowds and prefers them to go out on their own.'

'Can you not tell by the way Tara talks about him?' June said, blowing smoke high up into the air. 'You know the way some women look when they're talking about blokes they're really keen on.' She leaned across the table and tipped Bridget's hand, then nodded towards Angela. 'Does she look all starry-eyed and in love, the way her sister does when she's talkin' about Aiden Byrne?'

They all laughed, then Angela said, 'I think she's keen enough on him. She must be – Tara's not the type to go off lightly to Paris with a man.'

'Well, she deserves a break,' Bridget said, 'and I'm sure he must be nice enough, because it's not every fella that Tara will look at. And it's the first one since Gabriel died.'

'What do you make of Frank Kennedy?' Angela suddenly asked. 'Is he still keen on Tara, or do you think she's managed to put him off at last? I haven't seen him in the Cale Green Hotel for a long time.'

Bridget gave a wry smile. 'Whatever Tara does, she will never be able to put Frank off,' she told her two friends. 'Oh, she might keep him at a good distance, and she could even go a year or two without seeing him, but Frank will never forget her. The closest he ever came was with Kate Thornley, because I know he thought the world of her, but his feelings for Tara were too strong for him to marry someone else.'

'It's unbelievable,' Angela sighed. 'And in a way it's very sad, because she's never going to look at him. But Gerry McShane is a fine-looking man and he's got a lot going for him – good job, money and everything. I reckon he's the one she'll settle down with in the fullness of time.'

Bridget got up from the table and went over to the sink to wash up the tea things. 'Well, if she does, I'll be delighted for her, but I'll be sorry for poor oul' Frank. He's as decent a man as you'll ever find.' She turned back to face the two women at the table. 'When I think how kind he was to me after losing the baby, sending flowers and a basket of fruit. And any time him and Fred go to the wrestling or the boxing together, he always leaves a few pounds on the mantelpiece for the kids.' She shook her head. 'I know he's made mistakes, but they weren't made out of wickedness. And I know it's caused rows between meself and Tara, but I still can't help what I think. Frank Kennedy is one of the best men I've ever met – and nobody will tell me any different.'

Chapter 67

✃

The call Angela had been waiting for eventually came.

'The court case is next Friday,' Aiden told her. 'So we'll know one way or another what's going to happen.' He had paused. 'If it all goes OK, I promise I'll make it up to you, but if the worst comes to the worst, I'll let you know straight away and you will be free to find somebody that won't ruin your life. If things turn out bad for me, my business and my reputation in the area will be ruined. You're only a young woman and you don't need to be burdened with my problems.'

'I don't care what happens,' Angela had told him. 'It won't change my feelings for you.'

'We'll see,' he had said, sounding very distant.

Angela had been like a cat on hot bricks all week, waiting for it to be over and done with. When she woke on the Friday morning, after another broken night's sleep, she felt physically sick and couldn't face any breakfast.

'You must have something,' Tara told her as they sat in the dining-room in the house. 'You can't go out on an empty stomach. At least have a piece of toast or a bowl of cereal.'

Angela had told Tara all about the court situation when she came back from Paris, and had been relieved to find her sympathetic and supportive.

'Tea is all I can manage,' Angela said, her face pale and drawn. She was dressed smartly in her navy working suit and a blue, tie-necked blouse, and had done her best to lift her appearance with a brighter than usual lipstick, but her anxiety was stamped on her face. 'I'll have something to eat when I get into work.'

'Why don't you get a taxi and come over to the Grosvenor for your lunch?' Tara suggested. 'It would break the day for you and help to take your mind off things for a while.'

Angela thought for a few moments, then shook her blonde head. 'Thanks anyway, Tara, but Aiden doesn't go into court until eleven o'clock, and I'd rather be beside the phone in case he rings.' She gave a little weak smile. 'Maybe we could have a celebratory lunch next week if everything goes OK?'

The morning and the afternoon crawled by without a word from Aiden or any of his family. All Angela managed to eat all day was half a piece of toast and a few mouthfuls of potato and chicken. Her mind flitted from one disastrous scenario to another as she wondered what was happening.

Several times her hand hovered over the telephone as she debated whether to ring Aiden's office to see if they had any news, or to ask whether they might have his mother's phone number. But each time she had chickened out. What if the staff didn't know that he was in court?

And what if the unthinkable had happened? What if Aiden had been given a jail sentence?

Suddenly it was five o'clock. Aiden's office would now be closed; there was no point in ringing now. Angela tidied up her desk, put on her jacket, and lifted up her handbag. All she wanted to do now was go home and go to bed. She would fill a hot water bottle and take it upstairs with her, then she would pull the blankets up over her head and lie and wait.

Eventually, she felt, she would receive the phone call that would confirm all her hopes and dreams regarding Aiden Byrne were smashed to pieces.

When she heard the rapping on her bedroom door, Angela didn't know where she was or what time of the day or night it was. Somehow – after tossing and turning, and agonising over all the possibilities – she had fallen into a deep sleep.

The bedroom door opened and Tara's curly red hair appeared. 'Can you come to the phone, Angela?' she said in a low, serious voice. 'There's some news for you.'

Then, before Angela could think of the right words, she was gone – presumably to ask whoever was calling to hang on for a few minutes.

Angela threw back the covers and sat up in bed. She glanced at the window and was amazed to see how dark it was outside. She switched on her bedside lamp and looked at her watch – it was half-past eight. She was amazed to see she had been sleeping for several hours. She moved herself to pull on her blouse and skirt, and slip her feet into her shoes, then she went downstairs to face whatever news awaited her.

Whoever had rung to speak to her had obviously hung up, because the phone lay silently in its cradle, on top of the hall table. Angela gave a small, weary sigh and headed towards the kitchen to make herself a cup of tea. As she passed the sitting-room door, Tara came out.

'Angela, I know you're probably not in the mood to chat,' she said in a quiet, serious tone, 'but if you wouldn't mind coming in here for a few minutes ...'

Angela caught her breath. *Tara knew something.* She'd obviously spoken to one of Aiden's family on the phone. With a shaky hand she tucked a wing of her blonde hair back behind one ear, held her head up and walked into the room.

For a moment she thought she was back in bed dreaming. How could Aiden Byrne be sitting on the sofa all dressed in his smart business suit with an overnight bag on the floor next to him? A large bottle of champagne stood on the coffee table in front of him, as well as three champagne flutes. Angela stared at him with wide, amazed eyes, then her gaze moved back to Tara, who was now grinning from ear to ear.

Before she could utter a word, Aiden was on his feet and coming towards her with open arms. 'It's all over,' he told her in an unfamiliar, choked voice. He pulled her close into his chest and held her tightly. 'The judge dismissed the case as self-defence before it had hardly started.'

'How?' Angela said.

'There was a witness who had been outside and heard what passed between me and the girl,' he explained. 'He knew the family of the lad who broke his leg. Initially, he decided to keep out of it, but, at the last minute, his conscience got the better of him and he went to the Guards to make a statement.'

'But how did you get here so quickly?' Angela asked, still unable to take it all in.

'I decided to take a chance,' he told her, beaming. 'I went home from the court, packed a bag and drove straight up to the airport. Luckily enough, I got a standby flight to Manchester within a couple of hours.'

'I can't believe it,' Angela whispered.

'The champagne!' Tara interrupted in a cheery tone. She felt conspicuously in the way at the moment, but knew that she couldn't just disappear. 'I'll have a quick glass to celebrate with you,' she told them, 'then I'll leave you in peace to chat.'

Aiden kissed Angela lightly on the forehead, then went back to the coffee table, lifted the bottle and quickly popped the cork. He poured the bubbly liquid into the three glasses and handed them around.

'To the future,' he said, holding his glass out to clink with the other two.

They were halfway down their glasses when he reached for the champagne bottle to re-fill them again.

'No, no,' Tara said, covering the top of her glass with her hand. 'Honestly, I have enough.'

'Ah, you must,' he said, looking directly at her. 'The first toast was only one of relief – to say thank God that justice was done. But I have another toast, a more important one, and I would really like you to join in.'

Tara obediently held out the half-empty glass.

When the glasses were all refilled, Aiden and put his down and reached into his inside pocket. 'On my way to the airport, I made a little detour into Dublin,' he said, 'to buy you this.' He held out a small square package to Angela.

Quickly, she put her crystal flute down on the table, then took the package from him with trembling hands, and opened it to find a small jeweller's box. She looked up at Aiden before opening it, hoping to find a clue in his eyes. But he simply smiled back and she could tell nothing at all from his expression. She looked over at Tara, who was smiling expectantly and hugging the champagne glass in both her hands.

Angela took a deep breath and opened the box. There, safely tucked in the purple velvet lining, was a three-stoned, glittering diamond ring.

'Angela,' Aiden Byrne said, in a slightly nervous tone, 'now that we have all the obstacles out of the way, I'd like to ask you to be my wife.'

A short while later, Tara hugged both Angela and Aiden again and wished them all the best for their future together. She left them in the sitting-room along with Vera and a nurse who was boarding at the house. Both women, very suspicious of alcohol, were daintily sipping their glasses of champagne after offering their very best wishes to the happy couple. Oblivious to the trials and tribulations that Angela and Aiden had suffered over the last few months, the two women had stumbled upon the engagement celebration and had been delighted to join in such a happy occasion.

After her one and a half glasses of champagne, Tara walked down to Bridget's and told her old friend the good news.

'Thank God for something to celebrate,' Bridget said, joining her two hands together as though in prayer. She paused for a few moments, then said, 'I know you don't approve of me drinking, Tara, but surely we can't let Angela's engagement go by without a little toast?' Then, before Tara had time even to think about it, she rushed out to the small cabinet in the sitting-room and come back clutching a bottle of sherry.

But by the time Bridget had followed the first drink with a few more, her mood had descended into one of melancholy. This time she was depressed over the recent Aberfan school disaster in South Wales.

'All those poor little innocent children,' she cried, her words slurring. 'Where is God, Tara, at times like these? Is there a God at all, you have to wonder?'

Then she repeated her usual list of woes, which, by now, everyone dreaded hearing. In her rational moments she knew there was nothing that could be done about the baby she lost, the baby she gave away, and the situation regarding Lucy and Lloyd. And yet, she couldn't stop herself.

'The one good thing that came about that weekend was meeting Thelma Stevens,' she said, giving Tara a watery smile. 'She's been a great help to me. She phones me every few nights. Tara, the woman is a real inspiration when you hear the life she's had. All the trouble she's been through with that daughter, yet she's up every morning and running that lovely boarding house of hers, looking as if she hasn't a care in the world.' She rubbed her hands over her tear-stained face. 'She reminds me for all the world of Ruby Sweeney, and I only wish she lived nearer to me, because she has such an understanding heart.'

Tara reached across the kitchen table and squeezed her friend's hand. 'The reason she is friends with you is because you have such a lovely, understanding heart, too.'

Bridget lifted her gaze to Tara to say something, but the words failed to manifest. Instead she laid her head on her arms and cried like a baby.

An hour and a half later, Tara left Maple Terrace with a heavy heart. Bridget had drunk three large glasses of sherry in the time it had taken Tara to drink one, and there was no disguising the effect it had on her.

Chapter 68

❧

MID-DECEMBER 1966

Tara glanced around the glittering, festive function room in the Grosvenor Hotel, and was gratified to see that every single table was full. All the important people in Stockport were there – the bankers, the estate agents, the building contractors, the local newspaper staff, and all the companies that had been involved in the extension work and the refurbishment of the hotel. All these people had been invited for an exclusive dinner-dance to celebrate the group's first Christmas in the hotel business.

The newly refurbished foyer of the Grosvenor was magnificently decorated, with a huge Christmas tree hung with frosted white bells, bows and candles. Festive greenery tumbled over pictures and banisters, and trailed down the sides of the ornate mantelpiece. The circular marble table in the centre of the entrance hall held a breath-taking display of different-sized glass vases filled with creamy-white lilies. The white theme was carried through to the function room, and on each circular table stood a tall vase of more lilies.

John Burns and his wife were sitting to one side of her, and Gerry McShane on the other. Next was the quiet member of the group – Eric Simmons – and his wife, while Frank Kennedy was sitting opposite her. All the men were smartly dressed in tuxedos and bow-ties, and Tara had bought a beautiful green velvet gown with a matching stole and evening bag especially for the occasion. Her only jewels were emerald and diamond earrings, and she had piled her red hair up in a loose style with a few loose tendrils at the nape of her neck. She knew when she bought the outfit in Manchester that it was very special, and she was left in no doubt about it when she saw the look of admiration in Gerry's eyes.

The six-monthly report on the Grosvenor Hotel's finances had been very favourable, and there was no doubt in anyone's mind that the venture had got off to a very promising start. There had been a meeting in the hotel earlier that afternoon, and when the reports on the work schedules showed that they were actually a little ahead of time, it had added to the positive atmosphere.

Tara and Gerry McShane had been very discreet where their relationship was concerned, and had kept it strictly out of office. On nights like tonight, when they were at group functions, they made a point of mixing with the others.

Frank had kept a good distance between himself and Tara since the summer. In fact, he had only called into the hotel on a couple of occasions – mainly for the business group meetings or discussions with the contractors – and had kept well away from Tara's office. Gerry had mentioned that Frank was involved in a big building project over in Galway, and had been spending a lot of time travelling back and forth. Whatever his reason for not being around, Tara was grateful for it.

Tonight, since she had been the person behind all the organisation for the dinner-dance, Tara had made a special effort to be as friendly to Frank as she was to the others. When she had been chatting generally to everyone around the table, she had made sure to include him in conversations, and had addressed him directly on one or two occasions. But as the night went on and the dancing got underway, it became quite apparent that Frank had taken Gerry McShane's message to heart.

He danced with John's and Eric's wives several times, then he had gone to the bar, where he had stood chatting to various people for a large part of the night. He made no move in Tara's direction.

Towards the end of the evening, Tara was on her way back from the ladies' room when she saw Frank coming towards her across the hotel foyer. For a moment she wasn't quite sure what to do and slowed her step. Then, as they were about to pass each other, she tilted her head towards him. 'It's been a very successful night so far, don't you think?' she said, in a distant but reasonably friendly tone.

Frank nodded. 'Indeed it has,' he replied, in what could only be described as a subdued manner. 'Yourself and the staff have organised it brilliantly.' He gestured around the foyer. 'You've done a great job on the hotel generally, just as I knew you would.'

'Thank you,' Tara said, suddenly feeling awkward. She fiddled with the little strap on her evening bag for something to do.

There was a small silence then he said, 'The reports were all very encouraging, so I hope you feel your investment in the Grosvenor was a sound one.'

'I do, actually,' Tara said, carefully stepping to the side to let a couple pass by.

'I mustn't detain you,' Frank said, starting to turn away. 'There are still a few more dances to go, and I'm sure there will be people waiting for you.'

Something about him suddenly Tara struck. He looked different. And yet, she wasn't quite sure why. It wasn't an obvious physical change. Then, as he lifted his gaze towards her, Tara saw quite clearly that the difference was in his eyes.

The brilliant, piercing eyes that had once entranced her were now clouded, and she was taken aback to see a naked vulnerability in them.

'Frank,' she suddenly heard herself say, 'I should have said this before … I want to thank you for offering me this business opportunity. It has worked out very well, and … I'm very grateful to you.'

Frank inclined his head, his gaze moving somewhere behind her. 'I knew it would work out, Tara, or I would never have asked you to get involved. I also knew you were the best person for the managerial role.' He ran a hand through his thick dark hair. 'You're a very clever, competent woman.' He paused. 'And I want you to know that I would never have let you lose on the deal. I had put money aside to cover any losses you could possibly have incurred.'

Tara caught her breath. 'There was no need for that,' she said, a touch of indignation in her voice. 'I'm perfectly capable of organising my own finances.'

'Oh, I know that,' he said, his eyes coming back to rest on her again. 'But I also know how much the old house back in Ireland means to you, and I wanted to make sure that, whatever happened, you would always be able to keep it.'

Tara looked at him, a ripple of confusion running through her. If it were anyone else, she would have felt overwhelmed with gratitude and amazement at their kindness. He was right: if she lost everything else, Ballygrace House would be the one thing she would want to hang on to.

Why she wanted to keep it she was never quite sure, because the old house had been the source of sadness and unhappiness at times. And yet, she was not able to let go of it. The house seemed to measure how far she had come in life. It had chalked up the milestones she had travelled since she was a young, motherless girl.

And Frank Kennedy was one of the few people who knew what it meant to her. Not only that, but he had been willing to lose thousands of pounds of his own money to ensure she kept the house in which she had lived with Gabriel.

But even as she stood in front of him, she couldn't give him the satisfaction of feeling that she was in any way beholden to him.

'I had already checked out all the risks I was taking buying into the Grosvenor,' she told him, feeling a quiver in her voice, 'and I was fully prepared for any losses that would come as a result of it. There was really no need for you to feel in any way responsible for me.'

'Well,' he said, in a flat, almost defeated tone, 'I've obviously made yet another mistake where you are concerned, Tara. But I was willing to take that risk because I've learned that there are certain things in life that *can* be prevented and some that cannot. You losing your house was something I could prevent happening – and if the worst had come to the worst, it was the least I owed you.'

'You owe me nothing,' she said quietly.

When he saw the familiar defensive look on her face, he held up his hands. 'I know it was only money. And when you have a certain amount and are able give it away, gestures can become meaningless.' He shook his head, his face now taut with emotion. 'You don't have to tell me, Tara. Believe me, I've heard it before from other quarters.' He shrugged. 'I did it for no other reason than I wanted to protect you from any ill-judgements on my part. I'm under no illusions as to what you think of me.'

Tara looked at him wordlessly for a few moments, then he looked her straight in the eye and said, 'I wish you all the good things you wish yourself – at this time of the year and always.'

Then he bowed his head, and she watched him stride on down the corridor.

As she turned back to join the others, a wave of emotion suddenly hit her, and, to her horror, hot tears started to stream down her face. She stood for a moment, brushing them away with the back of her hand, but the tears came faster than she could dry them. And they seemed to be coming from somewhere other than her eyes, some sad place buried deep inside her perhaps.

Totally confused, she found herself rushing back to the ladies, terrified she would meet someone on the way or in there. Thankfully, it was empty. She headed for the cubicle at the far end. After locking the door with fumbling, shaking hands, she flushed the toilet, then let the tears she had been holding in flow freely.

For a good ten minutes Tara stood in the cubicle, her head and hands pressed against the expensive wall tiles as her shoulders heaved with great, wracking sobs, while she tried to stem the tears with handfuls of the tissues that sat on the window-ledge.

What on earth is wrong? she asked herself. Why the hell am I crying like this?

But she had no answer. At least, no answer that she would allow herself to accept.

Deep down she knew it was to do with the kindness that Frank Kennedy had just shown her, but it made no sense to her that she should cry over him.

Instead, she rationalised her emotional outburst by reminding herself that her period was due in ten days' time. Usually, she felt slightly emotional for two or three days before. On this occasion, she decided that her monthly cycle must have gone skew-whiff.

Eventually the tears stopped and Tara dried her face. She came out of the cubicle and went to the end mirror beside a window, opening it so that the cold night air cooled her red, swollen face. And then she carefully re-applied her make-up, using a double layer of foundation and a thick coat of powder.

When she was satisfied that she would pass in the dimly-lit function room, she took several deep breaths and made her way back.

Chapter 69

Angela had assured Tara that she would still be in Stockport to manage the Cale Green Hotel over the Christmas period. This was something that she had promised when she took on the job, under no circumstances would she let her sister down. She knew Tara had to give all her energy to her first Christmas in the Grosvenor, and was relying on Angela to make sure that the usual standards prevailed in the smaller hotel.

It would be a working Christmas for them both, the only relief being Christmas Day, which they planned to spend down at Bridget's, enjoying a family Christmas with Bridget and Fred and watching the children open their presents from Santa Claus.

Tara was well aware of the sacrifice Angela was making on her behalf. 'I feel bad that you can't be in Ireland with Aiden and his little girl for Christmas,' Tara had said, as they walked back from Mass the Sunday before Christmas. Both women were wrapped up in thick coats, scarves and hats against the chill wind. 'And I truly appreciate your loyalty.'

'After all you've done for me, it's the least I can do for you,' Angela told her. Then she took a deep breath. 'But I can't guarantee that I'll be around next Christmas ...'

Tara looked at her and smiled. 'I should hope not,' she said in a brisk manner. 'Hopefully by next Christmas you'll be either planning a wedding, or you'll be already married.'

'Can you imagine it?' Angela said, putting a gloved hand up to her mouth to stifle her giggles. 'Who would believe that I'd be getting married to somebody sensible like an accountant? And moving back home to Ireland? I thought I'd be here for years and years, and end up marrying an Englishman. It's amazing how things turn out, isn't it?'

'Life is constantly full of surprises,' Tara told her, 'and my loss is Aiden Byrne's gain.'

They walked along in the winter morning air, chatting companionably about possible wedding plans, then Angela suddenly asked, 'Do you see yourself ever getting married again, Tara?' Before she had a chance to answer, Angela had rushed on, terrified of offending her. 'I don't mind if you feel it's none of my business. I would never have asked such a personal question before ... It's just that Aiden lost his wife, too.'

'It's OK, Angela,' Tara had answered lightly. 'It's a natural enough question to ask after all this time.' She paused, considering the question. 'Maybe,' she said, a cautious note in her voice, 'if I met the right person.'

Then, emboldened by Tara's open manner, Angela asked, 'Do you think that Gerry McShane might be that person? You've been going out together for a while now.'

'Oh, I'm not sure about that,' Tara had quickly said. 'It's much too early to tell.'

'You've been seeing him for nearly as long as I've been seeing Aiden,' Angela said, although she knew she was pushing the point. 'And you took him down to Bridget and Fred's recently. And you've been to York a couple of times to meet his family, haven't you?'

'True,' Tara said, 'and they're all lovely people. And Gerry McShane is a lovely man, but I think it takes a bit longer to get to know someone when you're older. Or maybe it's just me.' Then she gave a sidelong grin. 'Besides, Angela, it's manners to wait until you're asked – and so far the subject has never arisen between me and Gerry.'

'It's coming up to Christmas,' Angela reminded her, 'and that's always a romantic time of the year.'

The following night Tara and Gerry went to a ballet of *The Snow*

Queen. Afterwards Gerry drove them back out to the Grosvenor. He had rung her an hour before picking her up at the house in Cale Green, saying, 'Bring your things for work in the morning. I have an early meeting in the hotel tomorrow, and I've booked one of the suites.' His voice had softened. 'I'd love someone to keep me company overnight.'

As soon as Tara and Gerry McShane arrived in the entrance hall of the Grosvenor Hotel, they were greeted by a uniformed member of staff, who spirited away Tara's suede coat with the luxurious fur collar, Gerry's sheepskin coat, and both their overnight bags. The bar was busy, but they were quickly shown to a table by the window, which the staff reserved for special customers.

They were sitting quietly chatting over a glass of wine when Gerry suddenly nodded towards the bar. 'I see Mr Kennedy has just come in with some friends.' He leaned forward. 'He's with a rough-looking chap that I'm sure I recognise from somewhere.' He raised his eyebrows.

Tara glanced over. 'It's Bridget and Fred,' she said in a high, surprised voice. She had been speaking to Bridget the previous night and she hadn't mentioned anything about coming out for the evening with Frank Kennedy. Tara suddenly felt uncomfortable on a number of levels. For a start, she didn't like the way Gerry had referred to Fred, and secondly, she couldn't ask Bridget and Fred to join them without asking Frank. 'The couple are very good friends of mine,' she told him, 'and Fred is a lovely man. You must know him from the Cale Green Hotel; he's my head barman. I'll get them to come over.'

Gerry sat up straighter in his chair. 'They'll probably be happy in their own company,' he said. 'And anyway, it's hardly worth getting into a big social with them, when we're heading off to bed shortly. If we just sit quietly here, they probably won't notice us.' He gave a small laugh. 'I'm sure you don't want to have to sit and make small talk with Mr Kennedy and his companions.'

Tara felt a stab of irritation. 'But I can't ignore Bridget,' she said. 'She's my oldest friend.' She stared at Gerry now, obviously annoyed.

When he saw the look on her face, he shrugged. 'By all means call them over, if that's what you want. I was only thinking of you, because it's late and you're working in the morning.' He gave her a lazy sort of smile now. 'I didn't mean anything against your friends. It's just that I know you like your beauty sleep ... and I was being a little selfish, as I want you all to myself.'

Tara smiled and her shoulders relaxed. She craned her neck to see over to the bar, and, when Fred caught her eye, she waved him over.

Bridget came first, and her face was glowing when she sat down beside Tara. She was dressed up in a striking, double-breasted purple dress, and had been to the hairdresser's that morning; her hair was tinted a warm chestnut colour. The young hairdresser had also clearly talked her into having her hair cut a bit shorter, with sharper peaks at the sides and the back of her neck.

'You look fabulous,' Tara told her, admiring her outfit. 'And I love the long black boots.'

'So does Fred!' Bridget said, rolling her eyes and giggling like a schoolgirl. She put her gin and tonic down on the table and made herself comfortable in the chair. Tara then made the introductions and, after shaking hands, Bridget turned towards Gerry.

'I've heard all about you,' she said, winking at him. 'But I thought I was never going to get the chance to meet you. I think she's keeping you hidden away.'

Gerry laughed and made an appropriate comment, and Tara was relieved to see her friend in such good spirits, although she could tell by her sparkling eyes she had had a few drinks. Still, she reasoned, it was Christmas, and everyone was having a drink, including herself.

'Frank rang up last night to say he'd booked a table for us as a special Christmas treat,' Bridget explained, looking over to Gerry to include him in the conversation, 'so I rang June and she said she would come down and babysit for us.'

Fred came across to the table now – pint in hand – and kissed Tara on the cheek, then he held out his hand to shake Gerry's. 'I see you often in the hotel. Nice to meet you again,' he said, giving his usual beaming smile. He sat down on the sofa beside Bridget. 'We had a beltin' meal in at the restaurant tonight, didn't we, love?'

'Fantastic,' Bridget agreed, lifting her glass and taking a good drink from it.

'Big change from when I worked in here,' Fred told them. 'You wouldn't know the place.'

'What did you do?' Gerry asked.

'Barman,' Fred said. 'And Bridget was a barmaid, weren't you, love? And that's how we met.'

'Love across a crowded bar,' Gerry quipped.

'It wasn't so crowded then,' Fred told him. 'They're certainly doing a lot more business these days.' He looked at Tara. 'You've done a champion job on the place, you know. It's fantastic – really classy.'

'Although, in fairness to the previous owners,' Bridget said, 'it was always a nice place.' She looked at her husband now, a fond expression in her eyes. 'Do you remember the big sports do they had in here that Christmas, when they gave you your award? Do you remember all the lovely decorations and things they had?'

'That was a wonderful night,' Tara said, her eyes soft as she remembered the occasion. 'Fred was truly the star of the show.'

'Aw, go away with the pair of you,' Fred said, embarrassed but delighted at the compliment.

'And you're right about how well the hotel looked, Bridget,' Tara said. 'It was beautiful that night.'

Frank Kennedy suddenly appeared at the table, dressed in a casually expensive dark suit and a subtly striped blue and navy shirt. 'Can I get anyone a drink?' he asked, his manner slightly distracted.

Tara glanced up at him but he kept his gaze averted, looking back towards the bar. She wondered if he had heard them talking about the night of Fred's award. He had been there, of course, with Kate Thornley on his arm. It had been the first night they had appeared together in public.

Gerry held up his half-empty wine glass. 'We're fine, thanks. I should imagine that we'll be heading off to bed soon.'

Just as Tara was finishing her drink, Bridget suggested that they go to the ladies' together. Tara recognised that it was a signal for a private word, so she lifted her handbag and told Gerry she'd only be a few minutes.

'You're not going to believe what Frank has been telling us,' Bridget said as they walked along the thickly carpeted corridor. 'His ex-wife died last month.'

'Really?' Tara said, suddenly wondering if that was the reason he had looked so different.

The went into the ladies' now, which was empty, giving them the chance to talk freely.

'And you're not going to believe what caused it: sclerosis of the liver. Seemingly she had been drinking in secret for years, and even though she was warned, she kept it up.' Her eyes widened. 'Frank has been back and forward to County Clare these last few months.'

Tara's brow wrinkled. 'But I thought they had nothing to do with each other since they divorced?'

Bridget shook her head. 'Not at all. He's always kept in touch with her and the family, especially when he realised she had a problem. His kids are all grown up now, and he's set every one of them up in their own home – all bought and paid for. And the girl who was sick as a child, is now fully recovered and married with a child of her own.'

'I often wondered what happened there,' Tara said quietly.

Bridget nodded. 'Seemingly he looked after his ex-wife very well, gave her a big house and everything. Generous considering that she was the one who wouldn't move over to England to be beside him in the first place. That's what broke them up.' Bridget shook her head. 'He's very private and has never said much about her, but from what he told us this evening, I believe he's been through an awful time.'

'I didn't realise that he kept you up to date on all his personal news.'

Bridget gave an embarrassed little shrug. 'He's always told me and Fred bits and pieces, but I didn't like to say anything to you, because I know you hate me even mentioning him.'

'Well, I wouldn't wish that kind of bad luck on anyone,' Tara said quietly. 'And I'm sorry to hear about his wife.'

'He tried everything he could to help her. Last year he organised for her to go into a drying-out centre with the nuns down in Cork,' Bridget went on, 'but she wouldn't stay. Then he got her over to a private clinic in London earlier this year, but again she wouldn't stay.' Bridget's face tightened a little. 'There was nothing more he could do.'

'What eventually happened to her?' Tara asked.

'She collapsed at home and was rushed into hospital. It seems she was in a kind of a coma for over a week before she died. Frank and the family were with her the whole time, and he's been back and forward every other week since the funeral.'

Tara bit her lip. 'I noticed a change in him – I could tell there was something wrong.'

'Don't say anything, especially not to the Grosvenor crowd,' Bridget suddenly said. 'I think he's kept it all to himself. He said he's only told a few close friends, like ourselves.'

'You know I don't have much to do with Frank, Bridget,' Tara said. 'I only talk business with him when I have to. I'm hardly likely to start having big emotional conversations with him now.'

'I know,' Bridget said, 'but I wouldn't like his private business to get around because of me.'

Gerry drained his glass and got to his feet when he saw the two women coming back into the bar. Then he and Tara said goodnight and left the others, as Fred went to order a final drink.

As they lay in the king-size bed together, Tara suddenly said, 'Somehow, I don't think you're too keen on my friends, Gerry. You seemed distant with Bridget and Fred.' She knew it was possibly going to spoil the remainder of the night, but was determined to make the point.

He moved to hold her at arm's length, a frown on his handsome face. 'What on earth makes you think that, Tara?' he asked incredulously. 'They're perfectly nice people.'

'It's just a feeling,' she replied. 'The same sort of feeling I had when we were with Kate in Paris.'

'But I was civil and polite to them,' he told her, 'and I was civil and polite to Kate and her Bohemian, arty friends.'

Something about the way he said 'arty' annoyed Tara, so she moved out of his arms to lie on her own side of the bed, her luxuriant red hair spread out on the pile of satin pillows. 'I just get the feeling that you don't approve of them.'

He laughed. 'Tara, for God's sake, I hardly know the bloody people.'

'But they're not just bloody people,' Tara said, her voice rising in anger, 'they are my oldest, dearest friends, and I want you to like them.'

There was a sudden silence. 'I'm sorry that I don't have the same social skills that you do,' he said in a strained tone. 'I'm obviously not as good at climbing up and down the social ladder to suit the occasion.'

Tara's eyes narrowed. 'And who exactly are you referring to, when you talk about climbing *down* the ladder?'

'Well, let's be honest,' he said, 'that Fred guy isn't exactly the sharpest tool in he box, is he? He's an excellent barman – I'll give him that.'

'I'm surprised at you saying such a thing, Gerry,' Tara said in a wounded tone. 'For your information, Fred had a serious accident a few years ago, and it affected his memory.'

'What happened?' Gerry asked.

'It was an accident in the wrestling ring. He used to wrestle at weekends.'

'Oh, my God.' Gerry shook his head. 'People have got to be mad to go into such a sport.'

'Well, Fred's neither mad nor stupid. He's one of the nicest men I've ever met,' Tara said coldly, 'and both he and Bridget are very special to me. Bridget and I grew up in the same village and we've been through a lot together.' She paused. 'As far as I'm concerned, social ladders have nothing whatsoever to do with real friendship.'

There was another silence, which was only broken when Gerry reached out and drew her back into his arms. Her body was stiff and unyielding. 'I'm really, really sorry, Tara,' he whispered into her thick hair. 'I didn't mean to offend any of your friends. You're quite right, Bridget and Fred are lovely people, and, if it helps, I'll make really a big effort to get to know them better.' He moved his hand up and down her bare back.

Then, as he felt her start to relax, he said, 'Why don't we go out with them for an evening when I come back for the New Year? If you like, we could even invite them over to my place in Didsbury? We could cook them something nice together.'

Then, pushing aside the hurt she felt at his earlier manner, Tara turned her face towards his and reached up to kiss his lips. 'That would be lovely, Gerry,' she told him. 'I'd like that very much.'

Chapter 70

❧❧❧

Joe arrived at Ballygrace House several hours later than he had anticipated. He had planned to leave Cork mid-afternoon, but just as he was ready to leave the parochial house a sick call came in. The parish priest was already out doing his weekly visit to the local hospital, so Father Joe Flynn did what he always did in these situations – put his own needs last and went out to tend to his flock. Even though he had been called to the same house three times the previous week, and knew that he had more chance of dropping dead himself than the hypochondriac Mr Flannery.

This particular visit was very different from his usual trips to stay in Ballygrace House. For a start, Tara wouldn't be there and so he would be staying in his sister's house all on his own. And the trip was not a social one. He had received a call from Tessie to say that his Aunt Molly was going downhill fast. The priest had made several visits up to Offaly in the last few months, thinking that Molly was breathing her last, only for her to rally round again. This time, Tessie assured him, there was a definite change, and the nuns running the nursing home had said they felt it was only a matter of days.

Tara had spoken to Joe on the phone the previous night and asked him to stay out at Ballygrace House. 'You would be doing me a favour, Joe,' she told him. 'I feel poor Ella is wasting her time going in and out, lighting fires and keeping the house dry and aired, when there's no one there. It would make me feel better and you more comfortable than if you stayed with Dad and Tessie. You'll have more space and privacy. Ella will call in the mornings to make your breakfast, and she'll do a nice meal for you at night. You'll have peace and quiet for a few days, not to mention comfort and warmth.'

After the busy week he'd had in Cork, Joe could see the sense in it, and the thought of a few days listening to music or reading a book by the fire in Tara's lovely front room appealed to him. 'Fair enough,' he said. 'When you put it like that, I'd be delighted to stay out at Ballygrace House.'

The journey up had been slow due to heavy rain, which gathered in huge puddles that started at the side of the road, then grew large enough to meet in the middle. The rain wasn't quite so bad by the time Joe reached County Laois, and it had eased off further by the time he found himself in Offaly.

As the car made its way up the winding drive towards Ballygrace House, Joe was surprised to notice that the trees and bushes looked straggly and overgrown, and the path was covered with dead leaves; on one occasion, when he put his foot on the accelerator, he felt the wheels slide.

Ella had left the outside lights on for him, and they threw a welcoming orange glow around the building as he approached it. He parked the car at the front of the big house, then took a few moments to glance around the gardens and shrubbery within his view. The word 'unkempt' came to his mind. And yet he knew his father was still tending the place. Joe shook his head and gave a little sigh. Everything was changing. Molly would soon be gone and Shay was getting old and not able to manage the things he used to.

Tara had told him in one of their regular telephone chats that she was going to get someone else in to help her father in the gardens this coming spring. She didn't care how much Shay protested; it was evident that things were getting too much for him. Any time she had broached the subject, Shay had argued and said that he could manage fine on his own. What did she want with strangers coming about the place anyway? he would ask. You couldn't trust people outside to do as good a job as members of the family. And you couldn't trust people about your property, either, for once they got a foot in the door and saw how things were, they'd be wheeling off barrow-loads of turf when nobody was looking, or helping themselves to anything else they fancied. And anyway, it wasn't as if he was on his own all the time. If there were any heavy jobs to be done, then Mick would always lend a hand.

But Mick, of course, wasn't getting any younger, either. As Joe lifted his leather bag out of the boot of the car, he decided that he would tell Tara that she was right to think of getting a younger, fitter gardener.

The fires in the main downstairs rooms were all banked up and, within minutes of poking them and adding small, dry lumps of turf, Joe had them blazing brightly again. He was particularly grateful to

Ella Keating for the fire in the drawing-room where the piano and the bookcases were, as it was his favourite room, and he planned to spend the remainder of the evening there, reading and playing the piano.

There was a welcoming smell in the kitchen. On investigating, Joe discovered that Ella had left him a pan of stewing steak along with several large potatoes; it sat over a pan of hot water on the edge of the range so that it wouldn't dry up. He raked the dead ashes from the grate and threw in some dry pieces of wood and light turf, and when he had got the fire going properly, he put the pan on the middle of the range to warm up.

He went upstairs to his usual bedroom and threw a few sods on the fire to keep the room warm until bedtime, before unpacking his few belongings. When he heard the rain splattering against the window, he went across to draw the curtains, and then noticed a pool of water on the window-sill. There was a damp area on the carpet beneath. He pressed his foot onto the carpet, and bubbling water came to the surface. There was quite obviously a leak somewhere, probably from the guttering or a loose roof tile.

Joe went over to his bag now and took out the *Irish Independent* he'd bought earlier in the day. He had only scanned it, but had read enough to last him until he heard the news on the radio tonight or in the morning. He opened the paper and spread the sheets over the damp area of the carpet. Then he went into the bathroom and got a couple of dark-coloured towels. He used one to mop up the puddle on the window-sill, then placed the dry one on it catch any further drips. He stood back and looked at the job, then, satisfied he had halted things for the time being, he went downstairs to have his supper.

Later on, when he had washed up his plate and milk tumbler, he poured himself a glass of red wine and took it out into the hallway while he phoned his sister.

'Is everything OK at the house?' Tara asked. 'Did Ella leave things all ready for you?'

'Absolutely perfect,' Joe told her, as he quickly debated whether or not to mention the leak problem. He decided that he wouldn't. He would speak to his father about it tomorrow and they would get a local workman to sort it out.

Chapter 71

❧❧❧

Joe drove out to his father's and Tessie's house after breakfast the following morning, and then they carried on to the nursing-home to visit Molly.

It turned out that she had rallied around yet again. They arrived to be told that the frail old lady had allowed them to feed her a liquidised breakfast and been able to drink tea from a beaker.

She was naturally very weak and had lost more weight, but her eyes brightened when she saw Joe, and she managed to whisper a few words to her visitors, and nod or shake her head at the appropriate time.

'She's a hardy oul' cratur, you have to give her that,' Shay commented as they came back out to the car. 'I suppose she could go on for another while. Not that you'd want her to.' He shook his head. 'Sure, what kind of life has she got?' Tessie shot him a warning glance, which he ignored. 'If it was me,' he went on, 'I'd sooner they just shot me and have done with it.'

Tessie ground her teeth together, thinking that shooting Shay might not be too bad an idea. There were times when he drove you mad with his tactlessness. You'd think he'd not be saying such unfeeling things in front of poor Joe – and him being a priest.

'God will take her in his own time. As long as she's comfortable and not in any pain,' Joe said quietly, 'that's the main thing.' After all these years, he was well used to his father's insensitive remarks, and it was like water off a duck's back. Joe knew it was hard for his father or anyone else to understand how he felt watching Molly – the last part of his childhood – slowly slipping away.

Molly and Maggie – Shay's two spinster aunts – had looked after him as if he were their own child, and had scrimped and scraped to buy him everything he needed for life in the seminary. They had built their whole lives around the young priest, and had given him everything they could with a heart and a half. Even Tara, who was the most understanding of his situation, couldn't feel the loss to the same extent, although Joe was sure she felt the same pain and more when she lost her grandfather, who had been the mainstay of her young life.

'You'll come in and have a bit of dinner with us?' Tessie offered, when Joe dropped them off at their house in Tullamore. 'I've a nice big piece of bacon cooked, and it won't take me more than half an hour to do the potatoes and vegetables.'

'That would be lovely,' Joe replied. Tara had told him that Ella would do a meal for him in the evening, so it would save him the trouble of making lunch for himself.

'How are things out at the big house?' Shay enquired, when they were all settled in the kitchen.

'Grand.' Joe decided that he would save mentioning the leak at Ballygrace House until they had had their lunch, otherwise Shay would be pontificating about it all through the meal.

Tessie was mashing the turnip and carrots together with big lumps of butter. The cabbage was already cooked in the leftover bacon juices, and a big bowl of floury potatoes in their skins was waiting in the middle of the table. She looked over at her husband. 'When you get time, will you check our own back door?' she asked, scraping the mixed vegetables into an oval dish. She turned back to the sink now to strain the steaming hot cabbage in a colander, then she put that into another dish and brought both to the table. 'I think it's swollen up. I'm finding it hard to close at times.' She gave a little laugh. 'Maybe we should just buy a new one and save you the trouble.' She went to the oven now and lifted out the plate of sliced bacon, which she put on the table alongside the potatoes and a small dish of butter.

'Never mind new doors,' Shay said, spearing a large potato onto his plate. He waved his fork about, emphasising the point. 'I'll have a look at it and see if I can shave down the bit that's sticking.'

Later on, Joe reluctantly ventured the bad news about the leak at Ballygrace House. 'Do you know anyone who could fix it?' he asked. 'Hopefully, it won't be too big a job.'

Shay rubbed his stubbly chin thoughtfully. 'It all depends on what's causing the damned leak. I checked all that guttering around September, and I'm sure there was no part of it that I missed. Surely it's not blocked guttering that's caused water to come inside the house?' Shay took everything to do with the maintenance of Ballygrace House very personally. 'Mind you, better if it is the guttering that's the problem as opposed to the roof. You could get a very hefty bill if it is the roof.'

'Do you know any workmen that would be available to have a look at it while I'm here?' Joe asked. 'I would hate to go away and leave it.'

'You're lookin' at the very man,' Shay told him, pressing his thumb against his chest.

'No, Shay,' Tessie said in a firm voice. 'You have high blood pressure and you're not to be going up on roofs, or doing anything dangerous like that.'

'Will you be quiet,' Shay retorted, his voice high with indignation. 'As if I have any intention of goin' up on a roof at this time of the year.' He shook his head. 'Women! They're always pokin' their noses in where they don't belong.' He looked at Joe very solemnly. 'Think yourself lucky that you never had to get married.'

Joe laughed lightly now, having found that it was often the best way to defuse the situation. 'Oh, I'm not going to say anything about that. Especially when I've just sat down to such a lovely meal cooked by your wife.'

'Thanks for that vote of confidence, Joe,' Tessie said, smiling at him.

'I'll tell you what,' Shay said, looking up at the clock. 'I'll take a run out to Ballygrace House with you now. We can stick the oul' bike in the boot and I'll cycle back.'

'You won't need the bike,' Joe told him. 'I'll gladly run you back home in the car.'

'Well, if you're sure it's no trouble,' Shay replied, 'because I don't mind cycling back home.' In truth, he liked the idea of his son, the priest, driving him through the town, so that anybody of any importance might see him in the front seat. It was the same when Tara came home with her big, fancy English car. Not that Shay gave a damn about impressing the big nobs in the town or anything like that. He preferred the down-to-earth, more ordinary people you could get a laugh with, but it was nice now and again to give the uppity types something to talk about. Shay stood up now and went out to the hallway to get his coat and cap.

'Don't let him go near that roof, Joe,' Tessie said to her stepson. 'The doctor has told him that he's to be careful doing things.'

Joe stood up and pushed his chair back under the table. Then he put a reassuring hand on her shoulder. 'I'll make sure he doesn't go up to the roof.'

*

As soon as the car pulled up outside Ballygrace House, Shay was out and standing at the problem area, his hands on his hips. 'It could be that feckin' oul' guttering,' he deduced, looking up at it. 'I can see some weeds or bits of twigs up there, just at the bit above the bedroom window. I wouldn't mind, but I gave all the gutters a good clean at the end of the summer.'

Joe came across the driveway to stand beside his father. 'You wouldn't think it would fill up again so quickly.'

Shay spat on the ground. 'Ah, ye couldn't be up to them oul' crows. When they're building their nests they're up on the roofs and the high trees, droppin' bits here and there and everywhere.'

Joe shaded his eyes with his hand and looked up at the roof area. He was rather at a loss as to what to say. In fact, if the truth be told, he felt fairly inadequate when it came to these kind of matters. Buildings and their upkeep were not something he knew much about. Thankfully, the men in his parish in Cork were generous enough of their time and working skills to keep the parochial house in good order. The most the priests ever had to do was to replace the odd light bulb or fuse now and again.

'So you think it's only the gutters?' Joe asked. 'A matter of getting someone in to clean them?'

'I'd say so,' Shay said, his eyes narrowed in thought. They suddenly felt a spit of rain. 'If you want to go on into the house and put the kettle on, I'll just take a walk around the back and check things out there.'

Just as he went to turn into the house, Joe heard another car coming up the drive.

'Who the devil could that be?' Shay said in a high, surprised voice. They both stood, looking towards the leaf-strewn driveway, until Mick Flynn's small car came into view. 'No show without Punch,' Shay said, shaking his head and sighing, although he was actually delighted. He would enjoy chewing over the gutter situation with Mick. While Joe was a nice and decent fellow, and Shay was undoubtedly proud of him, he was still a priest, and you couldn't get as much craic out of him as you would with Mick. Shay also felt he had to be careful with his language where his son was concerned.

When Mick alighted from the car – along with Kitty who was carrying a cake tin – the four stood chatting for a short while, but when the light spits of rain became heavier, Joe and Kitty headed into the house, leaving the two brothers to discuss the problem of the gutter.

Kitty had just put the kettle on to boil and had cut slices from her freshly baked rhubarb tart and cherry cake, when the brothers' voices could be heard out in the hallway. Then their footsteps sounded on the stairs as they made their way up to the bedroom to check the source of the leak.

'The tea will be ready in five minutes,' Kitty called as the two men headed back out of the house, 'so don't be too long, will ye?'

'We're just going to have a look at the bedroom window from the outside,' Mick called back.

Joe had gone into the drawing-room to check on the fire when he saw Shay pass by the tall sash window carrying the extending ladders. An unholy oath passed under his breath when he realised that Shay intended to go up onto the roof. 'Stupid old fool,' Joe muttered as he threw half a dozen small sods of turf onto the banked-up fire to get it going again. He put the fireguard back in place, then rubbed his hands together to shake off any bits of turf dust.

What a palaver the leak thing had turned out to be. Getting Shay involved had just made it into a huge affair, and now Mick was joining in. God only knew how long it would last. If they managed to locate a workman to repair it immediately, there was a chance the job could go on until he was due back in Cork.

Joe almost wished he'd just ignored the damp carpet and left it to be found when he was safely back in Cork, although he knew his conscience would never have let him do that to Tara. He had so looked forward to the thought of a couple of quiet afternoons and evenings in Ballygrace House on his own, enjoying his book and either playing or listening to some nice, classical music, but those precious hours were now dwindling away on mundane issues.

Father Joe Flynn got very little time to himself, because the parish priest was every bit as bad as Shay in his own way. Every time he saw Joe sitting down with the newspaper or a book, or occasionally – God forbid – listening to a radio programme, he would sideline him into helping with his Sunday sermon or try to engage him in some boring discussion about a parish event.

Joe went out into the hallway now and out of the front door to stop his father in his tracks. Thankfully, the rain had come to nothing serious and was still only the lightest of drizzles. He came around the side of Ballygrace House just in time to catch Shay checking that the old wooden ladder was steady enough to take his weight.

'Now, you keep a good grip on the bottom of it,' Shay was busy instructing his mild-mannered brother, 'and I'll go up as far as the window and take a quick look ...' He halted when he saw his son coming towards him.

'Now, Father,' Joe said, a look of exasperation on his face, 'what was the very last thing that Tessie said to you before leaving the house this afternoon?'

'Never mind Tessie,' Shay said, with a dismissive wave of his hand. 'She would have me stuck in a chair like a useless oul' eejit if she had her way. I'd be consigned to the knacker's yard long before me time.'

Joe moved forward and took a grip of the ladder. 'I can't, in all conscience,' he stated, 'let you put a foot on that ladder. Not after giving my word to Tessie that I wouldn't allow you to go anywhere near the roof.'

Shay moved a few steps away from the ladder, then looked around at Mick and gave an incredulous shake of his head. 'Sure, I'm not going *on* to the roof. Even Mick here will tell you that I had no intention of doing that.' He jabbed a finger up in the direction of the window. 'I'm only going to go halfway up and have a look at the oul' guttering.'

Joe moved forward until he was gripping both sides of the ladder and effectively barring Shay's way from stepping onto it. 'No,' he said firmly. 'If you were to suddenly feel dizzy when you were up that height, God knows what might happen.'

'Joe's right, Shay,' Mick suddenly chipped in. 'If you were to take one of them small bad turns when you were up the ladder, you could do yourself a power of harm. There's lads been killed coming off a ladder, and them only a few feet from the ground.'

'For Jesus's sake,' Shay said, sucking his breath in through his teeth. 'The way the pair of ye are goin' on, you'd think I was goin' up on a tightrope instead of a feckin' oul' ladder.'

'Why don't you leave it until the workman comes?' Joe told him. 'Let him go up and see what's wrong, and what needs to be done to fix it.'

'But they could tell us any old shite if we don't know what's wrong

379

ourselves,' Shay stated, 'and then they could charge us whatever the hell they like.'

Joe looked at his father and ground his back teeth together in frustration, feeling that he could cheerfully strangle him. How could he be bothered making such an issue of such a boring thing? Wouldn't it be the proper and straightforward thing just to bring in a workman who knew his business and get the job over and done with?

But, no, that would be far too obvious for Shay Flynn. He would much rather make a song and dance about it.

Joe finally reached the end of his tether. 'Right!' he said. 'I'll save us from all this argument – *I'll* go up and check the window and the guttering.' He gave the old wooden ladder a good shake to confirm that it was steady and then, before his father could say another word, he started on his way up towards the bedroom window.

A few seconds later he was standing right outside the bedroom window. He could immediately see the problem. The wood at the top of the window frame had completely rotted away, leaving a damp, splintery gap, which was allowing the water from the overflowing guttering to seep through. Simple.

'What can you see?' Shay shouted up. 'What's causin' the problem?'

Joe turned slightly to answer him. 'The window-frame,' he called down. 'It's rotted through.'

'Be-jaysus!' Shay exclaimed. He turned to Mick as though his brother hadn't heard the very same thing as himself. 'It's the feckin' oul' window-frame. Who would believe it? They were fine the last time I was up there. I checked each and every one.'

'Well, there's nothing we can do about it now,' Joe said, starting to come back down. 'We'll have to get a specialist workman in to do it.'

Later, neither Shay nor Mick could confirm or describe exactly what happened, but Joe suddenly seemed to lose his footing on the damp wooden ladder, and the next thing they knew was that the ladder was slipping away from them and sliding across the house wall.

Father Joe Flynn hung on for a few moments, as his father and uncle shouted, and then he lost his grasp on the ladder and plummeted backwards onto the stony path below.

The ambulance took almost half an hour to get out to Ballygrace

House, but by the time the two ambulance men were lifting the priest onto the stretcher, Kitty, Mick and Shay Flynn all knew that there was nothing could be done for him.

Seconds after his head hit the ground, Joe was dead.

Chapter 72

Tara was numb with grief as she retraced the same steps she had taken when Gabriel was buried. But this time, she couldn't afford to retreat into her own misery over her brother's death, to go back to that dark place in her mind. Since she was now the eldest child in the family, she had to share responsibility for her father and Uncle Mick, who were beyond themselves with guilt.

The fact they had allowed, almost encouraged, the young priest to climb the ladder that led to his death, had left the two elderly brothers haunted. Everyone said they had aged at least ten years in the last few days.

'Never, never will I forgive meself,' Shay sobbed as he looked at the coffin which lay in the middle of the drawing-room in Ballygrace House. He had had to be cajoled, almost dragged into the old Georgian house when his son's body was brought home from the mortuary. 'This feckin' house is cursed,' he had said to anyone who would listen. 'You only have to look at all the bad luck to befall everyone that's lived in it. It's only fit for burning to the ground.'

At one point Tara had to take her father into her bedroom upstairs, away from all the mourners, and sit him down with a large brandy to tell him a few home truths, in as kind a manner as she possibly could.

'I know you're upset, Daddy,' she'd told him, 'but we are all upset about what's happened, and I really don't need you to be spouting all that stuff about Ballygrace House being cursed.' She had gestured down towards the hallway where people were milling around, drinking tea and waiting in an orderly queue to pay their final respects to Father Joe. 'Young William Fitzgerald is down there with his stepfather – they've flown all the way over from London to be here for the funeral – and it would be terrible if he heard you saying all those things about his family's house.' She'd then put her arms around her father, suddenly seeing him for the frail, vulnerable man he had become. 'I know how you feel, and I'm heart sorry for you, but please, please keep your feelings about the house to yourself.'

When Shay had drunk the brandy and eventually composed himself enough to go downstairs, Tara closed the bedroom door behind him, went back across the room and threw herself down on the bed. Then she cried her heart out in wracking great sobs, for the kind, gentle brother she had loved so much. And this time she didn't even have her closest friend beside her. Bridget had crumpled into a heap when she heard the news and had taken to her bed, all the progress she'd made in the last few months seemingly unravelled by the news.

Angela had matured since the last tragedy, and she was the one at Tara's side on the plane and on the car journey down to Ballygrace.

When Tara eventually made herself go back downstairs again, the only thing that kept her going was the memory of the conversation she'd had with Joe last summer. The conversation during which they had both discussed their present lives, when Joe had told her how grateful he was that he had followed his religious vocation and that he had a life which had made him completely fulfilled.

There was not one other person that Tara knew who could have said such a wonderful thing.

The funeral was huge. People came from far and near to attend the young priest's passing. The whole family was there, dressed in black, and there were over a dozen priests in attendance, as well as the bishop of Offaly and the bishop of Cork.

The funeral service was held in the large church in Tullamore that Joe had attended when he was a young boy, living with his two great-aunts. Ironically, Molly had rallied round from her last brush with death, and was safely tucked up in her wheelchair in the nursing-home, oblivious to the fact that Joe was being buried.

Tara was grateful that at least the burial was in the cemetery in Tullamore and not in Ballygrace. Seeing Gabriel's grave while she was there with her brother would just have been too much.

There was a hot buffet laid on for everyone back at Ballygrace House, which of course brought back inevitable memories of the aftermath of Gabriel's funeral, but Tara just kept herself busy, going around talking to people and making sure they had something to eat and drink.

Kitty and Tessie both spoke privately to her about their worries over Mick and Shay; the men had hardly slept a wink since it had all happened.

'But it was an accident,' Tara said, for about the hundredth time over the last few days. What more could she say to them? What was the point of telling them that she felt every bit as guilty as her father and uncle, because it had been the guttering of *her* house that Joe had been checking. What was the point in saying that losing Joe so soon after losing Gabriel made her feel that she had been gutted with a ragged-edged knife?

Spilling out her raw emotions would only make the tragic situation even worse. She knew she had to be strong for everyone else.

Then, a thought suddenly came into her head. 'Would you mind asking everyone to go into the drawing-room,' she said to Kitty and Tessie. 'I'd like to say a few words.'

She waited for a few minutes while the women gathered all the mourners, then she took a deep breath and went in.

'Reverend Fathers and ladies and gentlemen,' she started. 'I've asked you all to come in as I'd like to say a few words about my brother, Joe . . .'

And then she told them all about the last afternoon she had spent with the priest in the dining-room in Ballygrace House, when Joe had advised her to stop mourning for Gabriel, to get out into the world and live life to the full. Then she told them how she had challenged Joe, saying that *he* wasn't living life to the full, that a priest lived a precious, closeted sort of life, and didn't know anything about real people and their hopes and dreams. Tara smiled and said how wrong she had been. She described the satisfaction that he told her he got from helping families and teenagers, and said how he had felt part of all the families in the parish.

'In short,' Tara said, 'Joe told me that he found everything he needed through his work, and that he was lucky to have found such a fulfilling life serving God.'

There was a contemplative silence in the room as she spoke.

'And I know,' Tara concluded, her voice started to waver now, 'that that is exactly how Father Joseph Flynn would like us all to remember him.'

There was another small silence, and then everyone in the room burst into a spontaneous round of applause, and the most enthusiastic clapping came from the hollow-eyed Shay Flynn. Tara's words had eased his pain and guilt for a little while on the worst day of his life.

When all the mourners and relatives had gone home, Tara was left in the house with William Fitzgerald, his stepfather, Harry, and Angela. Aiden Byrne had been at Angela's side all day, but, after offering his condolences to all the family once again, he had slipped away with the last of the crowd, saying he would call over again the following afternoon.

They were a solemn and sombre foursome as they pottered around, trying to do ordinary things around the house, but there was no point in pretending that the circumstances were anything but awful. And there had been no point in trying to bolster things up for young William and make out he was having some kind of a holiday in Ireland. He had grown up in many ways over the last year or two, and, after losing Gabriel, he was big and old enough now to realise that life could sometimes be tragic and often unfair.

Chapter 73

Tara and Angela arrived back in Stockport, tired and drained, at around eight o'clock on the Thursday evening. As they got out of the taxi which had brought them from the airport, Angela said that she was going straight to bed.

'I didn't sleep well last night and I'm absolutely exhausted,' she said, 'and Bridget will want to know how everything went.'

Angela came into the house for a few minutes to drop off her bag, then she left.

Tara could hear the piano when she came into the house, so she went into the sitting-room to have a few words with the very sympathetic Vera. Afterwards, she went straight up to her bedroom, not wishing to get into any further conversations about the funeral with the other women in the house.

As she closed the bedroom door behind her, it dawned on Tara that she would very much like to have her own privacy. In fact, she suddenly realised, she would like to have her own house. When she had been grieving for Gabriel she had hidden away in Ballygrace House until she felt ready to face the world again. Now, in the midst of this very raw tragedy, she was very aware that she had nowhere to go that was totally private, where she could come to terms with her loss.

Her sadness and crying would have to be stifled because of the other boarders, which she knew was an unhealthy state of affairs for a grown woman. Something would have to be done about her living conditions, but now was not the time to think about it. She took off her coat, hat and shoes, then lay down on the bed, numb and exhausted.

Some time later she moved herself to go and run a bath, then changed into her nightdress and headed straight back to the bedroom.

Tara was awake from five o'clock the next morning, and was first up in the house. She made her own coffee and toast, and was on her way out when the lady who organised breakfast was coming in.

There had been several messages left at the house from John Burns to say that Tara should take a few days off work, but she ignored them all and was in her office before eight o'clock. From her previous experience, she knew that throwing herself into her work was the only way to get through the next few months.

When lunchtime approached, one of the waitresses came up to Tara's office to see if she was lunching in the restaurant as usual.

'Not today, thank you,' Tara said, forcing a smile onto her chalk-white face. 'I'll just have a plain beef sandwich and another cup of coffee.'

The sandwich had only been ordered to save any discussion amongst the staff about the fact she hadn't eaten all morning. Eating was the last thing she felt like, but she had learned from the after-math of Gabriel's death, when her weight had plummeted so low that everyone had been very concerned for her health.

When the sandwich appeared she managed to swallow a few mouthfuls, then she threw it in the bin and continued for the rest of the afternoon on strong coffees.

The phone rang continually all day, and Tara forced herself to concentrate on each task as it came up. A lot of the calls had been personal ones from friends and business acquaintances, offering their sympathies and condolences. Again, Tara applied the 'one step at a time' ritual and found that, somehow, she managed to get through.

Gerry McShane had been her first call of the morning. 'I rang the house several times last night,' he told her in a concerned voice, 'but the rather formal teaching lady said you needed to rest and couldn't be disturbed.' He had paused. 'How are you, Tara? Are you sure you should be in at work today?'

She had simply explained that she *needed* to work. 'Having a routine helps me to get through the day,' she said quietly. 'Otherwise I'll just keep going over and over it.'

'Do you want me to call in to see you tonight?' he asked. 'I know you probably won't feel like going out for a meal or anything just yet ...'

'I think I'll just take it easy tonight,' she said in a quiet voice, 'and I'll ring you when I feel I'm better company.'

'Don't push yourself, Tara,' he had said kindly. 'You've been through a terrible ordeal. Just take everything as easily as you possibly can.'

'Thanks, Gerry,' Tara said softly, feeling grateful that this time she had someone special who cared about her – apart from her friends, of course.

Angela rang several times during the day, giving her updates on how things were going at the small hotel, and each time asking if Tara had heard from Bridget yet.

'No,' Tara said, 'but I know she'll feel bad about not being at the funeral.

Just before she left the Grosvenor, Tara decided to ring Bridget. In a way she was surprised she hadn't heard from her, but in another she wasn't surprised at all, for she knew that she would be feeling awkward about the situation.

June answered. 'Hello?' she said, sounding all breathless, as though she had just run down the hallway or the stairs.

'Hello, June, it's Tara,' she said. 'Could I have a word with Bridget?'

'Can you hold on?' June said, then there was a muffled sound and Fred's voice came on the line.

'Tara,' he said in a flat tone. 'You haven't heard anything from Bridget, then?'

'No,' she said. 'I was very tired last night, so I didn't come down with Angela.'

'Did you speak to Angela today?' he asked.

'Yes, I did,' Tara said, beginning to feel they were having a circular sort of conversation.

Fred let out a long, weary sigh. 'So Bridget's not been in touch with either of you? Nobody's heard from her.'

Tara suddenly felt very confused. 'Fred, is Bridget not there? Has she gone out for the afternoon or something?'

There was a silence, then Fred's voice came back on the line, sounding very fraught. 'She's gone, Tara,' he said, 'Bridget and Lucy. They've been missing since yesterday evening.'

Tara felt the room swim about her. She gripped the edge of her desk. 'Have you any idea where she might have gone?'

'We've no idea,' Fred's voice suddenly broke. 'She told June she was taking Lucy into Stockport for some new shoes, but nobody's seen them since.' He took a deep breath to steady himself. 'She's not been right, Tara. She's not been herself at all this last few days. Not eatin' or sleepin' – and she's been hitting the bottle every night since you left. She's the worst I've ever seen her.'

'I'm leaving the office now,' Tara said, reaching across the desk for her car keys and handbag. 'I'll be with you in ten minutes, and I'll pick Angela up on the way.'

Chapter 74

❧

Fred was in the sitting-room with Frank Kennedy when Tara and Angela arrived. June came rushing along the hallway, and asked Angela to come into the kitchen, to help her sort out some kind of a meal for the five lodgers who were due home from the building sites in the next half an hour. Michael and Helen were sitting at the kitchen table doing their homework.

'The kids don't know,' June whispered to Tara and Angela, as they stood out in the hallway, 'and I'm just tryin' to act all normal, like, in front of them.' She pursed her lips and shook her head. 'It's been a long twenty-four hours, and I think if we don't hear something soon, Fred's gonna have to phone the police. There's nowt else for it. Especially when there's a kid involved.'

Tara stepped back to look into the sitting-room, to make sure that Fred couldn't hear her. He was deeply engrossed in conversation with a very serious-looking Frank. She closed the door on them, then turned to June again. 'Have you any idea what's made her go?'

June shrugged. 'Well, I know she was right upset about your brother dying ...' She suddenly stopped, looked from one sister to the other. 'I'm really sorry. I meant to say it meself – offer my condolences, like – but with everything that's happened here ... You must think me right ignorant.'

'Of course we don't,' Tara said quietly. 'Thanks for even thinking of us at this time.' She paused. 'Have there been any more letters or phone calls from Lloyd? I'm just wondering, given that she has taken Lucy with her.'

June thought for a moment. 'There's been nothing that I know of, but then, she wouldn't have told me if there was. She's never mentioned that Lloyd fella to me at all. I think she felt very awkward about it.'

Tara moved towards the sitting-room door. 'I'll go and have a word with Fred.'

Fred was sitting on the sofa, his head in his hands. He glanced up when he heard Tara come into the room. 'I'm worried, Tara, I'm worried she's done herself in.'

Frank looked at her and shook his head. Tara sat down on the sofa beside Fred, and put her arm around his shoulder. 'We'll find her,' she said softly. 'No matter what happens. We'll find her.'

They sat for the next half an hour going over Bridget's last movements, and analysing anything that might give them the slightest clue as to her whereabouts. Frank had scoured all the shoe shops in Stockport, but no one could recall seeing them. He had also called in at Bridget's hairdresser's, and any other shops that she frequented in case anyone one had seen her around, but drew a blank in all cases.

Tara then urged Fred to phone anyone they could think of, including Thelma Stevens, and he went out to the hallway to make the calls, returning after each one to report that no one had seen or heard from her.

Angela brought in a tray with tea and sandwiches, and while Tara sipped at the tea and Fred was on the phone, Frank paced the room, trying to think of anything that might help.

Fred had just sat down on the sofa and lifted the tea cup to his lips when the phone rang. Michael, on his way back down the stairs from the toilet, rang to answer it. 'Daddy, it's that Lloyd fella,' he called into the sitting-room. 'He says can he have a word.'

Tara's green eyes shifted across the room to meet Frank's, and she immediately knew they were both thinking the same thing.

Fred gave a wearisome sigh. 'He's probably just ringing to say he's working around this area,' he said to them both, 'and wants me to meet him for a pint. That's what he usually does.' He stood up, then called out to Michael, 'Tell him I've got to go out, and ask him for the phone number he's at. Say that I'll give him a call back tomorrow or when I get a spare minute.'

Tara stood quickly. 'Hold on, Michael ... I wouldn't mind a word. I haven't spoken to Lloyd for ages and I'd like to hear how he's getting on.' She went out into the hall, carefully closing the door behind her.

Lloyd came straight to the point. 'Bridget turned up at my house last night with Lucy, and she was in an awful state.'

'In London?' Tara said. 'You mean she took Lucy all the way down to London?'

'She caught a train,' Lloyd went on. 'And then she made her way out to Brixton on the bus.'

'But why?' Tara asked.

'It was my fault,' he said, his voice croaky and upset. 'I sent her a letter saying that my mother was askin' for Lucy, and that I'd like us all to meet up sometime soon. I said that it was my mother's birthday this week, and maybe I could drive her up on the Sunday and we could meet for bit of lunch or somethin'.'

He paused. 'I didn't mean to cause all this trouble. It was only a suggestion, like. I never meant for Fred to find out or anything.'

Tara closed her eyes and held her breath. The stupid, stupid man ... What else did he think he was doing if not causing trouble? 'Where is she now, Lloyd?' she asked. 'And is she OK?'

'That's the thing,' Lloyd said. 'I'm not sure where she's gone. It was too late and she was too drunk to go anywhere last night, so her and Lucy slept in the spare room. I took the day off work to make sure they were okay, and then I drove them both into the train station this afternoon.'

Tara felt a huge surge of relief. 'So she's on her way home now?'

'No,' Lloyd said. 'She bought a ticket for Blackpool, not Manchester. She said she was going to meet someone.'

He shrugged. 'I thought it was Fred's mother or somebody like that.'

They spoke for a few minutes more, then Tara made him promise that he wouldn't phone Fred or get in touch again. 'You've caused very serious trouble, Lloyd,' she told him, 'so please don't make things worse.'

'Look, Tara,' he said, 'I only wanted my mum to meet Lucy. Now she has, she's satisfied. When she saw the state of Bridget last night, she said it would be best if we didn't have any more contact.' He paused. 'I won't be causin' any more trouble for anyone.'

After she hung up, Tara rushed down the hallway to the kitchen. 'Get Fred out of the sitting-room,' she said to June. 'Use any excuse. I need to talk to Frank on my own.'

June got Fred out into the backyard on the pretext that she thought she had heard someone calling his name, and Tara went back into the sitting-room.

Apart from herself, Frank was one of the few people who was aware the truth behind Lucy's parentage. She knew she could trust him. And she also knew that he would do whatever she asked without question.

'She's on her way to Blackpool with Lucy,' she told him without any preamble, 'and from what Lloyd has said, she's in a bit of a state. He says that Lucy's quite happy and doesn't seem to be aware of what's happening.'

'Why on earth has she gone to Blackpool?' Frank asked, his brow furrowed in confusion.

'At a guess, I'd say she's gone to the boarding-house that she and Fred stayed in last May,' Tara said. 'She got on very well with the landlady, Thelma. She's talked a lot about her and I know they phone each other regularly.' Tara thought for a moment. 'If one of us could get to Blackpool and pick them up, then Fred would be none the wiser that she was ever down in London. I can get the name and address of the boarding-house from June.'

'It'll have to be done without Fred knowing that we're going for her,' he stated, 'otherwise he'll insist on coming along with us, and he could walk into a situation he's not prepared for.' He sucked his breath in through his teeth. 'Whatever chance they have of surviving this, it could be lost if Bridget decides to tell him everything now.'

Tara closed her eyes, desperately trying to think of the best and safest solution. She looked at her watch. 'I could go to Blackpool right now, collect them and be back in three or four hours.'

Frank looked over at her. 'I don't mean to be telling you your business, Tara, but I don't think you should be driving such a distance under the circumstances. The road to Blackpool can be a tricky one at the best of times.'

'I've been driving for years,' Tara retorted.

He held up his hands. 'I know you have, but you've just been through a very hard time ... and I'm so very sorry about that.' He paused. 'I really don't know what to say ...'

'There is nothing to say.'

'Fred told me that you've only just got back from Ireland.' He stopped, trying to pick his words carefully. 'You look exhausted and I know you're very worried about Bridget. Why don't you let me drive you?'

Tara looked at him for a few moments, then she shook her head. 'No ... I don't think that's a good idea.'

Frank's eyes suddenly lit up with anger. 'For God's sake, Tara!' he exclaimed. 'We could be in a very, very serious situation here. Do you honestly think I'm going to pull the car over and try to seduce you? Is that what you think? Jesus Christ ...'

Tara saw the exasperation and the hurt written all over his face, and realised she had just done him a great disservice. But even though she knew she was wrong, it was as though she had no power to stop herself. 'I'll drive,' she said, walking over to the table to get her car keys, 'and Angela can come with me.'

Tara told Fred that she and Angela were needed down at the Cale Green Hotel. 'I'll be back in a few hours,' she told him. 'And if we haven't found them by then, maybe we should call the police.'

'I know she'd hate a big fuss,' Fred, said, absentmindedly running his hands through his hair, 'but if she's not back later tonight, then that's what I think we'll have to do.'

Tara paused at the doorway of the sitting-room on her way out. Frank was standing with his back to the window, his face thoughtful.

'If I hear any news,' she said, 'I'll ring and let you all know.'

'Hang on, Tara,' he said now. He opened his jacket and reached into his inside pocket, then he came towards her holding out a business card. 'Just in case things aren't as straightforward as we hope. My home number is on it. Call me any time and I'll do what I can to help.'

'Thanks,' Tara said, 'but hopefully it won't be needed.'

Chapter 75

Several times on the journey, Tara thought back to Frank's advice. Of course, he had been right. There was no doubt that she was tired, but determination kept her going. Angela dozed off, and Tara would have loved to have done the same, but she steeled herself and kept going.

As she drove along the quiet stretches of road, she found herself thinking about the last few encounters she'd had with Frank Kennedy, and realised that she had crossed the line with him on several occasions, said terrible things to him that she would never have said to another living soul.

What harm, she now asked herself, would it have done to let him drive them in his comfortable big car? What harm would it have done to let him help his friends?

Her stomach churned with guilt as she admitted to herself that she hadn't even had the decency to tell him she knew that his ex-wife had died, even though she had quite plainly seen the effect it had had on him.

A hot, burning feeling came over her as she realised just how viciously she had treated him, both recently and over the years. And he hadn't once tried to hurt her back. He had accepted that he had done wrong in deceiving her about being married and having a family, and he had allowed her to punish him for it, for all these years.

Maybe, Tara thought now, it was time to let it all go.

She should start to treat him with the respect she treated everyone else. He was a decent man. More than decent. He had been a good friend to Bridget and Fred, had been there for them through thick and thin. He had known about the situation with Lloyd, and he hadn't breathed a word for fear of hurting either of them.

Tara thought of Joe suddenly. He had said once that everyone should take happiness and contentment where they found it. Life was too short and too precious to waste it by worrying what people thought.

Too short to waste it by judging everyone else.

Then her tired, troubled mind suddenly jumped back to Gerry McShane in Paris, and his obvious disapproval of Kate and André. Then Christmas, and his obvious disapproval of Bridget and Fred.

She would talk to him. Gerry was a good man, and when she thought back to all the good times they had had together, she knew she didn't want to lose him. There were too few men around who could hold her interest, and Gerry was one of them. They had lots of things in common – business and cultural interests – and they enjoyed each other's company. She found him very attractive, and he had told her countless times how beautiful she was and how much he desired her physically.

Given that the world could be a dark, frightening place at times, she was very lucky to have found someone to fill the long, lonely weekends she had before she met him. Someone to make her laugh again. Someone to share her bed again.

As she came towards the lights of Blackpool, Tara decided that when this whole thing with Bridget was finished, she would start to look at Frank, Gerry and life in general in a different way.

Tara found the Seaview boarding house easily. She approached the harassed-looking red-haired woman behind the reception desk, leaving Angela to loiter in the entrance hall.

'I'm Tara Fitzgerald,' she said in a low voice, 'I believe you know a friend of mine – Bridget Roberts?'

'Tara! Of course!' Thelma's relief was palpable. 'Have you come for her?' she asked eagerly.

Tara's hand came up to still the beating in her chest. 'She's here? Thank God.'

'She's not at all well,' Thelma said, coming around to the front of the desk. 'I gave her a stiff brandy, then I made her go and lie down in one of the spare guest rooms. We're quiet at this time of the year.'

'Is Lucy OK?' Tara asked anxiously.

'She's with her,' Thelma said, putting her hand on Tara's arm in a comforting manner. 'The poor little mite didn't know if she was on her head or her heels. They both looked all in.'

Tara suddenly remembered Angela. She turned. 'This is my sister, Angela. We're both close friends of Bridget's.'

Thelma put her hand out to Angela now and shook it warmly, then she did the same to Tara. 'I feel as if I know you both,' she said, smiling. 'Bridget talks about you all the time.'

Tara suddenly warmed towards the woman, and could easily see what had drawn Bridget to her. There was definitely something of Ruby about her. 'What has Bridget told you?' she said quietly.

'Come into the office,' Thelma suggested. 'Nobody will disturb us there.'

When they were all seated, she explained how Bridget had turned up about two hours ago and poured out the whole story of Lloyd and Lucy, then had asked Thelma if she would mind Lucy while she went down to the church for a short while.

'To tell you the truth,' Thelma said, 'I was terrified she wouldn't come back. I nearly followed her, but a group of eight arrived in a mini-bus and I had to deal with them.' She lifted her eyes to the ceiling. 'Thankfully, Bridget came back about half an hour later, and she was a lot calmer.'

'Had she been drinking?' Tara asked.

Thelma hesitated, confirming Tara's suspicions. 'Not noticeably,' she said. 'I don't think the drop of brandy I gave her would have done her any harm.'

'If we wake her,' Tara said, 'do you think she'll come home with us? Did she talk as if she wanted to get back home to Fred and the rest of the family?'

'She was saying a lot of things,' Thelma said, 'but they didn't make sense.' She looked at Tara then at Angela. 'I don't want to say anything out of turn here, but what *is* the situation regarding the little one?'

Tara felt very uncomfortable now at the thought of betraying Bridget. 'What exactly did Bridget tell you?' she hedged.

'Well, to be honest,' Thelma said, 'one look at the little girl tells you all you need to know. She's not Fred's kid, is she?'

Tara folded her arms across her chest. 'As far as Fred is concerned, she is.'

Angela sat near the office door, just listening and saying nothing.

'From what I could make out,' the landlady went on, 'Bridget has got it into her head that the fellow in London is going to keep on and on about the child until Fred finds out different.' She suddenly stopped. 'If that was her only problem, it would be bad enough, but she's bouncing from one worry to the next. If you want my opinion, the poor girl's having a nervous breakdown.'

Tara suddenly felt her throat close over and she swallowed hard, trying to keep calm. Bridget having a nervous breakdown in a strange town, miles from Fred and miles from home. The whole situation was turning into a complete nightmare.

Angela looked over at Tara. 'That's exactly what I've been thinking, and June said it, too.'

'Well, whatever is wrong,' Tara snapped, 'it would help if we could just get her home and to the doctor. Maybe then we could prevent her getting any worse.'

'Tell you what,' Thelma said, standing up now, 'I'll go and check on them now, and we'll see how she feels after her rest.'

'Do you want me to come with you?' Tara asked.

The landlady thought for a moment. 'Might be best if I just look in on my own. If I think she's up to it, I'll explain that you're here and want to take her home.'

Thelma came back a few minutes later. 'She's still spark out, and so is the little girl. I reckon we should give them another half an hour. The sleep will do her good.' She looked at Tara now. 'I'm going to get you two a drink and something to eat. You're welcome to a meal in the dining-room, or I can get one of the girls in the kitchen to make you up some nice sandwiches.'

Angela glanced at Tara, hoping her sister would take the meal, as she hadn't eaten anything since lunchtime and was starving.

'I don't think I could manage anything.' Food was the last thing on Tara's mind. 'A cold drink would be fine.'

'Are you sure?' Thelma checked.

Angela looked at the landlady. 'I'd love a sandwich if it's not too much trouble,' she said.

Thelma went off to the kitchen and came back a short while later carrying a tray with three drinks in tall glasses with ice and lemon. She handed Tara and Angela a drink each. 'Ginger ale and lemonade,' she said, 'with a small dash of brandy to help the pair of you relax.

The sandwiches will be here in a few minutes.'

'If you don't mind, I'd prefer not to have alcohol,' Tara ventured. 'I'm tired enough as it is, and I've to drive back to Stockport.'

'Drink it up,' Thelma instructed. 'There's very little in it, and it'll do you the power of good. The brandy will revive you.'

Angela took a sip of the drink. 'It's lovely, Tara,' she told her. 'Nice and refreshing.'

Tara was too tired to argue, and took a small sip to be polite.

A plate of mixed sandwiches arrived along with a dish of chips. Angela tucked into them with relish, while Tara picked at one or two of the chips and a small sandwich triangle. Thelma had some things to sort out in the boarding house so left them to it.

'Do you think we should phone Fred and let him know where Bridget is?' Angela said.

'It might be best to give it a while until we've seen how she is,' Tara said, trying to work out what to do next. Then the tiredness suddenly crept over her, her eyes flickered shut, and she was startled as her body swayed and her head nodded forward. Quickly, she straightened up and took a mouthful of her sweet, fizzy drink. Then she walked to the front door to clear her head.

Sometime later, Thelma came back into the office, checking her watch. 'I think I'll wake them now,' she said. 'She's had a couple of hours' sleep.'

Thelma went upstairs and along the corridor. She rapped on Bridget's door, waited a few moments then rapped again. When there was no answer, she turned the handle quietly and went in.

The room was now in darkness, and she moved slowly and cautiously, giving her eyes a chance to adapt to the lack of light. Then, having worked out the shape of the two single beds, she tip-toed further in, afraid of giving the child a fright, and went over to the bed where Bridget lay.

'Bridget,' she whispered, gently shaking her. 'It's time to get up.'

But there was no response.

'Bridget,' she said, shaking her a little harder and raising her voice. 'Wake up.' Then, when there was still no movement, she moved closer and put her hand on both of Bridget's shoulders and gave her a much harder shake.

And then she realised that Bridget Roberts was not just sleeping.

Stopping only to glance at the sleeping child, Thelma flew across the room, out into the corridor and down the stairs as quickly as she could. She burst into the office where Tara was half-dozing and Angela was finishing the remainder of the sandwiches.

'There's something wrong ...' Thelma gasped, trying desperately to catch her breath. She had a pain in her chest from the exertion, as the furthest she ever walked these days was a sedate stroll with Jim along the prom. 'I can't wake her.'

Tara, wide awake now, was straight on her feet. 'Take us up to the room,' she said, her stomach starting to somersault. After what happened to Joe, it felt possible that the sky could now fall in.

'Will I get a glass of water for her or anything?' Angela said.

'Bring the drink that I poured for myself,' Thelma said, heading out of the office door.

All three made quickly for the stairs, Thelma holding onto her heaving chest and Angela stopping every so often to avoid spilling the drink.

'Do you think it's serious?' Angela asked.

'I don't know,' Thelma panted. She halted for a moment, hanging onto the handrail. 'But I gave her a right good shake and there was no response out of her.' Her voice faltered. 'And when I think back now ... there wasn't a kick out of the child ...'

'Oh, dear God,' Tara whispered. Gabriel and Joe and now Bridget ... A wave of panic rose inside her and she felt her legs start to shake. *Dear God ... Dear, dear God.*

They started off again, only to have to slow up when they got to the top of the stairs and met a group of three elderly women coming towards them.

'Evening, ladies,' Thelma said, in an amazingly calm voice. 'I hope you enjoy your night out at the bingo.'

'Oh, thank you, Thelma,' they all chorused.

Then, safely past them, they quickened their step again. 'It's the one with the door ajar,' Thelma said, as Tara and Angela overtook her. 'Go straight in. She's in the bed by the window.'

All three went into the darkened room now, leaving the door wide open to throw some light in. Tara, her heart now up in her throat, went straight across the room to the bed. 'Bridget!' she said in a firm, almost angry voice. 'Wake up now!' When there was no movement, she did exactly the same as Thelma, gave a few tentative shakes, then took

397

her friend by the shoulders and shook her almost violently. 'Bridget! For God's sake, will you wake up?' Bridget's head suddenly fell to the side. 'No ... no ...' Tara said, dropping her back onto the bed.

Angela, petrified, stepped back and hit the dressing-table, spilling half the drink down herself.

Thelma now pushed Tara aside and moved in to give Bridget a good slap on one side of her face and then on the other. Still no response. 'Bridget,' she said, 'come on now! Stop this nonsense.' Even as she said the words, she knew exactly how ridiculous she sounded, but she couldn't stop herself. Then, after giving her one final shake, Thelma suddenly started to cry. 'She's taken an overdose ... I know it.'

Tara moved forward again, but this time she bent down close to Bridget's face, to check if she was breathing. Then, unable to tell anything, she lifted her wrist to feel for a pulse.

'Oh, my God ... is she dead?' Angela moaned, voicing their unspoken thoughts. Then she looked over at the other bed. 'Oh,' she said, in a long, low wail, 'is little Lucy dead, too?'

Tara's face suddenly lit up. 'There's a pulse,' she said, sounding almost hysterical. 'There's a pulse!' She turned to Thelma, shouting now, 'Quick, get an ambulance.'

At that very moment, Lucy, startled by the noise, added to the mayhem by suddenly screaming.

'Thank God!' Thelma exclaimed. 'By the sound of her lungs, there's nothing wrong with her!'

Chapter 76

❧

While they were waiting for the ambulance, Tara left Angela consoling Lucy and Thelma splashing cold water on Bridget, before running downstairs to the office to ring Frank Kennedy. He would know what to do, and how to break the news to Fred. It was much too serious now for them to leave Fred out of the picture.

Frank answered straight away and listened carefully as Tara gave him all the details. 'Blackpool Infirmary,' he repeated. 'I'll go back to

Fred's and pick him up. We'll be there as quick as we can.' Then he asked, 'Are you OK, Tara?'

The kindness and concern in his voice suddenly hit a raw nerve, and Tara started to cry. 'I'm terrified, Frank,' she told him. 'I'm terrified that she's going to die.'

Suddenly, she wished he were with her. He above everyone knew what Bridget's friendship meant to her.

'Just try to hold on,' he told her. 'We'll be there soon.'

Then Tara heard the ambulance sirens, so she quickly hung up and rushed back up to the room.

Ever the businesswoman – and well used to dramas with her daughter – Thelma said to Tara and Angela, 'If any of the guests see them taking Bridget out on the stretcher, just tell them she's had an epileptic fit.'

When they arrived at the Blackpool Infirmary, the long wait began, as the comatose Bridget was whisked off to a private area to be checked out.

Frank and a shocked, dazed Fred arrived in the hospital a few hours later, by which time a doctor had come to tell the waiting group of women that Bridget had indeed taken an overdose of tablets.

How many she had taken and how much damage it had caused they still didn't know, but they had already pumped out the contents of her stomach and now it was a matter of time to see what happened.

Frank sat in the seat next to Fred in the waiting room. Angela held Lucy in her arms. Miraculously – after eating crisps and sweets – the little girl had dozed off again.

'Why? Why?' Fred kept asking, in between bouts of heavy, wracking sobs. 'Why did she want to die? Why did she want to leave me and the kids?' He reached over and stroked Lucy's legs.

'She didn't know what she was doing,' Tara said, coming over to stand beside him. Frank immediately got up and guided Tara into his seat. Then she sat, clutching Fred's hands between hers. 'She's had a nervous breakdown.'

'But why?' Fred repeated, as though unable to find any other words.

'Because of the baby and ...'

'And her hormones,' Thelma chimed in, trying to comfort the

poor man. 'It often happens to women when they lose a baby ... it can just tip them over the edge. I've seen it happen loads of times.'

'But she lost the baby last year,' Fred argued. 'She was getting better.'

'She was only hiding it,' Tara told her. 'She was hoping the feelings would go away ...' She stopped to wipe away the tears that were streaming down her face. 'All the business about poor Nora back in Ireland, and then, when Joe died, it was just the last straw.'

Fred's eyes suddenly opened wide, as if he'd just seen something terrible. 'She felt right bad about not being able to attend his funeral. She was crying non-stop, saying she was terrified to go back to Ireland.' Then he remembered. 'And she kept going on about the Aberfan thing ... couldn't get those poor kids out of her head. And the same with that programme she saw on telly, *Cathy Come Home* – it right upset her.'

'It's all down to her depression,' Frank said, in a calm and gentle voice. 'And hopefully, when she pulls through this, the doctors will sort her out properly. They obviously didn't know how bad the poor girl was.' He put his hand on Fred's shoulder. 'And your accident took an awful lot out of her, you know,' he said quietly. 'I wouldn't be surprised if that was the start of her depression. She thinks the world of you, and couldn't bear the thought of anything happening to you.'

'I don't know why she does,' Fred said, giving a watery, lopsided smile. 'I've never been good enough for her.'

'Of course you have, you big lummox,' Frank said, giving him a playful punch on the shoulder.

Tara glanced up at Frank now and smiled gratefully at him. He looked back at her, and, for the first time in years, their eyes met properly.

'Are you OK?' he mouthed silently to her.

Tara nodded, then turned away as her eyes filled up with tears.

At one o'clock in the morning the doctor came back to the waiting-room and told them that Bridget had started to pull round.

'She's turned the first corner,' the doctor said, 'and it's the most important one.' He looked at the waiting group. 'I suggest you all go home, get a good night's sleep, and come back in the morning. Hopefully, the news will be much better then.'

'You can all stay in the boarding house,' Thelma offered. 'I've several spare rooms.'

'But we have no spare clothes or anything,' Angela ventured, looking over at Tara.

'We'll last until the morning,' Tara told her. She gave a little shrug and smiled. 'I'm sure there's no one looking at us anyway.'

Having slept a good few hours already, Lucy was wide awake just after five o'clock in the morning, crying for her mother. Angela was in a deep sleep, so Tara stayed awake and tried to comfort the child until she heard the first people moving around for breakfast. Then she woke Angela and said they should all go down and have a decent breakfast before heading back to the hospital.

'We're going to look a right state in our crumpled work clothes and no change of clean underwear or anything,' Angela moaned.

'We'll live,' Tara told her, giving a wry smile. 'I have a brush and a bit of make-up, so we'll just have to do our best. As I said last night, I'm sure nobody's even looking at us.'

The hospital seemed a very different place in the morning light, with a constant stream of cars in and out, and uniformed staff bustling around. Fred, looking pale and drained, went to the ward office to see if they had any news, while Tara, Frank, Angela and Lucy all sat in the waiting room.

Some time later he came out, grinning from ear to ear. 'They've said she's awake this morning, and that I'm allowed to go in and see her. They said they have her in a little private room because of what's happened.' He gave an apologetic shrug. 'Only immediate relatives can see her for now.' Quarter of an hour after that, he returned, saying that she was asking for Lucy.

'Is there any chance of me seeing her?' Tara asked desperately.

'You can just say that Tara's her sister,' Frank suggested.

When Fred came back, he told Tara that she was allowed five minutes.

Bridget was lying – white-faced and tired – in the bed, propped up on several pillows. She started crying the minute she saw Tara. 'I'm sorry,' she sobbed. 'I've gone and caused a load of trouble again.'

Tara went over to her and wrapped her arms around her, and they both cried together. She held her for a few minutes, then she gently moved back to sit on a chair by the bed. She took a deep breath, aware that she had to pick the right words first time.

'Bridget,' she said, 'you are my oldest and dearest friend, and I want you to know that I love you very much.'

Bridget started sobbing again.

'No, no,' Tara said, reaching to the bed now to take her hand. 'You must listen carefully.' Then, when Bridget had composed herself, she started again. 'I need you, Bridget,' she told her, 'and if you succeed in killing yourself, you are going to ruin my life as well as Fred's and the children's.' She paused for a moment to let her words sink in. 'I have suffered enough losses recently, and I need you there to help me.'

Tara stopped again, wiping away her own tears now. 'I know I haven't always been a good friend to you. I've been so busy with the hotels and work that I've not always been there when you needed me.' She squeezed Bridget's hand now. 'And I know that at times – like the situation with Lloyd – that I've not wanted to listen to you. I didn't want to hear about certain things ... I wouldn't let you even mention Frank's name ...' She halted, swallowing hard. 'And I'm sorry if I made you feel uncomfortable at times, going on about you visiting Ballygrace when you didn't want to. I'm sorry for always thinking I knew what was best for you, Bridget. I'm sorry for so many things.'

'But, Tara,' Bridget said, her voice high with astonishment, 'you've been the best friend that anyone could have. You've never done a single wrong thing to me. Any time we had a difference, I knew you always had my best interests at heart.'

'But I did it all the wrong way,' Tara sobbed, 'I made you feel bad about Lucy, tried to shut you up because it made *me* feel uncomfortable.'

'But you were right,' Bridget insisted. 'I did a terrible thing. I've done a lot of terrible things in my life.' She shook her head. 'I'm not a good person.'

'Don't you dare say that!' Tara almost shouted. 'You're the best person in my life and I need you. Do you hear me, Bridget – I *need* you!' And then she broke down in great sobs. 'There's no one who knows me the way that you do. We were little girls together with no mothers, we grew up together. You knew my granda and Gabriel and Madeleine – you know everything about me. You know how much I wanted a baby. You know everything about all the important things in my life.'

Bridget stared at her friend.

Tara looked her straight in the eye. 'I can't face losing any more people that I love. I won't be able to carry on, so you'll only end up killing the pair of us.'

'Tara, Tara,' Bridget said, moving into a sitting position. 'I'm sorry ... I didn't think ... I never thought of the effect it would have on everybody else. I never knew you would be so upset, or that poor Fred would be in such a state. I thought you would all be relieved if I died. I thought it would give everybody peace.'

Tara grasped her friend's hand tightly. 'Promise me,' she said, 'that you'll never do anything like this again.'

Bridget stared at Tara now, as if seeing her for the first time. 'I promise you faithfully, Tara,' she stated, 'that I'll never, ever do anything like it again.' She lifted their joined hands together to her lips and held them there for a few moments. 'The doctors have told me that I can get all sorts of help for my problems.' She swallowed hard. 'I realise now what a lucky person I am. I've got a wonderful husband and family ... and the best friend that anyone could have.'

Chapter 77

❧❦❧

Bridget was to be transferred by ambulance to a special psychiatric ward in Stockport some time in the afternoon. The four other adults and Lucy now walked out into the car park, preparing to head home.

'If it's OK,' Fred said to Frank, 'me and Lucy will travel back in the car with you.'

'Why would you ask such a daft question?' Frank said, shaking his head and laughing. 'Isn't that the reason I'm here?'

Fred flushed. 'I don't want you to think I'm taking advantage, like, but do you mind if I stop off at the boarding house to let Thelma know how things are? She's been so good about everything.' He shook his head. 'I hope this hasn't ruined the poor woman's business.'

'Thelma Stevens is too good a businesswoman to let anything like that happen,' Tara told him. 'And don't forget that last year Bridget helped her to deal with a very awkward situation regarding her own daughter.'

Fred's face brightened at Tara's encouraging words. 'True,' he said, 'very true.'

Angela and Tara gave Lucy a kiss, then Lucy started crying, saying she wanted Angela to travel in the same car as her daddy.

'Go with them,' Tara said, 'I'll be fine travelling back on my own.' Then, searching in her handbag for her keys, she walked across to her car.

As soon as she sat into the car, Tara felt an overwhelming sense of weariness. She felt she could sleep for a solid week and it still wouldn't be enough. And even though it was cold, she wound the window down a little to keep her alert. Then she started up the car, got it into gear and prepared to move forward. And then, suddenly, as she pressed down on the accelerator the car hit a small wall in front. Tara was so tired she hadn't noticed it. She was thrown forward with a great jolt, her head crashing down on the steering-wheel.

The next thing she heard was Frank's voice. 'Tara!' He opened the door and, very carefully, reached in to her. 'Are you OK? Where are you hurt?' He gently touched her long red hair. 'Tell me what to do to help you.'

She felt a wet stickiness on the steering-wheel, and her right cheekbone was throbbing. When she lifted her head up and turned to look at him, Frank took a deep breath, clearly trying not to show his alarm. 'Don't worry,' he said comfortingly, 'it's not too bad.'

'I think I'm OK,' she said. 'I just got a bit of a bang on the head. It was my own fault. I was stupid – I didn't see the wall.'

Then Frank Kennedy gathered her up into his arms, and Tara gratefully laid her cut, aching head on his shoulder and wept.

Thankfully, the hospital casualty department was quiet. They quickly treated Tara with a local anaesthetic, six stitches and a sterile dressing. Then she was released with the strict instructions not to drive or do anything strenuous for the next forty-eight hours.

While she was being attended to, Frank organised for Tara's car to be taken to a local garage to be repaired.

'I know it looks bad at the moment,' the doctor who had stitched her cheekbone said, 'but after a while it will fade and you will hardly notice it.'

Tara felt so tired and dazed with everything that had happened that the possibility of being left with a scar on her face hadn't even touched her.

It was mid-afternoon when Frank dropped Lucy and Fred off at Maple Terrace, and then drove on to Cale Green with Tara and Angela.

'Don't worry about a thing,' he told Tara as he left her on the doorstep, 'I'll sort your car out and ring the hotel and let them know you've had an accident, and that you'll be back as soon as you're fit and well.' He paused. 'I don't think they had expected you in so quickly after the funeral anyway, so make sure you take all the time you need now.'

'I don't know how to thank you,' Tara said in a weary, uncertain voice. 'You've been so good.'

'Sure, there's nothing to thank me for,' Frank said, smiling warmly at her. 'Just look after yourself.'

And then, as he turned to go, Tara suddenly moved towards him and kissed him lightly on the cheek. Taking a deep breath she said, 'I'm grateful to you, Frank ... and I'm really sorry for having treated you so badly over the last few years.'

Frank stared at her, clearly taken aback.

Then Tara's gaze met his again and, as they looked at each other, she had an overwhelming urge to fall into his strong arms and ask him just to hold her – and keep her safe.

Gerry had called several times and left messages for her to ring back. Tara had a cup of coffee first and a couple of aspirin for the ache in her head, then she went to the phone.

Gerry had been quiet and subdued as she poured out the story about Bridget. She'd skirted around the Lloyd incident – instinctively knowing he would disapprove – saying she'd gone first to a friend in London and then straight up to Blackpool. Whether he had been shocked or uninterested, Tara wasn't sure, but she was surprised he didn't make any comment or ask for further details.

She was gratified, though, that when she told him about her accident he said, 'I'll be straight over.'

'Honestly, Gerry,' she said, 'I'm fine. It's a relatively small cut and it'll soon heal.' She didn't really mind whether he came over now or waited until later. The fact that he'd offered to come straightaway was enough. It told her that he cared.

After she had spoken to him, Tara went up to her bedroom and looked at herself in the wardrobe mirror. Her face was pale and drawn, apart from the area around the square white dressing, which was now turning into a purple and navy bruise. She stared at it for a while and then, for a brief moment, she considered removing the dressing to get a proper look at the cut, to see whether it was bad enough to destroy her looks.

Tears suddenly welled up in her eyes. It was bad enough to have gone through all she had without a constant reminder of the time etched on her face.

Then a little voice inside told her to stop being so vain and superficial. She wasn't a young, naive girl whose main concern was her looks. She was a grown woman in her thirties who had achieved a great deal in her life, more than most women she knew. And she had done it all by herself. The doctors had said that the cut would heal and eventually fade.

And if it didn't disappear completely, she wasn't going to let a small scar ruin her life.

Tara lay on her bed re-reading the same page in a magazine for the third time. She was trying desperately to keep her mind from thinking about Joe and Bridget again, because somehow they had managed to become muddled together.

She had never imagined feeling this way again after Gabriel died, but Tara now sadly realised that life was capable of throwing up tragedy at any time.

She had now come to the conclusion that the death of a loved one, and the immediate aftermath, was similar to being hit by a steamroller and completely flattened, then being told to pick yourself up again as if nothing had happened.

But some terrible things *had* happened, and Tara wasn't sure if she had the strength to pick herself up and start all over again.

She heard Gerry's car pull up as she was coming down the stairs to make a cup of coffee. When she heard the latch on the gate, she opened the front door.

'My God,' he said, unable to disguise his shock. He stood rooted to the doorstep, staring at her. 'I didn't realise it was so bad. You made it sound as if it was only a scratch. You're badly bruised as well.'

Tara's hand flew to the white gauze covering the stitches. 'It's not that serious,' she said, suddenly feeling extremely self-conscious. She opened the door wide to let him in, then brought him into the empty sitting-room.

Tara sat in one of the deep armchairs and Gerry sat on the sofa. 'How bad is the cut?' he asked in a strangely distant voice.

'Six stitches,' Tara said. 'The doctors said the scar will eventually fade.'

He shook his head. 'I can hardly take in everything that's happened.' He raised his eyebrows. 'Let me get this straight: your friend Bridget disappeared to London, leaving her family and friends, and then she travels to Blackpool to a boarding house where she takes an overdose.'

Tara nodded. 'More or less.'

'She sounds a very selfish lady to me, thinking only about herself. Surely she should have thought of the upset she would cause everyone?'

Tara's whole body stiffened. 'It wasn't like that at all,' she told him, suddenly feeling defensive. 'It was very, very serious. She's had a lot of problems in her life.'

'Don't forget, Tara,' he said, 'I've met your friends before. I know just the type of people they are.' His eyes narrowed now. 'You've run yourself into the ground trying to help this Bridget, and because of it, your beautiful face could be badly scarred for life.'

Whether it was the tone of his voice or the look in his eyes, Tara suddenly realised that the scar on her face mattered very much to Gerry McShane, that her looks must always have mattered to him. And she could now tell, by his whole demeanour, that she would not hold the same attraction for him if she were flawed, especially on her face.

Gerry's gaze moved to the window. 'While you're off work, Tara, I'd urge you to use the time to think a few things through. You need to look closely at the type of people you have as friends. Perhaps you might have outgrown them. To be honest, they're not in the same class as you.'

'That's where you're totally wrong,' she told him, 'but I have no intention of discussing my friends with you for a minute longer.' Tara stood up. 'Thanks for calling round, Gerry, but I think I could do with some time on my own.'

He got to his feet and slowly moved towards the door. 'Do you want me to call again tomorrow?'

'No,' she said, a decisive note in her voice, 'I don't think that will be necessary.'

As she closed the front door behind him, Tara felt resigned. She could see now that things would never work between them. Although Gerry was attractive and clever, fundamentally they were quite different. Deep down she had known that back in Paris, but she hadn't been ready to admit it then.

Tara instinctively knew that once the initial awkwardness between them was over, she and Gerry would get back onto an even keel work-wise. It wouldn't affect their business arrangements. Both of them were far too professional for that. And in any case, they had never really discussed their future together. It was one of those romances that had been fine while it lasted. It wasn't unusual – it happened to people all the time. But it had shown her that she was capable of being part of a couple again – if and when the right person came along.

But for the foreseeable future, Tara decided, she would rather be on her own.

Chapter 78

❧

APRIL 1967

The kitchen in Maple Terrace had been a hive of activity on the Saturday morning, as Bridget and June baked cakes and prepared sandwiches and a variety of party foods to celebrate Lucy's fourth birthday.

At two o'clock, half a dozen children were dropped off by various relatives, and all trooped in carrying wrapped presents or money in a birthday card. Michael and Helen had been allowed to bring a friend each, and Bridget had put the four eldest in charge of organising games and music for the little ones. After they'd eaten, the plan was for the adults to bring them all down to the park at Cale Green to play on the swings and the roundabouts.

Fred's parents arrived with the younger guests, and Angela and Tara came a short while later, having strolled down in the spring sunshine. They were both dressed casually, Tara in jeans and a fashionable skinny-rib, multi-coloured top and Angela in a pale-blue angora sweater, her new denim mini-skirt, and her gold locket with the little red stones that Aiden had bought her.

The scar on Tara's face had healed very well, and had now faded from a dull pink to a pinkish white. Careful make-up concealed the worst of it, but it would take more time before it became unnoticeable.

The adults all congregated in the kitchen where Fred had set up a small bar with bottles of beer for the men and small bottles of Babycham or Snowballs for the women.

'You seem very organised,' Tara said, sipping her Babycham. 'You've obviously been up at the crack of dawn to have all this ready.'

'Not at all,' Bridget said. 'I was up at the usual time, although June did come in early to give a hand. We got the lads' breakfast over with and everything tidied up, and then we started baking the little fairy cakes and things like that. The birthday cake was baked and iced yesterday, so we didn't have to worry about that.'

'It's lovely,' Tara said, looking at the table, which was filled with plates of different things, all waiting to be carried into the sitting-room at the appointed time.

Bridget pulled out one of the chairs now and sat down beside the other women. 'I can't believe she's four already,' she said shaking her head. 'The time has just flown.' She smiled. 'She was so excited last night I could hardly get her into the bed. It's the first year she's really understood about birthdays, and she's been going on about it since we told her she was going to have a party.'

'They sound as though they're having a great time in there, if the laughing and the giggling are anything to go by,' Angela said.

'Well, thank God they're enjoying themselves,' Bridget said. 'Because they didn't have too much of that over the last few months.' She rolled her eyes heavenwards. 'Although I'm not sure what I've let myself in for, because I've ended up promising that I'll give the other two parties as well when their birthdays come around.'

'Oh, you're a dab hand at it,' June joked. 'And you'll have all the mothers around the place complaining that they want parties like the Roberts kids.'

'I wouldn't go that far,' Bridget said, but she was obviously delighted by the compliment.

Tara looked over at her friend now and thought how much better she both looked and seemed. Bridget was now restored to the wife and mother she had been before. The correct medication and weekly meetings with a skilled counsellor had helped her put things back in place again. She was also beginning to understand that her early childhood had left her ill-prepared to deal with certain situations, and she was now learning different ways to cope with the stresses and strains of life.

She had also reached a stage where she could accept that she had done the best thing for her adopted baby at the time. Legally, she could do nothing about him now, and emotionally, she had finally come to terms with the fact that he would have had a better life with a settled, steady family than a naive, inexperienced young girl on her own.

And she was learning how to cope without resorting to alcohol. It wasn't that she constantly felt the need to drink, more a case of avoiding it when she was in the wrong mood.

The games had been temporarily halted and the food was being distributed on paper plates in the sitting-room when the front door-bell went.

'That'll be Frank,' Bridget called above the noise to Tara. 'Would you let him in?'

As always, when he first saw her, Frank's first reaction was one of hesitation. It was so deeply ingrained in him that he couldn't shake it off easily. Then, when he saw her green eyes light up and her face smile in a genuine welcome, he moved the bunch of flowers he'd bought for Bridget to his side and leaned forward and kissed her on the cheek. Just to the right of her scar.

'You look lovely, Tara,' he told her, stepping into the hallway. 'You get better looking every day.'

'Go away with you, Frank Kennedy, and your old Irish blarney,' she said, giving him a friendly push. Then they walked along the hallway and into the party together.

Aiden Byrne had phoned the house in Cale Green looking for Angela and was advised by Vera to phone Maple Terrace.

'I wasn't expecting to hear from you until later,' Angela said, in a surprised but delighted voice.

'I couldn't wait,' Aiden told her. 'I've been awake half the night thinking of an idea.'

'What?' she asked. 'What kind of an idea?'

'Well,' he went on, 'you know that we were talking recently about me moving to an office in Tullamore, and us finding a house out there for when we get married?'

'Yes.' Angela waited, having no idea where this conversation was leading.

'I was thinking about your career and the fact that there's not many openings around here for hotel management.'

'Aiden,' Angela said. 'What has that to do with finding a house in Tullamore?'

'I wondered,' he said, 'if there is any chance that Tara might consider selling Ballygrace House.'

Angela was stunned into silence.

'It's the answer to everyone's problems,' he told her. 'Tara told me she feels guilty at not being able to keep the house up, yet she doesn't want to sell it to total strangers.' He paused, gathering his thoughts. 'But I wonder if she might consider selling it to us. We could turn it into a lovely small hotel and build a modern house in the grounds for ourselves. It would mean that Tara could stay in Ballygrace House any time she wanted, and you would be running your own hotel.'

'Oh, my God,' Angela said. 'It's so unbelievable I can't take it in … Wouldn't it cost a fortune?'

'The sale of my own house would cover most of it and we'd work out the rest.' He laughed. 'Having an accountant in the family might just help a bit.'

'It sounds as though you have it all planned,' she said, 'but I've really no idea what Tara will think. She might be totally offended.'

Aiden pondered it for a few moments. 'Do you think it's worth taking a chance on asking her?'

Angela took a deep breath. 'Yes,' she said. 'Yes, I do.' She suddenly felt brave. She'd felt the sharp end of Tara's tongue before and had survived, and she could do it again. 'She's here now, why don't you ask her?'

When all the children had gone home and the women had finished clearing and washing up, Angela pulled Tara to the side.

'I hope you're not offended by Aiden's suggestion,' she said, her

411

face creased with worry. 'I don't want you to feel pressurised or anything, because, whatever happens, we're not going to live in Birr after we're married. Aiden says he feels awkward seeing people who were involved in the court case.'

'That's completely understandable,' Tara said. 'And the more I think about his suggestion, the more sense it makes. To be honest, I've been pushing it out of my mind for the last year, but I know I'll have to make a decision about the house eventually, and Aiden's proposal may be the very best I'm going to get.' She smiled at Angela. 'I just need a bit of time. I'm going to have a word with Frank about it before I make any hasty decisions. He knows the property situation back in Ireland, and I trust his judgement on these things.' She smiled. 'I've already mentioned it to him, and we're going to have a run out together after the party, sit somewhere quiet and talk it over.'

Later, when the party was over, Frank went to start up the Jaguar while Tara stood chatting on the doorstep with Bridget.

'So Lloyd kept his promise?' Tara said in a low voice.

'He did, thank God,' Bridget said, giving a little relieved smile. 'I've promised to send him a photograph every year on her birthday, and I'm going to do that this week when I get the party ones developed.' She looked at Tara. 'I've no worries about him now. He fully understands the situation and he doesn't want things ever to get out of hand again. He said he wouldn't do that to either me or Lucy, and thinks too much of Fred to rub his face in things that are better left unsaid.' She raised her eyebrows. 'I think the fact he has a serious girlfriend now helps. He says it's early days, but I wouldn't be surprised if it ends in wedding bells.'

'Talking of that,' Tara said, smiling now, 'you are definitely coming home with me for Angela's wedding in September, aren't you?'

Bridget smiled. 'Definitely. In fact, I'm even looking forward to it.' She smiled. 'I feel so much better about everything. That lady that I go to for counselling has helped me to see that a lot of the worries I had about people back home were way out of proportion.' She shrugged. 'I can see now that everyone is too wrapped up in themselves to be thinking about me all the time.'

'We'll have a big shopping weekend down in London over the summer,' Tara told her, 'and we'll knock them all dead at the wedding.'

'And I'm going to go to one of those really posh hairdresser's while

412

we're down there,' Bridget informed her, 'and get my hair done like that Twiggy's, only a bit longer and darker.'

'Listen to you,' Tara said, amused now. 'You'll be wearing tights instead of stockings soon if we're not careful. Angela has been trying to get me into them for months.'

'Now, Tara, you're not behind the door yourself when it comes to fashion, I've noticed your skirts are getting that little bit shorter every time I see you.' Bridget started to laugh. 'Angela will have to be careful, or us two old birds will take all the limelight at this wedding.'

'Ah, we're not quite over the hill yet,' Tara said, laughing with her.

Bridget looked back into the hallway now to check there was no one within earshot. 'By the way Frank was looking at you this afternoon, he obviously doesn't think you're anywhere near over the hill.' She nodded down to the car, where he was patiently waiting. 'He looked well today, didn't he? The sweater and jeans he was wearing were lovely. Casual but classy. I know he's always been very handsome, but he's back to his old self and more.' She looked straight at Tara now. 'I can see a big change in your attitude towards him over the last few months. Tell me honestly,' she held up her hand, 'bearing in mind I'm your oldest friend, what would you say if he asked you out properly?'

Tara put her head to the side. 'I don't know what I would say,' she said lightly. 'But don't worry, if it ever happens, you'll be the first to know.'

Chapter 79

❧

Since it was a nice evening, Tara suggested they take a walk out to Bramhall Park, where they could discuss Aiden Byrne's suggestion as they walked.

'I've been thinking it over,' Frank told her, as they strolled from the car park towards the old Elizabethan house and grounds, 'and while you were chatting to Angela I rang a fellow in Manchester who originally comes from Tullamore and knows the area well.'

'And?' Tara said.

'He think it's a great idea,' he replied. 'He said there's no decent hotel in the area, and Ballygrace House is well located for all the big towns in the Midlands.'

Tara pondered his words for a few minutes. 'I actually thought that myself, but I didn't want to agree to selling it too quickly after what had happened with Joe.' She looked up at him now, and her eyes clouded over. 'I have a kind of love-hate relationship with the place. It represents a lot of good and bad in my life, and in a strange way I feel very responsible for it.' She shrugged. 'I know it sounds silly. It's only a house, after all, but I couldn't bear the thought of letting it go to total strangers.'

'It's not at all silly,' Frank said, digging his hands into his jeans pockets. 'I understand.' He took a deep breath. 'I don't want to influence you either way, but it seems to me that by selling it to Aiden and Angela you have the best of both worlds. When it's up and running as a hotel, you can go back to it any time you want, without the responsibility of the upkeep and the maintenance. And it keeps it in the family.'

'That's very true,' Tara said, 'and I have to admit, Aiden seems to have thought it through very carefully. He has said that he and Angela will build a new house for themselves in the grounds, so that they're totally private, and then renovate Ballygrace House from top to bottom, as well as adding two sides.'

The fact that Angela wasn't going to be living in Ballygrace House had also been a major factor, because Tara knew that Shay would only worry sick about something terrible happening. He still reckoned that the house was cursed. But a hotel would be a very different matter, and, after a while, when curiosity got the better of him, Tara could picture him cycling out to keep an eye on all the renovation work.

'Twenty bedrooms is a nice number,' Frank commented. 'Around the same size as the Cale Green Hotel, and Angela has all the management experience necessary to run it, with Aiden looking after the financial side of things.' He smiled. 'And, of course, they have a very accomplished lady who can advise them on all the refurbishment side of things.'

Tara smiled. 'I have to admit it's the obvious solution, and the money from the sale will let me buy another house here in Stockport.' She shifted the strap of her bag higher up on her shoulder and tucked her hair behind her ears. 'I can't wait to move out of the house in Cale Green now. I've outgrown it and I'm ready for a fresh start.'

They started walking down the steps towards the lake. It was busier there, with couples strolling hand in hand, and family groups with the children throwing bread to the ducks.

'Have you any particular area in mind?' Frank asked.

'I'm not sure,' Tara said, 'but I want to move away from both hotels.' She crossed her arms over her chest. 'Maybe Bramhall village or Wilmslow – somewhere nice, but within easy driving distance of work.'

'I should imagine that Mr Pickford will be only too happy to advise you.'

Tara smiled now and rolled her eyes. 'I wouldn't dare go to another estate agent even if I wanted to.'

'What sort of size were you thinking of?' Frank asked now. 'Are you planning on taking in boarders again?'

'No, definitely not,' she told him. 'I'm too old for sharing. This is going to be my very own place. I want a nice big kitchen, dining-room and sitting-room, and maybe three bedrooms, so that I have room for when young William visits, or Angela and Aiden, or any of the family from Ireland.' She paused. 'It's important that the sitting-room is big enough, though.'

'Big enough for what?'

She paused. 'For my piano.'

'Do you still play?' he asked quietly.

'Not as much as I'd like to,' she said. 'I suppose I haven't made the time for it in recent years, but it's definitely one of the things I want to do when I'm settled in my new home.'

They came up to an old wooden bench by the side of the water. 'Shall we sit here for a few minutes?' Frank suggested.

Tara sat down first followed by Frank, who kept a careful distance between them. They sat in silence for a few moments, gazing ahead at the ducks and the swans, and watching the mothers help the children to throw crumbs into the water.

Tara turned to face him. 'Things will ease off at the hotel in the next month or so, after the official opening of the new extension is over. I'll have more time for myself, so I'll start looking at properties then.'

'You should be proud of yourself, Tara,' he told her. 'You've managed the Grosvenor very skilfully. A lot of places would have had to close and lose business while all the work was going on, but you've kept everything running smoothly. There's no man or woman in the business who could have handled it better.'

'It was exactly what I needed at the time,' she said. 'And I'm so glad that I eventually saw that.'

The sat for a while longer, then they moved and continued their walk on the circular path, talking over the details of the sale of Ballygrace House as they went.

Then, as they came towards the car park again, Tara suddenly said, 'Now I've made my decision about selling up, I feel as though a huge weight has been lifted off my shoulders. In fact, I feel like celebrating.'

Frank smiled at her. 'And so you should. Do you want to go somewhere for a drink?'

'Nope,' Tara said. 'I want something more celebratory than just a drink.' Her green eyes crinkled at the corners. 'I'm going to ring Bridget and Fred and ask them if they can get a babysitter, and we'll go out for nice meal tonight.' Her voice was excited now. 'Somewhere different. Maybe even into Manchester. I'll ask Angela, too, because she's got definitely got something to celebrate.'

Frank checked his watch, then he went to open the driver's side of the car. 'I'd better get you home now,' he told her. 'You're going to need time to phone around and organise your evening.' He got into the car and reached across to open the passenger side for her.

Tara slid into the cool, cream leather seats, a pensive look on her face. Then, as Frank started up the car, she suddenly turned towards him. 'I want you to come tonight as well.'

Frank was still for a moment, then he switched the car engine off and moved to face her. 'Are you sure?' he asked. 'I don't want you to feel obliged to include me. I've done nothing, only rang a fellow I knew for a bit of information.'

Tara nodded, her face starting to flush now. This wasn't easy, but they had to start somewhere, and she knew Frank would never have the courage to make the first move. 'Of course I'm sure. I wouldn't have asked you if I wasn't.' On an impulse, she reached her hand out and touched the side of his face. And then she looked into his eyes and felt a pang of guilt when she saw the familiar uncertainty there. All the old hurt. She leaned forward and kissed him on the lips.

'Tara,' he said, his voice low and hoarse, 'I'm not sure what to say or do ...'

'You don't need to say anything for now,' she told him. 'Just put your arms around me and hold me tight.'

Chapter 80

Tara took the summer months steadily and carefully. She spent time with Bridget, and was heartened to see her friend go from strength to strength. She also spent time back in Ireland with Angela, who had now moved back home, helping to organise her September wedding and finalise all the legal documents for the sale of Ballygrace House, to make sure that the transaction went smoothly.

She kept everyone informed and up to date on all her plans for the future. 'I'm not cutting my ties with Ireland or anything like that,' she assured Shay and Tessie. 'When all the renovations are finished, I'll be able to come back and stay in Ballygrace House any time I like.'

The mention of the house brought a dull ache to Shay's chest. It happened so often now that he was used to it. The ache was now a part of him and he thought of it as some kind of a link between him and Joe. 'As long as we still see you, Tara,' he said. Then he gave a little sigh. 'I suppose the best news about it all is that Angela will be home for good and living locally. We're lucky in that all the others are close by as well.' He shoved his cap back to scratch his head. 'Tessie has taken to little Clare, and I think she's hoping that once Angela and Aiden are married they'll have one of their own.'

Tara thanked God for the way things had worked out with Angela and Aiden. The wedding had helped to take everyone's mind off the tragic events that had happened earlier in the year, and had given them something hopeful to look forward to.

Tara also took time to spend with Frank. Slowly but surely over the last few months, their relationship had grown from a tentative friendship into a fully fledged romance once more.

417

Still hardly able to believe that he had been given a precious, second chance, Frank was like a young man again. He was attentive and caring without smothering her, and had regained his confidence, the twinkle in his eyes that had stolen Tara's heart in the first place.

They had spent the first few months just going out for the evenings – to the theatre, to the ballet and to concerts. And, on the quiet evenings that Tara spent at Frank's rambling house in Alderley Edge, they discovered a joint interest in experimenting with different types of cooking and listening to Bob Dylan, Simon and Garfunkel, and some of the other musicians that were now emerging. Frank was also educating Tara in the delights of jazz music, and they had recently started frequenting a jazz club in Manchester at the weekends.

Gradually, Tara found all the little icy parts she had held in her heart had begun to melt. The walls she had built against Frank Kennedy had crumbled. She could now look at him – at his still-handsome face and his well-kept, athletic body – and revel in the feelings of passion that he evoked in her. And she could now acknowledge the longing she had always had for him, the strong physical desire that she had denied and buried deep inside, the love that she had transmuted for too many years into hate. Joe's tragic death and Bridget's close call had taught Tara that life was too short and too precious to waste on hate.

They were into their third month of dating and spending evenings at Frank's house when Tara realised she was ready for the final barrier to come down. Without telling him, she booked a room at the same hotel in the Lake District where they had first made love all those years ago. She told him that they were going to a weekend conference and then, halfway there, she handed him the hotel brochure, saying, 'I think it's time we revisited some old haunts and some lovely memories, which I've never forgotten.'

'Tara ...' was all that Frank could say, and the emotion and gratitude that he felt was so overwhelming that he had to pull the car over to the side of the road and take her into his arms.

Their first night in the hotel was spent rediscovering the joy in each other, and their lovemaking was tender and slow. And over the next few days, as they made love again and again, Tara discovered heights of pleasure and intimacy with Frank Kennedy that she had never reached with any other man. Not even her beloved Gabriel.

And that realisation had come with more than a small pang of guilt.

To acknowledge in her heart that, while she had loved Gabriel dearly – and had enjoyed a comfortable and contented marriage with him – her feelings for him had stayed within a certain parameter. She now had to admit that they had fallen short of the passionate feelings she had always had for Frank.

As they drove back to Stockport from the Lake District on the Sunday afternoon, Tara realised that she and Frank were like both sides of the same coin. She could now clearly see what Bridget had said from the first time she met Frank, that they were so very alike in many ways.

And it was for that reason that she had put up no argument when Frank suggested that instead of buying a place of her own, she should consider moving into his house. 'I know it's too much to hope for that you would move in as my wife,' he told her, 'but I'll be more than happy to have you on any terms you like.'

There was a moment's hesitation. 'We might have to wait a little while,' Tara said softly. 'I wouldn't like to steal Angela's thunder. She's been planning her wedding for months.'

Frank looked at her with wide, surprised eyes. 'Do you mean it?' he asked in a hesitant voice. 'Would you really consider marrying me?'

'Well, neither of us are getting any younger.' She gave a small, teasing laugh. 'Especially you.'

His piercing blue eyes looked into hers for a few moments, then he drew her into his arms. 'I'm the luckiest man in the world,' he said, his voice hoarse with emotion. 'To have been given this second chance with you.' He hugged her close to him. 'And you will never, ever regret it ... I would kill myself before I would ever let you down. I've loved you since the first moment I set eyes on you, and I've never loved another woman since. You are everything, and more, than I could ever dream of. I love you with all my heart.'

Tara eased out of his embrace to look up at him now. 'And I love you with all my heart, Frank Kennedy. And in spite of how I treated you over the years, I've *always* loved you.' Her voice faltered a little. 'You were the first man I ever let make love to me, and, in marrying you, I want you to be the last.'

Frank closed his eyes now, forcing back the tears of emotion that had just formed in them. 'I am so deeply honoured,' he whispered. 'Because I know I have a very hard act to follow. I know how happy Gabriel made you.'

'I won't even try to deny that I was happy with Gabriel,' she told him. 'But you and I have something very, very special, Frank. And, if I'm painfully honest, I'm more myself with you than I've ever been with another human being. I think that was the reason for all the anger I felt towards you. I knew I'd lost something I'd never find with anyone else.'

They were silent for a while, Frank stroking her hair, then eventually he said, 'We could go away somewhere quiet if you want. We could even get married somewhere like Rome.'

For a moment, Tara's green eyes had a faraway look in them. 'I think I'd like to have it here in Stockport. Maybe a small, but nice reception in the Grosvenor.' She smiled at him. 'It's a place that has a bit of history for us, since it was one of the first places that we met.'

'It's part of our joint past and a big part of our present,' he told her. 'And I've no doubt it will see us well into the future.'

Chapter 81

ເຈ©ລ

BALLYGRACE MAY 1969

Angela and Aiden stood at the front door, watching as the brand-new, grey Jaguar made its way up the drive. It slowed almost to a halt as it passed the Ballygrace House Hotel, then continued around to the black-and-white, mock-Tudor, two-storey house at the far end of the grounds.

'Tara!' Angela called, rushing towards the car as quickly as her eight-month pregnancy girth would allow. Aiden followed behind, holding Clare by the hand.

Frank came out of the car first, wearing casual denims and a short-sleeved blue shirt. He gave Angela a hug and a kiss, and shook Aiden's hand, then he moved to open the back door of the car.

Tara swung her long denim-clad legs out, her loose red curls lifting in the light summer breeze, and she came to hug her sister and brother-in-law. 'I can't believe the change in the place,' she said, a catch in her voice. 'It's beautiful, far better than I could ever have imagined.'

'It's fantastic,' Frank told them, shielding his eyes against the sun to gaze at the new building. 'I can't wait to see inside. Congratulations to you both.'

Tara took her sister's hand, then stood back to get a good look at her. 'You're absolutely blooming.' Angela's long blonde hair shone in the afternoon sun, and a glow about her gave away her delight with her impending motherhood. She seemed very young and girlish-looking in a yellow T-shirt under a green-and-yellow checked maternity pinafore.

Angela smiled expectantly first at Tara then at Frank. 'You haven't come on your own, have you?'

'No, not at all,' Tara said, smiling back. 'The others are following behind.'

Frank looked down towards the large, ornate gates. 'They should be here any minute. They were behind us in Tullamore.'

'Tara,' Angela said, her eyebrows raised in question. 'I've been waiting all morning. Where's—'

'It's OK, Angela,' Tara said, laughing now. 'I suppose I'd better put you out of your suspense.' She strode back over to the car. 'The most important guest is fast asleep in here.'

Angela gave a little whoop of delight and followed Tara to the grey Jaguar. She opened the driver's door and leaned in, and there in the back seat, fast asleep in a little white Moses basket, was Noel Joseph Kennedy, Tara and Frank's baby son, named after Tara's grandfather and brother.

'Oh, my God ... he's beautiful!' Angela exclaimed, tears flooding into her eyes. 'A nose like yours, Tara, and jet-black hair like his daddy. Oh, he's a little dote! I can't wait to hold him.'

'You'll have plenty of chances over the coming week,' Tara told her. 'He's a little devil for attention.' She winked. 'Just like his father.'

Aiden and his young daughter came now to join them, Aiden lifting Clare up to get a better look at her ten-week-old cousin. She leaned over and carefully lifted the cream blanket to get a better look, then she tugged at the sleeve of Angela's dress. 'We're going to have a baby soon, Mammy, aren't we?'

Just as Noel started to stir, another car turned into the drive, a big, Ford family car. Like Frank's Jaguar, it slowed as it passed the hotel, then it continued round to the house and came to a stop beside them.

Angela's hand came to cover her mouth again, as Fred and Bridget emerged from the front of the car, then Michael, Helen and Lucy Roberts came tumbling out of the back, all rushing to hug and kiss Angela, and to exclaim how fat she had got.

Later that evening, as all the adults sat in the dining-room of the hotel – the old Ballygrace dining-room – Bridget kept looking around and shaking her head in disbelief. 'Never in my wildest dreams,' she said, 'would I have ever imagined Ballygrace House looking like this.' She looked over at Tara. 'Can you imagine what old Rosie Scully would have to say?'

Tara rolled her eyes. 'Oh, I certainly can. I'm sure she'd have plenty to say about it. And plenty to find fault with.' She saw the bemused looks on the men's faces. 'Rosie Scully was the Fitzgeralds' old house-keeper,' she explained. 'And the first time I came to Ballygrace House she ran me out of the place, saying that it wasn't for the likes of me and that I should know my station in life.' She laughed now, thinking back to the cranky old woman. 'Little did she realise that her advice only made me all the more determined to prove her wrong.'

'The driving force behind many a successful person,' Aiden said, smiling.

'I've arranged for you all to have a tour of all the main rooms down here and the upstairs rooms in the morning, after breakfast,' Angela told them. She squeezed her husband's hand. 'Aiden and I can't wait to have your opinion on all the work that's been done.'

'From what I've seen so far,' Frank told her, 'it's a first-class job. You have to look hard to see that the two side extensions aren't the same age as the rest of the house, as it all works so well together. And the car park and the landscaped gardens blend in perfectly. An excellent job.'

'And it's nice to see a hotel with a bit of green countryside around it,' Fred chipped in. 'The hotels in Stockport are lovely, but you can't beat open land and trees.'

Tara held her wine glass up. 'To the beautiful Ballygrace House Hotel,' she said, 'and to Angela and Aiden.'

*

The following morning, as the men were having a good look at the grounds, and Angela and Clare were out for a walk with the baby's pram, Tara and Bridget wandered around the old part of Ballygrace House.

'How does it feel to see everything so changed?' Bridget asked as they came out of the hotel kitchen, which bore no resemblance to the comfortable old room it had been before.

'Actually,' Tara said, 'it feels fine ... it feels right. It's given the old house a new lease of life.' For a few seconds her mind flitted back to Joe, to the time when she knew she needed to let go of Ballygrace House. 'A second chance.'

'Well, I'm delighted for the poor old house,' Bridget said. 'Because we all need a second chance.'

Tara looked at Bridget. 'And how does it feel to be back here again?'

'Grand,' she said thoughtfully. 'It was a lot easier to come back this year, when it went so well at Angela's wedding.' She smiled. 'It was good knowing that you and Frank would be here as well, and to be able to stay in the house with Angela. And it's totally different coming over with Fred and the kids. It sounds silly, but I feel safer with them around me. I don't feel so self-conscious, or that people are looking at me and talking about me.' She gave a little laugh. 'And even if they are, I don't care any more.'

'Oh, Bridget,' Tara said, touching her hand, 'I'm so pleased for you.'

Bridget looked out of the window at the side garden, where the three men were chatting away. 'Fred thinks all the locals in the pub in Ballygrace are very friendly, and the kids love it because they're allowed in the bar to play darts and pool. They've been going on about it for weeks now, and Michael can't wait to see William. Did Angela say when he's due down from university?'

Tara's brow wrinkled in thought. 'I think he's actually finished for the summer this coming weekend. She said he's coming to spend a month here before heading back to London. He's going to be working in the bar and the restaurant to give him some pocket money for the summer.'

'I believe he's given up on the idea of running his own hotel,' Bridget said.

Tara shook her head and gave a little bemused smile. 'The more

Elisha argued against it, the more determined he was. But when she eventually gave in and said that he could choose whatever career he wanted, the whole idea just fizzled out. I think he discovered that lawyers earn a lot more money for working a lot less.'

'Who would believe it?' Bridget mused. 'William Fitzgerald all grown up and a student at Trinity College.'

'He certainly has grown up,' Tara said, smiling now. 'He has a girlfriend now as well. Another student. From Cork, I believe.'

'Don't tell me!' Bridget said, shaking her head. 'You'll be making me feel all old.' She gave a little sigh. 'The next thing it will be our Michael havin' a girlfriend, and I can't bear to think of that.'

'You know we're going down to Clare for a few days to catch up with Frank's older children? They're all dying to see Noel.'

'Isn't it great that they took to you so well, Tara? You could see it at the wedding.'

'Thank God,' Tara said with some relief. 'And they were grand when we visited last October.'

They heard Fred giving a big laugh now, and both women looked out of the window at the three men laughing and joking.

'This is the sort of thing I dreamt of,' Bridget whispered. 'You and me, married and doing well, with all our kids together ...'

'I still wake in the night to look at Noel,' Tara said, 'and I have to pinch myself, because I still can't believe I have him and Frank. I thought it might be too late ...' She halted, pressing a finger to her lips. 'You know, all the hopes and dreams I had about owning the houses and hotels – owning Ballygrace House – they all mean nothing compared to having Frank and the baby. Oh, it's grand, – and I can't say I'm not proud of what I've achieved over the years, but the feeling I had when Noel was placed in my arms ...' Her eyes filled up now at the precious memory.

'We've been very lucky in many ways,' Bridget said, 'although we've not had it easy all the time. We've seen the two together – the good and the bad. But in all, I'd say we've been lucky.'